SUSANNAH KELLS

Coat of Arms

This edition published 1993 by
Diamond Books
77–85 Fulham Palace Road
Hammersmith, London W6 8JB

First published in Great Britain by
William Collins Sons & Co. Ltd 1986
First issued in Fontana Paperbacks 1987

COAT OF ARMS is based on a concept originated
by Richard Gregson

ISBN 0261 66203 1

Printed and bound in Great Britain by
BPCC Paperbacks Ltd
Member of BPCC Ltd

PART ONE

The old man lay dying.

He had been a man of many enemies and great foolishness, but now he slept. His curled hands twitched on the coverlet. Every few moments, unexpected and oddly obscene, he would laugh in his sleep, making Pearl wonder what dreams haunted death.

On the mantel an ormolu clock ticked, while beyond the rain-pocked windowpanes an early autumn gale whirled fallen leaves about the untended park and gardens. Above the wind's gusting came the throbbing note of bombers hidden by the low clouds. 'I didn't know they could fly in this weather,' Doctor Gordon said.

'They never stop.' Pearl stared at the sycamore trees that divided the park from the Home Farm. The wind had stripped the branches almost bare.

An American orderly brought a gift of a cylinder of oxygen. The Americans, Pearl thought, had colonized Howarth. They had been given the west wing as an Air Force Hospital for the war's duration, but they had slowly and subtly taken possession of the central block that was now used as an officers' club. They held wheelchair races in the Long Gallery, and in fine weather played softball on the croquet lawn where a diamond-shaped path was now worn into its precious turf.

The nurse put the oxygen mask over the old man's face, but he twitched away from it. 'It doesn't matter,' Doctor Gordon said.

Nor did it. The fourth Marquess of Arlington was dying. The family lawyer had been summoned and a message left for the eldest son, the Earl of Mountsorrel. There was nothing more to be done; within hours the old man would be dead and the Earl of Mountsorrel would be the new Marquess of Arlington, Earl of Arlington, Baron Howarth of Howarth, and owner of Howarth itself.

At lunchtime the old man still lingered on. The nurse wiped spittle from his lips and the Marquess seemed to shudder at her touch. Pearl, wanting escape from the astringent smell of incipient death, took her coat and walked down the great avenue of elms to the boarded gateway of the long drive.

Pearl wore black. Black shoes, black silk stockings, black dress, black gloves, black coat, black hat. It accentuated the height of her slim body and exaggerated her natural aloofness.

The black was not in anticipatory mourning for her father-in-law, but for her husband. The Lord Montague Howarth, younger son of the family, was missing in action and believed killed. The news had come just two days before and Pearl had come to Howarth to break it to her father-in-law, only to find him dying. His claw-like hand had touched Pearl's hand. 'There's hope, isn't there?'

She had told him that of course there was hope. Now, watching the rooks fly like torn black scraps above the tossing elms, Pearl felt a sudden shivering certainty that Monty was dead. It was an eerie feeling, a flicker of the supernatural like the chill of an opened grave, and, coming to a woman who prided herself on her hard, good sense, made her stop walking.

Pearl turned. She stared at the house with an oddly puzzled expression, as if she had never seen it before. Howarth. It was inconceivable that Howarth should be threatened, that mere death could make it as insubstantial as a rainbow. It was for this house, that would one day belong to her son, that Pearl had married; yet suddenly, as the dead leaves whirled about her, she saw that Howarth, like all things, could be lost.

It was beautiful. Howarth stood for order in chaos, for wealth and arrogance and immeasurable certainty in a world made tremulous by war. It was a house of pride and great loveliness, it was Howarth.

A cliff of white stone and windows, its pedimented portico was

8

topped by a pale dome from which there flew, still at full height, the standard of Arlington. The wings of the house spread east and west, sheltering the vast circle of gravel, and hiding, behind their Georgian severity, the sumptuousness of the rooms within. It was a house of dignity and beauty, the house of an aristocrat.

Yet it was a house in decline. Weeds had invaded the driveway. Within the great rooms damp seeped through fine paper and discoloured intricately moulded plasterwork. The fine pictures and great treasures had been crated and stored in the cellars against the ravages of war, yet the ravages of time seemed just as inexorable as any bomb. The house needed money. It needed a fortune poured into its magnificence if it was not to crumble and decay and fall. No wonder, Pearl thought, that the old man chuckled so malevolently in his dying sleep.

Pearl walked slowly back towards the house. The American bombers had long departed for Germany and the sky was strangely silent. Rain spat thinly on to the front lawns that had once been rolled and cut and pampered to perfection, but now were humped with molehills that looked like miniature burial mounds.

Taggart, the only servant left to the family, met Pearl at the garden entrance. 'Sir Michael Gooding telephoned, my Lady.'

Pearl let him take her coat and hat. 'From the station?'

'From London, my Lady. He missed the train.' The old man seemed to find a malicious pleasure in the news that the family lawyer would not be in at the death. 'He said he will try for the three-forty.'

'Did Mountsorrel ring?'

'I fear not, my Lady.'

Mountsorrel, the elder son, had still not telephoned when, at three forty-three by the ormolu clock, the fourth Marquess of Arlington died. Doctor Gordon punctiliously recorded the time of death in a small notebook, then took the crested ring from the dead man's finger. The nurse pulled the bedsheet over the sunken face. 'I'll lay him out after my tea.'

'Do,' Gordon said. He held the ring out to Pearl. 'That's Mountsorrel's now.'

Taggart, grumbling all the while, climbed to the small platform on the dome and pulled the flag to half-mast. Pearl insisted that it was done.

The dead man left three children. The oldest, Mountsorrel, should be on his way to Howarth. The youngest, Monty, was missing, believed killed. The third child was the Lady Sophie Howarth whom Pearl telephoned shortly after four o'clock. The phone rang and rang in Sophie's London flat. 'Sorry,' Sophie said when at last she answered it, 'I was slopping about in the bath. Any news?'

'He's dead.' Almost as an afterthought Pearl added that she was sorry.

'I can't say I am, darling.' Sophie had a voice that contrived to be laconic and acid at the same time, like a violin played high and flat. 'I suppose you've heard nothing about Monty?'

'No.'

'I wouldn't worry, darling,' Sophie said airily, 'not even Hitler could beat Monty.'

'Let's hope not.' Pearl heard a man's voice in the background, her sister-in-law shushing at it, then Sophie's clear, hard voice was loud in her ear again. 'When's the funeral?'

'I don't know.' Pearl shivered in a cold draught that came into the Marquess's study. 'Will you come?'

'I might.' Sophie sounded amused, and Pearl supposed that her sister-in-law was indeed tempted to dance on the grave of the father she had hated. ''Bye.' The line went dead.

Pearl rapped the telephone rest, impatient for the operator. When the village postmistress answered, Pearl dictated the number of Mountsorrel's London home. 'Who's that?' she asked peremptorily when the telephone answered.

'Hilary.' The Lady Hilary Howarth, elder of Mountsorrel's two daughters, was seventeen. 'Aunt Pearl?'

Pearl did not think the question needed an answer. 'I've been trying to reach your father all day. Where is he?'

'He's driving up to you. With mummy. They left at lunch-time.'

Pearl thought her brother-in-law might have had the courtesy to call Howarth before he left home. 'Shouldn't you be at school?' she asked Hilary.

'I'm taking an exam for Oxford tomorrow, so I'm staying the night here.' Hilary paused. 'How's grandfather?'

Pearl frowned as though the question was in bad taste. 'I'm afraid he's dead.'

There was silence for a few seconds, then Hilary's soft voice said how sorry she was.

'I think it's better you shouldn't mention it,' Pearl said, 'until your father has called *The Times*.'

'No, of course not.'

'Goodbye.' Pearl ended the conversation with the awkward curtness she generally used with her husband's family. It was ridiculous, she thought, for Hilary to be thinking about Oxford. It was not fitting. As the eldest daughter of the new Marquess of Arlington, she should be going into society, not mooning over books.

Pearl went to the Library where Doctor Gordon sat beside the tiny fire with a plate of sandwiches and a weak whisky. He stood as Pearl came in. 'Taggart knocked the scoff up for me. You don't mind?'

'Of course not.'

The elderly man, who had been the family's country doctor for a score of years, waved at the table. 'Paperwork's all done.'

The cause of death, Pearl saw, was put down as heart failure. Not that it mattered.

'It will be very odd,' Doctor Gordon said, 'to see John as the Marquess. Did he get your message?'

'He left London at lunchtime.'

Gordon took out the huge turnip watch with which, over the years, he had measured so many pulses. 'He's a bit late, isn't he?'

'He was always a slow driver.' Pearl took one of the sandwiches. It was, she saw with surprise, filled with thick, good beef and tart, dark mustard.

The doctor gave a sly smile. 'The Americans.'

'Ah.'

'Our allies, you see,' Gordon said happily, 'are not constrained by our rationing. There was a time when the British conquered the world on a diet of beef, now we toddle along on spam. The

Americans, on the other hand, eat beef, which is why they will probably conquer the universe. Will John move in here, do you think?'

'I would imagine so.'

'His wife never liked Howarth.' Doctor Gordon enjoyed family gossip. 'You say he's driving up?'

Pearl nodded. 'He gets a petrol allowance with his job.'

'Of course.' Gordon bit a vast mouthful of beef and wiped mustard from his lips. He chewed in silence, watching the fire, then seemed to think that the silence hung too heavily between them. 'Clocks go forward tomorrow.'

'Yes, they do.'

Gordon peered at Pearl over his spectacle rims. 'The children must have taken the news of their father hard?'

'Indeed,' said Pearl, though in truth she had left the breaking of the bad news about Monty to the head-teachers of her childrens' respective boarding schools. She assumed David and Caroline would be upset, but thought it best for the schools to deal with their grief.

Gordon made a vaguely sympathetic sound. 'David goes to Eton next year, does he?'

'Two more years,' Pearl said. If her earlier premonition was right, and Monty was dead, then her son would be the new heir to the Marquisate. The realization gave her little pleasure. David, she feared, was proving a dull, stuttering boy. It was strange that Mountsorrel's Hilary should be so like Monty and Monty's boy so like Mountsorrel. 'I think,' she said as she stood and crossed to the unlocked tantalus on the library table, 'that I'll have a whisky.'

Pearl left her sandwich untouched, sipping the whisky instead and listening to the hollow tick of the long-case clock. Gordon fed the small fire and made smaller talk. A man was dead, a son was coming to take up his inheritance, and Pearl's son was the new heir. There would have been a time, she thought, when the death of a Marquess of Arlington would have plunged the whole county into mourning, but no more. The glory of history had become trivial, and the thought made her look at a walnut frame that hung above the mantel.

Within the frame was an oblong of faded baize cloth upon which, behind ancient glass, a playing card was mounted.

'The *Caballo d' Espados*,' Doctor Gordon said. He had seen the direction of Pearl's gaze and smiled slyly.

'I'm sorry?'

'The card. The Knight of Swords. So much more poetic than the Queen of Spades, don't you think?'

'I suppose so, yes.'

'The Spanish –' Gordon was never happier than when he could display his erudition – 'still use the old suits. Swords, chalices, coins and batons. Borrowed from the Italian packs, of course.'

Pearl wondered whether, by keeping silent, she could stop the old man babbling on, but Gordon seemed to expect some sort of reaction to his information. 'I think,' Pearl said in her tartest voice, 'that it's all a nonsense.'

'A nonsense!' The doctor was tempted to argue, but Pearl's frigidity checked him. 'If you say so,' he said lamely.

But to Gordon, as to the old Marquess whose body lay cooling in the bedroom upstairs, the framed card was anything but a nonsense. With that one card, in 1812, the first Marquess of Arlington had taken Howarth and its estates from the nineteenth Baron de Conroy. In its day it had been a famous card game, a duel fought on green baize between the ancient family of de Conroy and the newly ennobled Marquess of Arlington, a man made rich through the Muscovy trade, and though the contest had long been forgotten by the rest of the world, it lived on in the memory of the two families.

Arlington had won, Arlington had taken the house, and ever since that day the playing card had hung above the mantel. On it was an engraved, hand-painted portrait of a mounted man, dressed in yellow silks and brandishing a sword. To the Howarths, and to men like Gordon who depended on them, the card was a talisman of the family's good fortune. It was unthinkable to despise the card, or to remove it from its old place, for to do so would be to risk fate's vengeance.

Yet Pearl had married into the family and the card did not hold a talismanic thrall over her. She hated gambling, despised gamblers, and believed that good fortune came from work and

13

cleverness. For her to accept that the proudest possession of her husband's family had come from the turn of a card was to diminish that possession, and Pearl was a woman who would not allow pride to be diminished. She had been born Pearl Gall, of middle-class stock, and while few women of the nobility had been as blessed with beauty as Pearl, none was prouder, for Pearl had schooled herself to rigid hauteur to compensate for what she saw as her lowly and ignominious birth.

At half past five, when it was darkening outside and the engines of the returning bombers filled the house with a muted, threatening thunder, an American orderly appeared and said that two policemen had come to the front door, thinking it was the entrance to the private rooms, wishing to speak with a member of the Howarth family. Pearl, remembering her shuddering premonition on the driveway, was certain that the policemen would be bringing news of Monty. His body, she thought, must have been washed up on the cold Adriatic shore. She went to the Entrance Hall. 'I am the Lady Montague Howarth.' Her voice betrayed none of the tremors that shivered through her.

The police sergeant was clumsily solicitous. 'You might care to sit down, my Lady?'

'I think not.' Pearl spoke icily, as if the policeman's consideration was a hint that she would not be strong enough to take bad news. She was determined to show nothing when they told her, for Pearl considered it tasteless to reveal emotions to her own class and downright stupidity to display them before lesser folk. 'Do go on.'

'Are you related to the Earl of Mountsorrel, my Lady?'

'He's my brother-in-law.'

'He's dead, my Lady. With his wife.'

'Dead?' For a second Pearl had the idea that the policeman had absurdly confused Monty with his brother. 'John's dead?'

'The Earl and Countess of Mountsorrel, my Lady. In a road accident near Thetford. Skidded, we think.'

'They're both dead?' Pearl wished she had sat down.

'Went straight off the road, my Lady. Hit a tractor.' Pearl said nothing and the sergeant took her silence for shock. 'Do you want me to call for a servant, my Lady? A cup of tea?'

'No.' Pearl shuddered suddenly, not so much at the ghastly news, as with the effort not to show any feeling whatsoever. She nodded coldly and, thinking that the men had done what they came to do, walked to the front door. 'Thank you for coming.'

'The bodies,' the sergeant said as he followed her down the steps, 'will have to be identified.'

'Of course.'

'And there's their property to be claimed.'

'The family lawyer,' Pearl said, 'will look after the formalities.'

The two policemen climbed back into their Wolseley car. 'She might have offered us a bloody cup of tea,' the constable grumbled.

'Or a whisky.' The sergeant stared moodily at the huge house. 'Cold sort, wasn't she?' The constable started the engine, put in the clutch, but suddenly the sergeant checked him with a raised hand. 'Hold it!'

Pearl was coming down the steps, almost running, waving to them in a decidedly undignified manner.

The sergeant rolled down his window. 'My Lady?'

Pearl stooped to look at the two policemen. 'At what time did they die?'

'Time, my Lady?'

'Yes. What time was it?' Her voice was urgent.

'Constable?'

The constable took out his notebook, wet his index finger, and turned the pages. 'As far as they can tell, my Lady, at half past four.'

'This afternoon?'

The constable bit back a comment that of course it had been this afternoon. 'Yes. Near enough, anyway. Might be ten minutes either side. There wasn't much traffic, you see.'

'Thank you.' Pearl stepped back. 'Good day to you.'

Pearl went back into the house and closed the huge front door as though she was shutting out the rest of the world. Half past four. The Marquess had died at three forty-three which meant that John, Earl of Mountsorrel, had unknowingly been the fifth Marquess of Arlington for all of three quarters of an hour.

Yet the conjunction of the times meant far more than that.

With the death of the fourth Marquess there would be a heavy bill in death duties. It was a bitter tax. Pearl, standing alone in the cold Entrance Hall, doubted that it could be paid without huge difficulty, but she was sure of one thing: the family could not pay twice. The Earl, by dying after his father, had made the family liable for a double burden of death duties and that would ruin the Howarths for ever.

She stood outside the Library with these urgent thoughts uppermost in her mind, and with the sudden realization that her claim on Howarth was now the best claim in the family. The title went to the next living male and the house went with the title, and either her husband or her son was the new Marquess. She clenched her hands, nails hurting her skin, as if summoning up all her strength for the battle she now faced. Pearl was Howarth now, and, though the house might have been won by a playing card, she would hold it by her own hard will.

Doctor Gordon looked up from his whisky glass as Pearl came back into the Library. 'Not bad news I trust?'

Pearl walked to the fire and held her hands to its warmth. She was shaking, but not from the cold. 'John and Louise are dead.'

Gordon thought he must have misheard. 'Mountsorrel?'

'He swerved off the road and hit a tractor. In Thetford.'

'Dear God.' The news prompted him to rise and go to the tantalus. 'Dear God! Both of them?'

'Both of them.'

The doctor poured two whiskies. 'I think you'd better have a drink, my dear.'

The clock between the high library stacks whirred as it geared itself to strike the third quarter. Pearl left her whisky untouched. 'He died at half-past four.'

'Wouldn't have been dark then, of course,' Gordon said. 'I've nearly killed myself a thousand times because of those damned silly little headlights, but it couldn't have been that.' He shook his head. 'Dear God! First Monty, then his father, now John.'

'John died,' Pearl said pointedly, 'after his father.'

Doctor Gordon stared at her, the whisky tumbler half-lifted to his mouth. Then, very slowly, he put the glass down.

Pearl said nothing.

Gordon knew what she wanted. He was an honest man, a church-warden, who had fought through the first war in the belief that death in the Flanders mud was better than a regime of lies. 'The police,' he said slowly, 'are certain of the time of death?'

'It was written in a notebook.'

Gordon stared at Pearl. He saw a woman who looked much younger than her age – which was somewhere in the mid-thirties. She had a classic face, the striking looks of the great beauty the younger son had wooed and won. She had hair the colour of saffron in the dawn, a skin unblemished by the wartime diet, and a backbone, Gordon believed, of tempered steel. 'The Marquess,' he said slowly, 'was unlucky in his recent investments.'

'I didn't know.' Pearl's father-in-law, in the last ten years, had been a most secretive man.

Gordon took a pipe from his pocket, tamped down the tobacco and lit up. 'He told me,' he said between puffs, 'that death duties would strike cruelly.'

Which was doubtless why, Pearl thought, the old man had been laughing as he lay dying. 'They cannot strike twice.' She had said it openly at last.

The doctor was honest, but not unsympathetic. To his mind it would be a tragedy if the Howarth family left Howarth. He feared the world that threatened after this war, a world in which victory would be made tawdry by socialized medicine if Labour had their way. It would be an even shabbier world if families like the Howarths were disinherited. Gordon had been reared in the belief of Britain's greatness, of a monarchy under God that had carried justice and decency across a globe, and he saw the great houses and their families as a part of that greatness. 'I could stretch a point,' he said dubiously, 'but there are witnesses.'

'Taggart's loyal.' Pearl was standing superbly erect.

'Mrs Mackenzie was in the room.' He reminded her of the nurse who, presumably, was now taking her supper in Taggart's small kitchen.

Pearl's blue eyes fixed on the doctor. 'I have lost Monty, his father, now his brother. You want my son to lose Howarth as well?'

Gordon thought of what must happen to Howarth if the family

17

left. The damp would finish its destructive work, the timbers of the roof would cave in and crash on to ancient floors, the weeds would grow where carpets now lay, and the claws of beasts would scrabble among the ruins. It was a vision of civilization destroyed by barbarism, and the vivid picture in his head made him sit at the long table. 'I suppose the lawyer will have to deal with everything now?'

'Yes.'

'Then you can give him this.' Doctor Gordon had taken a sheet of writing paper from his medical case. He unscrewed his fountain pen, tested it on the corner of the blotter, then wrote in a swift, untidy hand. He read aloud what he had written. 'To Whom it May Concern. Thomas John Carleton Montague Howarth, fourth Marquess of Arlington, died of natural causes this afternoon at 5.43, attended by me, who can attest that there is no need for a formal inquest. Signed, Andrew Gordon, physician.' He blotted the note and pushed it to Pearl. 'I could take two bottles of that excellent Scotch in lieu of payment for my services to the late Marquess.'

'Of course.'

Gordon put the pen away, then stared once more at the framed Knight of Swords. 'All these great houses were made by rogues, my dear. I suppose they have to be held by modern rogues?'

Pearl, her victory secure, smiled, and when she smiled her beauty could be heart-catching. 'Thank you again.'

The doctor left, then the lawyer arrived by decrepit taxi from the station. Sir Michael Gooding was portentous and patronizing; glad, as he verbosely said, to take the dismal burden of the arrangements consequent upon the sad deaths from Lady Montague's shoulders. But Pearl had already snatched the greater burden from Howarth; she had cheated the taxman, that enemy of all greatness, by her swiftness. Pearl would hold Howarth, playing card and all, because that was why she had married and that was her self-given purpose on this earth. She would hold Howarth.

Rain fell. It fell on Howarth's broken rooftiles, its parkland and on the long, weed-invaded driveway. It soaked the kitchen garden and puddled on the diamond-shaped path worn into the croquet lawn. Rain bounced on Howarth's steps and overflowed from the blocked gutters.

The rain soaked the black palls of the three coffins that were carried from the lychgate into the church. The tassels of the palls dripped water on to the church's flagstones. One of the tenant farmers, standing at the back of the nave, sneezed.

The coffins were let down unsteadily from the shoulders of the pallbearers on to the trestles. One, the Marquess's coffin, was laid hard by the altar rail. The others, those of his elder son and his daughter-in-law, were placed below the steps.

That was the proper order of things, just as the commoners were at the back of the church, the gentry in the middle pews, and the family at the front.

Pearl was the chief mourner. If her husband lived then he was the Marquess and she was Marchioness, but if Monty was dead then the child on her right was the new lord of this parish. David was eleven years old, a stutterer, and he stared at the three coffins with a child's wide-eyed fascination with death.

In the same pew were the Ladies Hilary and Ann. They were the daughters of the dead Earl and Countess of Mountsorrel. Hilary, the elder, was seventeen and had been given the beauty of this family: the straight tall slim body and golden hair of the Howarths.

The organ groaned into quiet. Rain hammered at the old windows and sighed among the bells that had been silenced for the war, while, far off, a bomber droned about a damp sky.

The bishop, medal ribbons bright beneath the strip of his scapula, recited the old words of the service.

The church door banged open, caught by the wind to slam with a clash of iron bolts against a stone pillar. The same gust slewed a cold slap of rain on to the flagstones as a tall man limped into the church. He pulled a soft black hat off his head to show a thin face and dark hair sleeked back over a narrow Norman skull. He carried an ebony stick which rapped on the stones with every step. About his shoulders, draped like a cloak, was a fur-collared greatcoat.

One of the villagers at the back of the crowded church offered the man space in their pew, but the offer was ignored. Instead the latecomer stood at the back of the aisle and stared at the three coffins.

High in the nave great wooden panels bore the coats of arms of the aristocracy who had lived and died in the parish. The same crests were repeated on the memorial stones about the walls of the choir and side aisles. To the colonel of Howarth's American hospital, come to the funeral out of Allied politeness, the old shields were much of a muchness, all part of England's quaintness, but to the peerage who had come to see a marquess buried the escutcheons told a bitter story.

Three generations of Howarths had carved their coat of arms in this church, stamping it in marble like a sign of ownership on God's house. Latin epitaphs told lies about old lives, but always the proud coat of arms was blazoned above the incised words.

Yet there was another, older coat of arms in this church: an older banner, a repetition of three black martlets that was the badge of the de Conroys. On the east window, against which the inclement wind hurled hard rain, the three martlets in stained glass had been placed before the Stuart monarchs reigned in England. There were martlets on the stone pulpit, on the capitals of the nave's pillars and cast in brass on the tombstones of the choir.

The Barons de Conroy had built this church. The Conqueror had given the land to a de Conroy, and de Conroy money had brought stone in ox-drawn wagons from the Midland quarries to make a church where their Saxon serfs could worship. They had ruled here until the nineteenth Baron had come home from the wars against Napoleon, a pack of Spanish playing cards in his baggage, and played a simple game of cards with the first Marquess of Arlington.

And lost to the Knight of Swords. Conroy had become Howarth, a feud had begun, and there had never been forgiveness.

Yet, in death, the Howarths rested in the vault where eighteen generations of de Conroys had been laid to rest. In life, like the leashed hounds of rival packs, they snarled and snapped at each other while in death they corrupted peacefully in a shared darkness.

The American colonel, remembering the neatly tended grave-yards of his home-town, shivered at the sight of the open vault. Farm labourers, wearing the boots they wore in the turnip fields, splashed through the water on the vault floor to receive the three coffins, and shoved them gratingly on to the waiting stone shelves. 'I am the resurrection,' the bishop said, and the rain seemed to seethe on the hammer-beam roof as if God, on this stormy day, wanted to bring the old church crashing down on to the mourners.

The organ's hand-pump wheezed and clattered, then a great chord vibrated through the church, defying the wind and rain and the sigh of hanging bells. The funeral was done.

The lesser folk left first, raising umbrellas in the porch and running through puddles towards the Conroy Arms. The inn sign, showing the three martlets, swung in the wind.

The gentry lingered. There were not enough cars to carry every invited guest to the funeral meats that awaited them at Howarth. 'I suppose we could take turns?' Sir Michael Gooding said hope-fully.

The American colonel diffidently offered the use of the officers' club bus, but the offer was not taken up, perhaps because the thought of a busride was simply too undignified.

'Able-bodied to walk,' Lord Whitney Mackerson said. 'Bit of rain never hurt anyone.'

The organist finished with a flourish as the remaining mourners shuffled uncertainly towards the porch and the waiting weather. The man with the ebony stick was still standing at the back of the nave where faded black curtains hid the bell ropes. He watched Pearl.

Within the space of three heartbeats it seemed as if each of them noticed him. They stopped, astonished. Except for the turmoil of the rain-laden wind there was silence in the church.

The man had an air of easy arrogance and he seemed, alone in the church, to be enjoying himself. He was handsome, but there was something in his dark, saturnine face to suggest a savage temper that might suddenly flare into quick violence. It was also a face that was known to every person in the church:

the face of a man who was of their own kind, an aristocrat.

He still looked at Pearl, then bowed. 'Lady Montague.'

'Lord de Conroy.' Pearl's voice was as hard as the stone on which the old Marquess now rested. The bitter enmity, that had seeped through the generations since de Conroy's ancestor accused the first Marquess of Arlington of cheating at cards, now accounted for the hostility with which they all confronted the solitary, sardonic man.

De Conroy had lost the lower part of his right leg at Dunkirk and the ferrule of his stick clacked on the stones as he limped towards Pearl. 'I have come,' he said grandly, 'to offer my condolences.'

Trapped by the Baron's politeness, she could only bow her head in recognition.

He continued to stare at Pearl, ignoring the other members of her family. 'In these past months,' he said in his deep voice, 'I became quite close to the Earl and I mourn his death.'

'To the Earl?' Pearl's astonishment that her dead brother-in-law should have had dealings with a de Conroy was shared by the others. Some looked at Hilary, the dead Earl's daughter, as if for confirmation, but the girl's face showed nothing.

'And as for your husband,' de Conroy spoke to Pearl in a voice that suggested much practice of speaking low confidences to women, 'he was a very brave man.'

The compliment was generous, the voice sincere, and around Pearl there was unstiffening of shoulders and a sigh of relaxation. That was handsome, they all thought. De Conroy had come to make his peace. Amid the turmoil of a great war a feud was being ended, and Pearl recognized the significance of the moment and held her hand out to the Baron. 'Thank you.'

De Conroy took her hand, raised it to his lips, and kissed the air a half-inch above her gloved fingers. The strange tableau was broken only by the arrival of the clergy from the vestry. Pearl, her hand released, turned to thank the bishop, courtesies and regrets were exchanged, and it was agreed that the weather was dreadful. 'Can I give anyone a lift to the house?' the bishop offered.

'That would be most kind.' Pearl turned to see which elderly relatives might best benefit from the bishop's offer and found that her family's erstwhile enemy was still standing at her elbow.

'My car,' Lord de Conroy said, 'is at your disposal.'

Pearl hesitated. No Howarth had ever let a de Conroy step into Howarth, yet the rain seethed, the funeral meats awaited, and the Baron's gesture in coming to the funeral had been noble. So, abandoning one hundred and thirty-two years of enmity, Pearl smiled her acceptance.

The rain flooded the parkland, seeped into the great house, and brought down a plaster ceiling in a bedroom of Howarth's west wing. A marquess was dead and, for the first time in more than a century, a de Conroy was coming home.

The Library was the largest of the rooms left to the family by the war's exigencies and thus the place where the funeral meats were served. It was also Howarth's warmest room, provided with two fires and insulated by the shelves of books that the third Marchioness had re-arranged so that no male author should rub leather binding with a female writer. Jane Austen stayed chastely far from Thackeray. Queen Victoria, visiting Howarth in the final decade of her reign, had applauded the idea.

Lady Calamore, a close neighbour who looked uncannily like the late Queen in her mourning dress of black bombazine and lace, surveyed the splendid food that had been fetched from the American canteen. 'Pineapple!' she said with surprise. 'You see, David? Pineapple!'

'Yes.' David Howarth, his fair hair stuck to his scalp by the rain, stared at the glistening yellow rings.

'Have you ever eaten pineapple?' Lady Calamore asked.

'N-n-n-n-no.' David's stammer was always worse in company.

'My late, dear husband had a stammer,' Lady Calamore said with blithe tactlessness. 'He cured it by filling his mouth with pebbles. Have you tried that?'

'No.'

'Wash them thoroughly, of course. Ah! Ham. I think I might taste just a little of that.' She piled slice after slice on to her plate, wondering if she could secrete some of it in her handbag for her dogs. The poor things suffered so badly because of the rationing.

'How do the worms,' David suddenly blurted out, 'get into the coffin?'

'What an extraordinary question! You'd better ask your dear cousin. Hilary knows all about wildlife. Or perhaps you'd better not.' Lady Calamore added the caution hastily, remembering that Hilary's parents were in two of the coffins that had been lowered into the vault. 'It's so very nice to see your Aunt Sophie again, isn't it?'

'Y-yes.'

'I remember when she was very little she used to steal the damsons from our garden.' Lady Calamore also remembered when the Lady Sophie had been expelled from Howarth and disinherited. The village gossip said Sophie's father had found her in Howarth's stables, long legs spread and knees raised, with a footman plunging into her slim body while a stable boy waited his turn. 'They said she charged a shilling!'

'What?'

'Nothing, dear boy! Carry my plate, will you? Is that port? I do believe it is.'

Lady Calamore was not the only person to recall the episode of Sophie's shillings. There were men and women in this room whose titles stretched back to the Tudors and even beyond, and all had heard the whisper rippling through society that Arlington's daughter was a whore. She had been sent, the story went, to a Swiss sanatorium where a doctor, specializing in the nervous diseases of the very rich, had administered bromide and then been seduced. Sophie had returned to Howarth rejuvenated, had repeated her offence, and been banished for ever.

A viscount, whose forebears had stood in the steel line at Agincourt, looked slyly across the room and opined that Sophie was a damned fine-looking woman. The viscountess stored the remark up to use in their next argument.

Lord Creed, who mourned Monty more than he did the dead Marquess, thought that sin suited Sophie very well. His wife agreed. 'Perhaps I should sin more, dear?' she said innocently.

Lord Creed smiled at her. 'You look as if you sin quite enough already.' Which compliment pleased the Lady Creed. She had even more reason than her husband to mourn Monty, but her mourning would have to be as secret as its cause.

It was a meeting of a clan. Old men with ancient titles greeted cousins and agreed that the war had played hell with the coverts. An earl, who had lost all his sons to enemy guns, shrugged off condolences, enquiring instead of the American officers present how many German towns they had bombed in the last month and encouraging them to greater efforts while there was still time to wreak revenge. His wife brightly discussed with Pearl a recipe for restoring the faded covers of leather books.

The war, the possibility of restoring the pheasant stocks, the American food and Sophie's presence were all lively topics of conversation, but none could rival the fact that a de Conroy had come to a Howarth funeral. Lord Mackerson, a cousin of the dead Marquess, had stiffly refused to greet the Baron, and now glared with distaste across the Library. 'Bastard.'

'Whitney!' Lady Mackerson said in hopeless remonstrance.

'Gambler! Wastrel! Degenerate!'

'Whitney, please!'

'Man's not fit to be in society.'

Lady Mackerson, who suspected that her husband was jealous of de Conroy's wealth and gaming luck, sighed. 'He was very gallant in church.'

'He's gallant all right. Full of running at the off, isn't he, but no staying power. Two stiff fences and he's hacking for home.' The equine metaphor referred to the Lord de Conroy's two marriages, both of which had led to scandalous divorces. One ex-wife had died, while the other lived in seclusion and rumoured madness on the Cornish coast. 'At least,' Mackerson said with satisfaction, 'he's the last of his line.'

'He has a daughter, doesn't he?'

'Daughters don't count.'

Lady Mackerson watched the tall Baron who was staring at the framed playing card over the mantel. 'He's not old, Whitney. Mid-forties? He could have a son.'

Lord Whitney lowered his muzzle into his whisky, then

laughed. 'No he couldn't. Jerries saw to that, didn't they? The bloody mine took more than his foot, my dear, and a DSO's no compensation for mangled balls.'

'Whitney!'

Pearl, beautiful in sheer black, moved among the guests with stately ease. She found her son balancing a plate heaped with food and felt immediate disgust for the child. 'I do dislike greed, David.'

'It's not m-m . . .'

'And don't answer back. Ah!' She turned, smiling, to thank the lord lieutenant for his attendance. Out of the corner of her eye she saw de Conroy limp from the room and felt relief that he was leaving. However handsomely the Baron had behaved in the church, Pearl nevertheless felt that he had over-reached himself by coming into the house, but at least he had not outstayed his welcome. She told the lord lieutenant that there was no news of her husband.

'Shot down, wasn't he?' he asked.

'Indeed. He was going to parachute into Yugoslavia and it seems a night-fighter caught them over the coast.'

'He was a most brave man,' the lord lieutenant said, and it was true. Monty had won an MC before Dunkirk and a DSO in the Western Desert, and some men said the DSO should have been a Victoria Cross. Monty had once told Pearl that an aristocrat had only two duties; to amuse the populace and die for his country, and Monty had done both with a splendid panache. It was typical of her husband, Pearl thought, that he would volunteer to parachute behind enemy lines and she could only hope that his death had been swift.

She turned and saw her father deep in conversation with Sir Michael Gooding, and Pearl knew that the two men were discussing the inheritance of the dead Marquess. She sheered away from them, not wanting to think about the ruined legacy of Howarth.

The dead man had speculated and lost, so now the great Howarth estates were mortgaged and the government would be sharpening its claws for the death duties. That thought reminded Pearl that she must speak with Hilary and Sophie. Only those two, of all the family, knew that the Marquess had died before his son and their silence must be ensured. Pearl blamed herself for making the telephone calls, but the breaches in her lie were not irreparable. Sophie would be the most difficult, for a Sophie warned of trouble might take a perverse delight in stirring the pot. Pearl looked for her sister-in-law, failed to find her in the Library, and felt relieved. Perhaps, she persuaded herself, it was a case of the least said to Sophie the soonest mended.

Hilary was another matter. 'A word in private, if you don't mind?' Pearl said.

She led the girl into the small Library that Pearl planned to make into her own study. 'I've been speaking with Sir Michael about your future. You and Ann will be living here, of course.'

'Thank you.'

Pearl sat on the edge of a dust-sheeted sofa. She found such conversations very hard. Any show of emotion was difficult for her, threatening to chip away at her elegant façade. 'Once all this business has died down I think we can be very happy.'

'Yes, I'm sure.' Hilary, at seventeen, was horribly confused. She had wept for her parents, yet she was assailed by the unworthy conviction that she regretted her Uncle Monty's death far more. Monty, not her parents, had been the light of her childhood; the player of games, inventor of stories, and Hilary's tutor of the countryside. He had shown her where the grebes twisted sinuously beneath water, where leverets lay while the hare fed, and where the star-of-Bethlehem grew. Monty had taught her to fish, how to tie and cast a fly, and had applauded her first salmon. Everything Hilary knew about the countryside, her deep passion for the mysteries and secrets of nature, she owed to him.

'Is it true your father knew de Conroy?' Pearl suddenly asked.

'I think it was, yes.' Hilary had a guileless, open face, imbued with honesty and intelligence. At seventeen her beauty was already remarkable and made all the more enticing by the quality of innocence that informed her fine-drawn features. 'I don't know what they talked about, though,' she added.

Pearl had only asked the question to delay the real reason for this conversation. 'I thought it wise,' Pearl said, 'to clear up a small misunderstanding.' Hilary stared at her aunt, saying nothing. Pearl's voice was sharp and imperious. 'You will remember we spoke on the day of your father's death?'

'Yes.' Hilary was too young and too sad to notice Pearl's embarrassment.

'I was wrong to tell you your grandfather was dead at the time that I rang you' – Pearl plucked at the dust sheet with a nervous right hand – 'or Doctor Gordon was wrong. Your grandfather was in a very deep sleep, and didn't die for another hour or so.'

The information seemed so trivial to Hilary that she did not know what to say. She shrugged instead.

Pearl watched the girl. 'One simply doesn't want silly rumours, you understand?'

'Of course.' Hilary did not understand at all.

Pearl stood. 'You and Ann are returning to school tomorrow?'

'Yes.'

'You'd both better have an early night. And you'll remember what I said?'

Hilary nodded. 'Of course.'

Pearl was glad when the conversation was over. She was a woman happiest on her own or in a crowd, disliking the intimacy of a small room with just one other companion. She congratulated herself on an unpleasant task well done and, once again seeing no sign of the Lady Sophie, decided she had achieved enough for the moment to prevent the taxmen discovering the deception that would save Howarth from a further tranche of death duties.

For Howarth must be saved. Pearl, whom some people thought incapable of love, loved Howarth. That evening, like many of the funeral guests before her, Pearl wandered through the great rooms where furniture was draped with dust sheets and tall windows were shuttered. She folded back the shutters to cast a watery, fading light on cracking paint and threadbare carpets. The walls showed great rectangles where paintings had hung. In one room a priceless Chinese wallpaper showed dark stains of damp. Chandeliers, too big to take down and protect against the bombs that had thankfully never fallen, were thickly misted with spiders' webs.

From the Ballroom to the Red Dining Room she wandered, from the Music Room to the Long Gallery to the Withdrawing

Room to the Billiard Room. Mice had gnawed into wainscots, wiring hung ugly from cornices, and the damp smelled faint and foul in the cold air. In the State Rooms, the plaster had been boarded over, but in other chambers there were chunks of it lying forlorn on parquet floors. Yet this was her son's inheritance, it was for this that Pearl had married, and she saw its sublime grandeur beneath the decay. She would hold this house, she would lie and cheat for this house, and she would not lose it, because it was Howarth.

The Lady Sophie had not stayed long in the house from which her father had expelled her twenty-two years before. Howarth, she found, had become dark and dispiriting, filled with old people and decaying memories, a house of death. She had brazened out the stares of the curious, she had fulfilled her vow to attend her father's funeral, and she had left.

That evening she sat before a looking glass in a strange house. Caton Hall was scarcely a century old. It had the heavy timber and over-decorated look beloved by Victorian builders. Wood panelling sheathed every wall and timber columns rose to painted ceilings. Blackout curtains mercifully hid the stained glass in the tall windows. The rain had stopped, but a night wind tugged at the casements and sighed among the chimney pots on the wide roof.

At times, alone in her Kensington flat, Sophie would stare into a mirror for an hour at a stretch, hating every minute of the years that were taking beauty from her. It was a miracle that her looks had lasted as long as they had, yet every morning she feared the mirror and every night, between soft sheets, she let a man tell her that the long years had made no difference. She was forty-five this year, and though men told her she looked not a day over thirty, she felt as old and worn as the hills.

She put rubies into her ears. Red suited her. Sophie had not been given the golden hair of the Howarths; hers was black, raven black, sleek as jet, untouched by grey. She had dark eyes that promised challenge and an amused line to her mouth. She grimaced into the looking glass, wondering if her coming to this

29

house was wise, but knowing that she could never resist such mischief.

Sophie, as the clocks in the house struck seven, emerged from her bedroom and descended the great staircase. Tiger and lion skins lay on the hall floor. Weapons were displayed as trophies: assegais and knobkerries, Mausers and flintlocks, swords and leather shields; all testifying that the men of this house had killed and killed again to keep the Empire's frontiers safe and the world's map red.

Caton was a house of great wealth and male comfort. It was a place of fishing rods, guns, tobacco jars and saddle-leather. Sophie liked such places, knowing that, like a jewel set into gun-metal, they made her femininity glow.

She pushed open the double doors of the drawing room to be greeted by a great fire that roared up to meet the wind above the chimneys. Its heat touched her bare shoulders above the black dress.

'You used to drink gin, I remember,' Lord de Conroy said.

'And still do.'

Kynaston de Conroy was slim in evening dress. He poured her drink, then limped across the floor. 'Your most excellent health, dear Sophie.'

She touched the rim of her glass on his, then sat in a leather chair beside the fire. She had met Lord de Conroy exploring Howarth, just as she had been exploring it after the funeral, and he had smiled, tilted her chin to his friendly kiss, and invited her to dine.

'I shouldn't,' she had said.

'The war has made you virtuous?'

So she was here, because she could not resist the piquancy of the invitation. Yet the Baron and Sophie were not strangers to each other. They had met in the casinos of Deauville and Biarritz before the war, they had bumped shoulders on the dance floors of a dozen countries, and their casual acquaintanceship had been given spice by their families' enmity. But this meeting, in the house that the de Conroys had built to replace the lost Howarth, was not casual, for tonight, for the first time, Sophie was alone with de Conroy.

And that, she thought, was strange, for Kynaston de Conroy was the kind of man Sophie adored. Before the war, in the days when wealth gave blessing to irresponsibility, he had led a fast pack of aristocratic predators who had moved in an elegant phalanx through high society, secure in their arrogant certainty that no finer horsemen, marksmen or seducers existed in the world.

'How long has it been?' de Conroy asked. 'Six years? Seven?'

'You're going to tell me I haven't changed one little bit.' Sophie put her right leg over her left and smoothed the black silk over her thigh. 'It is eight years, Kynaston. You were at the Regina Hotel in Munich, going to dine with Ribbentrop, and trying to grow a Hitler moustache to confuse the peasants.'

He laughed. 'We ate at the Walterspiels', I remember, and agreed there would be no war in our lifetime. You were with your princeling, weren't you?'

Sophie nodded. 'We ate thrushes in Boettner's restaurant. The bastard deserted me in Vienna. He went off and married some simpering little virgin.'

'My grandfather,' de Conroy said, 'believed that bedding a virgin . . .' he checked his words as the door opened and an elderly woman ushered in a small girl who was swathed in a tartan dressing gown. De Conroy stood. 'Lady Sophie? My daughter Christine.'

This was evidently an evening ritual when de Conroy's daughter was presented by her nurse at her bedtime. The girl was skinny and plain, with mousy hair brushed into a shine. Her father gave her a cursory, bored inspection, and ordered her to curtsey to the Lady Sophie. Christine obeyed, then let her father kiss her forehead. 'You will say your prayers?' de Conroy asked.

The child nodded solemnly. 'Yes, father.'

'Then goodnight to you.' De Conroy gestured to the nurse who took small Christine's hand and led her from the room. De Conroy waited until the door was closed. 'Not much, but mine own.' The undisguised savagery betrayed his disappointment that his only child should be a daughter and not the son who would carry on the de Conroy line.

Sophie sipped her gin. 'You can have other children, can't you? The Americans haven't taken all the nubile girls.'

De Conroy's affable mood had been broken by his daughter's appearance. 'No,' he said, 'I can't. The gun still works, but it doesn't have any bullets.'

'I'm sorry.'

He shook his head to show that her pity was misplaced. 'I was lucky. My sergeant will never walk, see, or make love again.'

Sophie took a cigarette from a pewter box beside her chair. A pair of dice lay on the table, and a pack of playing cards, both reminders that de Conroy was a famous gambler. A gambler, a rake, and a nobleman, with a reputation for riding his women as he rode his horses on the hunting field: to exhaustion. The de Conroys had always had that reputation, and the portraits in this room, some fetched from Howarth when the house was lost, showed the same Norman face going back through the centuries. It was easy to imagine a de Conroy at Hastings, hacking with a broadsword at the fair-skinned Saxons, or at Crécy, riding down the French knights in blood and terror. The de Conroys were the old nobility who despised the Tudor upstarts and had no time for johnny-come-latelies like the Arlingtons. Such old aristocrats, who had made their titles with swords instead of money, were still the most dangerous.

'Odd sort of day, wasn't it?' de Conroy broke the silence.

'Yes.' And an odd evening, Sophie thought. She had come here expecting to be amused, to re-create a sliver of the pre-war carelessness, but de Conroy's biting wit, rather like her own, seemed to have been dampened by the rain and the funeral.

'And an odd family,' de Conroy said. 'No men left in it, did you notice? Only the old ones, anyway, and that child.'

'David.' Sophie laughed softly. 'He seems a dull little thing. One can hardly believe he's Monty's son, but he has to be. I can't imagine Pearl doing a whoopsy behind the screen, can you?'

'I don't know Pearl.'

'She did come from nowhere,' Sophie said cattily, 'so it's hardly surprising you never met her. But she's a rare beauty, don't you think?'

De Conroy's answer was cut off by a servant, clad in black,

who announced dinner. It was served in a dining room that had another great fire in the hearth, a fire that cast strange shadows on the carved beams of the high ceiling.

Dogs were let into the dining hall at the meal's end and the Baron tossed them scraps of meat from the carving plate. It seemed to Sophie, watching him, that he took more pleasure in the dogs than he had from his thin, plain child.

'Brandy in the drawing room?' de Conroy offered.

'That would be pleasant.'

The servant had built up the fire and turned off some of the lights. The dogs were excluded. Bitter coffee and old brandy waited by the hearth.

De Conroy cut himself a cigar. 'Pity about Monty.'

'A pity?' Sophie was astonished, not just by the sudden mention of her brother, but by de Conroy's evident sincerity.

'He was a brave man.'

It was said as a high compliment, and Sophie took it as such. 'He might not be dead.'

'He's dead.' The Baron drew on his cigar till it glowed evenly. 'I spoke to a fellow at the War Office. They haven't got a body so they can't make it official, but he's gone. I never knew him well, of course, but he was always civil. He shot damned well.'

'Yes, he did.' Sophie lit a cigarette and sat back. It had been a long time, she thought, since she had dined so well or in such comfort.

De Conroy looked at her. 'Why did he marry Pearl?'

'Because she was the most beautiful girl he'd ever seen, because a dozen others wanted her, and because Monty could never resist a challenge.'

He smiled in understanding. 'So it wasn't love?'

'How very vulgar of you to suggest that Pearl could be so feeble as to fall in love.'

He liked that. 'So why did she marry him?'

Sophie paused. She suspected, in the lazy warm post-prandial ease, that de Conroy was not making mere conversation, but had brought her here to ask just these questions. She shrugged. 'Because she knew she'd get Howarth one day. Monty was the younger brother, the elder brother was no longer welcome in his wife's bed. Therefore there would be no inconvenient sons to stop Monty becoming Marquess one day. And if not Monty, then certainly her own son. It was a very long view, but she's a very cool lady and likes to take the long view.' Sophie sipped her brandy. 'And if Monty had not so inconveniently died, then Pearl would be Marchioness now.'

De Conroy thought about it, then shrugged. 'Your elder brother was a fool.'

'Did you really know him?' Sophie remembered his statement in the church that morning.

The Baron nodded. He put his brandy down and crossed to a desk in the shadows beneath the blackout curtains. He pulled open a drawer, found a folded paper tied with red ribbon, and brought it to Sophie. 'You'll enjoy that,' he said.

She untied the lawyer's ribbons and found that she held a typed agreement, filled with the circumlocutions so loved by the law, the heretofores and hereinafters, the parties of the first and the second part, but despite all the long-winded phraseology and ponderous sentences, the meaning of the document was very clear and very startling.

John, Earl of Mountsorrel, had agreed with Kynaston, Baron de Conroy, that immediately upon John's accession to the Marquisate of Arlington he would sell, for the sum of fifty thousand pounds, the house, gardens, parkland and farms of Howarth to the Baron.

Sophie read it again. It truly did astonish her. Her brother, she thought, must have known just how shredded the inheritance was, and de Conroy's offer must have been a godsend to have made him discard the old antipathy and deal with the family's enemy. 'You think this makes John a fool?'

'I'd have gone to seventy-five thousand.' De Conroy laughed. 'And the place isn't worth more than thirty.'

Sophie thought how very much he must want to restore Howarth to its original family. She folded the paper. 'You came so very close, Kynaston.'

'Didn't I?' De Conroy took the paper from Sophie. For an instant he seemed to be tempted to throw it on the fire, but then

34

he tied its red laces again. 'And if the silly bastard had lived two hours longer, it would have been mine.'

Something flickered through Sophie's consciousness, a thought that seemed amusing but which would not quite articulate itself. She shrugged. 'Why did he agree to it?'

'Why?' De Conroy seemed astonished she should ask. 'The place is a disgrace! It's on the way to ruin! Your family's broke, my dear, cleaned out. That old fool wasted everything that was left and your brother knew it. Better to sell fast and cut the losses.'

'So you were not being quite so gallant as we thought this morning?'

He laughed, then limped across the room and restored the document to its drawer. 'For one hundred and thirty-two years, Sophie, my family has sworn to regain that house.' He came back to the fire trailing cigar smoke. 'Before I die I will own Howarth, as you call it. I will give it the old name, put our crest back on its walls, and I will leave it to my daughter.'

'So the feud isn't ending?'

'There's more than one way to skin a cat.'

Sophie laughed softly. The fire cast a warm glow on the panelled walls and a red sheen on the varnished portraits. One picture showed Howarth behind the sitter's shoulder; an older Howarth, without the portico, but still graceful and lovely. She looked back into de Conroy's thin face. 'If the feud isn't over, Kynaston, then I shouldn't be sitting here.'

'I don't fight women,' he said.

'If you want Howarth, then you'll have to fight Pearl, and you'll find she's a great deal tougher than the rest of us.'

'Tougher?'

'She's not a fool.' Sophie gave him a deprecating smile. 'John was dull, I'm whatever I am, Monty was a feckless rogue, but Pearl! Ah, Pearl is middle-class!' Sophie laughed. 'She'd hate to be told it, but she is. She'll squeeze a much higher price out of you. That's if she'll sell at all.'

'She has no choice. The death duties will finish her.'

'She has a rich daddy,' Sophie said mockingly. 'Besides, you forget something. Pearl married for Howarth. Do you really think she'll give it up because of the bloody taxman?' Again the amusing thought stuttered at the edge of her consciousness, and again it would not come clear. 'And Pearl, being middle-class, would rather live in decayed aristocratic glory than move to a brick house. She came from a brick house, Kynaston, and though her father got himself a knighthood, he's still a factory owner with grimy hands in her eyes. She has risen in the world, and she won't slide down gracefully.'

'I never knew any woman,' de Conroy said savagely, 'who could not be bought.'

'And I never knew any man,' Sophie said, 'who could not be made to beg.'

There was silence between them. The wind gusted at the window and the logs, cut from Caton's timber, spewed bright sparks into the chimney. From somewhere deep in the house the sound of the wireless droned, then was cut off.

De Conroy stood in front of the fire, flinching slightly as his stump chafed on his false leg. 'I want Howarth,' he said quietly, 'and before I die I wish to restore it to my family. Is that so bad?'

'No.'

'So I will offer Pearl what I offered John.'

'And she'll refuse it. Then what?'

'Then I am an enemy,' de Conroy said simply.

'And what does that make me?' Sophie asked. 'Your spy?'

He frowned. 'You think I asked you here to tell me about Pearl?'

'Yes,' Sophie said.

De Conroy shook his head. He paused, watching her, then gave her a crooked, friendly smile. 'Do you remember the car race in Rome? The night we were all drunk? Who were you with, Teddy Hobbs?'

'He's dead.'

'Or the night we took up all the carpets in the Badrutt Palace? Dumped them in the snow and that silly manager was hopping around wetting his trousers.'

Sophie tossed her cigarette in the fire, stood up, and kissed him. 'Poor Kynaston.'

He put an arm round her shoulders. He had spoken of those

36

days before the war, when a fast car and a champagne bottle encompassed all the future. 'It's going to be a drab world now,' he said. 'That's why I invited you. To pretend nothing's changed.'

She wanted to believe him, yet Sophie knew the de Conroys were never quixotic. Kynaston could play games with the fastest, but beneath the elegant façade there was a drive of steel. She smiled. 'I'm spoken for.'

He stroked her cheek. 'So I hear. An American general?'

'Very fat, very rich, very generous.'

'Do I take that mention of your lover,' de Conroy asked, 'as a dutiful note of reluctance proper in a woman about to be seduced?'

'Yes,' Sophie said, 'you do.' And later, as she had known she would, she lifted her hips to his hard body and clawed his back as they twisted on the stiff flax sheets beneath the smoke-darkened beams of his bedroom. Afterwards, in the heart of the autumn night, he slept with his right hand curled about her left breast and his stump resting on her thigh. Sophie, awake, stared through the uncurtained window at the ragged clouds that swept across the moon's face in the storm-swept night.

She moved gently, trying not to wake him as she eased herself out of the bed. He groaned once, but slept on.

Sophie walked in the darkness to the tall window. She would go to her own room now, a necessary part of the old pretence that nothing had happened in the night. But first she leaned her forehead on the welcome coolness of the windowpane and saw how the moon silvered the sheetlike water which flooded de Conroy's park. A tiny gleam, made by the slitted headlamps of a lorry, showed far beyond the park's boundary and Sophie knew it was on the same main road that her elder brother had skidded in his Humber and died in a tangle of metal and glass.

The thought came then, suddenly as if a light had been switched on, and Sophie held the breath in her naked body, stared into the night, and saw how clever Pearl had been. Dear God, of course! The telephone call had come at four, and John had not died till half past, and Sophie, now wide awake and filled with laughter, turned to stare at the dark, slim body sprawled on the

37

rucked sheets. De Conroy owned Howarth! Pearl had lied to better effect than she knew, and she, Sophie, could prove it.

She looked back into the night, the delight at her knowledge bubbling inside her. The lawyer's paper downstairs, duly witnessed and stamped, gave Howarth to de Conroy and he did not know it. To tell him, Sophie thought, would be a joy worth having.

De Conroy woke silently. He watched her, seeing how the moon shone pale on her long thighs and flat belly and small, taut breasts. 'You're very beautiful,' he said.

She almost told him then, almost blurted it out because she enjoyed stirring a pot into a witch's brew, but de Conroy reached for his cigarettes beside the bed and that mundane movement, so soon after his compliment, checked the words in Sophie's throat. 'You can drive me to London tomorrow?' she said instead.

The lighter flared on his thin face, then he nodded. 'You're welcome to stay.'

If she stayed, Sophie thought, then she would tell him and he would take Howarth and there would be nothing for her. Her knowledge, she thought, was best kept secret. She scooped up her clothes from the floor. 'London tomorrow, and time to observe the proprieties now.'

He nodded. 'Thank you.'

She kissed his cheek. 'The gun works very well, Kynaston.'

He smiled. 'Goodnight, my Lady.'

She walked naked to her room, filled with the secret of Pearl's deception and wondering how best to turn it to her advantage without betrayal. The fox was outside the chicken house and Sophie held the key, but she was not sure she wished to use it. She was an outcast, but she was a Howarth, and though she had hated her father and her elder brother she had loved Monty and he would have wanted Howarth held, for Howarth was the prize, the tarnished jewel Sophie could not yet cast to her family's enemy.

The dawn brought a pale, clear sky and a wind that plucked at fallen branches and dried the puddles on the flooded lawns, while Sophie, her peace kept, went home.

The pastures needed nitrogen. 'Why?' Pearl asked.

'So the sheep don't die, my Lady.'

'There's grass there.'

'It bain't be the grass, my Lady. It be the clover.' Harold Dyson, standing with his hat clutched in mud-soiled hands before her desk, spoke with ill-concealed impatience. 'We always does it. Right till June on these fields.'

'We have to?'

'Of course we has to! It's the nitrogen, see? Clover don't start putting it into the soil till June so we has to do it till then. And it's needed now. Ewes are feeding their bellies for lambs, aren't they?' It was an enormously long speech for Mr Dyson, one that he later scathingly described in the Conroy Arms as 'educating them that should know already'.

'Very well.' Pearl gave in, though God alone knew how it would be paid for. At least the seed for the spring barley had come from the seed merchants owned by the family, though that merely transferred a debt further from home.

'She be feeling the pinch,' Mr Dyson said that night in the taproom. 'You mark my words, she'll be out of that big old place before the lambs are sold.' Mr Dyson expected to take Howarth's lambs to market at the end of May and it was now mid-February. The old Marquess had been six months in his grave, and the villagers could sense the despair in the big house. 'Pity Lord Monty ain't here. He knows which end of a hoe to hold.'

Which dubious compliment was scorned by the landlord. 'Lord Monty? All he was ever good for was losing money on a horse! Pity about him, all the same.'

It was hard for Pearl to admit that she was beaten, yet the balance sheet was inexorable. The inheritance of Howarth, all but for a handful of houses, a seed merchants, and a small brewery with its tied pubs, was mortgaged. Pearl might save

Howarth if she sold everything the family owned, but she would be left with the decaying shell of a great house and no income to keep it.

Yet she fought on. Hilary, alone with Pearl now that the younger children were at boarding school, heard her aunt's voice raised in anger to the family's lawyer one day. 'My name is Howarth. This house is Howarth. I don't care what other properties we lose, but we will not lose the one thing that bears our name! Nor will I be the Howarth who reduced this family to the level of mere country gentry.'

It was a breath-taking but hopeless arrogance. The Divorce, Probate, and Admiralty Divisions of Chancery had granted Pearl's request that she become the principal trustee of the shrunken Howarth Trust, but she used her position solely in the service of her determination not to abandon Howarth. Her father, a gloomy Midlands industrialist who had made his own fortune from nothing, refused to help. He would need all his cash, Sir Reginald Gall claimed, to turn his factories round to peacetime production. 'Sell the place!' was Sir Reginald's advice. 'Gooding tells me you've got an offer.'

'I'll sell Ash first,' Pearl said grimly, not caring that the words were cruel. Ash, a beautiful Queen Anne house with nine bedrooms, stabling for a dozen horses, and three hundred acres of arable land, had been Sir Reginald's wedding gift to his daughter and Monty.

Pearl used up her savings in Howarth's service. She knew she was being stubborn, but she had a vision of a Howarth restored, made luminous again, of a house fit for her ambitions. To sell it would be to settle for second best and the second best was failure to Pearl.

She made economies. Hilary was one victim of them. It was ridiculous, Pearl said, for her to think of going to Oxford, and so she was peremptorily pulled out of school to save the fees, and told to prepare herself for the first social season of peacetime during which, Pearl fondly believed, the girl could be married off. 'There's plenty to do in the meantime,' Pearl said, 'you won't be idle.'

Pearl had it in mind that her niece could be her companion; a genteel occupation suitable for a young lady, but Hilary rebelled. She insisted on working on Howarth's farms instead, joining the Land Army girls who had been drafted into agricultural service.

The farm work was Hilary's solace against misery. War, death and uncertainty had plagued her young hopes, but nothing had depressed her so much as her guardian's blank refusal to let her attend Oxford. So, as the Western Allies fought across the Reichswald in the murderous battles of the Reich's dying throes, Hilary worked.

'Little thing like you,' Mr Dyson liked to say, 'shouldn't be doing work like this.'

'I'm taller than most of your workers, Harry.'

'Ain't tallness that counts, my Lady. It's muscle. Some be born to it, but not the likes of you.'

Hilary liked the Land Army girls, who said she was not stuck up like some they could name, but not common either. It was odd, Hilary thought, how such contradictions were expected of her because she had a title. At lunchtime, one winter's day, when the land was hard with a February frost and the trees were black traceries against a steel-grey sky, Hilary saw an American Mustang fighter, bellied like a fish full of roe, stagger overhead with greasy smoke spewing from a faltering engine. 'I hope that ain't your fellow,' Daisy, one of the Land Army girls, said to Hilary.

'My fellow?' Hilary looked up from the hay she was slicing for cattle-food.

'You know!' Ruby, Daisy's Birmingham friend, said. 'The one what fancies you!'

'Stephen?' Hilary was friendly with an American pilot who would come and walk the long frost-rimed fields of Howarth with her. She laughed. 'He's only a friend.'

'All right you lot! This is a bloody farm, not a gossip shop!' Harry Dyson, gaitered and booted, strode towards the hayrick. 'Sorry, my Lady, didn't see you there. But I was wanting you.' He waited until Daisy and Ruby had moved away. 'You wouldn't do me a favour, would you?'

'Of course.'

'We needs the vet fast.' Harry seemed nervous.

'Grass sickness again?'

41

'I've got a dozen ewes on Low Ground. Shivering like aspens, they are.'

Hilary understood his nervousness. There was a pile of unpaid bills at Howarth and Dyson could not bear asking the vet to come on yet another unprofitable visit. Pearl would have to make the telephone call herself, and Dyson did not want to ask her. No one liked dealing with Pearl, and increasingly Hilary was the go-between. 'I'll ask her.'

'Good girl.'

Hilary did not like asking either, but there was no choice. If the vet did not inject calcium into the ewes, they would die. Even with the injections their survival was chancy, and their lambs would be stillborn, but the effort had to be made.

She rode an ancient bicycle to the big house where a Daimler stood in the snow on the gravel drive. There were evidently guests to luncheon, who would be told their thin fare was because of the food rationing, rather than poverty.

Hilary let herself into the back of the house and went to Pearl's study, unwilling to interrupt the luncheon. She could hear voices in the Small Dining Room next door and, as the door was ajar, she crept close to it and listened.

A man, fruity-voiced and smooth, was talking money. Pearl was evidently listening intently, rarely interrupting. 'The sum on offer, dear lady, is fifty thousand pounds.'

'From de Conroy?' Pearl's voice revealed her distaste for whatever was being discussed.

'I would venture to suggest, my Lady, that his Lordship's offer is twice Howarth's market value.'

There was silence, except for the scrape of a match as a cigar was lit. 'De Conroy, I presume,' Pearl spoke in her iciest voice, 'is not wanting to buy Howarth as an investment?'

'Indeed not,' the man chuckled.

'And the Baron is not without money,' Pearl said. 'What does the family own? 200,000 acres?'

'Something like that.'

'So his income must be in the region of a quarter of a million a year?'

'I really couldn't say,' the man said evasively. 'All I will say,

42

your Ladyship, is that if Lord de Conroy chooses to send me to you, then he is willing to negotiate. Understand that, and anything is possible. I do not come with an irrecoverable offer, but as a reasonable man willing to explore any pathway that can bring satisfaction to every party. We do not need to talk vulgar money!'

But whatever else was to be discussed, and Hilary could think of nothing so immediate as vulgar money, she did not have a chance to discover for, with a suddenness that made her scream, a pair of strong hands gripped her waist, turned her, and a man kissed her swiftly on the mouth before shouting his triumph. 'A spy! A spy!'

'Let go of me!' Hilary twisted from the man's grip, but he held his arm firm about her waist as he kicked the door fully open.

He was a young man, leanly good-looking, in naval uniform. 'My Lady,' he said proudly, 'I have caught a spy.'

'Hilary,' Pearl stood up, frowning, 'what on earth are you doing?' She looked at the young man with a flicker of distaste at his horseplay. 'Do let go of her, Lieutenant. She's my niece.'

The naval officer seemed astonished. He had assumed that the girl, as beautiful a creature as he had ever seen, was a servant. It was not an unreasonable assumption, for Hilary's khaki trousers and shabby sweater were littered with straw. 'I'm sorry,' he said awkwardly.

'Dyson sent me.' Hilary ignored him, speaking to Pearl instead. 'I'm afraid he wants you to telephone the vet. We've got ewes down with grass fever.'

'Whatever that is,' Pearl said lightly, and Hilary realized that her aunt did not want to display poverty in front of these visitors. 'One day,' she said, dropping her napkin, 'Dyson will doubtless conquer his fear of the telephone. Very well, Hilary, perhaps you'll pour coffee for Sir Nicholas?'

Sir Nicholas Fenton, the man with the persuasive, subtle voice, introduced himself as Lord de Conroy's lawyer. He had come to Howarth with his son, Lieutenant Edward Fenton, who was on leave from his London job as an admiral's aide-de-camp. Edward, formally introduced to Hilary, was suddenly eager to gain her approval. He had chauffeured his father to Howarth because he

43

wanted to see the famous house and had explored its chill glories while his father discussed its future with Pearl. Now, as a means of earning Hilary's approval, Edward Fenton gave the house lavish praise. 'You're very fortunate to live here,' he said.

'Yes.' Hilary, still offended by the memory of his kiss, was studiedly cold with the lieutenant.

'It's such a pity,' he went on, 'that the place has to be seething with Yanks. All the best places are these days.'

'They're mostly wounded Americans in Howarth,' Hilary said with icy challenge.

Sir Nicholas, plump and smooth as butter, watched the two of them. The girl, he thought, was truly an exquisite beauty, despite her frightful clothes and the faint smell of the fields she had brought in with her. It was a beauty, Fenton saw, that was unbalancing his son who, in his eagerness to impress the girl, was stumbling into voluble foolishness.

Sir Nicholas, embarrassed for his son, smiled sympathetically. 'Is there any news, Lady Hilary, of Lord Montague?'

'No.' Or rather, Hilary thought, the news was all bad. The Germans had pulled out of the southern Balkans and neither the Allied missions nor the Yugoslavs had discovered any sign of Major the Lord Montague Howarth. Hilary gave a wan smile. 'The Red Cross say he isn't a prisoner.' She shrugged. 'I think we've all rather got used to the idea that he's dead.'

'I'm so very sorry.' Sir Nicholas drew on the cigar that he had picked from the dead Marquess's cedar-lined cabinet. 'I met your uncle a few times and he was always such a very good companion.'

'Yes, he was.' It was astonishing, Hilary thought, how even now she clung to the ridiculous hope that Monty was alive, and that his idiotic enthusiasms would once again lighten her life. She wondered, as she had wondered a hundred times during these last six months, why Monty had married Pearl. Love, she thought, was a mystery.

Pearl came back into the room. 'That's looked after. I never knew sheep could be so troublesome. Thank you, Hilary. Tell Dyson that Mr Billings will be here within the hour.' Hilary, glad to be relieved of the company of the lawyer and his over-confident son, stood to leave, but Pearl checked her with a hand and looked

44

towards Edward. Pearl wanted him out of the way while she continued her discussions with his father. 'You said you wanted to see the estate, Lieutenant. I'm sure Hilary will be glad to show it to you.'

Hilary, trapped, could only agree. Sir Nicholas waited until she and his son were gone, then smiled at Pearl. 'She's exceedingly beautiful, my Lady.'

'And tiresome. She wants to go to Oxford, which is ridiculous.' Pearl spoke brusquely, as though Hilary's future was a small matter; then she took Sir Nicholas, a most subtle and ingratiating lawyer, into her study. There they talked, as the winter day faded into chill dusk and as the American bombers came thundering home from the east.

They were still talking when the blackout curtains were drawn and as the RAF bombers climbed towards the spreading cloud cover that would hide their journey into Germany. And at their conversation's end Pearl felt hope.

The Lord de Conroy had sent an emissary; the emissary was a clever man, and Pearl dared to think that a bargain could be made, a feud ended and Howarth saved. That above all. The sheep might sicken in their winter pastures and men might fall in flames from the cold night above Germany, but Pearl would keep the house her husband's ancestor had won with the Knight of Swords; she would keep Howarth.

In April, accompanied by Sir Nicholas Fenton, the Lord de Conroy came to Howarth again.

His Rolls-Royce, the three martlets lacquered on to its front doors, was parked in the drive while his Lordship was closeted with her Ladyship.

'It was a quite ridiculous feud,' Pearl said to Hilary that evening.

'Is it over, then?'

'It should never have begun.' Pearl eyed the playing card over the mantel, hating everything it stood for. 'Kynaston and the Fentons are coming to luncheon on Sunday. I hope you'll be here? I know he'd like to meet you.'

'Of course.'

There was money suddenly, and Hilary learned that it was a bank loan, evidently advanced against the happy conclusion of the negotiations that were going on between Pearl and the twenty-third Baron de Conroy. Hilary knew no details of them, only that there was now a feeling of hope that Howarth would be saved and Pearl's obsessive ambition realized. At Sunday's luncheon, for the first time in one hundred and thirty-two years, a de Conroy voiced his belief that the first Marquess had won Howarth by cheating at cards and no Howarth voice was raised against the slander. Pearl merely laughed, while Edward Fenton, who seemed to be able to take a day's leave whenever it pleased him, gave the Lord de Conroy a sycophantic smile.

In May peace came to Europe. Fighter planes stood redundant on the margins of airfields, tank engines cooled in churned fields, and London's street lamps glowed for the first time in six years. The crowds in the victorious capitals of the West surged with aimless joy. In the East, the Allies still fought the Japanese, but in Europe there was victory. The church bells of Britain, silenced for so long, pealed the news that, at long last, there were bluebirds over the white cliffs of Dover.

With the announcement of peace Pearl moved to London, to the Brick Street house where Hilary's parents had lived and which was part of Howarth's shrunken inheritance. Hilary, by her own choice, stayed in the country where Pearl was happy the girl should remain, insisting only, for propriety's sake, that she sleep at Lady Calamore's house.

On the first Friday after the German surrender Hilary donned Monty's old fishing waders and started to hack out a clogged drainage ditch that was thick with weeds. Pollarded willows made it hard for a tractor to pull a drag line through the ditch, and Hilary had volunteered to tackle the job. 'You won't get ten feet, my girl!' Mr Dyson had said.

'A shilling a foot over ten, Harry?'

'Go on with you.'

She did at least fifty yards before midday and had the satisfaction of a hard, physical task well done. She pulled the waders off, ate her lunch, then leaned back on a willow bole. She slept.

Ten minutes later she woke to a kiss.

She screamed in fright, sat up, and reached for the machete she had been using on the worst tangles in the ditch. 'Oh, it's you.'

'That's some welcome.' Edward Fenton, dressed in faded cricket whites, grinned at her. 'Hello.'

'I'm busy.'

'You were sleeping. I hacked my way through the brambles and awoke you as all sleeping beauties should be woken. 'Are you going to the village dance tonight?'

Hilary struggled back into her waders, and stepped down into the ditch. 'I am, yes.'

'With me?'

'I'm not going with anyone. An American lieutenant is giving me a lift there, but that's all.'

Edward rolled on to his belly and watched her. He thought he could gaze at her for ever, that he would never tire of Hilary's delicately delineated mouth, her innocent eyes, or her smooth, honey-gold skin. 'Come with me instead. I've borrowed a car.'

'No.' Hilary raked cut weed from the ditch bed and watched the brown water gurgle and swirl into the cleared space. It was, she thought, very satisfying work.

'Do you get paid for doing this?' Edward asked.

'No.'

'So you could take the afternoon off,' he said. 'We could go to the river, yes? There's a boatyard I know where we can get a sail.'

'I've promised Dyson I'll do this.' She hacked down with the machete, driving Edward back with its muddy splash. She laughed at him. 'Sorry!'

She wondered why she disliked Edward Fenton. This was his fourth visit to Howarth, and the first time he had come without his father or pretending that he brought legal papers on his behalf. Ever since their first meeting he had been eager to impress and please her, yet she instinctively shied away from him. He was handsome, and tried hard to be friendly, but he had a kind of glossy arrogance, a cockiness, that Hilary did not like.

Edward lit a cigarette and watched how the rise and fall of the

47

machete strained the cotton shirt against her breasts. He began talking about the Lord de Conroy, and it struck Hilary for the first time how much he hero-worshipped the older man and modelled his behaviour on the Baron's confident haughtiness. 'He really is the best sort of Englishman,' Edward said in an echo of his public-school housemaster, who had been very keen on the best sort of Englishmen.

Hilary bent to cut a thick stem with her clasp knife. 'If there is such a thing as a best sort of Englishman,' she said, 'then Monty was that.'

'I never knew him.'

Hilary dragged the cut weed on to the bank. 'He wasn't unlike de Conroy,' she said thoughtfully. 'He shot, he hunted, he fished, and he did them all very well. But he was never arrogant. He used to make us laugh a lot.' She thought how inadequate that description was; how it skimmed round Monty's infectious insouciance, his grace, the common touch that had characterized the apparent ease with which he did the difficult well.

Edward fixed on just one thing she had said. 'He was like de Conroy?'

'In a way.' Hilary thought she might have said the wrong thing, but did not care to correct the impression.

'That's probably why Pearl likes him so much.'

Pearl liked de Conroy, Hilary thought, because he had money. 'Probably,' she said.

'Don't you think it's odd,' Edward said, 'that he's prepared to lease the house to Pearl?'

Hilary thought that Edward was trying to make her gossip about her family, and said nothing. 'Don't you?' he asked again.

'I really don't know.'

Edward would not be deterred by her evasiveness. 'I mean if he really wants to live in the house again, and he does, why is he letting Pearl take a lease on it?'

Hilary straightened up, wiped a muddy hand over her forehead, and leaned on the bank opposite Edward. 'I truly don't know.'

Edward thought she looked unutterably beautiful: a dirty, bedraggled Venus in a ditch. 'Do you think,' he said archly, 'that there's a secret clause?' He enticed Hilary with his words, seeing that she was becoming interested despite her show of indifference. 'Like marriage?'

'But she's not certain Monty's dead!' Her words were a protest, but one that was useless against the sudden sense Edward's words made. Marriage was the perfect solution, and it explained why Pearl had been so confident in these last few weeks, so imperious and brusque. De Conroy's fortune would be married to Howarth's dilapidation and Hilary wondered why she had not suspected such a thing before.

'Of course it isn't official,' Edward said, 'but I'll lay ten guineas to one of yours that it will be within the month.'

'I don't gamble,' Hilary said, feeling rather prissy as she said it.

'But you do dance?'

'Yes.'

'And you are going to the village hall tonight?'

'On my own,' Hilary said very distinctly, which was not entirely true for, later that afternoon, Stephen Ruckmeister came to Howarth to fetch Hilary from work, and drove her to Lady Calamore's in his shining red MG of which he was inordinately proud. Ruckmeister was an American Mustang pilot, uncomplicated and cheerful, and content to be Hilary's companion rather than her lover. He admired Lady Calamore's garden while Hilary bathed and changed, then drove her to the dance that would celebrate a war's ending. Edward, dressed in his naval uniform, watched the red MG come into the main village street.

The victory dance was hardly different from the weekly village dances that had been held throughout the war. The small parish hall was draped with the flags of America and Britain, and, because the war was won, the rector grudgingly gave permission for the American servicemen to bring alcohol into the hall. As they had always done so, despite Reverend Kite's disapproval, it really made small difference.

The music, as ever, was twofold. The evening began, in the lemonade-drinking presence of the rector, with a three-piece band of drums, accordion and violin played by the village butcher, his brother, and a local teacher. At half past eight, when Reverend Kite left for his supper, the American musicians took over. The dancing, which had earlier been sedate enough for any clergyman's taste, turned into jitterbugging.

Edward privately thought of such village dances as peasant fare, yet this evening was a chance for him to be with Hilary. She had arrived at the hall with an American, but Edward saw that she did not stay at the pilot's side. She danced with almost any man who asked her. Edward drank the free, sour-tasting bourbon and told himself that tonight, with Pearl absent in London, Hilary was his for the asking. It was for this reason that he had abandoned the capital's pleasure and come to the village.

For Hilary the dance was an event at which she dared not show partiality to any man. She was from the big house, there were obligations that went with that privilege, but they were not ones she found hard to assume. The other girls, combing their shingled hair in the small mirror tacked up in the porch, might sigh over their men, but Hilary was not in love.

It was a night of happiness, for the war had been won, but there was also sadness because the Americans were leaving. Some were going home while others, like Ruckmeister, were being sent to the Pacific. The dancers drank to victory and drowned parting's sorrow in liquor.

'They're drinking too much,' Hilary said.

'In righteous celebration, surely?' Edward had waited for his moment, seen that she was bereft of partners for a while, and positioned himself possessively at her side. The music slewed into a fast, jazzy beat. Edward, thinking that her refusal was negotiable, drained the whisky so that the glass would not encumber him. 'Let's dance?'

Hilary laughed. 'This is my party piece.'

'Your what?'

But Stephen Ruckmeister, who had not danced with Hilary all evening, swooped across the floor, held out his hand, and Edward could only watch as the two of them went into a quick, practised Charleston that, judging from the spectators' expressions, was indeed Hilary's party piece. She danced it beautifully and with a contagious enjoyment.

She laughed aloud, daring the musicians to go faster. The other couples stepped back, enjoying the performance, and clapped with the music's rhythm.

Edward watched. He thought the American pilot had an ugly square head and a frightful cropped haircut and a stupid snubbed nose. Edward found a discarded glass full of whisky, drank it, and let the jealousy sear through him like the flush of the liquor.

And Hilary, he thought with sudden illumination, was a tease. She was so heart-achingly beautiful, by far the most lovely girl in this shabby hall, but she was a bloody tease all the same. A tease in a white skirt and a pale blue sweater that made her sun-bleached hair look even blonder. Each smile she gave to another man tore at Edward's soul like a bullet. He had stalked her these last weeks so softly, not wanting to scare her off; he had thought her so innocent and guileless, but now she flaunted herself in front of these damned peasants with a square-headed Yank who had a chest of medal ribbons that the Americans, in Edward's view, seemed to give away with the morning bloody cornflakes.

Edward was drunk, but thought he was sober. He believed himself to be in love with Hilary, which might have been true, and also believed, in his drunkenness, that she was mocking him, which was not true. He could not bear to think of her in another man's favour, that she preferred the snub-nosed American to himself.

He wanted her. He had wanted her since the moment he had seized her by the waist in Pearl's study. He woke each morning with the same lust for Hilary, and daydreamed of heroic acts that would impress her. He had believed her to be shy, retiring and innocent, yet seeing her dance so skilfully and gaily he believed he had been wrong. She was knowing all right, and she had hidden it. She was a bitch, he told himself as he knocked back the last of the whisky.

The music finished on a blaring crescendo and the hall cheered. Hilary and Stephen, laughing at themselves and filled with the pleasure of the moment, clasped each other in a friendly embrace.

Edward watched them walk towards him. He was ready for a fight. Ruckmeister, seeing the thin, dark face so full of anger, swerved away from the Englishman. 'Want a drink?' he said to Hilary.

'I need one.'

Stephen plunged into the press of bodies at the drinks table. 'I'll be back!' he called affably.

Hilary waited, watching the irrepressible Daisy locked in a wrestler's grip with a hulking American sergeant, then her own elbow was gripped and she turned to see Edward grinning at her. 'My turn for a dance,' he said.

'In a minute.'

'Dance.' He pulled at her, his smile vanishing. 'My turn.'

Hilary tried to ease her elbow free. 'You're hurting me.'

'I want a dance.' All Edward's sense had fled with his sobriety. He only knew that he, heir to his father's baronetcy, had been slighted by this girl in a hall of peasants and vulgar Americans. To his addled brain they had all noticed the slight, and everyone could see that the Lady Hilary Howarth despised the only man of her social class in the hall. 'My turn.'

'Let go, please.' His fingers were hurting her arm.

'You OK?' Stephen Ruckmeister, a tumbler in each hand, emerged from the scrum of bodies.

'She's dancing with me,' Edward said. Part of him knew that he was acting badly, but the liquor-fed surge of lust was irrepressible.

'I'm not,' Hilary said, and her pointed refusal acted like a spur on Edward's anger. He reached for her with his other hand, as if by physical force he could get his own way, but Ruckmeister simply dropped one of the drinks, soaking Hilary's shoes, and gripped Edward's wrist. 'That's enough, fella, OK? Let's keep it pleasant, right?'

'Fuck you.' Edward let go of Hilary and swung his fist, Ruckmeister pulled him off balance and the Englishman stumbled, flailed into thin air, then fell.

There was a rush of bodies, not to join the fight, but to stop it. Harry Dyson, who had promised the rector he would keep an eye on these dances, dragged Edward away by his collar. 'You all right, Lady Hilary?'

'I'm fine, Harry.'

'I'll dump him outside to cool off.' Edward was struggling, but

Harry Dyson had lifted too many straw bales to be overpowered by a twenty-year-old boy. The dancers parted to watch the naval officer being ejected.

'I'm sorry,' Ruckmeister said.

'For nothing. Thank you.'

'I guess he was a little steamed up, right?'

'Yes.' Yet the incident cast a sudden shadow over Hilary's evening: it was so unexpected and out of character. Edward, she had always presumed, was a gentleman, 'a public-school man' as Pearl liked to call him, and Hilary was sure that he would be back, sobered by the night air, contrite and ready to offer an apology.

But there was no apology. The dance went on and the episode was forgotten by the other dancers. At midnight, after 'God Save the King' and the 'Star-Spangled Banner' had been belted out by the American band, the dance ended and Stephen Ruckmeister bowed to her. 'I have a carriage for your Ladyship.'

'It's a ten-minute walk, Captain.'

He made an ominous face. 'The night is dark, your Ladyship, and the peasants are revolting.'

'Nonsense.'

'It's an exquisite MG,' he said. 'Very pretty, and it needs the exercise. Besides, I'll be gone in a week.'

She laughed. 'OK.'

It was a spring night, beautiful and calm, and the smell of wild garlic rose from the churchyard. The moon was at the half, pale and high, casting a quiet silver light on the street. Two trucks, headlamps unnaturally bright now that the blackout was needed no more, were taking their cargoes of men back to the airbase. Other men, more fortunate, faded into the night's shadows with their girls. Constable Pearson, his belly belted tightly over four pints of ale, watched benignly as the jeeps accelerated drunkenly southwards.

Ruckmeister led Hilary towards the lane beyond the church where his car was parked. 'We could make a detour?'

'To where?'

'I don't know. London? Paris? Berlin?'

She laughed, then stopped abruptly.

The red MG had been savaged. Its tyres, including the spare one strapped to the rear, were slashed and flat. The leather bonnet strap was cut and beneath it was scratched the message 'Yanks go home'.

'Oh God!' Ruckmeister stared in the moonlight.

'I'm sorry. I'm so sorry.' Hilary felt desperately ashamed of her own country. She tried not to believe what she suspected, yet it could only have been Edward. The evening's celebration of peace had been destroyed by rage, lust, and jealousy. 'I am so very sorry.' Her voice was misery itself.

Ruckmeister took her to Lady Calamore's gate. 'I kind of wondered,' he shrugged, 'you know?' He hesitated, then found the courage that was never lacking when enemy planes threatened, but spilt like water when he looked into Hilary's calm eyes. 'You don't want to go back to Howarth tonight?'

'No –' not to Howarth with its empty, waiting bedrooms. She refused, not because she did not like him, but because she would not use her body to give a casual comfort. She looked into his eyes, and smiled. 'You might get more pleasure by looking for Lieutenant Fenton in the Conroy Arms.'

The American returned her smile. 'Thanks.'

She kissed him goodnight, and watched him walk towards the darkened inn. He was a friend, and he was going to another war that might take him just as the war in Europe had taken Monty.

All the best were going, Hilary thought, and she would be left in Pearl and de Conroy's world, a moneyed world where the only merit lay in winning and no thought was given to how the victory was won. They would deny her Oxford, they would want her to marry what they called the best sort of Englishman; but she was a Howarth, she had a Howarth's nerve, and she would go her own way and decide her own fate.

A skein of Canada geese crossed a peacetime moon and Hilary went to her rest.

Peace in London was lights. Lights blazing from buildings, reflecting on the river, blazoning the revellers who thronged the streets in celebration of victory. It did not matter that the city was tawdry, broken by bombs, exhausted by the war, for now it was lit by street lamps that gilded the shabbiness with a magical, almost forgotten sheen. It was peace.

And at the Savoy, there was plenty. There were hams and salmon and cheeses and pies and fruit and pure white bread rolls. There was food brought frozen across the Atlantic, such as had not been seen in years. There were salads and hot plates and serried bottles of wine and white-coated waiters who carried glasses of whisky and rum and gin and champagne. The Americans were giving this ball, and in this tired, drab city, they would make a celebration of peace to match the brightness of the lights outside.

An army band provided the music: it blared slick tunes to make the weary dance. Balloons and streamers littered the River. Room, while exuberant Americans turned what might have been a staid, polite evening into a riot of joy.

Pearl, the widowed Lady Howarth, arrived late, judging the moment of her entrance to perfection so that no one in the room could miss her, not just for her startling beauty, but also because of the dress she had chosen. At a time when all clothes were subject to ration coupons, Pearl had dared to come to the victory ball in a dress of lavish splendour. It was of black crepe trimmed with silver, high-waisted in front and cut low behind, its breast-hugging bodice swelling into a lavishly pleated skirt that reached to her silver shoes. It was a dress that spoke of half-forgotten Parisian luxuries. This night, celebrating the war's ending, Pearl was sinuous, elegant and superb.

She was in mourning. The War Office had written to say that her husband was now considered to have been killed in action. It tendered its regrets, and had the honour to enclose a pamphlet which outlined the benefits available to war widows.

Lady Mirabelle Hare, who had probably launched more malevolent rumours than any woman alive, saw Pearl's dress and whispered to her companion on the margin of the dance floor. 'It's de Conroy, of course. Pearl couldn't afford a frock like that! The last time she was in town she was positively in rags!'

'It's Kynaston's money, of course,' a duchess, who had no

shortage of the stuff herself, said. 'Poor Pearl would be lost without money, but is any amount of it worth sleeping with that libertine?'

'The duchess says that, dear,' Lady Mirabelle confided in Sophie, 'because Kynaston said he'd rather go to bed with a poxed nun than with her. Is it really him? You must know.'

'She's dining in his suite,' Sophie said.

'There you are then!'

And when, after dinner, Pearl appeared with de Conroy's party, the rumour about an impending marriage hissed round the ballroom, was weighed in the scales of gossip and jealousy, and found to be a sensible idea. Pearl and de Conroy looked superb together: she in her shimmering dress and he in his regimentals. Her icy beauty matched his darker arrogance. Just such couples, Sophie thought, must have stalked Augustan Rome or stirred the envy of Versailles.

De Conroy, an hour later, made his bow to Sophie. 'I can just about stagger through a waltz.'

She took his arm and they went out on to the floor. The Baron looked at the elderly females who lined the tables at the floor's edge. 'What are the old bats saying?'

'That your impending marriage is a good thing. Sexless, but good.'

He gave Sophie a sardonic smile. 'It isn't official yet.'

'After tonight, Kynaston,' Sophie adjusted her steps to de Conroy's one-legged efforts, 'what do you have to do to make it official? Copulate on the steps of St Paul's?'

A smile flickered and went. 'You're angry with me?'

'Dear Kynaston, you flatter yourself.'

'I might have told you about this before.'

'Don't be ridiculous. I'd have only gossiped.'

He smiled, bowed to her when the music ended, then escorted her to a table that overlooked the river. Sophie, strident this night in a tube-tight dress of black and scarlet, stared at the unusual sight of lights shaking their reflections on the Thames, then looked at de Conroy. 'Are you starting another rumour, Kynaston?'

He laughed. 'If a man can't drink with a future relative, what

56

can he do?' He clicked his fingers, took champagne from a passing waiter, and sat. 'Would you believe me if I said I'd missed you?'

'Of course. I know my ravishing effect on men.' Sophie lit a cigarette. 'But thank you all the same.' After her one night at Caton Hall she had received flowers, then silence for a winter.

De Conroy lit a cigar. 'Are you well?'

'As you see me.' Sophie shrugged. Her American was leaving, going home to his plump wife in Minnesota, and when he went Sophie's income would plummet. She had been wondering how she could cash in on her secret knowledge of Pearl's deception, but that seemed like a spent weapon now. Sophie was perennially short of money, and knew only too well that she had depended on her looks. There had been a time when she could come to a ball like this with a mere ten minutes of preparation, but these days it took an hour's work on her face before she would stalk her old hunting grounds.

De Conroy watched that face, remembering the silver sheen on her naked body in his bedroom. 'I wish it had been you who inherited Howarth.'

Sophie laughed at the compliment. 'You don't sound happy about your third wife, Kynaston. Has she driven a hard bargain?'

'Very.'

'I did tell you she would. But you get what you want, don't you? Howarth.' Sophie turned to watch Pearl who was now dancing with the middle-aged heir to a dukedom. She thought that Pearl's beauty was that of ice, or steel, or whatever is cold and hard and impenetrable.

'Do they really say it will be a sexless marriage?' de Conroy asked.

Sophie heard a proud male's fear of a slight being cast on his virility. 'Yes, Kynaston, they do. Naturally you'll get a quickie on the honeymoon night, but that's probably your lot.'

He flared up at her. 'God damn it, they're wrong!'

'You don't have to convince me, my darling.' Sophie smiled. 'Pearl might be harder to persuade, though.'

Lord de Conroy twisted in his chair. Pearl, walking from the dance floor, had a refined grace. She was beautiful, desirable, and he could not believe she lacked the passion that ought to turn that tall, lithe body into an instrument of ecstasy. 'I'll have her tonight.'

'A hundred guineas says you won't,' Sophie said instantly.

'Done,' he said, just as fast, and offered his hand.

Sophie hesitated. 'A hundred guineas?'

'The deed to be done before dawn.' His dark eyes lit up suddenly with a gambler's joy.

'How on earth,' Sophie said, 'will I ever know?'

'You will have my word,' de Conroy said proudly. 'My family, unlike yours, has never, ever cheated in a wager.'

Sophie shrugged. 'Your word's good enough.' She touched his outstretched hand with a casual finger. 'One hundred guineas that you don't lay her before dawn,' Sophie tapped ash from her cigarette, 'though I can't see why you bother.'

'Because she'll be my wife.'

Sophie crowed with delighted laughter. 'Don't be ridiculous, Kynaston. You're not marrying Pearl for sex. You get Howarth! Isn't that what you want? Isn't that what your family's wanted for a hundred and thirty wasted years?'

Kynaston de Conroy had thought so, but the whispered, malicious gossip had touched a raw nerve. He had negotiated with Pearl because he wanted Howarth, because his family's passion for the lost house had never abated, yet now, now that he had achieved what all his ancestors had failed to do, he felt he had struck a bad bargain.

The price, he thought, had been too high. He had never encountered a woman who fought as she did. The fight had been conducted by lawyers, but it was Pearl who instructed hers, who had been inflexible in her demands, and who had given not an inch in the long negotiations that would lead to a dynastic marriage.

A marriage that was, in truth, a most elegant, most satisfying solution. De Conroy would regain Howarth, Pearl would keep it, and her son would inherit it. The Baron had wanted his daughter to inherit the house, but Pearl had broken off negotiations until he yielded that point. She knew how desperately de Conroy wanted to call Howarth his own, and she had played on that need to get just what she wanted.

De Conroy would buy Howarth from Pearl. It would cost him seventy thousand pounds, more than double the estate's worth, but even when it was bought it would not be his, for Pearl, in a masterstroke, had demanded a ninety-year lease. He would buy the house at an inflated price, while she would buy her lease at market rates. De Conroy would own it, but Pearl would be the occupier, the tenant.

'A lease!' de Conroy had asked. 'Why in hell's name does she want a lease?'

Sir Nicholas Fenton had shrugged. 'I think it gives her some protection, my Lord, against your buying the house, then not marrying her. Naturally, my Lord, the wedding will invalidate the lease and you will repay the balance of the monies.'

'To hell with the ninety years. She can buy the lease then refuse to marry me! Make it five years. And she doesn't get possession of the park or the farmland.'

They settled on thirty years without the farmland, but with the park.

Pearl then insisted on a document, signed and sealed and locked in her lawyer's safe, that protected her hold on Howarth against the possibility of divorce. Every confounded way, de Conroy thought, the woman had trussed him and beaten him down. 'Is she a God-damned Jew?' he had asked Sir Nicholas.

'I believe the family is wholly English, my Lord.'

'What it comes down to,' de Conroy had growled at his lawyer, 'is that I give the woman seventy thousand pounds for the privilege of living in her house and sharing her bed.'

And now, the Baron thought, the London gossip said that he would not even share her bed. He watched Pearl now, seeing how sinuous her body was in the black and silver skirt. She was a damned proud and superb bitch, but she might have bargained for more than she wanted.

At one in the morning Pearl announced her departure. 'Perhaps you'd send someone for my coat, Kynaston?' she said.

'Fetch it with me. I want a word.'

'Of course.'

They took a lift to de Conroy's suite, kept for his London

visits. 'I do trust,' Pearl said, 'that Fenton hasn't found some last-minute problem?'

'Not that I know of.' He opened the door and ushered Pearl inside. 'The sale will be complete in two weeks. It's astonishing how fast lawyers can move when they smell money.'

'Indeed it is.' Pearl took her coat and offered it as though she expected de Conroy to help her put it on. 'You wanted a brief word, Kynaston?'

'If you don't mind.' De Conroy ignored the coat and led her to the sitting room. He poured himself a brandy. Pearl refused a drink.

'I just thought,' de Conroy said, 'that we've been so busy with the lawyers and their nonsense that we haven't had time to get acquainted.' Which was not really what he had meant to say. Indeed, he had not truly planned on saying anything at all, thinking it best to simply tip this golden-haired beauty on to the sofa and pluck up her skirts, but there was a chilling, formidable quality to Pearl that put a tremor of apprehension into him. The hundred guineas, he thought, might take a little more winning than a swift pounce.

'That's entirely true.' Pearl put her coat on the sofa, positioned herself beside the fireplace, and smiled. 'I think I might have a little brandy after all.' She watched him cross to the cabinet. 'We do have the party in a fortnight.' The Americans were withdrawing from Howarth, and Pearl planned a small farewell party that had swollen to a mammoth gathering, which would also be the occasion when the open secret of their engagement would be made public. 'We'll have plenty of time to talk then,' she said as though that took care of his worry.

De Conroy brought her the drink. 'There are some things, my dear, that are best not said in public.'

'How very true. Thank you,' she said, taking it from him.

'I'm not even sure,' de Conroy said, 'that I've told you how very glad I am to be marrying you.'

'It's entirely mutual, Kynaston.' Pearl's voice was matter-of-fact, but her eyes seemed huge to him, and the sconced lights threw soft shadows beneath her cheekbones.

'You're very beautiful,' he said and leaned forward to kiss her.

She turned her head an inch so that he kissed her cheek instead of her lips, then raised the brandy glass and thus forced his head backwards.

She lowered the glass. 'I'm so glad Christine gets along with David.'

'That's splendid, yes.'

'I'm sure we'll be very happy,' Pearl said in a voice that expressed no particular joy, though she was, in fact, speaking the truth. De Conroy, after all, was not so unlike Monty, and Pearl did not believe her life with this man would be very different from her well-ordered life before the war. Then, each year had begun with the London season, after which Monty and Pearl would stay with friends for Ascot before departing in wagons-lits for the Continent. Late in August they would return to Britain and take a night-train to Scotland where, on the Howarth estate, Monty fished for salmon and shot grouse. November saw them at home in Ash where Monty delighted in the high, fast birds. At Christmas they went to Howarth. In the New Year Monty hunted with the Quorn, then, with the point-to-points over and the Colonel's Cup safely back on Ash's shelves again, the season started once more and the trunks were packed and the cars run down to London.

Pearl did not shoot or fish, and disliked horses. Monty enthusing over his Game Book did not amuse her, but nor, she admitted, could she interest him in the paintings she bought. Put like that, she thought, it sounded as if it had been a bad marriage, but that it had never been.

It had not been ecstatic, but neither Monty nor Pearl had been so foolish as to expect ecstasy. Monty had never been anything less than kind, nor anything less than a friend. He was a gentle, attentive lover who, sensing that Pearl took little pleasure in sex, used his skills on other women. He never did it to hurt or embarrass her. Above all things, she thought, Monty had been a gentleman, and that was not a bad epitaph.

And de Conroy, she was sure, was also a gentleman; an excessively wealthy one, which would happily ensure that the future would be as predictably privileged as the past. He was also, at this moment, demanding Pearl's body.

Pearl had expected it, knew it was a reasonable demand, and even thought it handsomely polite of de Conroy to display such eagerness. Yet at this moment she could not think of anything that was more unwelcome or more inconvenient. Making love, for Pearl, was an activity that needed to be planned, to be fitted into a timetable, and she had never taken pleasure in what she privately believed to be impulsive messiness. 'I was hoping,' she said, trying to postpone his ardour, 'that you would stay on for the weekend at Howarth after the party?'

'It will be my greatest pleasure,' the Baron said, and he took the brandy from her hand, put it on the mantel, then put his arms around her. If he tried to talk her into coming to bed, he thought, he would be here till the second coming. So he kissed her instead.

Pearl seemed to move backwards, or else his false leg betrayed him, for suddenly she lost her balance and fell against the wall beside the mantelpiece. De Conroy had to flail for support. Neither was hurt, and Pearl laughed as if in embarrassment as they untangled themselves. 'Dear Kynaston,' she said.

'It's the damned leg.' De Conroy had taken her hand and he drew her towards him, then downwards till she could either fall over or sit on the sofa. Pearl chose to sit, and he kissed her again with such force that she went backwards until her head was on the cushions and she lay thinking how extraordinary men were to put such stock on carnality.

De Conroy's lips slid from her mouth to her neck and from her neck to the swell of her breasts above the stiff silver-black brocade of the bodice. His right hand was on the silk at her ankle, sliding up, while his left explored the skin his lips had kissed, then pushed beneath the cloth to finger her breasts. 'Dear Pearl.' He kissed her again, to still any words she might utter, and his right hand forced up her skirts until, with astonishment, he found his path obstructed by the elasticated band of a pair of *directoire* knickers. Such a garment, he thought, should not stand between a man and his hundred guineas and he forced his hand beneath the elastic and on upwards till he felt the warm, smooth skin above her stockings and he thought, with sudden joy, that this was a woman of extraordinary, splendid beauty, and he knew he would have her, that she would be his.

'My darling.' De Conroy tried to ignore the ludicrous situation, telling himself that passion would come when the silken obstruction was gone. He unclipped the stocking's suspender.

Pearl put a tentative hand on to his black, oiled hair. It was most undignified, but sex was always that. Monty, she thought, had at least made her laugh sometimes. 'Dear Kynaston,' she said as an experiment, but he was too busy trying to find her other breast to reply.

A second suspender clip went, his breath was warm on her pale skin, and the knock, at last, came loud at the door.

'Damn them,' de Conroy growled.

'If only I'd known,' Pearl said. He had raised his head when the knocking sounded, and she used the space to sit up, tuck her breasts back into her dress and then to give him a swift kiss on the cheek. 'Do tell them I'll be right out, will you?'

'You?'

'Of course!' She twisted lithely around him, dragging herself free of his elastic-trapped right hand, and stood. She looked into the mirror to pat her hair into place. 'Coming!' she called out.

'You rang the service bell?' De Conroy was still on his knees.

Pearl decided her stocking was safe with its one remaining suspender clip. 'I wanted to order a cab. I didn't realize we might have something more thrilling to do.' She swept up her coat, blew him a kiss, and walked to the door. 'I shall wait for the taxi downstairs. Two weeks, my dear, yes?'

De Conroy, when she had gone, looked at the service bell by the mantel and saw that it had not been his leg giving way, but Pearl who had pulled him off balance so that, while he kissed her, she could press the bell behind her back. God damn it, he thought, but what a magnificent woman! He heaved himself to his feet, and thought that in two weeks' time he would have the clothes off her and all of that tall, pale body would be revealed and then, perhaps, the price of Howarth would not seem so very steep after all.

He took her glass of brandy, added it to his own, and thought how superb her breasts were, how tantalizing that one glimpse of long thigh had been, and relished the taming he would give her in just two weeks.

Thus Sophie won a bet, and Howarth was sold.

The valley was a place of stones. A stream coursed from the barren hilltops, foaming white around the rocks and tumbling bright and cold towards the lush, lower pastures where pomegranates flowered and ilex grew at the meadow margins. In summer the stream-bed would be dry, but the spring had been late this year and the meltwater still filled the valley with its roaring, hurrying sound.

A herd of sheep and goats grazed the valley. It was a mystery what they ate, for the grass was pale and tightly cropped, yet the animals survived. The rams had bells tied to their collars and their mournful clanging rang harsh by day and night.

There was a village in the high valley, a miserable place of stone shacks and steep, mud-slicked streets. At the top of the village, next to the church that had been bombed by the Germans, was the big house. It was built round a courtyard where heathers grew between the cracked stones.

There, Corporal Horton died.

Monty wept for him.

Horton had lived so long and endured so much since the German night-fighter had shot down the Mitchell bomber carrying the British military mission to its dropping zone. Only two men, one of them the radio-operator, Horton, had fallen safely from the plane. The wind had swept their parachutes across the coastline and the two men had landed high in the hills above the sea. Horton had received a sliver of the Messerschmitt's cannon fire in his belly and Monty, no doctor, had saved the corporal's life with crude surgery.

The winter had come early in 1944. The two men, Horton

slowly recuperating, had taken shelter in a high village. They tried to find Tito's partisans so they could continue their war, but the Germans had found them instead. Armed only with a single sten-gun and two miserable spare magazines they had fled into the snow.

They had gone south and east, struggling into a howling blizzard that blanketed their tracks and froze snow on their soaked clothes. They had crossed a high ridge and there Horton had collapsed again. Somehow Monty had carried him down the mountain to a village.

A Cetnik group had found them. The Cetniks were running from the Germans and the Communists, and had unwillingly carried Horton away from the expected German pursuit, as far as this village near the Greek border, where they had left the two Englishmen.

A doctor came once a month from the valley, and he had re-opened Horton's wound, stitched it again, and sprinkled sulphur powder on the swollen, foul flesh around the stitches. 'He will live.'

Monty had believed it. Horton had believed it. Slowly, painful day by painful day, the corporal had seemed to recover. Monty had worked through that winter, earning their keep by unblocking a well that had been filled with stones by a German explosion, and each evening he would feed Horton and talk to him of life after the war.

Horton would go back to Birmingham. His job, he said, was waiting for him, thanks to the union.

'Not thanks to the boss?'

'Bloody hell, no!' Horton had laughed, then hissed as the pain seethed through him. 'And you?'

'I don't know,' Monty would say, but then he would talk about Howarth, how its rooms looked out on to the park, and its gilded pillars rose to painted ceilings; how it was so very beautiful.

'I wouldn't mind seeing it,' Horton said.

'You will. Bring the wife.'

Horton had laughed. 'She won't believe I know a toff, will she?'

In March Horton had climbed out of bed for the first time and soon he was walking from the house to the well where he sat and watched Monty work. Monty was glad he had not surrendered the corporal to the Germans. He had thought of doing it at one time, sure that the Germans would put Horton into a hospital and treat him well, but the corporal had begged him not to.

The Germans had retreated. That news came to the village, and when Monty asked the doctor to send a message to the Allied front that two Englishmen were in the high hills, he promised he would. Later he said it was difficult. Some Greek communists, fighting a civil war across the border, had retreated to the safety of Yugoslavia. 'They don't like the English,' the doctor said. It seemed British troops had thrown the communists out of Athens. 'You stay a little,' he said, 'you're safer here.'

So they stayed and then Horton died. It happened very suddenly. One night he was sitting at the table, laughing with Monty and the woman they lodged with, and the next morning he was dead. He had bled to death, a massive haemorrhage, and he lay in his bed with a faraway, placid look on his face.

Monty buried the corporal. He insisted on digging the grave himself, and he hacked down through rocky soil until he reached the bedrock. He had made a shallow scrape over which, the body laid within, he heaped earth and stones. The villagers, sensing his grief, watched him.

They saw a tall man, made cruelly thin by the war's exigencies, with hair the colour of angels' wings. Before the Germans came, there had been a mosaic of angels in the village church and their wings had been made of thousands and thousands of golden tiles that had been blasted into powder by the German machine guns and hand grenades.

Monty had a face that could crease into laughter more easily than any the villagers had ever known. The women all thought him handsome, not just because of his swift smile, or his thin, fine-drawn features and eyes the colour of a summer sky, but because of his strange, soft courtesy that made each of them feel, when he spoke with her, that she was the most important person in the world. One man had thought the Englishman soft because of his solicitousness with women and would carry a knife scar to his dying day because of the mistake. The villagers had seen

Monty's easy manner turn to a merciless, quick cruelty in the blinking of an eye.

At the head of the grave Monty placed a cross and a flat-faced stone in which, with a blunt knife, he scratched Horton's name. It was a duty. He scratched deep, cutting and grazing his fingers. The work saved him from thinking, and for that he was glad.

The war was ending. The great battles that had flowed and ebbed across the continents were smouldering into embers now. The time had come for him to return home, and he found no gladness in the thought. He had not liked the war, but Monty did not think he would welcome the peace.

He was a younger son, and the war had given freedom from that role. He had fought, as he had lived before the war, without thought of the morrow, but now the morrow was come. One part of Monty wished he could go on, ever on, walking eastwards into new places and new adventures, seeing strange city walls and hearing the waves break on exotic shores. The war had given him adventure and companionship and extremes of passion, and now he must face the smaller world of family and duty. He would go from a banquet to short commons.

That night Monty packed the few things he possessed. He took Horton's dog tags, his boots, and the sten-gun. He put them by the door, ready for the morning.

'You're going,' the woman said.

'Yes.'

She was a widow. Her husband had owned the big house, and the Germans had stood him on the cracked flagstones and shot him. The woman refused to clean the blood from the stone that had faded to a dull, pale brown. 'If the communists catch you,' she said, 'they'll shoot you.'

Monty slid his hands down her hunger-thin body, kissing her breasts and her belly. She reached for him, wanting to hold him and to be held. The wind sighed at the sacking-covered window and stirred sparks in the tiny fire.

'Do you love me a little?' she asked.

'A lot, and for all time.'

The woman looked into his eyes. He had the brightest blue eyes she had ever seen and a gaunt, hawk's face and he made love as though he would make the pleasure last till eternity. She guessed that he made every woman feel that way. It was a gift some men had, and this man had it. 'Are you really a lord?'

'Really. My father and my brother are greater lords, but I am a lord.'

She held his face in her hands. 'The other man was not a lord?'

'No.'

'But you cried for him?'

'He was a friend.'

She smiled, not truly understanding. 'I won't cry when you leave me, Englishman.'

'Then I shall cry for you.' He felt her body push up beneath his and he slowed his movements to make her pleasure last and when it was over, and she was crying, he held her against the dark night.

He left in the morning. He carried his pack, his gun, and a half-loaf of bread. He walked past the stones heaped on Corporal Horton's grave and did not look back.

He did not know who was a friend and who an enemy in this bare landscape. The Greek communists would kill him, the Yugoslav communists celebrate with him, and the Cetniks, if any were left, might do either, so he kept to the high paths and used his soldier's skills to stay hidden.

On the third day he was above a high valley. An aeroplane flashed in the sunlight beneath him and he took his binoculars from his pack and saw the barred star on the wings. It was parked at the end of a makeshift strip hacked out of the cornfields and Monty, his sten-gun shouldered, scrambled down the mountain.

The plane's American crew was one of the last teams searching for downed airmen in these inhospitable mountains. They were packed and ready to leave as Monty walked into the farmyard which had been their temporary headquarters. Their leader, a captain, stared at the tall, bright-haired man who wore a sheep-skin jerkin and carried a machine gun. His face was tanned the colour of mahogany, he looked like a bandit, but he spoke crisp English. 'Jesus Christ,' the American said, 'who are you?'

Monty grinned. 'Major Monty Howarth. Inniskilling Dragoons. Is the war over?'

'You bet.' The captain looked at Monty's clothes and laughed. 'You planning to stay, Major? Or do you want to fly to Rome?'

'Rome? Now?'

'We're leaving in two minutes.'

'Rome!' Monty smiled seraphically. 'There used to be a brothel off the Veneto which had the most beautiful whore in Europe.'

'Let's go find her!'

The whore, like the brothel itself, had gone, but her existence was confirmed by a local bar-keeper who offered the two men a much-thumbed photograph as proof. Monty stared at it, listened to the strange sound of traffic out ide, and thought how much the world had changed. He was the Marquess. He had been told as much at the British headquarters where, in half an hour's time, a telephone call was booked for him, to Howarth.

Then it would be time to go. The Lord Montague Howarth, Fifth Marquess of Arlington, Earl of Arlington, and Baron Howarth of Howarth, would take possession of his fiefdom, of his land, and of his house. Monty was alive, and he was going home.

The formal farewell to Howarth's American hospital had become Pearl's celebration of her own victory. Howarth would be restored in all its grandeur, and she would be confirmed as its chatelaine. The vast wealth of the de Conroys, old money, would be hers.

Amidst the continuing rationing and drabness of a country drained and exhausted by war, her party, catered by the Americans, would be a lavish beacon that promised a return to normality. The invitations, which had at first been few in number, multiplied with Pearl's burgeoning ideas. The Americans, whom she had treated heretofore with scant courtesy, were badgered into ever greater generosity. Honey-roasted hams were brought from Virginia, oranges from Florida, and there were even lobsters fetched from a US Naval base on England's south coast. Servants, in desperately short supply, were supplied by the orderlies of a nearby British officers' training camp.

The training camp's officers had to be invited, as did the senior officers of a dozen American or British airfields in the vicinity. The local gentry needed to be shown that Howarth was once again to become the grandest house in the county. The bishop was summoned from his palace, and Howarth relatives, even the most distant and half-forgotten, were called to witness this renaissance of Howarth's fortunes.

The de Conroys would come. Gentry from a dozen shires, all tracing their ancestry to the French lord who had fought with the Conqueror at Hastings, would come to see the house the family had lost and never thought to regain. The bitter feud would be drowned in champagne and ended in celebration.

Pearl's father, told privately of her engagement to the Lord de Conroy, was delighted. 'Always knew you were a clever one!' His laughter crackled down the telephone line. 'You're a grand girl, lass! Proud of you!'

'So you'll come?'

'Wild horses wouldn't stop me!'

'And mother?'

'She's poorly, lass.' Lady Gall had been poorly ever since her wedding day. 'Have a word with her.'

The invitations went out and a surprising number of people were willing to endure the privations of a war-torn travel system to see Howarth's rebirth. The day before the great event, Pearl added up the acceptances and harried the Americans into yet more largesse.

'I make it three hundred,' Hilary said.

'At least.'

'And more than forty have asked if they can stay the weekend.' The party was on a Friday and the celebrations, Pearl hoped, would linger through till Sunday.

'They can't all stay. The linen isn't aired.' Pearl keenly felt the lack of servants. 'Did you phone the Conroy Arms?' At least, she thought, the stubborn refusal of the local inn to change its allegiance would no longer gall them.

'They're keeping six rooms. And Mr Thomas at the Spread Eagle has four reserved.'

'I'm putting Kynaston in the Blue Room,' Pearl said briskly.

In keeping with her implied promise of a fortnight before, the Blue Room adjoined her own suite of rooms.

Hilary, knowing it, said nothing.

Pearl pulled the lists towards her. 'Would you mind sleeping out?'

'Not at all. I'll go to Lady Calamore.'

'She'll like that.' The telephone rang. 'Can you answer it?'

Hilary picked it up. 'Howarth six four.'

An American sergeant put his head round the door to ask whether her Ladyship wanted the protective boards taken down from the plasterwork in the Long Gallery.

'I thought that was done!' Pearl said.

'Not yet, ma'am.'

'If you'd be so kind, Sergeant. And be careful about it! That plasterwork is older than your White House and a good deal more precious. And, Sergeant!'

The cropped head wearily reappeared. 'Ma'am?'

'The paintings. Are they fetched up from the cellars yet?'

'All done, ma'am.'

'And hung?'

The sergeant, wishing someone would hang her Ladyship, affirmed that the paintings, stored against bomb damage for so long, were back in place on the walls.

'Splendid. I shall come and inspect them. Who is it, Hilary?'

Hilary shrugged and held out the telephone. A succession of crackles, far louder than usual, sounded from the earpiece. 'I thought,' she said, 'that I heard Italian.'

'Italian? Must be a crossed line. The Post Office can't do a thing right! Sergeant! We'll start in the Music Room.'

Hilary shouted the number again, thought she heard a faint reply, but when she listened again, heard nothing. She waited two minutes, then put the telephone down.

The next day dawned fine and stayed fine. Pearl had the main entrance, lacking its fine wrought-iron gates, unboarded. The few Land Army girls left were bullied into weeding the half-mile of gravel beneath the avenue of elms. Howarth, as far as it could be, was ready. The drink arrived in American trucks, directed by Pearl's command to the kitchen door so that the great sweep of the forecourt would not be gouged by their tyre-marks.

Pearl made a last inspection of the house and gardens. Mr Dyson was ordered to cut the lower terrace finer. He sniffed. 'Mower blades are rusted up, aren't they?'

'Then unrust them.'

'And there's no petrol, your Ladyship. Not for mowers.'

'See Colonel Meyers. Tell him you need gas. That's what they call it, Dyson, gas. Well, go on, man!'

One of the tablecloths in the Banquet Hall was deemed to be crooked. All the silverware had to be removed so that the cloth, a redundant bedsheet from the American hospital, could be straightened. The orderlies were paraded for Pearl's inspection and instructed in their duties. Mrs Carline, leading a press gang of women from the village in cleaning and airing the bedrooms, complained that some of the pillows were falling apart. 'No Christian could sleep on 'em, my Lady!'

'Needle and thread in the sewing room!' Pearl said sharply. 'Hilary will show you where they're kept. Where is she, by the way?'

'Sweeping out the Garden Room.'

'Have Dyson's men painted the furniture there yet?'

'I don't know, my Lady.'

'Remind him if they haven't.'

Taggart, alone for so long in Howarth, could not cope with the influx of people. He retired to the butler's pantry with a bottle of American rye whisky and was asleep long before the party began.

The Baron de Conroy arrived at midday, Pearl greeted him on the steps and looked approvingly at his Rolls-Royce that shone in the summer sunshine. She thought it looked apt on Howarth's forecourt. 'I think your man might leave it there, Kynaston.'

'Of course.'

'The servants will be looked after in the kitchen,' Pearl said to the chauffeur. 'This way, Kynaston.' He limped with her through the newly swept corridors, leaning on his ebony stick. The house would soon be his.

Sir Nicholas Fenton, his wife and Edward arrived next. Sir Nicholas, like de Conroy, had come early for the important business of the day. Edward had the remains of a black eye. 'I fell downstairs,' he told Pearl.

'That was careless. If you want Hilary I think she's in the Garden Room.'

Lady Fenton was given tea in the Yellow Drawing Room while Pearl took the lawyer to the Library where de Conroy waited. Sir Michael Gooding was due at any moment.

Sir Nicholas poured himself and the Baron a whisky while Pearl opened a folder. 'You might like to look at that, Kynaston.'

It was a list of the staff Pearl wanted for Howarth. Footmen, parlourmaids, cooks, gardeners, grooms, boilermen, a clockman and laundry girls. De Conroy stabbed down with a finger. 'Five hundred pounds a year for a housekeeper?'

'Howarth deserves the best. If you agree,' Pearl said, 'I thought we'd talk to an agency next week.'

'Absolutely.' He pushed the folder back to Pearl. 'Whatever you think best, my dear.'

It was that open-handedness that Pearl liked. Kynaston de Conroy, she was sure, would be happy with his guns and fishing, his horse-racing and his friends, and Pearl would be free to restore Howarth as she wished. A vision of grandeur was her blueprint, a vision that would take the kind of money only a de Conroy could provide. The thought warmed Pearl, making the prospect of this night's lovemaking the more endurable.

'Gooding's late, isn't he?' Sir Nicholas said.

Before Pearl could answer, the telephone jangled in her study next door. She frowned. 'That will be someone else wanting to come. Hilary!' Hilary was out of earshot and the telephone went on ringing. 'Where's Taggart?' Pearl demanded of no one in particular. She sighed and went into the study.

'Howarth six four.' Her voice betrayed her annoyance at having to answer the telephone herself.

There was a chuckle down the line. 'Pearl?'

Pearl went cold all over. She felt the blood surge through her like a tide of chill water.

'Pearl?'

She thought she would faint. She was shivering, and goose pimples prickled on her skin.

73

The Baron de Conroy, drink in his hand, smiled at her as he came into the room. He stared uncomprehendingly at a Manet that Pearl had brought from Ash.

'I can't speak now,' Pearl said. Her thoughts were racing. She was sure that her consternation must be so obvious, so very, very obvious.

Monty was alive. He was talking to her. His laugh, a bit puzzled because of her words, was echoing in her ear. She felt sure that de Conroy could hear Monty's voice, but he still stared at the painting above the mantel. 'Where are you?' she asked.

'Bummed a lift home with the Yanks. I've just landed in Suffolk.'

'Tomorrow,' Pearl said desperately. If she did not sign the lease today then she would lose Howarth. God knows there could be no marriage to de Conroy now, but she would hold Howarth if it was the last thing she did.

She had insisted on leasing Howarth, because she thought the lease would stand even if the marriage fell. It gave her possession of the house. She told herself that the marriage would have changed nothing, that she needed the seventy thousand pounds, and she knew she must keep this call secret or else the poverty of Howarth would drown her.

Monty was alive! She shivered.

Her blood raced like ice-water, yet her mind was clear. If she could hide this astonishing news then de Conroy would buy the house, the money would pay off the death duties, Pearl would get her lease and Howarth would be safe for thirty years. A lot, she thought, could happen in thirty years.

'Pearl?'

'Tomorrow!' she said sharply. Tomorrow she would show surprise, astonishment, regret, but the house would be saved.

Then, in a counter-flood of turmoil that made her body shake with anger, she knew this call must be a hoax. A cruel, damned hoax. Of course it was. 'Tomorrow,' Pearl said. 'Call me tomorrow, you understand?'

The man began to speak, but Pearl put the telephone down. Her pulse raced and her ears were singing. She held the handset down with both hands as if she could block out the horror, and the Lord de Conroy, alerted by the strain in her voice, turned from the painting. 'Is everything all right?'

'Yes.' It took a huge effort for Pearl to say it.

'Who was it?'

She had never thought faster. 'David. He's fallen over, silly boy. Playing cricket. He always makes too much of a fuss.' She knew the lie was inadequate, that it did not live up to her flushed, tense appearance or the breathlessness in her voice. So stupid, she thought. So stupid and so unfair! She had fought for this house. She had negotiated a settlement of such beauty, such utter beauty – and now this! All that money waiting to be poured into Howarth, the servants who would tend it like acolytes, the future: all was threatened!

De Conroy frowned. 'He fell over?'

'I can't stand crying children. It upsets me.' Pearl still held the telephone. She was dressed in black, becoming, widow's black, because her husband was dead. Today she had planned on being the noble, grieving, calm widow, and Monty was alive. It must be a hoax, it must be!

The Baron sipped his whisky. 'I shouldn't be upset,' he said with rough sympathy. 'A few knocks and bruises are good for children. Toughens them up.'

'Exactly.' Pearl let go of the telephone and, to her relief, it did not start ringing. 'I'm afraid David's prep school doesn't use the cane enough.' She thought she must sound hysterical. Alive? For God's sake! She would have to back out of this transaction now, she could not go on with it and deceive this man. But there was the bank loan; and there were the hundreds of guests arriving in an hour's time, and there was Howarth which, without her signature on the paper, would be lost for ever. Even thirty years, she told herself, was better than nothing.

Then, in a whirl of apologies, the wing-collared Sir Michael Gooding arrived and Sir Nicholas, his round face beaming, knocked on the study door and suggested that perhaps the moment was opportune.

Pearl took a deep breath. It was a hoax. Of course it was. There were cruel people who would enjoy inflicting such pain on her, and no credence could be put upon such a stupid jest. If

75

Monty was alive then the War Office would have said so. It was a hoax. She nodded. 'Of course.'

She walked into the Library and stood silently while the lawyers arranged their papers on the long, mahogany table. 'My Lady?' Sir Nicholas offered Pearl a gold-nibbed fountain pen. 'I've marked the spaces that need your signature. I apologize that there seem to be so many, but one can't be too careful.'

'Indeed not.' She took the pen, bent, and seemed to watch her own hand write her name. It was a practical joke, of course, just the sort of stupidity that Monty's old friends would find amusing. Damn them! Yet tomorrow, she consoled herself, she would look back on this panic as silly. Pearl signed again, and again, and again. Tomorrow, she thought, she would wake up in de Conroy's bed. She hoped he was gentle. She signed for the last time, the blood pounding in her ears, then, very calmly, laid the pen down, thinking, as she did so, of the moment last year when another pen had forged a time of death on this table. All for Howarth. Everything was for Howarth.

Sir Nicholas offered the pen to de Conroy. 'My Lord?'

No one spoke. The gold nib scratched on the paper. Sir Michael, assiduous and attentive, followed the pen with a blotter attached to a wooden rocker.

The last paper was signed and Sir Nicholas smiled. 'May I use your telephone?'

'Of course.' For a wild moment Pearl thought he was telephoning Monty, then she thrust the idea away. It was a hoax!

They waited. Sir Michael inspected the blotter, de Conroy smiled a secret smile, and in the garden a lawn mower coughed into life. Pearl jumped at the sudden noise.

Sir Nicholas came back from the study. He poured whisky into four glasses and, with a smile, handed them round. 'I have just confirmed,' he said, 'that the monies have been released into your Ladyship's account, less, of course, the price of the lease.' He bowed, triumphant, to de Conroy. 'You will be delighted to know, my Lord, that the cheque did not bounce.' The small joke released the tension and Pearl, smiling, raised her glass.

'A moment!' de Conroy said harshly, and panic fluttered back into Pearl. 'I won't drink to this happy moment yet.'

Pearl knew it was over then, that he had known she was lying about the telephone call, but the Lord de Conroy said nothing. Instead he took a clasp knife from his pocket, walked to the mantel, and grunted as he levered the framed playing card off the wall.

No one spoke. They watched as his Lordship splintered the frame, cracked the old glass, and finally succeeded in wrenching out the Knight of Swords. He tossed the broken frame and playing card into the hearth. 'It's over,' he said.

Pearl forced a smile, and raised her glass. 'To Howarth.'

'To Conroy.'

Pearl saw that the whisky was shaking in her glass. She tossed it all down and knew that the call had to be a hoax. A hoax, a hoax, a hoax, and Howarth was sold.

The warm weather allowed the guests to saunter out on to the wide terraces above the ornamental lake. 'I don't know,' the Earl of Fleet, a cousin of de Conroy, said to Pearl, 'how you kept your lawns in such good shape. Mine are quite foul.'

'We grazed sheep for much of the war.'

The Earl turned to stare at Howarth's garden front. The stone was pale, the carving delicate, and the afternoon sun was warm on the house's beauty. 'It's good to see the place back in the family.'

It was a feeling shared by many of the guests. A few family members, like Lord Mackerson, had refused to come, saying that it was unfitting for Pearl, an interloper, to be the one to end the feud, but that opinion was rare. Most of the two families, like warring tribes discovering they had no cause to fight, mingled in new amity.

There was a band in the Ballroom and another smaller band on the upper terrace. Lights had been strung from the Garden Room roof to the portico that led out from the Yellow Drawing Room. They would be lit in the evening, for this party would stretch from the sun's zenith to the paling of the moon. Everything that could be done, Pearl thought, had been done.

There were guests strolling on the lawns and by the ornamental lake, and the house was filled with music and laughter. This, Pearl thought, was how it should be, and she had achieved it. There was much yet to be done: there was painting and gilding and plastering, but this day she was giving the county a glimpse of the magnificence that was Howarth. She saw more guests arriving and, still nervous after the hoax telephone call, watched to make sure that no tall, golden-haired man was among the newcomers. But it was a party from London, led by the Lady Mirabelle Hare who gave Pearl a kiss on the cheek. 'Positively nothing, darling, would have kept me away. Black suits you.'

'Thank you.'

'But it suits anyone, doesn't it? Kynaston looks well, doesn't he?'

'I think so.'

'Marriage always has suited Kynaston. It spruces him up for a time. So charming.'

But no sour jealousy could spoil this day for Pearl. Her mood, as the afternoon shaded into a perfect evening, lightened with each moment. Of course it was a hoax! If Monty had been in Suffolk he would be here by now. The clock over the stables struck seven and she felt an immense reassurance that the call had been nothing but a cruel and tactless jest. She smiled on life. Howarth, shabby as it was, looked splendid. This evening, the great house alive with guests, music, and entertainment, was a foretaste of all that was to come.

'Your children,' an American colonel asked, 'are not here?'

'They're at school. David's in Oxfordshire and Caroline's in Berkshire.'

The colonel looked at the great façade that was now touched by the sinking sun. 'Some place for your boy to inherit.'

'Isn't it?' Praise of Howarth was balm to Pearl.

The officers gave the party colour, their dress uniforms bright and their gallantry displayed in the rows of shining medals. Lord de Conroy's friends, tall, loud men with confident voices and condescending eyes, congratulated him on his engagement. 'She looks a cracker, eh?' the Earl of Fleet said.

'Not bad.'

'Wouldn't mind a hack on her myself, what? Good God, that's Sophie.'

Sophie had arrived with a man in a uniform of ornately ancient grandeur who claimed to be a Polish count. He ensconced himself in the billiard room with a British officer. 'He's going to win a lot of money,' Sophie said.

'At billiards?' Hilary asked.

'He's very good, but pretends he can't play. It's a living, though.' Sophie shrugged. They were walking together on the lower terrace. A warm wind rippled the lake and beat tiny wavelets on to the mossy bank. 'Wouldn't it be funny,' Sophie said, 'if Monty were to walk in?'

Hilary laughed. 'Poor Monty.'

'Darling, he's in hell and seducing all the she-devils.' Sophie stopped and stared at Howarth. 'He'd hate this.'

'Hate it?'

'All these de Conroys. I can't really think that Monty would approve.'

'Did he like Howarth?'

'I don't think so,' Sophie shrugged. 'Not that much, anyway, but it was the bone the family dogs were trained to guard and I don't think he'd approve of it being tossed so easily to Kynaston.'

Hilary smiled sadly. 'Pearl's putting up a memorial stone.'

'Don't tell me.' Sophie grimaced. 'Monty remembered in marble and de Conroy sleeping in the Blue Room?'

'Yes.'

'What a treasure you are to have told me. Mind you, he deserves his reward for paying all that money. If you can call cuddling Pearl a reward.' Sophie gave Hilary a sideways glance. 'It must be like going to bed with the Venus de Milo. Cold as stone and no arms to hug you.' She laughed, remembering de Conroy's prompt cheque for a hundred guineas and the amusing note that had been folded round it. 'When will they marry?' she asked.

'No one's actually mentioned a date.'

'I can't see him delaying long, not while Pearl has a lease and he can only visit with her permission.' Sophie laughed again and decided she liked Hilary. She had rarely met her elder brother's family and had thought that Hilary would prove a priggish, dull young woman, but she liked her niece's intelligent innocence. It would be sad if that goodness was sullied. Sophie found herself surprised at choosing that word, yet Hilary did emanate a kind of goodness. 'I hear,' Sophie said carefully, 'that I might have cause to congratulate you.'

'Me?'

'Wedding bells?'

'Mine?' Hilary was so astonished that she checked her walk to stare at her aunt.

'I was talking to Kynaston's lawyer. The fat one with a voice like butter going down a drain? He said his son was frightfully struck by you.'

'Edward?'

'If that's what the callow youth is called, yes. But I probably read too much into his words.'

'What words?'

Sophie made a vague gesture with her furled parasol. 'Oh, Sir Nicholas said something about his son having a head start in the race for your hand. What's the boy like?'

'Quite foul. You'll recognize him because he's in naval uniform and has a black eye.'

'Your work?'

'In a way.' Hilary smiled.

'Good for you. So I don't need to save up for a wedding present?'

'Not for me,' Hilary said grimly.

'God alone knows what one gives Pearl the second time around. A dose of Spanish fly perhaps?'

Hilary laughed, then turned to look at the house. The dusk had not yet faded into darkness, but in the soft, dying light Howarth shone like a jewelled cabinet decorated with bright moonstones. There were dancers on the terrace and beneath the Ballroom's sparkling crystal chandeliers.

The bishop danced with Pearl and congratulated her on her engagement. 'Is Lord de Conroy a churchgoer?'

'Not that I know of,' Pearl said, 'but neither was Monty.'

'One does hope his Lordship is,' the lord bishop said, thinking of de Conroy's fabled wealth and of all the dilapidated churches in the diocese, 'one fervently hopes so.'

De Conroy watched Sophie walk into the house with Hilary. He bowed to them, encouraged Hilary to go off to where the food was being served, then offered his arm to Sophie.

'*Directoire* knickers,' Sophie said.

'I didn't think anyone wore them these days!' De Conroy's cigar smoke trailed back down the terrace. 'At least no one under fifty. Got my damned hand caught in them.'

Sophie laughed with delight. 'I did warn you.'

'She'll have to be broken, won't she?' De Conroy spoke lightly, but Sophie heard the steel in his voice. 'If that woman thinks she can take my money and have a headache every night, she's wrong.'

'Most women survive happily like that,' Sophie said.

'Not my women,' de Conroy said grimly. 'It's my house and I'll have things done here my way. She's not going to prettify it, not on your life. Dogs and horses, that's what makes a house! Not bloody wallpaper and rugs. If I leave it to her it will look as if a pansy lives in the place.'

Sophie laughed. 'Pearl won't be easily broken, Kynaston.'

'She will be.'

Sophie perched on the stone wall that edged the upper terrace. She wore a dress of white silk that hugged her slim figure. Around her neck was a black choker studded with gems and in her hair, a spray of white silk flowers. In the lengthening evening shadows she looked sultry and desirable, still emanating the musky invitation to sensuality that de Conroy remembered. She smiled. 'Pearl's cleverer than you think.'

'She'd like me to think so, I'm sure.' De Conroy sat beside her. 'But clever women can be broken.'

'Perhaps. But she's already cheated you once, Kynaston.'

The dark, thin face turned and frowned. 'Cheated me?'

Sophie looked into the harsh, proud eyes and wondered whether she should say anything, but then the devilry in her provoked her. Everything was signed and sealed, and her secret could harm no one now. 'It took me a long time to work it out, Kynaston, but our darling Pearl told a monstrous lie.'

'A lie?'

'John died after father.' Sophie saw the shock that the news brought de Conroy, and lit a cigarette. She blew smoke into the darkling air. 'I really should have been brighter. You see she telephoned me when the old boy snuffed it, and now I think about it, that call must have been earlier than half past four, which was when John and Louise were killed. I think she changed the death certificate, or whatever one does in those circumstances, and all to save the death duties!'

Lord de Conroy stared at Sophie. She was telling him that Howarth would have been his anyway, and for a much lesser price, for a price that would not have contained marriage and a lease. God damn it and God damn it again. 'You might have told me,' he said bitterly.

'Don't be a fool,' Sophie said sharply. 'If I'd have thought of it earlier, of course, I would have told you! What do you think I am?'

'A bloody Howarth! A cheat!'

She jumped up and walked away from him.

'Sophie! Sophie, please!'

The 'please' stopped her. She turned.

De Conroy stood, flinching as his stump took his weight, and limped towards her. 'I'm sorry.'

'You think I'd have kept it secret?'

'I apologize.' His voice was still bitter and taut with the knowledge that he had been duped. 'Are you sure?'

'No, I'm not. I could be entirely wrong. And how would you prove it anyway? I only told you because I thought it was amusing.'

The Baron forced a smile. 'I couldn't prove it, and you're right. It is amusing.' He did not think it was amusing at all. Once married, he thought, he would have the truth from Pearl and he would exact a revenge on her body.

'Don't say anything to her, Kynaston.'

'Of course not.' He looked down into Sophie's provocative, beautiful face. 'It's sad your memory served you so ill.'

'Isn't it?'

'I think you should make it up to me.'

She laughed. 'Why not? Next week?'

He took her hand and kissed it. 'I think I should join my bride and look happy.'

Sophie watched him walk away. Once he was married, she thought, that tale would make a pretty morsel to serve to London's gossips.

One of those gossips, the rotund Sir Nicholas Fenton, had discovered the fourth Marquess's cabinet of cigars in the Smoking Room. He rolled one between his fingers, breathed a sigh of ecstasy, and lit it. He had not tasted a Monte-Cristo in four years. And today of all days, when the Lord de Conroy had sealed such a splendid triumph – he saw the Lady Hilary pass the door and called out to her.

She came in. 'Sir Nicholas?'

'Dear Lady Hilary.' Sir Nicholas patted a chair beside him. 'I seem to have appropriated a bottle of champagne. Might I tempt you?'

'A little.'

He poured her a glass. 'I have good news for you.'

'Really?' Hilary, remembering what Sophie had told her on the terrace, wondered if Sir Nicholas was about to propose marriage on behalf of his son, but instead the plump lawyer told her she would be going to Switzerland.

'Switzerland!' Hilary said in astonishment.

'Lord de Conroy has funds in Switzerland. I have contacts in the Foreign Office who will give you a travel permit, and you can go to the finishing school in Verbier!' He spoke as though he was unveiling a delicious treat to a mentally defective child. Pearl had suggested the finishing school, and de Conroy had agreed to pay the fees. 'It's such a good idea,' Sir Nicholas said. 'You can ski!'

Hilary smiled. 'I don't think so.'

'You don't like skiing? Skating, then?'

'No. Not in Switzerland.'

'But . . .'

'If I can't go to Oxford, Sir Nicholas, I certainly won't waste anyone's money in Verbier.'

'But . . .'

'I'm going to Oxfordshire, to the Ponsonbys.'

Sir Nicholas, who had warmed to the notion of this beautiful girl emerging from finishing school as a suitable bride for his son, gulped. 'Lord Ponsonby?'

Hilary nodded. 'He's re-opening his stud and wants me to help with the horses.' She smiled beatifically. 'Isn't that good news?'

'Your dear aunt knows?'

'Not yet. But I'm going next week.'

'But my dear Lady Hilary, it's an egregious mistake!'

'Nonsense.' Hilary stood. 'If you sent me to Switzerland I'd run away with a cuckoo-clock maker and disgrace you all. Aren't you coming to dance?'

'Later, perhaps.' Sir Nicholas shrugged. It was her funeral, he decided, silly girl. If she wanted to become a stablehand, then let her, but she would regret it when the Lady Pearl de Conroy cut off her allowance. He must, Sir Nicholas thought, have a quiet word with Pearl before this evening ended.

Hilary, happy at the defiant stand she had taken with the lawyer, walked into the Ballroom to come face to face with his son. Edward stiffened, frowned, then gave her a wooden bow.

She peered at his naval tunic and pretended delight. 'Isn't that the Atlantic medal ribbon? What did you do? Sink a U-boat since the war ended?'

Edward had the grace to blush. 'I had to borrow the jacket. My fool of a steward spilt gravy on mine.'

'How sad. What a pity your friend didn't have the VC.' Edward, who had told himself a thousand times in the last two weeks that he hated this girl, felt all the despair of thwarted desire as he saw again her blue eyes and the perfection of her face. 'I think I should apologize to you.'

'Whatever for?'

'The last time we met. I was . . .'

'I know what you were. Did Stephen find you? Or did you fall downstairs?' Edward said nothing, and Hilary walked away from him. One of the American doctors, who had spent the last eight months in vain pursuit of the Lady Hilary, asked her to dance and, to his astonishment, was accepted. Edward could only watch and suffer.

84

The night came gently, the sky shadowing into watercolour perfection over the wide park. Birds flew home, and two swans, as if knowing that this evening needed their grace to complete its wonders, turned on arched wings and floated down on to the lake's glittering surface.

The orchestras played, the food was plentiful, and the laughter was contagious. The party, even the most scornful were forced to admit, was a great success. Champagne and lights, ballgowns and uniforms, splendour in the gathering dark.

And in the gloaming no one noticed the thin man, dressed in a foul sheepskin jerkin and old paratrooper's trousers and boots, walking up the drive.

The US Air Force, who had rescued Monty out of Yugoslavia, were flying from Rome to England the next morning. No one else seemed to know what to do with the Marquess of Arlington so, his telephone call from Rome cheated by the bomb-torn land lines, Monty had accepted the offered lift home. He flew to an airbase in Suffolk.

He left his sten-gun at the base and accepted the loan of an old bicycle. He had no money, except a few lire. All afternoon he cycled north through the gentle countryside. The bicycle chain broke and he walked the last six miles through a gentle English dusk, watching the wild geese cross the sky and wondering why Pearl had been so terrified when he telephoned her from the American base at lunchtime.

He climbed the front steps of Howarth. A young couple, sitting there with a bottle of wine, smiled at him. He smiled back. 'Good party?' he said.

'Very good.' They watched him go inside and thought that the strangest people gate-crashed parties.

He walked through the Entrance Hall and into the Ballroom. He saw a blur of people, of uniforms, of faces. He walked through them and no one recognized the Marquess of Arlington with his brigand's clothes and his wind-hardened face.

Monty stopped by one of the tall windows. On the terrace, beneath the strung lights and as superb and beautiful as he had remembered, was Pearl. And on her arm, possession written all over his dark face, was the Lord de Conroy. They were sur-

85

rounded by laughter, by adulation, by admiration. It was impossible to escape the message of that commanding touch upon Pearl's
arm and Monty, at last, understood why she had behaved so
strangely on the telephone.

The Marquess of Arlington stared at his black-dressed wife.
For months now he had dreamed of this moment. He had smiled
sometimes to be indulging in fantasies of that old cliché, the
warrior's return, yet indulge he had. In his dreams Pearl had
been coming towards him, smiling, her arms reaching for him,
and he had fantasized that her emotional coldness would be
broken and all her beauty deployed for his welcome. Instead he
stood in his own home, a stranger, and watched her on the arm
of another man.

The American band, brass blaring, played 'We'll Meet Again'.

Monty had the strangest compulsion to simply walk away.
They thought him dead, of course. Rome Headquarters had told
him that. He did not belong here, he was in a dream, and if he
walked away now then no one would ever know that he had even
been there.

The music ended, there was applause, and a man touched
Monty's elbow. 'You OK, fella?'

He turned. An American was staring at him. Monty forced a
smile. 'Yes.'

'Some thrash, eh?' The man gestured about the Ballroom.

Monty turned to look. 'Indeed, yes.'

Someone screamed. The band, about to strike up another
tune, paused with instruments raised. Conversation froze
throughout the huge room and two hundred faces turned to look
at Hilary who had screamed involuntarily with shock. She stared,
across the gleaming floor beneath the bright chandeliers, at a
painfully thin man in sheepskin and khaki who had walked out
of the grave.

Monty stared back at his niece. In her childhood he had been
Hilary's joy, the uncle who had scared her with ghost stories,
listened to her, treated her, not as a child, but as a valued
friend.

She had gone white.

Monty smiled. 'Hello, squirt.'

'Monty?' Hilary ran to him, arms outstretched, and he picked her up, and whirled her round, feeling the prick of tears in his eyes.

Hilary was crying. 'You're alive!'

'That's just a rumour.'

There was silence. Everyone in the room looked at the delight on a girl's face and at a tall man, dressed like a bandit, who cried and laughed at the same time.

From the open terrace doorway Pearl stared at him. She had gone pale as death. Monty looked at her. Hilary was still in his arms and his vision was blurred by the tears of homecoming. His wife did not come towards him, did not smile, did not reach out with her arms. 'Hello, Pearl,' he said.

The glass fell from Pearl's hand and shattered into a hundred fragments.

The two families, who had come together to end an ancient feud, edged apart like wary dogs.

Sir Nicholas Fenton and Sir Michael Gooding stared at the apparition and then thought of the fat lawyers' fees this coming home would bring.

The Lord de Conroy knew he had been cheated, and his world flamed red.

For Monty, Marquess of Arlington, had come home.

The shotgun hammered into de Conroy's shoulder and a flower-pot, standing on the parapet of Caton Hall's terrace, disintegrated into red shards, twitching soil and shredded scraps of geranium. 'She knew. The bitch damn well knew!' The second barrel flared and another geranium was snatched off the balustrade. 'She knew! God damn it! She knew! I was in the same damn room when he phoned!'

'You don't know that,' Sir Nicholas Fenton suggested gently.

'Do not tell me what I know and do not know!' Lord de Conroy turned furiously on the lawyer who was sitting in the shade of the panelled drawing room. 'They think I'm a fool!'

'It was extremely foolish of you,' Sir Nicholas said equably, 'to lose your temper.'

'I should have killed her.' De Conroy broke the gun, pushed fresh cartridges into the barrels, and looked for something else to shatter. His ten-year-old daughter, Christine, cried upstairs and he frowned at the noise. 'You know a decent boarding school for girls, Palliser?'

John Palliser, de Conroy's second guest at Caton Hall, shrugged. 'Alas no.'

'Damn bitch,' de Conroy said, evidently thinking of Pearl rather than of his daughter. 'God-damned cheating bloody bitch.' He emptied both barrels at a moss-covered sundial, causing stone to splinter away and his daughter to cry even louder.

Sir Nicholas Fenton had once been close to the fall of a German flying-bomb. He remembered how it had taken time for the world, broken into a million shards, to settle into reality again, except that in that moment of shattering explosion, when the intolerable pressure of the gases had blasted bricks and iron and glass, reality had been changed for ever.

Lord Montague Howarth was alive, and even a fortnight after that dreadful night at Howarth Sir Nicholas still felt as if a bomb had exploded in his life. His client had bought a house, sold a lease, with the net result that the Marquess of Arlington now possessed Howarth for the next thirty years.

'If you had not been so precipitate,' Sir Nicholas said chidingly, 'Monty would probably have settled by now.'

'Who cares if he settles? Damned jumped-up family! Fifth bloody Marquess!' The twenty-third Lord de Conroy poured scorn on to the word 'fifth', then fired again to drive over a garden chair with lead shot. 'Made their damned money in trade! They're not real aristocracy, Fenton! The real aristocracy came here with the Conqueror, not by toadying to George the damned Third!'

'I'm sure that's fascinating.' Sir Nicholas wrinkled his nostrils at the acrid smell of the gunsmoke that drifted through the open

French windows, 'but *arriviste* or not, I suspect Monty will now be stubborn.'

'Then I'll bloody destroy him.' Bang went the gun again, and the fallen chair twitched under the shower of lead.

'You probably will.' Sir Nicholas sighed, remembering that fearful night at Howarth. When Pearl had dropped her glass in the open doorway there had been silence in the ballroom.

De Conroy had lurched forward. He had taken Pearl's elbow, forcing her to look into his face, and he had asked her a question in a voice too low for anyone else to hear. The guests saw her shake her head. He had asked again, more urgently, and again she had shaken her head, in even more emphatic denial, and then, infuriated beyond endurance, he had brought his left hand round and slapped her face with a crack that echoed like a pistol shot in the room's frozen silence.

Sir Nicholas remembered the gasp that had sounded round the ballroom when de Conroy hit Pearl. It was a moment, the lawyer reflected, when the atavistic savagery of the old aristocracy had been stripped bare, like the velvet glove taken off a steel-clad fist. In that moment the Lord de Conroy was like one of the barons who had plunged mediaeval England into blood and barbarity.

Monty had let go of Hilary.

De Conroy had turned, hand raised, but Monty hit him swiftly and his false leg, no ebony stick to support it, had given way. The Earl of Fleet had jumped to his cousin's aid, but Monty slammed an elbow into the Earl's belly, brought his left hand back into his face, then sent him sprawling over the fallen de Conroy and he crashed, flailing, on to the terrace.

No one else moved. The fight had been so swift, so silent and savage, that some people had missed it entirely, merely thinking that the Baron and his cousin had tripped over as Monty advanced towards them.

The Marquess of Arlington looked down on de Conroy. 'You raise a hand against any of my women again and I'll kill you.'

An odd phrase, Sir Nicholas had thought, 'my women'. For Monty too, it had been a moment of atavism, a sudden stripping away of civility in a room where the de Conroys had moved to one end and the Howarths to the other, with only the bemused Americans left in the middle. It had been then that Monty turned and drove the enemy family from Howarth, barking the command like a soldier, chivvying embarrassed, silenced guests out to their waiting cars.

Monty had fought for his family's honour, not for his wife's, for he made plain his displeasure with Pearl. He had ordered her to find the Knight of Swords and replace it on the wall, and the old feud, with the playing card, was reinstated.

'The marriage,' de Conroy now said with sudden savagery, 'was your idea.'

'Yes, and you agreed to it.' Sir Nicholas was too eminent and had been too well rewarded by the law to be frightened by de Conroy. 'If you're unhappy with my advice, my Lord, I will recommend another solicitor to your service.'

De Conroy broke the gun again and threw it on to a leather sofa. He dropped into a chair and looked at the man who sat to the lawyer's right. 'I never even had her.'

John Palliser gave a slight frown. He could never quite accustom himself to aristocratic mores, even though his merchant bank was popular with the landed gentry and he had many dealings with them. The banker could think of nothing intelligent to say in reply to this open admission of sexual failure, so he said nothing. 'Mind you,' de Conroy went on, his temper evidently exhausted by the shotgun blasts, 'she probably isn't worth having.' He lit himself a cigarette and looked cheerfully at Sir Nicholas. 'So! We'll sue the bastards till they scream, right?'

Sir Nicholas reflected how tiresome the Barony of England must have been before there was the law and Parliament to restrain their simple-minded brutality. 'The very worst thing you can do, my Lord, is to sue.'

'For Christ's sake, why?'

The lawyer's affable smile hid a mind as sharp as an assassin's knife. 'I took the liberty of lunching with Gooding, entirely without prejudice you understand. Their defence will be to suggest that you took advantage of a penurious woman, apparently widowed by war, who was in desperate financial straits, and to whom you offered matrimony because of your well-known wish to regain Howarth.' Sir Nicholas's eyes were closed, and his face was happily benign. 'To persuade her to accept your hand, you deliberately devised a lease of such strict and onerous conditions that she, with nowhere to turn, and, indeed, distracted by her grief, accepted.' The shrewd eyes opened suddenly. 'I might dare to suggest, my Lord, that not only would you lose, but that their Lordships might see fit to allow the Howarths full possession with damages.' Sir Nicholas smiled his most subtle smile. 'So don't sue.'

De Conroy had listened to him with commendable patience, but now he shook his head. 'Damn the lease, sir. I want them sued for forging the old man's time of death.'

'That is a criminal matter and for the discretion of the Director of Public Prosecutions.'

'Then fix it! That's what you're supposed to be good at, isn't it? Have lunch with what's-his-name, take him to your club!'

Sir Nicholas smiled into de Conroy's angry face. 'Your grasp of legal procedure is most impressive, my Lord. I can doubtless interest the DPP in the case, and I can probably influence him with some judicial lobbying, but the law has an inconvenient habit of requiring proof, and the hearsay of a well-known London gossip is no longer sufficient, I fear, to bring about convictions in the court.'

The news that the Howarths might have cheated the Treasury out of death duties piqued the banker's interest. 'How much will the duties be?' he asked.

Sir Nicholas shrugged. 'Sixty thousand? Maybe more.'

'And they'd have to pay twice?'

'If it was proved the son died after the father,' the lawyer said carefully, 'yes. Though the second set of death duties would be halved because of the closeness of the two deaths.' He shrugged. 'They couldn't pay anyway.'

'And if it were proved that the elder son succeeded,' de Conroy said hopefully, 'then my agreement with Mountsorrel would be valid and those bastards will have to scuttle out of Howarth.'

'If,' Sir Nicholas said, 'we can prove it.'

'We'll prove it.' De Conroy only had Sophie's word as evidence, but he planned to pursue it. The Lady Sophie, he had decided, was the weakest link in the family chain, and he would use his wealth like a hammer on that link.

Sir Nicholas knew that the idea of forcing the Howarths into a criminal court on a charge of fraud appealed to the gambler in the Lord de Conroy, but he was less sanguine about the chances for a successful prosecution. Pearl in the witness box would be a formidable opponent, more than capable of using her femininity to coax sympathy from a jury. 'The object of the exercise,' the lawyer now said in his careful, plummy voice, 'is to evict the Howarths from Howarth and to do it as expeditiously as possible. If we must use the law, we will succeed, but the law is susceptible to delay. I prefer to attack their finances. John?'

Palliser drew papers from his briefcase and, in a dull voice, read out the list of vast properties of Howarth that the fourth Marquess had mortgaged. There were estates in the North Country, manors in Wiltshire and Somerset, a moor in Scotland, and housing in London. There was arable land in the Midlands and orchards in Kent; and this roll of vast wealth that had once been Howarth was now held by bankers. 'I would suggest, my Lord, that we buy those mortgages now and immediately foreclose. My information is that the family is in no position to make any payments.'

'Will the holders sell?' de Conroy asked.

'After last week,' the banker said grimly, 'they'd be delighted to sell.' The British people had just surprised themselves by electing a Labour government and ejecting Winston Churchill from Number Ten. The new government, dazed by their own success, promised a managed economy in which the people would be rewarded by ownership of all the important industries. Britain, it was said, would slough off the old evils of capitalism and show the world how freedom and socialism could prosper hand in hand, and the first fruit of this new freedom was a disastrous panic among the finance houses.

The Baron nodded. 'Buy them. We'll strip the bastards bare.'

Palliser nodded and de Conroy had the grim satisfaction of knowing that he would flense from Howarth every damn property it owned and, at the same time, Sir Nicholas would give surveyors instructions to go over the house itself with a toothcomb. Every last defect, down to a missing carpet-tack, was to be found, listed and costed, for by the terms of the lease tenants had to pay for repairs and de Conroy would make those repairs prohibitively expensive. He would attack his enemy with money and, if money did not work, there was always the chance that he could prove Sophie's startling allegation.

'We won't need to go to court,' his lawyer said calmly.

'We won't?'

'The new Marquess will do our work for us.' Pleased with the decisions taken, Sir Nicholas walked to the window and stared at the serenity of Caton's parkland. 'We couldn't hope for a better opponent!' He chuckled. 'Howarth's hopeless with money. He believes, God bless him, that there is a giant tap in the sky out of which flows an endless succession of half-crowns and guineas. He will spend with abandon and nothing that his wife can do will stop him.' Sir Nicholas turned back to de Conroy. 'He is, in short, an irresponsible spendthrift, a playboy! Pursue this business of the death duties by all means, but I promise you, my Lord, that long before the case can come to court the Marquess of Arlington will be dog-broke and begging you to let him off the lease. You will see him ruined, and you will see him on his knees. I promise you.'

De Conroy looked dubious. 'His father-in-law's rich.'

'The marriage is in tatters! There'll be no help from that quarter.' Sir Nicholas smiled reassuringly. 'Arlington's already started to destroy himself. He's abandoned the Marchioness and taken himself off to what passes these days for fleshpots in London. I do assure you, my Lord, that the Marquess will bring about his own destruction.'

'And when he's down,' de Conroy said, 'I'll kick him in the bloody teeth.'

'Precisely,' Sir Nicholas said. A banker, a lawyer, and a wealthy lord were now Howarth's enemies, and all Howarth had was its playboy back from the wars, its Knight of Swords, Monty.

The letter was addressed to the Marquess of Arlington at his London house. It was written in a careful copperplate script and had the honour to suggest that, should the Marquess happen to be passing his bank, he might care to step inside and discuss his private account.

Monty threw the letter into the empty grate. Damned banks.

He wondered why he even bothered to open his mail these days; it brought nothing but bad news. Damn the lawyers, damn the banks, and damn the bloody horses that were running slow.

A second letter had the honour to inform his Lordship that the mortgages held by the undersigned on the Howarth property had been purchased by Palliser's Bank Ltd, of Lombard Street. The undersigned thanked his Lordship for the privilege of having been able to serve his Lordship's family for so many years, and expressed the sincere hope that Messrs Palliser Ltd would continue to extend to his Lordship every courtesy that the undersigned had striven to supply in the past. 'Damn you too,' Monty said, and threw the second letter after the first.

It was slowly dawning on him that he was poor.

He had come back from the war expecting to find Howarth, as it ever had been, replete with money. Instead, there was none. He wondered who in hell Palliser's Bank was, and why they had bought his mortgages.

'Coffee, my Lord.' Hammond, who had been Monty's batman before he disappeared into the Special Forces, put coffee and *The Times* on the breakfast table. He had appeared, newly demobbed, at the Brick Street tradesmen's entrance and declared that he wished to be Monty's valet, chauffeur, and gentleman's gentleman. 'The going's firm at Goodwood,' he now said hopefully.

'When did I last pay you, Hammond?'

'So far, my Lord, I have not received any wages.'

'So how the hell can you have money for Goodwood?'

'The dogs ran well last night, my Lord.'

Monty grunted. He had a hangover, but he usually did these days. 'You're probably richer than I am.'

'It's very likely, my Lord. Might I suggest that Tinker's Daughter in the third race might be worth a bob or two?'

When he was alone again, Monty stared at the newspaper and

wondered what on earth an atomic bomb was. He turned to the racing page instead.

He supposed he would have to draw on Howarth's tax account again. Pearl had begged him not to, but what the hell? The money was his, not hers. The account contained the money the Lord de Conroy had paid for Howarth, and was being kept for the death duties, but Monty was not in any mood to humour the Marchioness of Arlington. He would damned well spend it if he wanted to.

The dining-room door opened and a brunette, wearing one of Pearl's dressing gowns, yawned. 'Good morning.'

Monty glanced up and nodded. 'Good morning.'

The girl sat at the far end of the table. Hammond, alerted by the sound of her feet on the stairs, brought in coffee, toast, and his own copy of the *Daily Mirror*. She smiled her thanks. 'I'm not here, Hammond.'

'I know that, madam,' he replied, sounding offended.

Monty saw that Tinker's Daughter was quoted at nine to one, which usually meant that the bookies didn't know what to make of the beast. 'Might go to Goodwood,' he said.

'Lucky old you. I told Roger I'd be getting the two thirty back from Bristol.'

'I hope he's not at Paddington to meet you.'

'He would never do that!'

By the time Roger and his wife were reunited, Tinker's Daughter had come in sixth. Monty tore the ticket in two.

Monty was approaching forty. That fact depressed him. He did not feel forty; he felt young, full of life, and depressed. His skills amounted to a killing tennis serve, a deadly aim with a shotgun, one of the finest cover drives on the cricket field, and a superb ability to kill Germans just so long as they were not in Tiger Tanks. If they were, then Monty could reverse out of sight faster, as Hammond liked to say, than shit off a shovel. He could cut a throat pretty well, too.

He could make a whore feel like a princess and, as he had once proved in Naples, make a princess feel like a whore. He could dance well. He considered himself a fair judge of horseflesh. He could hold his drink like a trooper, and knew a good wine from an excellent wine. They were the skills of a soldier, of a bright young man of the Thirties, and of a bachelor; they were not the skills demanded of a man come home to find himself, unexpectedly, Marquess of Arlington and guardian of a family's shrunken inheritance.

To guard that inheritance he had a ten-pound note and a single ten-shilling note in his wallet and a bank that was decidedly nervous about his personal account. He thought about his responsibilities and decided they were best met by putting all ten guineas on the nose of a horse in the last race, which was a selling plate. The horse was a mare called Pearl Necklace and was quoted at sixty-six to one. 'Hot tip from the stable, guv?' the bookie asked him.

The Honourable John Lancaster, a man with whom Monty had burned many candles at both ends in pre-war days, laughed at the choice. 'Her trainer says she's only good for dog-meat, Monty. Still, your money, old boy.'

There were faces missing, the faces of men who were buried in Burma or the desert or Normandy, but so much seemed the same to Monty. His old friends had rallied round in sympathy because he had come back from the war to find his wife out of line. Many men had done the same thing. Doubtless, it was assumed, he would give Pearl a deserved thrashing and everything, in time, would get back to normal.

That was the greatest assumption, that everything would return to normal. Times were hard, of course, and a Socialist government was a rather quaint discomfort, if not a downright insult, but in the end the natural order would re-assert itself. 'We were thinking, Monty darling, of buying and racing a very fast gee-gee,' the Lady Henrietta Creed greeted Monty with a kiss outside Goodwood's parade ring. 'Lots of us together. You want to share the loot?'

'I'm really not sure I can.'

She reproved him with huge eyes; those same eyes, Monty remembered, that had stared at him across the pillow before the war. She smiled sympathetically. 'Times are hard, are they?'

'Slightly.'

'Golly! If the Arlingtons are suffering then we'd all better tighten our belts, hadn't we?' She walked beside him, arm in arm. 'You'll shoot with us this autumn?'

'You've got birds?'

'A few.' She shrugged. 'It won't be like before the war, of course. But we could have a jolly nice time, yes?'

'Yes.' He smiled at the prospect. The Creeds had a rambling Cotswold house with boards that creaked most of the night as guests tiptoed between the bedrooms.

Henrietta looked mischievously up at him. 'Mirabelle Hare says you're divorcing Pearl. Is it true?'

'No.'

'That's a very unconvincing denial, darling.'

'I'm really not.' Monty, in truth, had given little thought to his marriage. He was disgusted with Pearl for treating with de Conroy, but he had never contemplated divorce. 'I couldn't get a divorce, anyway.'

'Why ever not? It's not as scandalous as it used to be. Tom and I talk about it all the time!'

'I rather like being admitted to the Royal Enclosure at Ascot.'

'There is that, of course,' Henrietta admitted. 'Oh, look! Isn't that your scandalous sister? I must say your family wears well, it's most unfair. She's as slim as you are!'

Sophie was resplendent in white with a parasol over her dark hair. 'I'm here with my disastrous Pole,' she said.

'Where is he?' Monty asked.

'Doing what all Poles do when they find a bar unexpectedly open. How's your luck?'

'Very down.'

Sophie laughed. 'It runs in the family this afternoon.' She took his arm and, at the first opportunity, separated him from Henrietta. 'Thank you for what you did for Hilary.'

Monty shrugged. He had taken some of the Howarth purchase money, the money that Pearl had begged him not to touch, and put it into an account for his niece. The money would pay for three years at Oxford. He wished his own problems could be as easily solved.

Sophie had half-hoped to find her brother here, and half-dreaded it, but now that she had him to herself she put off the moment of truth, asking about his children instead.

Monty grimaced. 'David's plump, nervous and stammers. Caroline stares at me with disapproval.' Not, he thought guiltily, that he had seen very much of either child in this, their summer holiday.

'And Pearl?'

'I just put a tenner on a horse with her name. My last one.'

Sophie laughed. She stopped him short of the crowd at the paddock amongst whom she saw a score of people who might want to talk to them. 'I've got a problem, Monty.' Her face still wore its bright, happy look, but her voice was grim.

'Go on.'

'It's the old problem, really.' She forced a laugh. 'Money.'

Monty looked down at his sister and saw that there was a fine network of lines around her eyes. 'You need money?'

'Oh Lord, lots and lots.' Sophie watched the horses being led into the ring. 'I had a frightfully generous American, but he's gone back to his plump wife. My Pole's fun, but he's got less than me. I've also got an overdraft and a very trying bank manager. The last one was a charming little creature, but this new manager hasn't got any sense of humour at all, none!'

Monty raised his hat to the wife of a friend, then looked back at his sister. 'How much?'

'Three thousand.'

'Christ Almighty!'

''Tis a bit, isn't it?' Sophie gave a brittle laugh. 'It sort of got run up after father died. I told the bloody little man that I'd inherit part of the plunder, and the moron believed me.' She lit a cigarette and the wind whirled her smoke towards Monty. 'I don't know where banks find their managers. Do you think they make them wear barbed-wire knickers? I can't believe they're born nasty, but perhaps they are.' Sophie watched the jockeys file out of the weighing room. 'I'm also being thrown out of my flat.'

As a catalogue of disaster, Monty thought, it was pretty comprehensive. 'For God's sake, why?'

'It belonged to a chap I knew. He was rather sweet, really, but the Huns went and killed him at Anzio. Anyway his ghastly wife has inherited it, discovered me inside, put two and two together very accurately, and now I'm being tossed on to the street.'

'When?'

'Not right away. I mean there's a shred of civilization left, isn't there?'

Monty looked down at Sophie. He sighed. 'So you're homeless and broke?'

'A bit, yes.'

He smiled, took out his wallet, and showed her the empty note compartment. 'I have a bank manager, too. And house problems.'

'Poor Monty.' Sophie watched the owners and trainers bending to harangue their stone-faced jockeys. 'The thing is, you see, that I could solve all my little problems in one nasty coup.'

Monty sensed that Sophie was reaching the real reason for talking so urgently and privately with him. 'Go on.'

'Kynaston de Conroy's being rather sweet to me. Flowers and champagne, you know?'

Monty laughed. 'You're asking my permission?'

'No.' Sophie drew the word out.

'What then?'

She prodded the worn turf with her parasol. 'There's a sort of price attached, if you see what I mean. Not just in bed.'

Monty did not see what she meant, and said as much.

Sophie sighed. 'It's about father's death.'

'What about it?'

Sophie stared at the paddock where the first jockeys, in bright silks, were pulling themselves into their saddles. 'He died an hour or so after John, right?'

Monty nodded. 'Very conveniently, yes.'

'Well, he didn't,' Sophie said flatly. 'He died in the early afternoon.'

It took a second for the impact of what she was saying to hit him. 'Oh, Christ.'

'Yes. I don't know exactly when, to be honest, but I know Pearl phoned me around four o'clock. John didn't die till half past.' She delivered the disastrous news very calmly.

Monty watched Pearl Necklace's jockey shorten the stirrup leather. The mare was blinkered and nervous. The lad was having a struggle to hold on to her. Monty frowned. 'Pearl changed the time?'

'Must have persuaded dear old Gordon to do it. She didn't tell you?'

He shook his head. 'We're not exactly close these days.'

'I can't say I blame you.' Sophie stared straight through a man who was trying to catch her eye. 'But I fear Kynaston knows. And if he can prove it you'll have to give up Howarth because of that agreement –' on the night of Monty's return Sophie had told him about their elder brother's arrangement with de Conroy – 'and you'll have to pay a whole lot more tax, and . . .' Sophie's voice tailed away in misery.

'De Conroy knows? How the hell does he know?'

Sophie sighed again. 'Sort of me. That was before, you know.' She looked up at her brother with wide, falsely innocent eyes. 'Hell, Monty! How was I to know you'd been resurrected! They were planning to put up a marble plaque to your memory!'

Monty pushed the point of his shooting stick into the ground. It was softer than he had hoped and the racecard said Pearl Necklace liked very firm ground. Jesus Christ, Pearl had lied and de Conroy knew about it!

'Now,' Sophie said miserably, and in a very small voice, 'Kynaston wants me to give him an affidavit.'

'Oh, bloody hell.'

'Rather, yes.'

The eleven runners for the selling plate were out on the course now. Ten cantered down smoothly while the eleventh, Pearl Necklace, shied against the rails. The favourite's odds had shortened to evens. Goodbye, Monty thought, to ten guineas, but what did that matter? If Sophie wrote her affidavit, and if the government got hold of it, Howarth could kiss goodbye to everything. 'What have you told him?'

'I've told him I'll think about it.' Sophie's voice told him that she would provide the affidavit, and that she could see no way, short of a windfall of several thousand pounds, to refuse de

Conroy because de Conroy had offered to solve all her financial problems, and Monty, sensing it, knew he could not compete with his rival's wealth.

'Pearl's been rather naughty,' Sophie said. 'She knew you were alive when she signed the lease, didn't she? And she forged father's time of death. I mean the art of these things is not to get found out, isn't it?'

Monty would not respond to any criticism of Pearl. She was his business, no one else's. 'Don't give de Conroy the affidavit yet.'

'I can't hold him off for ever.'

'Give me a week,' he said, 'maybe two.'

Sophie looked up at her brother. He had changed, she thought. To the casual eye he looked as carelessly elegant as ever, but she saw a steel in him that had not been there before.

A stir in the crowd made Monty turn. The starter's tape had snapped up and the bright silks bobbed on the far rails. One horse was already losing ground.

'I'm sorry to be so bloody,' Sophie said.

'I'll talk to Pearl.' Monty spoke without hope, but he decided that, before disaster struck, he would force the truth out of his wife. Perhaps, he thought hopefully, there would be a simple explanation, but he doubted it. Sophie's information of a lie told to protect Howarth rang very true.

'You do know,' Sophie said, 'that Pearl didn't go to bed with Kynaston?'

'No, I didn't know.'

The first shouts sounded at the turn. Monty heard the drumbeat of hooves and could see clods of earth being hurled high behind the knot of galloping beasts.

'Well, she didn't,' Sophie said. Monty didn't react so she dropped the subject. 'Which horse did you back?'

'Pearl Necklace. I think she's ambling behind.'

'What colours?'

'Black spots on yellow. Black sleeves.'

'She's leading!' Sophie forced a passage to the rail.

The mare was indeed leading by a neck, and running as if the dogs of hell were at her heels. Her jockey, astonished to have clear turf in front of him and fearing a faltering stride, raised his whip.

'Don't cut her!' Monty's voice was lost in the roar of the crowd.

The whip slashed down. Some horses might have checked at that touch, but Pearl Necklace actually lengthened her stride and pulled a length away, then two, and was first past the post as if, all her young life, she had been winning races.

'Dear God!' Monty looked at his ticket. 'That's six hundred and ninety-three quid!'

'Lucky old you.'

'Dinner? The Ritz?'

'That would be delicious.' Sophie put her arm through his and walked towards the bookmakers' rails. 'What are you going to do, Monty?'

'Fight the bugger, I suppose. It's what we've always done.'

'And my affidavit?'

'Give me a little time.'

Sophie nodded, hating the trap that had closed round her. 'So you fight him and I bed him?'

'That's about it, yes.' Though how he was to fight, and with what weapons, Monty did not know. It was just in the blood, an obstinacy from the past, that a Howarth did not bend to a de Conroy and a man did not surrender just because he was beaten. God alone knew how, but Monty would fight.

Monty drove to Howarth the next day. His petrol licence claimed he was a salesman for Lackertons seed-merchants, a firm still owned by the Howarths, and the licence was a useful lie that made him reluctant to part with the dubious assets of the company that was a part of his threatened inheritance.

His Jaguar had been stored on blocks throughout the war. Monty folded the hood down and drove the long, silver-bonneted car fast. It howled over the Breckland, touching a hundred miles an hour on the empty, straight road. Monty loved this car; it was a toy, a snarling thing of beauty that brought envious glances from other, slower motorists and the petrol-licence-bereft pedestrians who waited in village streets for a country bus.

102

He stopped a half-mile from Howarth, letting the engine tick over. Sunlight bathed the landscape, glinting from streams and throwing harsh shadows from the concrete pillboxes which had been strung over this flat land against the German invasion that had never come. The sun shone on Howarth.

It looked serene, a house in its glory, and it was a mill-stone about his neck. Sir Michael Gooding, speaking to Monty in his chambers a month before, had encouraged him to give it up. 'There won't be a problem surrendering the lease, Monty.'

'I know.'

'It's too big,' the lawyer had said, 'and you can't afford it. Why don't you move back to Ash?'

Monty had not replied, not knowing what to say. Good sense, prudence, all the conventional virtues of economy told him that Sir Michael was right, but Monty did not like the idea of surrender.

His brother, he thought, had not balked at the thought. He had been ready to sell Howarth, even to a de Conroy, but John had always worried about money. Damn money, Monty thought, and damn de Conroy, and everyone else who wanted to take his family's house away from him. He was a marquess, he had inherited this grandeur, and he would not give it up because the bores told him it was the prudent thing to do. He put in the clutch.

He parked on Howarth's forecourt and switched off the engine as his twelve-year-old son ran up to the car. 'D-d-d-d-daddy!'

Monty ruffled David's hair, then lifted his valise out of the passenger seat. 'Think you can drive it?'

'Yes.'

'Put it in the coach-house yard, will you?'

'I've got a Mosquito.'

'A what?'

'You know. A p-p-plane. It's a model.'

The boy was plump. His hair straggled down over his forehead and he had puppy-dog eyes that pleaded for approval. His socks had fallen down and his shoes were scuffed. Something, Monty thought, would have to be done if the boy was to make a decent

103

showing. 'Don't scratch the paintwork, for God's sake. And don't use anything but first gear.'

'I won't.'

'Where's your sister?'

'In her bedroom. Reading.'

'And Hilary?'

'Riding Lady Calamore's horse.' David, receiving a nod from his father, pressed the starter button and the big engine snarled into life.

The clutch plates grated foully as Monty walked away. He forced himself not to turn round, and listened instead to the uncertain engine note as the sports car crept away under his son's tremulous, excited control.

Monty dropped the valise in the Entrance Hall. 'Where's her Ladyship, Taggart?'

'In her study, my Lord.'

'I don't want us to be disturbed, you hear?'

'Very good, my Lord.'

Monty had seen Pearl only twice since the June evening when he had walked back into her life. Their meetings had been icy with politeness, strained with unsaid words, and lacking all promise of any future contentment together.

She looked up as he came into the study, then stood. 'Monty, what a surprise.'

He closed the door. The air was heavy with the smell of mown grass that came through the open window. 'Pearl.' He said her name tonelessly.

'You'd like some tea? I'm sure Taggart will make some.'

'No.' To annoy her he went to the cabinet where he knew she kept her drink. He poured himself a whisky. 'I won on a horse yesterday.'

'I'm so glad,' she said, though she could not keep the disapproval out of her voice.

He turned. Pearl wore a dress of pale blue cotton print that looked cool and formal. A white cardigan was knotted about her shoulders. There were pearls in her ears and about her neck. 'The horse,' he said, 'was called Pearl Necklace.'

'Hilary spotted it in the paper,' Pearl said. She had taken her

104

defeat over Hilary's future with unnatural meekness. Her hair was looped below her ears and coiled lavishly on her head. She looked chillingly beautiful. Monty remembered the first time he had seen her, by a polo-field in the Indian hills, and how he had been physically struck by her. She had seemed so sinuous, so fresh in the heat, so beautiful. Even now, after nearly fifteen years of marriage, he found her looks startling. She was, Monty thought, a thoroughbred, but there was a flaw inside, deep inside; a flaw that had let her sign the lease knowing that he lived.

She capped the fountain pen with which she had been writing. 'I'm glad you've come.'

'You are?' he said with ill-concealed mockery.

'My father telephoned an hour ago. He tried to reach you, but Hammond told him you were coming here.' She was speaking without her usual economy, made garrulous by nervousness. 'He's found a man who'd like to buy the seed-merchants and the brewery. It's a very good offer indeed.'

'It is, is it?' Monty stood in the window, one hand in his trouser pocket, watching blades of a binder rise and fall in the field beyond the park. Howarth should be buying a combine harvester, he thought, and then came the bitter memory that the field no longer belonged to Howarth. It belonged, like the rest of the Home Farm's acreage, to the Baron de Conroy. Only the house, its park and gardens and the Dower House was covered by the lease.

'We have to sell Lackertons and the pubs,' Pearl said.

Monty did not reply, staring instead at the plume of dirty smoke belched by the binder's tractor. The smoke drifted westwards. An east wind, Monty thought. In winter that would bring freezing wind from the Russian steppes and the boilers in Howarth needed descaling and coal was horribly expensive. Damn the bloody place, he thought.

'Sir Michael telephoned as well,' Pearl said.

'Really?'

She persevered against his callous tone. 'You heard that Palliser's Bank has taken over our mortgages?'

'Yes.'

'That's de Conroy's bank. He's going to foreclose on us.'

'Like as not, yes.'

'We have to do something!' Pearl protested. 'Will you let me handle the sale of Lackertons?'

Monty turned round. 'You'll do nothing without my permission.'

'But . . .'

'This is my house. Even if only under your crippling lease, you understand?'

Pearl faced him, her own anger sparked by his sudden harshness. 'We have to pay for the lease. We can't do that if you're drawing on the tax account.'

'Damn the tax account.' His voice was as sharp as a whip-crack. 'What happens, Pearl, when the Treasury sues us?'

'Sues us?'

'Because you lied about the time of father's death.'

Pearl stared at him. She felt, suddenly, just as she had felt in this very room when Monty had telephoned. 'I . . .' she began, but there was nowhere for her words to go. If Monty had found out, she thought, who else might know and what trouble might be brewing? She shook her head.

He was vicious. 'It'll take Ash, take Brick Street, it will take everything! We'll be paying death duties again, and we'll be fined, and you'll be damned lucky if the word prison isn't mentioned.'

'No!'

He ignored her protest. 'Because de Conroy, Pearl, your precious bloody Kynaston, is gathering the damned evidence. Now what, pray, do you intend to do about that?'

Pearl had never seen Monty like this. She wondered if the war had put this edge of savagery into his soul. 'They wouldn't dare prosecute!' she said, rallying her courage.

'Wouldn't dare?' Monty laughed at her. 'We've got a Socialist government. Of course they'll dare! They can't wait! They want to strip us of everything. It's called revenge, the politics of envy, and de Conroy will help them.' He was standing above Pearl now. 'They'll sue us, Pearl, and they'll take everything. All your pictures, all the furniture, even these!' He seized the necklace, twisted his hand, and the pearls clattered on to the polished floor boards. 'Everything.'

106

The breaking thread hurt Pearl's neck, but she was too proud to betray the pain. Instead she looked up into Monty's face and pleaded with him. 'I did it for Howarth. I wanted it for David!'

Rather, Monty thought, Pearl wanted it for herself. She wanted to make it beautiful again, a setting fit for her own chill loveliness. 'So you lied? You cheated? All for David?'

'It's ours, isn't it?' Pearl's temper flared. 'It's ours for thirty years! A lot can happen in thirty years!'

'A lot happened in four, didn't it?' Pearl's anger had acted like the flicker of a match flame against the wick of Monty's rage. 'Christ! One year ago I was fighting a God-damned war and what were you doing? I come back to find what? David's a mess, Caroline creeps around like a bloody nun, and you're sniffing round de Conroy like a bitch on heat!'

'Monty!' There was a real fear in Pearl now. She thought he was going to hit her and flinched from his raised hand, but Monty twisted away from her with a look of such disgust that it cut into Pearl's soul. She had taught herself to behave with icy coolness and haughty pride, for that was how she thought an aristocrat should behave, but Monty had raised her to the nobility and he was the one man who could slice through her diamond-hard carapace. 'I didn't . . .' She started to speak, but could not finish.

Monty turned back to her, contempt in his eyes. 'Didn't what?'

Pearl shook her head like a puzzled child. 'With de Conroy.' She could not say what she wanted to say.

'You pathetic bitch!' Monty's temper, that he had tried to check, was suddenly unleashed again. 'I couldn't have cared less if you'd bedded the whole Brigade of Guards! What I do care about is having my name dragged through the courts because you told a stupid, bloody lie. So tell me about father's death.'

She hesitated, as though tempted to try on him the story she had told Hilary, but the look of fury on her husband's face prompted her to the truth. 'Your father,' she said slowly, 'died at three forty-three.' She told him the whole story of the letter Doctor Gordon had written for the lawyer, that lied about the time of death.

Monty scribbled on a sheet of her writing paper. 'Who else knows?'

'Taggart, of course.' Pearl frowned, 'And Sophie. I telephoned her.'

'*The Times*?'

'Sir Michael dealt with them later.'

'There was a nurse, wasn't there?'

Pearl nodded. 'She left the next day.'

'You've got her address?'

Pearl shrugged, as if such a personal matter was beneath her dignity. 'And I phoned Hilary, but I told her that it was a mistake.'

'Jesus Christ! Why didn't you just tell the whole bloody world?' Monty looked at the notes he had made. 'So the false certificate says five forty-three?'

'Yes.'

He walked to the window and stared into the gardens. Legally, Monty thought, Kynaston de Conroy should be living in Howarth even now. If the truth were told and the law enforced, then Monty had no right to be in this house, none, because Howarth had been sold at the instant the fourth Marquess died.

A lie had helped Pearl keep a tenuous grip on the house, a thirty-year grip that was now threatened by de Conroy's knowledge, and Monty knew the time had come to make a decision. He could abide with the truth, acknowledge his wife's offence, and walk away from Howarth.

Or he could fight.

Morally there was no choice. The moral thing, the good thing, would be to surrender.

But de Conroy had slapped Pearl. He had stalked this house as if he had won a victory and he was head of a family that feuded with his.

Monty should have been considering his choice, wondering whether to side with truth or fight despite the truth. Instead he found himself thinking that Taggart would lie to God in his Heaven for the Howarths. And Hilary? Monty was not sure that the girl could tell a lie, but perhaps Pearl had already defused Hilary. Doctor Gordon had lied once, so why not again? Sophie was the problem; Sophie and the damned affidavit that would solve her financial problems.

He turned back to Pearl. Atavism would triumph. Honour, pride and devilment were more precious to an aristocrat than the law, and Monty would fight de Conroy just as de Conroy would fight him if the tables were turned. An idea glimmered in his mind, an outrageous idea. 'Was there a clock in father's bedroom?'

'That Empire clock that used to be in the Small Dining Room.'

'Do you have last year's diary?'

She nodded. 'In the top right-hand drawer.'

He found it and leafed quickly through the pages that recorded the committee meetings of Pearl's wartime charities. He found the page he wanted and bit his lower lip as he stared at the week in which his father had died. He turned to the next page, then back again. The idea suddenly burgeoned inside his head, blazing as clear as a parachute flare over a battlefield. 'You will say,' he said quietly, 'that you told Sophie father died at three forty-three according to the clock in his bedroom. Understand?'

'Sophie? Why Sophie?'

Monty did not want to reveal to Pearl that Sophie would now be swearing to an affidavit. 'She's bound to be called as a witness, isn't she? So you say that you told her it was at three forty-three.'

Pearl thought that Monty was insisting she take all the blame for the lie. She wanted to argue, but did not dare to cross him in this savage, strange mood. She nodded. 'If you say so.'

'I do say so,' Monty pulled the whisky across her desk, 'and I think we might beat the bastards.'

Pearl stared at him. 'Beat them?'

He shut his eyes. 'God Almighty, Pearl. This is Howarth. Of course we bloody fight!' He was thinking that he might just win, he might just turn it around and make his enemies look fools. He opened his eyes and stared at the woman he had married, whom he supposed he loved, whom he would not desert. She had been wrong to lie, but she had done it for his family, and for his son. Now Monty, back from the wars, must continue her fight and show the world that an aristocrat could still win battles and hold what was his: Howarth.

The Baron de Conroy was a man who liked disciples. He had inherited estates in Britain, South Africa and Canada; estates where gold was mined and timber cut. Lawyers and managers and bailiffs ran those estates leaving the Baron free to follow the life his father and his father's father had led.

He shot, he drank, he gambled, he went from whore to drawing room, and he believed that with his title came a dispensation from the trammels that held other men. A de Conroy had once gambled away an estate, another had challenged a Prince of the Blood to a duel, a third had boasted of playing the two-backed beast with a king's mistress and suffered the axe for his foolishness.

He styled himself on his ancestors, for his inheritance gave his life meaning. He could pretend a disdain for the world because he had the wealth to transcend the world's shifts, and if that disdain threatened loneliness then he was never without sycophantic young men who modelled their conduct on his, and believed his wild assertions about the nature of man and the world in which man lived. 'The thing about women,' the Lord de Conroy now said, 'is that they don't have bottom.'

'No,' Edward Fenton said.

'No belly for the long haul. Twitchy things, women.'

'Yes.'

'A dog, a woman, and a walnut tree,' de Conroy said sagely, 'the more they're beaten the better they be.'

Edward, though he had heard the old rhyme a dozen times before, laughed as if it was new to him.

The two men, followed by a pair of de Conroy's dogs, were walking along the border between the leased Howarth Park and the ploughed fields that now belonged to the Baron. It was a crisp autumn day, cold and sharp, with high cirrus clouds drifting overhead.

'Take Sophie!' de Conroy said. 'To look at her you'd think she had some style, wouldn't you?'

'Indeed, yes.'

'The woman dresses well, she's amusing, and she's intelligent.' He admitted the last quality as though he was being both honest and generous. 'But it's all a façade, Edward, all a façade!'

110

'It is?' The lawyer's son was delighted to be given this rare chance to be alone with his hero. Edward, released from the Navy, was about to go up to Cambridge, and de Conroy had asked him to walk about the Howarth estate he had become familiar with when he was vainly courting Hilary. To Edward this walk marked his acceptance into the privileged world of upper-class manhood. He stole surreptitious looks at the Baron, admiring the hard lines of the dark, narrow face, envying the older man's easy certainty about matters that were still a mystery to him.

De Conroy barked a short, knowing laugh. 'Sophie's got no rationality, Edward, none. The truth is that if you bed a woman with a bit of panache then she's yours for life. The real trick is not to make too much fuss of them. Smother them with kindness and they'll bite you. Give 'em a kick for every kiss, my father used to say.'

It was all music to Edward's ears, and intended as such. The Lord de Conroy was pitching his words for a young man's hearing, feeding fantasy and lust, painting a picture of a world where women were as well-schooled and tractable as the two dogs at his heels. If he cared to be more truthful, Kynaston found the battle between the sexes to be a far more equal fight than he now pretended, but he sensed that Edward wanted to admire him and so he laid on the flannel with a will. 'I'll bet you a fiver you can't drop that seagull,' he now said.

Edward squinted upwards, saw the gull, and tracked it with his gun. The sound of the shot carried far over the flat land over which the seagull, squawking in alarm, raced off unhurt. The dogs, expecting to retrieve game, quivered expectantly.

De Conroy laughed. 'That's thirty quid you owe me now.' He lurched round on his false leg, searching the sky. 'Where does the prevailing wind come from round here?'

Edward was not sure, but did not like to show his ignorance in front of the Baron. 'There,' he said, pointing after the indignant seagull. It seemed as safe an answer as any.

'Right.' De Conroy marched on, aiming for a point that would bisect a line between the source of the prevailing wind and the house that looked so calm across its parkland. 'The extraordinary thing is,' he said, returning to the subject of Sophie, 'that all it took was an offer of cash and a weekly tupping and she's ready to betray her family! Rotten lot, the Howarths. Always were. Cheat at cards, cheat at law, cheat at any damn thing.'

Edward smiled. 'You got your affidavit?'

'Didn't I just!' De Conroy laughed. 'Lady Montague telephoned and told her that the old boy died at three forty-three in the afternoon. No doubt at all!'

'So you've got them.' Edward stared at Howarth. Sunlight flared off the glass panes of the Garden Room and made crisp shadows of the stone carvings above the windows.

'Your father reckons we need more evidence,' de Conroy said sourly. 'Sophie's evidence is hearsay. Must have eyewitnesses.' The truth was that Sir Nicholas was still dubious about pursuing the matter of the timing of the two deaths, reckoning that financial pressure would be a far more effective weapon. De Conroy now held all the Howarth mortgages and had already foreclosed on two. The rest, he was sure, would all be foreclosed by the year's end.

They stopped at the edge of a wide dyke that separated the park from the farmland. 'Does this water feed the ornamental lake?'

'Up there,' Edward said, pointing to the winding gear of a sluicegate a hundred yards away on the other bank. 'That's the inlet.'

De Conroy hunted around for a scrap of straw, found one, and tossed it into the still water. It drifted very slowly in the opposite direction from the sluicegate. 'Let's keep going,' he said. 'I've bought Sophie a house, did you know?'

'My father mentioned it.' Sir Nicholas had been astonished that the Baron had provided Sophie with a mews cottage close to Knightsbridge. 'The man's a slave to his glands!' he had remarked tartly.

'That was her price,' de Conroy now explained. 'Cheap, too. Never hurts to reward treachery. Do you think she'd be too old for you?'

Edward, embarrassed and startled by the question, laughed. 'She's very beautiful.'

112

'Always was. Prettiest girl in London back in the Thirties, and a damned good lay,' de Conroy said fervently. 'If you want to call on her, do.'

'That's frightfully kind.'

'Not at all.' Edward could be useful to him, and his Lordship wanted to bind the loyalty of Sir Nicholas's son by gratifying his young lust. Sophie might even be grateful, de Conroy thought, to have this handsome young man sent her way. 'Take her a bottle of bubbly and she'll probably open her legs for you. I won't tell her I sent you, you understand, but you're welcome to have a stab at her. I'm off to South Africa next week, so she's yours for the winter.'

'It's really most kind.' Edward felt a warm glow at this sign of his acceptance into the world of hard, fast men that surrounded his hero.

De Conroy stopped a few yards upstream of the sluicegate and clicked his fingers so that his dogs sat obediently behind him. 'Here, I think.'

'Here?' Edward was puzzled. They stood on a featureless stretch of dyke, arable behind them and Howarth Park in front. De Conroy stared at the house, remembering the night Monty had come home and feeling again the nerve-twitch of humiliation that he would repay a thousandfold.

'Dung,' he said. 'Manure. I will build here the biggest dung-heap in the world.' He spoke with stately pomp, as though he planned a great monument. 'I'll put in bloody great walls there and there,' he indicated the bank either side of him, 'and pour the filth in between. God will do the rest.'

The wind would carry the stench of rotting dung across the park to soak Howarth with its filthy smell. The liquid would seep into the dyke, and thence to the sluice that fed the lake so that the Arlingtons would either have to drain it or live with a cesspool of liquid sewage in their garden. De Conroy shook with delighted laughter.

Edward laughed too. The thought of the crisp Marchioness wreathed in the fumes of decaying excreta was wondrous.

'I'll teach them. Cheating bastards!' De Conroy thrust his ebony stick into the ground as if staking out the place where he would build his masterpiece. 'Perhaps I'll put a pig-farm here. The biggest pig-farm in England.'

'Cast your swine before Pearl,' Edward said, but the jest was lost on the Baron who stood with his head tilted back as though he already smelt the filth wafting towards Howarth.

'Hilary,' de Conroy said suddenly.

'Hilary?'

The dark face jerked towards Edward. 'Still see her, do you?'

Edward could not bear to admit that she had rejected and humiliated him. 'We meet now and then,' he said guardedly, as though protecting something precious and fine in his life.

'Damn pretty filly!' de Conroy said with genuine admiration. 'There used to be a whore in Deauville who looked like her; face of an angel, and what a vulgar little slut she was! Married some Italian count, last I heard. Had her yet?'

'Hilary?' Edward knew he hesitated too long for a lie to be believable. 'No.'

'You will. Persevere! It's just like the gaming tables, Edward! Red has to turn up in the end. Every time you ask you're rolling on a fifty-fifty chance. They might say no a hundred times, but the next time it'll be yes. God, I chased Nettie Forshaw for three years! Three years! Even went to church with her! But she fell in the end. Made love like a palsied cow, so it was hardly worth it. But you're friends, eh?'

'Oh, yes.' Edward's pride would not let him admit to anything less.

'I was wondering, you see, whether you'd have a word with her.' De Conroy, whether Sir Nicholas approved or not, intended to pursue the matter of the time of the old Marquess's death. The case would not only win Howarth for him, but would be the ultimate humiliation for the Marquess of Arlington. 'Find out if Lady Montague telephoned her. Find out if she knows who was at the deathbed. Sniff around. I make myself clear?'

'You do indeed.'

'I'll see you're looked after.' The Baron fished a card from a pocket of his tweed jacket. 'Drop me a line if you learn anything.' On the card was the address of the de Conroy estate in Cape

Province where his Lordship planned to spend the winter. 'Perhaps you'd like to come out at Christmas?'

'That would be splendid!'

'Fleet's coming, and a few of the other fellows. You ought to know them. Good company. Ah!' He had espied a grey heron that flew up the line of the dyke. 'Double or quits?'

'You're on.'

'But wait till it's past that willow-stump on the far bank.'

Edward raised the gun. The heron, wings beating slowly, flew past him with its long legs trailing behind. He judged the wind, waited until the bird was clear of the willow-stump, then fired.

The bird twitched, its head jerked up, then the beautiful line of spread wings crumpled into feathers and death as it fell with a splash into the dyke.

'Bloody good!' de Conroy said. 'I'll send you a cheque, if I may.'

'Thank you, sir.'

'And talk to that Hilary! Make her talk. Let's have some havoc, Edward, havoc!' De Conroy spoke the word like a warcry, a challenge across the dyke towards the house his family had built and his enemies now held.

Before the war Lord Creed had held some memorable shoots. Posts would be set up a couple of hundred yards from the coverts, each post given an engraved card that bore the gun's number. The white-smocked beaters would flush out the game, the guns would start to sound off and the loaders would be ready with the second gun before the first one emptied. In '39, Lord Creed remembered, they had taken three thousand pheasants off the estate. 'Damned lucky to get a brace these days. Can't get beaters! Beneath their dignity. Bloody Labour government! Yours!'

A cock pheasant clattered up from a brake of alders fifty yards away. Monty admired the droop of the tail-feathers as it climbed.

He let the bird get high, wanting it to pick up speed so there was an element of sport in the kill. He turned as the bird went over him then dropped it with his right barrel.

'Bloody good,' Creed said grudgingly. 'You haven't lost your eye, have you? I suppose you practised on the Hun.'

'Something like that.' Monty picked up the dead bird that his dog dropped at his feet. He walked with Tom Creed along a frost-rimed margin of a field that had once been a paradise for guns, a place where the old King would come to display his marksmanship. The war had put paid to that splendour: the gamekeepers had been drafted into the forces and the foxes had decimated the carefully tended coverts. 'Of course,' Monty said, going back to an earlier conversation, 'they don't make them like that any more.'

'No.' Creed looked vainly for a bird. 'It's in fair shape, is it?'

'It's splendid.' Monty hated being a second-hand car salesman, especially for a machine as beautiful as his sports car, but needs must, he thought. 'Three and a half litres, six cylinders, overhead valves, 125 horsepower, knock-off hubs. One careful owner and never driven above thirty miles an hour.'

Creed barked a dutiful laugh. 'What have you got out of her?'

'Hundred and six. Gets a bit twitchy on the corners if you go faster.'

Creed whistled. 'When did you buy her?'

''37. Cost me £450.'

'And you want six hundred?'

'Not a penny under, Tom. You can't get them now, and it's in lovely shape. Hood needs a bit of work, but any seamstress can patch that up.'

Lord Creed wanted the Jaguar so badly it hurt. He had just begun a formal affair with a girl half his age, and the car, he believed, would give just the right impression of careless youth that his forty-two years belied. He had hoped the Marquess's penury would bring the price toppling, but Monty would not budge. Giving up the hunt for more pheasants, Creed turned back towards the house. 'I'll have to ask Henrietta. Can't spend a bloody penny these days without her say-so.'

At two in the morning Monty himself asked Henrietta. She

116

was the daughter of an Irish peer and had the flaming red hair of her country of origin. 'He wants it desperately,' she said.

'I was hoping so.'

'You're evil, Monty. I was hoping he'd buy me a fur coat.'

'You'd be happier with the car, darling.' He stroked the smooth skin in the small of her back.

She pulled him into her arms. 'Life tough, Monty?'

'Pretty awful. Flogged a picture last week, though.'

'Poor Monty.' She pulled the bedclothes over them both, making a warm, soft cocoon. 'What happened?'

'De Conroy, of course.' Monty shrugged. 'Bought all my father's mortgages; foreclosed on the lot. We've lost all the tenancies, everything.' And with the tenancies went the rent, and with the rent went any hope Monty might have had of paying the cost of the lease, the ground-rent and the repairs that would have to be made to the house.

Henrietta frowned. 'There's a mad streak in that family.' She ran a finger down his forehead, down the spine of his hawklike nose. 'I'm glad the Germans didn't get you.'

'I am too.' He smiled.

'So what will you do, Monty?'

He gave a small, mocking laugh. 'Become a businessman. I own a brewery and a seed-merchants, so I shall go into trade.' His voice did not disguise the aristocracy's distaste for mere trade.

Henrietta laughed, then kissed him. 'I'll tell Tom to buy the car.'

Monty might find it distasteful, but he would be a businessman, so he took some of the money being kept for death duties and invested it in lorries for the brewery. He bought ex-army Bedfords, three-tonners that would be more efficient than the old horsedrawn drays, but the trucks proved bad bargains. They rusted in the yard while, as they ever had, the heavy horses hauled the barrels out to the public houses.

He sold a Canaletto in December. Pearl watched it leave Howarth with barely disguised anger, an anger that was fuelled by the derisory price the picture fetched at auction. The bad

117

news did not end there. In the New Year a fire roared through one of the seed-merchants' warehouses and, though the stock was insured, the failure of the firm to deliver the spring wheat and barley seeds to the Midlands farms meant a permanent loss of business. Monty was failing.

In April he dined with Sir Michael Gooding in the Cavalry Club. 'Get out of Howarth!' the lawyer said.

'I'm too stubborn.'

Sir Michael sawed at his beef. 'My dear Monty, you cannot afford to be stubborn.'

Afterwards, taking his coat in the hallway, Monty heard a lazy, mocking voice behind him. 'Didn't know they were admitting tradesmen to the club?'

Monty turned. Lord de Conroy, his face darkened by the South African sun, laughed and walked away.

The following May the death duties had to be paid and, all that summer, Monty struggled to raise the money. To supplement what was left of Howarth's purchase price, he sold twenty-seven more pictures and, in the autumn, was forced to sell the brewery and the pubs which, despite the rusting lorries, was Howarth's most profitable holding. His haste to sell fetched a bad price and, in desperation, he took from his bank's vaults the gold dinner service that had been presented to the first Marquess by the Czar of Russia. That did fetch a decent price, but no pleasure. Sophie, ensconced in her new mews house behind Harrods, shrugged. 'Kynaston bought it, darling.'

'Jesus.' Monty did not blame his sister for her new liaison. The family could not help her, so she helped herself. She had shown Monty a copy of her affidavit in which she had said exactly what Monty had asked her to say.

'He likes to eat his chitterlings off our coat of arms.' Sophie laughed sourly. She had no news of de Conroy's progress in proving Pearl's deception. 'Perhaps he's forgotten, my love. Or else he thinks you're committing suicide quite nicely without his help?'

Monty prowled the small living room. The drinks cupboard, when he opened it, lit up and played the tune of 'Happy Days Are Here Again' on a small music box.

'It's very dinky, isn't it?' Sophie said. 'Kynaston's little love nest. He's taking me to the Negresco next week.'

'Lucky old you.' Monty wondered if he would ever again have the money for Continental travel. He had bought himself a pre-war Morris 10 to replace the Jaguar, and every time he slid into the cramped seat he felt the loss of the silver car like a bitter pang.

The death duties were paid, but then came the mocking bills from Lord de Conroy. The ground-rent was due, and immediate repairs were needed to the house. A Sevres dinner service was sold, then another picture, and still there was not enough money. David went to Eton, because Pearl insisted her son must follow Monty there, the bills mounted, and so the Chippendale furniture from the Music Room went to the auction block.

'If you sell Ash,' Sir Michael Gooding said during the luncheon he was giving Monty at White's, 'you'll fetch what, twenty thousand?'

'We're holding on to Ash.' Monty did not like to say that his father-in-law had just bought Ash for twenty-five thousand and immediately given the house back to Pearl. The twenty-five thousand was their new reserve for when the Ministry of Supply issued the Release Notes that would flood Howarth with precious building supplies and the big repairs could be made. Monty was praying that the rationing of bricks and plaster and wire and timber would go on for ever.

'Sell Brick Street.'

'That's where I live,' Monty said. He liked to have a London house, somewhere that Henrietta could come and the other women who were so sympathetic to his predicament, even though they all expected him to have found caviar and champagne on the black market for their entertainment. 'Perhaps I should mortgage it?'

'If anyone will touch you.' Sir Michael shrugged. 'You'll have to sell the seed-merchants, then. What's Lackertons worth? Twenty thousand?'

'Twenty-two according to the books.'

Sir Michael carefully cut his sole into portions and scooped tartare sauce on to his knife. 'I'll instruct agents, shall I?'

'I suppose you'd better.'

Sir Michael laughed. 'There are my fees, Monty! We lawyers do have to live.'

'For ever?'

Sir Michael laughed politely. Privately he thought Monty a fool. The man had no business clinging on to Howarth, but lawyers had become rich in the past on aristocratic folly, so Sir Michael was content to wait until the last assets of a once great family were on the market.

Winter came early and bleak, howling blizzards across the flat land from the North Sea. Howarth froze. The rooms the Americans had occupied were left empty and unheated, the VD posters still stuck on the distempered walls. Two downstairs rooms were heated with electric fires, but the bedrooms had to stay cold. Pearl complained, but it was she who had let de Conroy take the Knight of Swords off the library wall and Monty believed the old legend that predicted ill-fortune if the card was touched. 'If it's too cold,' Monty said, 'then move out.'

She bristled immediately. 'Is that what you want? To surrender?'

He shrugged. Frost made brittle patterns on the windowpane and the wind fretted at the doors of Howarth. Monty had failed, and for the first time since his homecoming he saw into what folly his aristocratic pride had led him. 'It might be better,' he said slowly, 'if we let Howarth go now, when we've still got something to salvage.' He hated saying it, but the future seemed inexorable.

'You've found a buyer for Lackertons?' Pearl asked.

'We've had an offer.' Monty stood close to the single bar of the fire that glowed a dull red. 'Twenty-three thousand five hundred. I'd like more.'

'That gives us time,' Pearl said.

Time for what? Monty wondered. For the money from Lackertons would be soaked up like a great sponge, and after the seed-merchants the Brick Street house would have to go, and when that money was spent there would be nothing and on that day the Howarths, for all their defiance, would creep ignominiously from Howarth. A new banner would be raised over the dome, the Knight of Swords would be brought down, and de

120

Conroy would chip with hammer and chisel at the moulded plaster that covered up the shield of the three martlets throughout the house. Monty shook his head. 'I don't need time, I need income. We're selling every asset, everything! Whatever makes us money, we sell because we have to, because the house needs the money. We're bleeding ourselves to death!'

Pearl would have no truck with such defeatism. She walked to the window and, despite the freezing wind that scoured about the house, threw it wide open. 'Look.'

Monty looked. He fetched the binoculars through which he had searched the desert for Rommel's men and saw, beyond the main dyke on the far side of the park, scars in the frosted earth. Two wooden walls had been built thirty yards apart at the water's edge. 'What is it?'

Pearl's voice was suddenly, extraordinarily, close to tears. 'He's going to build a manure silo there. Dung, Monty, dung! By summer it will stink!'

She was not near to weeping because of a dung-heap, nor even for the poverty that threatened their hold on Howarth, but for the dream in jeopardy. Pearl did not see Howarth as a cold, decaying mansion, but as a possession of glory. Alone in the great corridors, while Monty pursued his fading hopes in London, she walked beneath the damp plaster and saw the splendour that could be made from the dilapidation. She saw magnificence in broken stucco where others saw only bills. She did not see a broken, sad house, but a radiant, bright monument to the imagination and skills of the men who had built it.

Pearl was cold and proud, but she had an artist's eye and her father's stubbornness, and she would make this house into a work of art. She might be out of step with a Britain that struggled to make small houses out of bombsites, that celebrated the plain, thrifty virtues imposed by war's exhaustion, but Pearl's ambitions could not be confined to the economies of utility. Inheritance and marriage had given her a jewel, and the jewel was Howarth, and she would leave this house more glorious than she had found it. If she caused offence by arrogance in the service of that dream, then so be it, for the result would be a thing of such beauty that, for generations to come, her work would be admired.

It was an artist's dream, and it would be pursued with an artist's single-mindedness, and against it were the forces of economy and sense. All over Britain the great houses decayed; their owners forced to abandon history's glory for smaller, lesser buildings. The stately home, the pundits said, must become a school or a museum or a lunatic asylum. Such mansions must be useful or they must be destroyed. But Pearl would keep their stately home both stately and a home and Monty, sensing it, walked to his wife and put his arms around her.

She turned and let him hold her. Monty kissed her forehead. 'I never thanked you,' he said, 'for all you did.'

She looked up, puzzled. 'All I did?'

'Without you,' he said, 'Howarth would have been lost.'

The compliment jarred Pearl so that the tears she had fought back suddenly flowed. All that she asked was that Monty understood. Howarth was worth more than good behaviour, more than a carping government, more than a lease. Howarth was a treasure for all time.

And Pearl's fight had become Monty's fight. It would take money, more money than he dared dream of, but he thought of the law's insidious threat, of the efforts being made to discover Pearl's lies, and of all the estates de Conroy had taken from Howarth in these last months, and he thought of his failure with the brewery, of his sold car, of the fact that Howarth had become a derelict house beside a dung-heap, and against it he weighed Pearl's obsession and her hopes. Those hopes, he suddenly knew, were his as well. So, like a boxer who had been knocked down, but who struggled up, bleeding for the final round, Monty would fight on.

'There is a gentleman to see you,' Hammond said in such a way that Monty knew that his visitor was no gentleman. The man, whoever he was, had made no appointment.

Rain fell on Brick Street. Winter seemed unending. Monty, with nothing else to do, studied the next day's card for Market Rasen, wondering how much money he would make if he put a fiver to win on all rank outsiders. He was invited out for dinner, already changed, and had forty-five minutes to kill before friends fetched him in their car. He nodded. 'Can't hurt.'

Hammond, whose loyalty to Monty was such that he overlooked the smaller matter of wages, did not trouble to hide his contempt for the man he ushered into the drawing room. 'Mr Solomon Linsky, my Lord.'

A small, rotund, middle-aged man came towards him. He wore thick-lensed spectacles, a black coat with a velvet collar, and held a soft black hat in nervous hands. He gave an awkward bow. 'My Lord.'

'Mr Linsky?' Monty was making sure of the name.

'Sol Linsky,' Sol Linsky said. 'At your humble service.' He bowed again, hands fluttering at the brim of his hat. 'You're very good to see me, my Lord.'

'Do take your coat off. You'll have something to drink?'

The round face adopted an expression that suggested Monty had offered great honour. 'A gin, if it's no trouble.'

Monty had his usual Scotch. He limited himself these days, such being the expense of whisky, but a man could not give up every pleasure just because of poverty. 'I don't have a geat deal of time, Mr Linsky.'

'Business,' Sol Linsky said, as though the word explained everything. He smiled again nervously when Monty waved at a chair. The man seemed terrified to be in this room.

'Business?' Monty asked.

'You don't mind,' Solomon Linsky asked earnestly, 'if I smoke?'

'One of these?' Monty overcame his distaste for the small man and offered a box of cigars, but Solomon Linsky preferred to light the dark, foul-smelling cheroot that he had taken from his jacket pocket.

Monty was regretting inviting Linsky into the house. There was something unsettling about this small, shrewd-eyed man who seemed so very, very humble. Monty, as a marquess, was not unused to people being scared by his title, but Linsky's cringing obsequiousness was grating. 'You've come far, sir?'

'The East End, my Lord.' Linsky seemed ashamed to admit that he came from this poverty-stricken area. His clothes did not suggest poverty, but rather solid success, and even though his voice certainly betrayed a Cockney origin, it was overlaid with an oily eagerness that was so very offensive.

'Perhaps,' Monty said, 'you could tell me the purpose of this visit?'

Linsky nodded eagerly. 'I have a charity.'

Bloody hell, Monty thought. The bastard wants money. 'Indeed? Do I know it?'

'It's possible,' Sol Linsky said. 'We rescue orphans from the German occupied countries, my Lord. Jewish orphans. I myself am of the Jewish persuasion.'

'Really?' Monty asked politely.

'I am, indeed. We take these young people, my Lord, broken by barbarism, and we give them new lives, new hope, education, a future!' Sol Linsky leaned eagerly forward and he listed the benefits of the charity for which he did, indeed, work part of the time.

Monty looked surreptitiously at the clock. He was constantly approached by charities, all aristocrats were, but in the last months he had been unable to give a penny. 'I hate to disappoint, Linsky, but I usually like to have a prospectus for any charity that wants a donation.'

'Donation! Who said I come as a beggar?' His eyes, behind the thick lenses, were reproachful. 'Can I be frank, my Lord?'

'I'd appreciate it.'

Linsky paused, as though he was unaccustomed to talking business. 'I hear you've got a property for sale.'

The sudden change of tack took Monty by surprise. 'A seed-merchants, yes.'

'Lickertons?' Linsky asked.

'Lackertons.' He lit himself a cigar. 'But I have to tell you we've got an offer on it.'

'Twenty-three thousand five hundred, yes?' Sol Linsky seemed to think he had spoken too quickly, for he laughed in embarrassment, shrugged, then looked apologetically at Monty. 'One hears, you see, one hears.'

'I'm sure one does,' Monty said icily, wondering how the

124

details of his business were so well known in the East End of London.

'Have you accepted the offer?' Linsky asked.

He almost said yes, just to get rid of the little man, but honesty prevailed. 'Not yet. I probably will tomorrow.'

'If I could beg your Lordship's attention?' Monty gestured as if to say that he already had his attention, and the small man swallowed a mouthful of gin, coughed, then smiled ingratiatingly at the tall aristocrat in his evening dress. 'Could I offer twenty-four thousand?'

Monty was so astonished that he said nothing.

Mr Solomon Linsky blinked behind his spectacles, waiting.

'Twenty-four?' Monty repeated, for want of anything better to say.

'The trustees of the charity wouldn't let me go higher.' Linsky shrugged as if to intimate that, if it was up to him, he would pay a king's ransom for the failing seed-merchants.

Monty was now quite lost. 'I'm not sure I entirely follow you. You want to buy Lackertons?'

'Yes.'

'For your charity?'

Linsky stared at Monty, then, very slowly, hit his own forehead with the heel of his right hand. 'I'm a putz.'

'I'm still at sea.'

'A putz! That's what I am!' Linsky's gesture had shaken ash from his cheroot that fell from his trousers on to the carpet. 'We want a London office, my Lord. For the charity. Have you tried to find offices in London? It's like pork in Golder's Green! Yes, my Lord, we want to buy Lackertons because it has a head office in London and we can use it. Fenchurch Street, yes?'

Monty nodded. 'I believe so.' He had never visited the seed-merchant's head office, but he remembered its address. 'I can't split the property up. We're asking the purchaser to take on the head office, the provincial warehouses, everything.'

'I understand that.' Linsky nodded eagerly. 'We'd sell the provincial properties. We'll make a loss, no doubt,' he shrugged as if that was the way in a cruel world, 'but our young people

125

need help, and we need an office, and so, my Lord, I have great pride in offering you twenty-four thousand pounds.'

Which, Monty thought, was five hundred pounds more than the existing offer. Perhaps Linsky's intervention would drive the price up again? He sipped his whisky to hide the small elation he felt at this good news. 'You'll forgive me, but we'd require some reassurance that your principals have that kind of money.'

'You businessmen!' Linsky said in an apparent attempt at familiarity. 'We poor charities will never be able to pull the wool over your eyes, will we?' He chuckled, put down his gin and cheroot, and fished inside his jacket pocket. 'Will that do, my Lord?'

To Monty's astonishment Sol Linsky hauled out a thick roll of notes, bound with a rubber band. 'Seventeen thousand,' he said. 'I'll have the rest by Thursday.'

'Cash?'

'Was when it left the bank,' Linsky said, peering at the massive wad of notes.

'You're offering cash?'

Worry immediately showed behind the spectacles. 'It's not good enough?'

'My dear Linsky, of course it is.'

Sol Linsky peered eagerly at Monty. 'I'm not used to property dealings, my Lord, so I don't know how these things are done. Do we make a deal now?'

'You talk to my lawyer first thing in the morning.' Monty scribbled Sir Michael's number on a scrap of paper. 'I'll speak to him tonight, so he'll be expecting your call.'

Linsky looked at the paper. 'Sir Michael Gooding! I've never met so many toffs! Marquesses and knights!' He pushed the paper, with his money, into his pocket. 'Thank you, my Lord. It's really most kind of you.'

'It's good of you to come.' Monty stood, indicating that the meeting was over. 'You'll telephone Sir Michael in the morning?'

'I will, I will indeed.'

Monty rang for Hammond who brought the man's coat and hat, and saw him out.

'The man's mad,' Monty said when he returned. 'He was carrying seventeen grand in his pocket!'

Hammond stared. 'Cash?'

'Notes! In a rubber band!'

'Jesus Christ!'

'He's quite mad!' Monty began to laugh. 'He wants to pay cash for Lackertons! He's paying a monkey over the best offer and he's paying cash!'

'Hooray,' Hammond said.

Monty clapped his hands in delight. 'God send me more madmen! Perhaps our luck's turning!'

'About time, my Lord.'

In the dark streets outside, Sol Linsky climbed into the passenger seat of a small van. 'Bloody toff,' he said. He thumbed his lighter to re-ignite the cheroot, and the flare of the flame lit up the peroxide-blonde hair of the girl in the driving seat.

'What's he like?' she asked.

'Like the rest of them!' Sol shrugged. 'Good-looking sort of fellow, but a putz! What a putz!' Linsky chuckled. 'He don't know nothing! Thinks he's God's anointed just because his daddy was a lord. He thought I was a bit of dog-shit! Talks in that plummy, bloody voice, all la-di-da, and the bleeding house is freezing! Freezing! Hang on a moment.'

A Rolls-Royce had stopped outside the house. Its horn gave a peremptory toot and the girl leaned forward as the front door opened.

His Lordship, a cape over his evening dress, stood in the hall light for a moment, evidently talking to someone in the house, then turned and came down the steps.

'He is good-looking,' the girl said.

'He's a putz, Gloria!' Sol Linsky said cheerfully, 'and we'll make a bleeding fortune out of him.'

'Roll on Christmas,' Gloria said.

'Whatever that is,' Sol replied happily. He watched the Rolls-Royce pull away, then nodded. 'Home, my love, and thank you for driving me.'

'My pleasure, Sol.' The Austin jerked forward, spluttered, and Linsky thanked his God for aristocrats who did not understand business and for fools who thought they made money when he walked into their lives. Marquess of Arlington, indeed! A putz!

The ball seemed to hang in the cold, damp air. It turned slowly, end over end, then fell towards the pitch. Oxford University was playing against the Royal Military College, Sandhurst. As most of the Oxford players were ex-soldiers, hardened by war service, while the RMC team was largely comprised of young men fresh out of school, the game was confidently expected to be a push-over.

But Oxford was losing. The play of Sandhurst's fly-half was responsible. He had the ball now, sidestepped through the Oxford forwards, then released a long, flat, fast pass to his centre. He looped behind his backs, took an inside pass from his left wing, and ran the ball over for a try. 'He's too good for us,' said Hilary, her blonde hair hidden by a woollen hat, as she applauded with mittened hands.

'Hugh was always good at rugger,' Janet Campbell said.

'His people were missionaries. Died in 1940,' Janet's mother said. 'They were torpedoed coming back from the Gold Coast. We knew them rather well. Oh, well played, Hugh!' The Sandhurst fly-half had just converted his own try.

Janet Campbell, like Hilary, was an undergraduate at Oxford. Her parents had come up for the weekend and tonight Hilary was invited to dine with them. She was rather looking forward to it as the college food, provided with the help of the students' rationbooks, was ghastly. The Reverend Charles Campbell stamped his cold feet on the duckboards. 'If I had known Hugh would be here I'd have invited him to dinner tonight.' A moment before he had been exhorting the Oxford team to break Hugh Grimes's leg.

Janet looked at Hilary and laughed. 'Hilary would have liked that.'

'Oh?' Mrs Campbell was delighted with the insinuation. 'Do you like the look of him, Hilary? He is such a nice boy, but he must be younger than you. He was born when, Charles? Just after you took over St Peter's?'

128

'Year after, I think.' The Reverend Charles Campbell, who had once played Rugby for Oxford, bellowed at the University to put their backs into it.

Janet laughed at his friend's face. 'You are struck.'

'Nonsense.' Yet Hilary did rather like the look of Hugh Grimes. He was short, muscled, and played rugby with an intense enthusiasm, urging his team on, hurling himself into every play as if the bruises and cuts that scarred him were nothing.

Mrs Campbell, who was solicitous of Hilary because the girl was an orphan, prodded her well-wrapped husband. 'You could ask Hugh to dinner, Charles.'

'He's probably going back to Sandhurst.'

'You won't know unless you ask.'

'Mother!' Janet said.

'Not at all, dear. I always liked Hugh.' Mrs Campbell spoke of Hugh Grimes as fondly as she spoke of her dog sitting obediently at her heels. 'And Hilary doesn't mind, do you?'

'Of course not.' Hilary laughed to cover her embarrassment.

In the second half Hugh Grimes scored another try and collected another cut on his forehead. By now he was bleeding and battered but grinning with victory. 'Come on, then,' Charles Campbell said, 'let's ambush the brute.'

The Campbell family left their dog in Hilary's safe keeping and set off across the muddy pitch. Contented, she watched them go. Oxford, though cold and damp and ill-fed, had made her happier than she had ever been. She had friends nearby who let her ride at the weekends, and she found her academic work agreeable. There were times when she thought of Pearl's old plans for her, finishing school and marriage, and could have laughed aloud.

'Hilary!' The voice came from behind. 'Hilary? It is you!' She turned to see Edward Fenton smiling at her. He wore a Cambridge College scarf around his neck. 'You do look well,' he said.

'Thank you.'

'Your pooch?' Edward stooped to pat Cardinal who rewarded him with muddy sweeps of his tail.

'He belongs to friends of mine.'

Edward straightened up. 'Jolly good match, eh?'

'If you didn't want Oxford to win, yes.'

'That fellow Grimes, eh? Quite something.' Edward had not gone to South Africa at Christmas after all because he had failed in his errand to speak with Hilary and the Lord de Conroy had expressed displeasure. In truth Edward had funked it, suspecting that she would be less than responsive to his approach, but this fortuitous meeting was too good a chance to miss. 'I'm spending the weekend at New College,' he said. 'Can I walk with you?' Edward said the last few words on the spur of the moment, driven to them by Hilary's beauty. He had told himself repeatedly over the last year that she could not be this lovely, but standing so close to her he was overwhelmed again.

'I'm waiting for friends.'

'The pooch's owners?'

'Yes.'

Edward felt hopelessly tongue-tied. De Conroy, he thought, would know just what to say, but Hilary's face turned his thoughts into jelly. 'Can I give you dinner tonight?'

'That's very kind,' Hilary said, 'but I'm spoken for.'

'Sad.'

'Ah, a Cambridge man, I see!' Charles Campbell espied Edward's scarf as he hurried back across the muddy pitch. 'You must have been delighted to see Oxford's fall from grace?'

'Good afternoon, sir,' Edward said.

Hilary, somewhat reluctantly, made the introductions. The Reverend shook his hand warmly. 'You're a friend of Hilary's?'

'We go back a couple of years, sir.'

'An eternity to you young folk, what?' Campbell laughed. His wife and daughter still chatted with the mud and blood-spattered Hugh Grimes and Hilary wished she was with them rather than with the elegant Edward Fenton.

'I was hoping,' he was saying to Charles Campbell, 'that I could tempt Lady Hilary to dine tonight.'

'You're too late! I'm afraid we bagged her first, but you're very welcome to join us, most welcome indeed!'

'Thank you, sir.' Edward had hoped for just that invitation.

'It'll balance us nicely,' Charles Campbell said. 'Three fellows and three maidens, what? Oh!' he looked at Hilary. 'I should

130

have told you. Young Hugh's delighted to come. Good news, yes?'

'Indeed,' she said, yet somehow the shine had gone out of the prospect of the evening for Hilary. When Edward had hailed her so unexpectedly she had tried to judge him, not by the past, but by the present, yet there was still an unsettling smoothness to him she did not like.

It was a smoothness that was readily apparent in the Randolph Hotel dining room that night. Hugh Grimes, sitting between Mrs Campbell and Janet, seemed gauche beside Edward's silky charm. 'You'll make a career in the army, will you, Grimes?'

Hugh Grimes appeared tempted to ask why else would he be at Sandhurst, but nodded instead. 'Yes.'

'Funny time to choose, what?' Edward smiled. 'Just after the ref has blown the final whistle on the big game?'

'You were in the Navy, Mr Fenton?' Mrs Campbell asked.

'Indeed, ma'am.' Edward smiled modestly, somehow suggesting that he had endured endless watches on the freezing bridges of destroyers out in the deep Atlantic.

Hugh, in an ill-fitting dinner jacket that looked as if it had belonged to his elder brother, if not his dead missionary father, concentrated on his Brown Windsor soup. He looked once or twice at Hilary, but spent most of the meal talking about old times with Janet. His face was scarred with dark blood from the rugby game.

It was, Hilary thought, a very good, honest face. She wondered what mystery it was that attracted her, why suddenly she wanted to see more of this man, to see him smile. She sensed that Hugh Grimes disliked Edward and wondered if that was merely wishful thinking. He reminded Hilary of Stephen Ruckmeister, now back in the States, who still wrote her wry letters. Ruckmeister was engaged to a girl who, he wrote, reminded him of her.

Edward, when the roast lamb had been carved, asked Hilary about her uncle and aunt, and Hilary gave him bland news of Howarth. 'You might remember,' Edward said to the table at large, 'the frightful fuss when Lord Monty came home?'

Hugh had not the first idea what he was talking about. 'Lord Monty?'

'The Marquess of Arlington.'

'Ah.' Hugh remembered now, and he glanced at Hilary as if realizing, for the first time, that she was titled.

'It was rather a jolly evening!' Edward said, intimating that he and Hilary shared a glittering privileged past.

'Who on earth is he?' Janet asked Hilary in the lavatory when they were en route to coffee in the lounge.

'I can't stand him!' Hilary powdered her face as she told Janet about Edward. 'He's a pest! He wangled this invitation.'

'That's not hard with daddy.' Janet pushed grips into her black hair. 'I'll try and head him off in the lounge. And get Hugh to walk you home.' She was not going back to the college, but staying with her parents in the hotel's comfort.

But at the evening's end, when the time had come for Hilary to leave, Edward was first to his feet and loud in his protestation that Hugh should stay and finish his port. Sleek in his evening dress, he bowed over Mrs Campbell's hand, thanked the Reverend Charles Campbell for his generosity, then held his arm out to Hilary.

She gave Janet a despairing look, but Charles Campbell, oblivious of the tiny drama, was talking rugby with Hugh and Hilary had no choice.

The night was cold and misty, the pavements slick with rain, and Hilary tucked her elbows firmly by her sides so he could not take her arm. They walked in silence for a hundred yards, then Edward cleared his throat. 'I wanted a private word with you.'

'I'm not sure,' Hilary said with a firmness she did not feel, 'that we have anything private to discuss.'

'It's about my mother,' Edward said. 'She's very ill.'

She immediately felt a stab of guilt for the unkind tone of her voice. 'I'm sorry.'

Edward shrugged, suggesting that fate had to be met with fortitude. 'It's just that I seem to remember Lady Montague saying your grandfather had a very good private nurse. Was that right?'

Hilary nodded. 'He had a nurse, yes.'

'You wouldn't know her name?' Edward felt delight that his hunch had paid off. He knew that a direct question would have elicited no response, but the fiction of a sick mother, he had reckoned rightly, might open up Hilary's defences. 'Father wants

132

to find a nurse and it seems stupidly hard to find anyone reliable.'

'I don't know who she was,' Hilary said, 'but Doctor Gordon might know. He probably found her.'

'She was there to the end?'

'I imagine so.' It seemed an odd question, and her guarded tone reflected it.

'You weren't there?'

Hilary shook her head. 'I was in London.'

'Yes, of course.' Edward was following a thread into a dark place, a fragile thread that could break if he put the smallest pressure on it, and he chose his words with exquisite care. 'I'm trying to prepare myself, you see. It's quite hard.' He walked a few paces in silence, head bowed, then gave the thread another tentative twitch. 'So the first you knew about your grandfather's death was when your aunt telephoned?'

Hilary glanced at him, her face lit by the misty aureole of a street lamp. 'Yes.'

'That must have been very, very hard?'

Hilary shrugged, still imagining that Edward explored the subject in preparation for his own mother's death. 'I was never very close to grandfather. He was a strange man, really. I mean I suppose I ought to have felt something more, but . . .' her voice faded as it ran out of words.

'Oh, Lord!' Edward stopped in the street and stared at Hilary with an expression of remorse. 'How very clumsy of me. That was the day your parents died, wasn't it?'

'Yes.'

Edward's voice was full of a sympathetic concern. 'That news came later, of course?' he said.

'Yes.'

It was time for the final twitch. 'I suppose it was a blessing really,' Edward said, 'that your grandfather died before his son. I mean the news would have been a terrible blow, wouldn't it?'

'I'm sure it would,' Hilary said.

And Edward let go of the thread to lunge forward in victory. 'Because your grandfather did die first, didn't he?'

And Hilary felt her world wrench out of true, knew that all Edward's sympathy had been a pretence leading to this moment, and she suddenly remembered that weird conversation with her aunt on the day of the funeral, and for the first time Pearl's words made sense and Hilary saw what she had never seen before, that there had been no mistake and that her grandfather must have died before her father.

She stared at Edward, her breath misting in the street. Pieces tumbled into place in her head, making a picture of deception and lies. She wondered if Monty knew.

Edward, watching her in the light of a street lamp, thought he could read her face like a book. As intelligent as she was, she was no dissembler, and he thought there was something pathetic about the dawning of realization on her features. 'Didn't he?' His voice was harder now, sharp with the demand for the one word he needed.

Hilary looked at the thin face above the white silk scarf. 'This has nothing to do with your mother, Edward.'

'He died first, didn't he?'

'Thank you for seeing me this far. I'll manage the rest on my own.'

Edward moved to cut off her progress, trapping her between himself and the high college wall. 'I'm staying till Monday,' he said, 'suppose we have luncheon tomorrow?'

'Thank you, but no.'

The street was almost empty. A few voices were loud in the mist to the right, and in the other direction a car backfired. Hilary knew she could not outrun him, and was astonished that she should be in this situation. 'Supposing,' Edward said, 'I was to tell you that the Marquess is about to be dragged into the courts, that the Marchioness may face criminal charges, that they'll lose Howarth and be stripped of every last penny they own?'

Hilary heard the note of triumph in his voice and she knew, from what she had just understood, that he was not exaggerating. 'I don't know what you're talking about,' she said. It was a feeble response, and she knew it.

'And suppose,' Edward went on, 'that you could stop all that happening. You.' He pointed his finger at her. 'I think you do understand me, Hilary. So why don't we talk about it tomorrow? At luncheon.'

'No.'

He stood close to her, too close, and his dark eyes were shadowed by his hat brim. 'Criminal charges. Disgrace. Scandal. And you can stop it.' She stepped away from him, but he moved, keeping her trapped against the wall. 'Luncheon, tomorrow. I'll pick you up at twelve. We'll go to the Spread Eagle at Thame.'

'No.'

Edward laughed. He did not have the absolute proof he wanted, the admission that the Marquess had died before the Earl, but he had more than enough to please Lord de Conroy, and maybe enough to pull this delicate beauty off balance. 'You don't understand, Hilary. Your family's between the devil and the deep blue sea, and I'm offering you a boat.' He was delighted with himself, imagining that he acted as de Conroy would have done, using any weapon to take what he wanted.

And Hilary knew what he wanted, and she remembered the streak of violence in him and felt a shiver that was not the night cold. 'No. Now excuse me.'

'Hilary . . .' Edward began.

'She said no.' Hugh Grimes appeared as if from nowhere, stepping silently out of the mist like an apparition.

Edward whipped round. 'Grimes! Taking a walk, are you?'

'I think you should, Fenton.'

Edward was four inches taller than Hugh and he had drunk enough to feel confident that his extra height could serve him well against the younger man. 'You're interrupting us, Grimes. Now be a good fellow and cut along.'

Hugh looked at Hilary. 'May I see you home?'

'I'd be grateful, thank you.'

'We haven't finished,' Edward said to Hugh before turning back to Hilary. 'Midday tomorrow, then. Luncheon.'

'I'm lunching with Hugh,' Hilary said, hoping that Hugh would not dispute the bald statement. He did not. Instead, in a gesture that was more expressive than any angry blow aimed at Edward, he took Hilary's willing arm. They walked away, leaving Edward alone beneath the mist-shrouded street lamp.

'Your penchant for the middle classes won't save your family!'

135

he shouted.

'Ignore him,' Hilary said.

'I've no intention of doing anything else,' Hugh Grimes said, as though beating the hell out of Edward was too simple a matter to be worth his attention. 'Janet sent me. You don't mind?'

'Mind?' She looked at him, sensing that he was as strong as Edward was rotten. Hilary, who had once sworn she would make her own path in the world, smiled at Hugh. 'I'm delighted.'

He smiled back, and Hilary was too nervous with this sudden happiness to see that he was just as happy as she herself was.

'Are we really lunching tomorrow?' Hugh asked.

'I think that's a very good idea.' And Hilary had the irrational certainty that this stranger, never glimpsed before that day, was someone who might change her life and she did not understand it, but just knew it was a wonderful feeling and a very good idea indeed.

Pearl telephoned to discover whether Monty knew that Hilary had disappeared for a week to Scotland.

'Yes,' Monty said, 'I know. She's in Tom Creed's cottage, birdwatching. She's hoping to see an osprey.'

'With a man! Unchaperoned!' Pearl's voice was livid with outrage. 'What if the gossip columnists find out?'

'I imagine they'll be impressed by him. He's a splendid chap!'

'You've met him?' Pearl sounded surprised.

'Took 'em to dinner before they went. I must say I did like him.' Monty had indeed liked Hugh and it had been pleasurably obvious that Hilary adored him.

Pearl, thrown by Monty's encomium, paused. 'Are they wealthy people?'

'Who?'

'This man's parents! Are they wealthy?'

'They're dead people. Missionaries. Went to heaven courtesy of a U-boat back in '40.'

'That's hardly respectable,' Pearl said tartly.

'Can't think of anything more respectable!' Monty said. 'One can hardly imagine Ma and Pa Grimes having a knees up in the bible class, though one never knows these days, does one?'

'You know what I mean, Monty.' Pearl sniffed. 'Well if the girl gets herself into trouble, she'll only have herself to blame.'

'It's all right,' Monty smiled into the telephone, 'they promised to take anti-baby precautions.'

There was an absolute silence from Howarth for all of ten seconds. 'Lucy Carraby telephoned,' Pearl then said in a blithe change of subject which insinuated that Monty, once again, had been guilty of gross bad taste. 'She's found some nineteenth-century cotton percale in her attic. It's in perfect condition, and it's just what I've been looking for.'

'We can't afford it!'

'Don't be ridiculous, Monty. I only want enough for my bed-room walls, and Lucy says she'll take twenty pounds.' The imminence of the sale of Lackertons had triggered Pearl into a flurry of spending plans, most of which had come to nothing. Monty knew how desperately she wanted to travel to Paris to explore the mysteries of Dior's New Look, but Howarth simply could not spare the money. He doubted whether they could even spare twenty pounds, the equivalent of a fortnight's unpaid wages for Hammond, but he could sense how much Pearl wanted the percale and, after the privations of the long cold winter and the fun he had extracted from the dead missionaries, he decided she deserved some recompense, so he said the cotton percale sounded like a splendid idea.

'There's a problem,' Pearl said then. It seemed Lucy would be away for a month, putting her Irish horses out to grass in the Meath country, so would Monty please drive to her house near Southend and collect the rolls of cloth. 'I'd get a carrier to fetch it,' she said, 'but you know how unreliable they are.' And how expensive, Monty thought as he agreed to go. 'It'll have to be tomorrow,' Pearl said, 'Lucy's going the next day.'

'I'm signing the sale papers tomorrow!'

'That's not till midday! If you go in the early morning you'll be back in plenty of time.'

Monty, suddenly knowing what it felt like to be a nagged husband, went early the next day. He admired Lucy's stables, agreed it had been a dreadful winter, and crammed the cotton on to the tiny back seat of the Morris.

'You can't stay for luncheon?' Lucy boomed at him.

'Not a chance, but thank you.' He promised to come for a summer luncheon party, then swung the starting-handle.

The Morris would not start.

Monty let the flooded carburettor drain, checked the plug leads, and tried again. Nothing. 'Damn it.'

Lucy, an enormous woman who hunted with the Essex Farmers, gave the car a massive thump with a booted foot. 'Try again.'

Nothing. Monty stripped the distributor, reassembled it, then swung the handle again.

'I could fetch a little man from the village,' Lucy said.

Monty looked at his watch. He might just make London on time if she ran him to the station. 'The car will be safe here?'

'Who'd want to steal it, Monty?'

He caught the train with thirty seconds to spare, not even time to buy *The Times*, but he knew he would just make Sir Michael's office by midday. Monty was not over-concerned with punctuality, believing like most of his class that men would happily await his coming, but Solomon Linsky was paying his deposit in cash, hard cash, and the lure of the folded notes was a wondrous spur to timekeeping.

Somewhere on the marshes beyond Canvey Island the train hissed and puffed and clanked to a halt.

Monty waited. The steam of the engine drifted over the desolate landscape, then died altogether. The guard walked to the side of the track. 'Dunno, guv!' was his answer to any query as to why they were delayed.

They waited. A rusty merchant ship inched its way up the Thames beyond the marshland. Monty was tempted to walk back to the last station, but the temptation was checked by a sudden lurch of the carriage and the clank of couplings. Then silence again.

It was past one o'clock when the train finally steamed through the bomb-torn desolation of the East End, inching its way across viaducts weakened by explosions, over rows of small houses torn by great gaps where weeds grew about dirty brick-strewn pools, and on end walls pathetic scraps of wallpaper still blew in the breeze. It seemed extraordinary that anyone had survived. The scorched shells of warehouses rose gaunt above the small streets stretching down to the docks that had been the German target. Monty saw a church opened to the sky, a hospital sliced in two like a child's toy house kicked half to destruction, and everywhere the great beams that shored up half-shattered buildings above the new pre-fabricated housing that squatted like cheap army huts among the ruins of London.

At Fenchurch Street Station Monty found a public telephone, pushed his tuppence into the slot, pressed the A button, only to be told that Sir Michael had given up and gone to lunch.

'Bugger,' he said, hanging up. Sir Michael was a famous trencherman and would doubtless still be tucking into Stilton at half past two. Monty thought about a taxi to Brick Street, then realized that he was in the same street as the offices he was selling and, on a whim, decided to look at the premises that would give a new lease of life to the dying Howarth.

It took him ten minutes to find Lackertons, but eventually he stood in front of a three-storeyed brick building with grimy windows and filthy steps leading down to a cellar. The main door was open.

The offices were Dickensian. They were panelled in dark, dirty wood and lit by tiny light bulbs inserted into old, swan-necked gas-jets. Mottled glass divided the main office into cubby-holes where clerks bent over ledgers. 'Sir?' A clerk in a wing collar came to the counter.

From the bowels of the building came a horrendous crash that made the clerk wince. 'What was that?' Monty asked.

'We have new owners, sir.' The clerk sniffed disapproval, knowing that the seed-merchants was being closed down and that his job, like all the others in this dark office, would be lost when the sale was completed. 'They are making improvements, sir.' His lugubrious countenance made Monty feel guilty, for these diligent men, scratching in their books, had provided Howarth with a tiny income, yet this was the very first time he had ever come to their dusty workplace. He did not give his name. The crash sounded again, echoing through the building. Solomon Linsky had insisted that, from the moment contracts were exchanged, work would start on the improvements he planned for the offices. He must suppose that Monty had signed the papers at the appointed time. 'What are they doing?' Monty asked after another resounding bang.

'I have no idea, sir. Can I help you?'

The next crash was a hollow, booming noise like a shell-burst inside a tank. 'They're in the cellar?' Monty asked.

'Indeed, sir.'

'How do I reach it?'

'Sir?' But Monty had already lifted the counter flap, walked through, and now waited expectantly. The clerk, evidently a man much used to being harried through a dull life, pointed to a door. 'It's that way, sir.'

Stairs led down to a cellar that was filled with old papers and records of the firm. A few chairs and a gas ring showed that the basement had been an air-raid shelter in the war when life under the bombs must have sounded much like the crashing that echoed through the building now. Monty had to stoop as he went down the steps. He turned at the bottom and saw a huge man wielding a sledgehammer against one of the brick pillars that held up the ground floor. The man saw Monty as a shadow in the gloom. 'That you, Sol?' When Monty walked into the feeble light of a naked bulb the big man checked the swing of his massive hammer. 'What the hell do you want, mate?'

Somehow the greeting sat ill with Mr Linsky's desire to use the offices for charity. Monty suppressed the angry retort he was about to make, and decided it was time for guile. 'Sol sent me.'

The answer was evidently entirely satisfactory, for the man swung the hammer again in the narrow confines of the cellar to crack its sixteen-pound head against the pillar that spurted dust and chips into the air. The man inspected the damage. 'What do you think?'

'Wonderful.' Monty stopped and saw that the bricks were cracked.

'I mean I couldn't wait all day for Sol,' the man said. 'I've got things to do!'

'I'm sure.'

'So the putz signed, did he?'

The putz, for Monty assumed he was the person under discussion, nodded. 'Oh, yes.'

''Cos if I hang around, you know, I lose the next job, don't I? Sol knows that!'

'He does indeed.' Monty, without a clue as to what the hugely muscled man was talking about, thought he was holding up his end of the conversation rather splendidly.

The man nodded at the pillar. 'You think it's all right, then?'

'You've certainly knocked it about,' Monty said.

He had evidently knocked other parts of the cellar about for the man now nodded proudly towards a vast crack that ran up a cement-faced wall at the front of the building. 'Lovely bit of work, that, lovely!' He spoke of the destruction in the same tones that Michelangelo might have used of the Sistine Chapel. 'One big bang and it cracked something lovely!'

'Didn't it just?'

The man, gratified to hear praise of his work, lowered the sledgehammer to the ground, took a half-smoked cigarette from behind his ear and re-lit it. 'You Sol's lawyer?'

'No.'

'Oh!' He laughed. 'You're the district surveyor! Well, pardon me! No harm done, though, eh? I mean Sol looks after you, doesn't he?'

'He does indeed.' Monty looked at the man's huge forearms that were thick with tattoos, amongst them the insignia of a famous regiment. 'You were in the Rifles?'

'That's it, guv. Normandy and the Rhine.'

'Pity to die now, having survived so much.'

The big face frowned, slow on the uptake. 'Eh?'

Monty prudently pulled the handle of the sledgehammer towards him. 'Why the hell are you smashing up my cellar?'

The man was built like Goliath and Monty did not fancy his chances as a David. He made his voice officer-crisp, hoping that ingrained army discipline might cow this huge man, but it was more probably the sledgehammer in Monty's hands which persuaded ex-Corporal Harry Cockerel that truth might prove a prudent saviour. It took ten minutes, some undignified dodging between the pillars, and one threatened blow with the hammer to drag

141

the facts out of Cockerel, but the facts, when they came, were worth all the wait. 'I'm a distresser, guv.'

'A what?'

Harry frowned at Monty's woeful ignorance. 'I make 'em look as if the Jerry bombs cracked 'em up, guv. Like a close miss, you know?' He waved at the cellar walls that did indeed look as if they had been weakened by the nearby fall of a German bomb.

And it was done, Monty learned, because the government would now pay for these offices to be rebuilt on the grounds that they had suffered war-damage. 'And the district surveyor,' Monty said, 'confirms that they're unsafe?'

'That's it, guv. Slip him a pony and he'll sign anything! Mind you, you've got to batter the places up a bit.' He waved at his handiwork.

Monty felt like the biggest fool in creation. 'And Mr Linsky has a lot of buildings?'

'Christ, yes, guv!' Harry Cockerel, sensing that this toff was not planning to call the police, was becoming expansive. 'He's a fly one, very fly! Nice man, though! Nothing wrong with our Sol.'

Which was a matter of opinion, Monty thought. 'And what's a putz?'

'East End Jewish, guv. A clot. Idiot. You know.'

The putz knew indeed. 'And Mr Linsky buys buildings, distresses them, and gets the government to rebuild them?'

'That's it. Then I suppose he flogs 'em. Makes money, anyway.'

'Bloody hell.'

'Clever man,' Harry said, 'very clever!' He touched the side of his nose as if in proof of his assertion. 'Mind you, he'll be bloody livid when he finds out you ain't signed the papers.' Harry looked despairingly at the work he had done in imitation of German bombs.

'Mr Linsky's coming here?' Monty asked.

'Said he was, guv.'

Monty held out the sledgehammer and added a pound note. 'Why don't you go on to your next job, Mr Cockerel, and I'll wait for Mr Linsky.'

He waited an hour before feet sounded on the outside stairs and an agitated voice shouted into the cellar: 'Don't touch a bloody thing, Harry, that toffee-nosed bastard's disappeared!' So Linsky, no longer the humble, suppliant Jew, ducked under the low door. 'Sodding bastard's done a disappearing act, hasn't he?'

'Hello, Linsky.'

Sol Linsky whipped round, saw Monty, and sagged. 'Shit.'

'The toffee-nosed putz is here.' He moved to cut off Sol's retreat by the front steps.

Linsky had a dead cheroot in his mouth. He re-lit it, using the time to think fast, and decided attack was the best defence in the face of the evident destruction of Monty's premises. 'So why didn't you sign? You ever heard of breach of promise? Verbal contract, my Lord! Just as good in a court of law as a signed piece of paper!' He puffed smoke happily. 'Best thing you can do, my Lord, is to get up to the West End and scribble your moniker on the papers!'

Monty smiled. 'Funny you should mention the law, Linsky. I wonder what they'd make of Mr Harry Cockerel and the district surveyor? I wonder what would happen if the law decided to inspect all your buildings, Linsky, and compare them with real bomb-damaged sites? I know it would only be my word against yours, but who do you think they'll believe? You? Or the Marquess of Arlington, Earl of Arlington, Baron Howarth of Howarth, MC, DSO, and not quite the putz he was yesterday.'

Sol Linsky thought about it and decided that the toffee-nosed bastard knew a great deal too much. He grinned. 'So why haven't you called in the law, my Lord?'

'Monty.'

The bespectacled face looked puzzled. 'Monty?'

'Partners should be on first-name terms,' Monty said, 'don't you agree, Sol?'

'Partners!' Linsky shouted the word in disgust.

'Either that or the law, Sol.'

'Partners!' he mocked him. 'I don't need a bleeding layabout!' He took the roll of notes from his pocket and peeled a wad from the top. 'We'll forget about it, right?' He held the money out. 'You go and buy yourself a new coronet and I'll forget we ever met.'

143

'But we did meet,' Monty ignored the proffered money, 'and we're partners. Or else it's five years down the Scrubs, Sol.'

'Bleedin' 'ell.' Sol looked at his Lordship, then grinned. 'You're a gentleman, right?'

'One tries,' Monty said.

Sol Linsky stuffed the notes into his jacket pocket, then fished into his trouser pocket to produce a handful of change. He selected a shining penny. 'A gentleman's wager, then. Tails you're my partner, heads you forget all about this?' He looked at him quizzically.

Monty nodded. 'Spin it, then.'

The bright penny flickered in the cellar's gloom. At the last moment, as Sol was about to catch it, Monty snatched it from the air.

'Hey!' Sol shouted.

Monty smiled. He held the penny before Linsky's bespectacled eyes and turned it slowly. 'I haven't seen a double-headed penny in years, Sol. So what's it to be? Partners or prison?'

Solomon Linsky took the penny, grinned, and resigned himself to the inevitable. He held out his hand. 'Partners.'

'A wise decision,' Monty said.

'But if you're a partner, you bleedin' work, right! So for starters you can bust the light bulbs. Harry always forgets to do that, and we don't want the district surveyor to see too well, do we?'

So Monty broke the light bulbs and thus the Marquess of Arlington went into trade.

The putz, under Sol Linsky's tuition, learned fast.

They tossed a coin to decide whether their company would be called Linhow or Monsol. Monsol won. They rented two rooms in Dover Street which was their office. According to Sol they had gone up-market because his Lordship wouldn't dirty himself by working in the East End, but the profits brought in by Monty's social connections were such that Sol did not mind. 'For a toff, he ain't bad,' he told Gloria.

Gloria was Sol's secretary, engaged to marry the obliging Mr

Cockerel, and in Gloria's eyes Monty could do no wrong. 'He's lovely!' she said.

'He's a bleeding two-timing twister, that's what he is,' Sol replied, but he said it fondly for he was a man who could not hold a grudge.

Linsky was a widower whose only son had died in the ill-fated Norwegian campaign, and who now poured his affections into the orphaned youngsters he rescued from the wreckage of the Third Reich. Sol was a philanthropist, but he was also one of the sharpest property dealers in London and, to his considerable surprise, he discovered that the esrtwhile toffee-nosed putz had a talent for this particular line of business. 'Were you really going to use Lackertons' offices for the charity?' Monty had asked him.

'Don't be a putz! You have to make the seller sympathize with you! Make him think he's winning the negotiations when you're slicing his feet off!'

Corners were cut, regulations twisted, and palms crossed with five-pound notes. 'You think no one else does it?' Sol told Monty. 'You think we need Inspection Notes, Supply Notes, Delivery Licences? You think your family became rich by grovelling to bureauputzes? Besides, so we're caught. It's a fine, yes? One hundred pounds? Maybe a thousand! A rap over the knuckles. So long as they don't find out about Harry and his sledgehammer, we're all right!' He re-lit his cheroot and chuckled. 'I've found us a perfect one. Fifteen provincial shops and premises off Holborn. I've given Elizabeth the details.'

Elizabeth Callaway was Monty's new secretary and, in Solomon Linsky's eyes, the ideal assistant. 'She's like you,' he said. 'She looks so very English, yes? No one suspects the English. She'll have Arthur Humbold eating out of her hand!'

'Who's Arthur Humbold?' Monty asked.

'He's our new putz. You'll hate him!' Sol took a peculiar and distinct delight in the guests he foisted on to Monty.

It was in the late summer of 1948 that a letter, bearing the crest of the Marquess of Arlington, invited Mr Humbold to take luncheon with his Lordship at Brick Street. Sol rarely attended such lunches, insisting that Monty and Elizabeth meet the clients while he and Gloria did the hard work in the back room. In

145

Dover Street, before Monty went to meet Humbold, Sol was touchingly anxious. 'You can go to thirty-five thousand, Monty.'

'Not a penny over thirty, Sol.'

'No one's that much of a putz!'

'Thirty,' Monty insisted. He, too, was nervous. He was always nervous at this point when the prospect, whom Sol had stalked and appraised, finally appeared.

Mr Arthur Humbold, when he presented himself at the Brick Street door, was a thin, uncertain man in his early thirties. He was dressed too carefully, in a grey suit that was shiny with use and a pearl tiepin.

Elizabeth Callaway met him. 'How very kind of you to come.' Her smile was overwhelming. 'You'll have something to drink?'

'Very kind of you.' Arthur Humbold stared in awe at the wood-panelled drawing room into which he was ushered. He was even more impressed by the tall, smiling girl with lustrous black hair who was so very solicitous of his comfort.

She took his coat and ushered him to a chair. 'His Lordship will be a few moments. I'm his assistant. Now we have sherry, whisky, gin. Anything, really. What would you like?'

Arthur Humbold stared at the array of bottles. He usually drank milk-stout, but said he would be very grateful for some sherry.

'I'll have some, too.' Elizabeth poured two glasses of the decanted cooking sherry, knowing full well that the amontillado would be wasted.

'You know, do you,' Mr Humbold was excruciatingly nervous, 'why his Lordship wants to see me?'

'Oh I'm sure he'd prefer to tell you himself.' Elizabeth sat in an upright chair and pulled her skirt a fraction too high so that her knees were revealed. 'And how is the photographic business?'

'Oh, so-so.' Humbold tore his eyes away from her legs and raised his glass. 'Cheers.'

'Down the hatch,' Elizabeth said. She slid imperceptibly forward so that the skirt rode another inch up her thighs.

On the table beside Arthur was a framed portrait of the King and Queen. In strong, black ink, written over the portrait's lower right-hand corner, was a dedication. 'To Monty, with our warmest wishes, George and Elizabeth R.' Humbold stared at it. 'He knows them, yes?'

'Of course!' She laughed as if the question had been unnecessary, though the truth was that Sol Linsky had written the inscription. Next to the portrait was a framed and genuine invitation to last November's Royal Wedding when the Princess Elizabeth had married Philip. Pearl, who had loved every moment of the wedding, thought that the framed memento was vulgar in the extreme, but Sol Linsky had insisted on displaying it. 'If I've got to have a bleeding Lord as a partner,' he said, 'then we might as well use it, right?' There were, Sol said, people ready to be impressed by such things: people like Arthur Humbold.

Thanks to a German bomb Humbold had inherited his father's chain of photographic shops. There had been a time, before the Box Brownie was invented, when old Mr Humbold's men photographed families the length and breadth of Britain, but of late the business had fallen on tougher times.

Sol had found the Holborn studios of Humbolds in January. He had stood in a doorway opposite, ignoring the bitter cold, just staring at the magic words painted on the shop's fascia board: 'Branches throughout the United Kingdom.'

There were two shopfronts and an office above. It was close to the Patent Office, to the Chancery Lane Underground Station, to Fleet Street, to a post office, and to the great slew of lawyers' chambers that curled up from the river. It was, Sol saw, run-down and decrepit. He pulled a small notebook from his pocket, a stub of pencil, and wrote down the shop's name.

He and Gloria spent two days with street directories until they had found the other properties in the chain. Then Sol disappeared to talk with lawyers' clerks and City of London employees, paying for scraps of information with big, white five-pound notes until Sol knew more about Arthur Humbold's business than Arthur did himself.

He knew that, over the years, Arthur Humbold's father had paid £21,000 for the freeholds of all his shops. That figure, which was partly based on guesswork and partly on information, was the key to everything.

The figure was ludicrously low, yet Sol knew that it almost certainly still appeared in the company's books as the actual value of all Humbold's premises. It astonished him that business-men never thought to have their buildings re-valued, and went on, year after year, assuming that a ten- or twenty-year-old price was still accurate. It was that assumption which would make Sol Linsky and his new partner their money.

Sol wrote down the figure £21,000. Next to it he pencilled in what he considered to be the real value of all the shops. £48,000.

Now he needed to reckon what Mr Arthur Humbold would accept as payment for his business, his stock, and the goodwill that went with them. Sol wrote down £10,000, decided that was generous but let it stand. The first and last figure made a total of £31,000, which left, on paper, a profit to Monsol of £17,000, though that was nowhere near the kind of money Sol intended to make. And the making of it depended on what happened in Brick Street when Monty, at last, confronted Mr Humbold.

'I see Elizabeth's looked after you. That's a very pleasant amontillado, is it not?'

Arthur Humbold looked at his glass and nodded eagerly. 'Very nice.'

'We kept a couple of pre-war pipes.' Monty could see that this one was a real putz. 'Let's have luncheon, shall we?'

Hammond served pâté, sole, and trifle. Monty kept the discussion firmly away from business, plying Humbold's glass with white wine and talking, instead, of politics. He agreed avidly with everything his guest said.

'This National Health Service now,' Arthur opined. 'Waste of time, isn't it?'

'Indeed,' Monty said.

'It will just encourage people to be poorly, won't it?'

Monty shook his head in admiration. 'I'd never thought of that. How clever of you to see it.'

Arthur shrugged modestly. He had never in his life been in the same room as an aristocrat, and he reckoned he was putting up a very good showing. The girl, Miss Callaway, was watching him admiringly. Arthur, whose girlfriend was a barmaid at the Station Hotel, wondered if he had set his romantic sights a little too low. He smiled. 'It takes a businessman to see these things.'

'You've got me there,' Monty laughed. 'I'm just a landowner. No head for business at all!' Throughout luncheon he had been saying the same thing, flattering Arthur Humbold's business acumen and decrying his own. 'Perhaps we can take our coffee next door and talk?'

'Of course.'

Back in the drawing room, Elizabeth offered Arthur a cigar. He let her cut it for him, then, as she held up a match to light it, cupped her hand in both his and noticed that she did not flinch from his touch. 'Thank you, very nice indeed.'

Monty smiled. 'You don't mind if Elizabeth stays? I have to delegate much of my work to her and I've no doubt she'll be dealing a fair bit with you in the next few weeks.'

Humbold had no objections whatsoever. He smiled at Elizabeth and was rewarded with a dazzling smile in return. She sat opposite him and, again, seemed oblivious of the fact that her skirt rode up her thighs.

'The thing is,' Monty said, 'that I want to buy your business.'

Arthur nearly choked on his cigar smoke. In the previous days, discussing with his barmaid why he had been summoned to meet a marquess, he had thought it probable there would be a photographic commission. But this? 'All of them?' he wheezed.

'Lock, stock and barrel.' Monty smiled and drew a sheet of paper out of a file. 'You understand that my dear father died recently. In his will he directed that free veterinary clinics should be established in certain towns. Charitable clinics for our dear pets. Do you understand?'

Arthur was in a daze, but he managed a nod. 'Yes.'

'And some of your premises, not all, of course, would be ideal for this purpose.'

Arthur wiped a shred of tobacco leaf from his lip. 'Animal clinics?'

Elizabeth Callaway leaned forward anxiously. 'You do think that's a good idea?'

'Oh yes, yes. Very definitely so, yes.' Arthur nodded. The aristocracy, he thought, must be barmy, but if there was a profit in it for him, who cared?

Elizabeth smiled. 'His Lordship is heavily involved with charity, Mr Humbold.'

'Yes, of course. Yes.'

'Splendid!' Monty behaved as if the deal was already done. 'I took the liberty, of having your business valued. Ringley and Barton did the job for me. You know the firm?'

'No.'

'They're in Bond Street,' he went on casually. 'They're pretty well established, but you might well want to find that out for yourself.' He looked to Elizabeth. 'Didn't they handle the sale of Lord Mallet's Oxford Street properties?'

'They did, my Lord.'

Monty smiled at Humbold in triumph. 'There you are! Telephone Tommy Mallet and mention my name. I'm sure he'll be entirely glad to tell you about Ringley and Barton.'

Arthur could no more imagine telephoning Lord Mallet than he could envisage flying to the moon. He muttered that there would be no need, and spooned sugar into his coffee.

'Ringley and Barton gave me their valuation and I must say,' Monty shook his head, 'that I was surprised.'

'Surprised?'

'It was low.' Monty frowned and held a sheet of paper towards him. 'There. £20,000. Too low, I think, don't you?'

In truth Arthur had no idea what his freeholds were worth. Somewhere, doubtless, the valuations were written down, but if Monty said they were too low, then he was happy to agree. 'Definitely low. Yes.'

'I'm quite prepared to take your word on it,' Monty said anxiously. 'I really don't want to be unfair. It would be a dreadful thing if the pets' clinics started on a sour note, wouldn't it?'

'Yes. Indeed, yes.'

'So I was thinking,' he said, 'of offering you £25,500. That's for the existing freehold premises, their stock, and of course the goodwill.'

'Ah yes, the goodwill!' Arthur spoke warmly, though in truth there was no goodwill left for Humbold's photographic shops. The customers had bought their own cameras, God damn them.

Monty suggested that Mr Humbold might go and talk to his

advisers; that he should consult his firm's books for his own valuation of the premises, and contact Elizabeth before the week's ending. 'There is a small matter of speed. The poor pets,' Monty was wondering how he would keep a straight face, 'are suffering.'

'I do see that,' Arthur said.

'And I firmly believe this is a very fair offer, very fair indeed.' Arthur Humbold nodded vigorously. 'Indeed, yes.'

'But you must be the best judge,' Monty went on, as though Arthur had not uttered agreement. 'We philanthropists can't pull the wool over the eyes of you businessmen!' He chuckled. 'But a man can live very well these days on £25,000, very well indeed!'

In the end, after a month's vacillation, Monty agreed on a price of £28,750. He sent a note to Mr Humbold that congratulated him on being a tough bargainer, then Sol went to work.

He declared that six of the provincial shops were rubbish. 'Too far from Woolworths!' He sold each one outright and netted £12,600.

Seven of the shops were happily close to bombsites and the sledgehammer-wielding Harry Cockerel was despatched to finish the Luftwaffe's unfinished work. Sol followed in Harry's wake, a pocket filled with five-pound notes, and inside three weeks all seven had been dutifully declared bomb-damaged by the various district surveyors within whose authority the shops lay. 'No one's honest these days,' Sol said piously. 'A sad world!'

The government duly funded the repairs and redecoration of the seven shops. Sol sold two of the rebuilt premises for £5,800, but the others he kept. 'We rent them and we wait!'

Yet the provincial shops were, he said, just birdseed. It was Humbold's old Holborn offices that he wanted, and into which carpenters, bricklayers, plumbers, painters, and electricians moved. There was no chance of declaring these offices bomb-damaged as they lay too far from the known fall of any enemy bombs, so Sol and Monty paid for the rebuilding. There was not a single government Release Note to be seen, the work was entirely illegal, and Monty became used to Gloria raiding the petty cash to pay brothers and cousins and other members of her sprawling tribe. Yet when the work was done they had a pristine

151

office in London, and London offices, as Sol had once told Monty, were rare and valuable things in these hard times.

An insurance company, looking for a safe investment, bought a twenty-year lease on the offices for £70,000. The deal was struck amidst the genteel old-world grandeur of one of Monty's clubs, where the Marquess of Arlington guaranteed the profitability of the insurance company's investment by renting the building back at an annual rent of £3,650. Sol then sublet the offices for £5,000 a year, and Monsol had already turned the Humbold property into more than £80,000 profit.

'Why don't people like Humbold have the wit to do it?' Monty asked.

'Listen to him!' Sol said. 'Did you have the wit to do it? I almost took you for twenty-three and a half! Besides, Humbold doesn't know the insurance companies, the banks, the surveyors, the plasterers. He's a putz!'

The business was a goldmine. Lackertons, Seedsmen, and a score of other undervalued businesses went the same way, yet Sol insisted this was just a beginning. 'When the economy revives,' he liked to say, 'just you wait!' Monty waited, he learned from Sol, and did his homework, yet always he was careful to present to the world a careless, lackadaisical languor. He became, as Sol proudly said, lethal.

Monty also enjoyed it. For an aristocrat to become a tradesman was, in society's eyes, an indignity, but he took to the piratical trade Sol taught him. Business, Monty found, was not dull men and commonplace routine, but depended on ruthless, swift decisions. Timid men who feared decisions went to the wall, while Monty, trained as a soldier and given the daring of his ancestors, flourished.

The Marquess of Arlington gave parties that summer. He celebrated Hilary's degree and Gloria's birthday and obliged Sophie by not giving a party on her fiftieth birthday, but bought her a necklace of rubies instead. He took Sol to Ascot, taking pride in introducing him as a friend in the Royal Enclosure.

Howarth was fed with Monsol money. Hilary found a job in the British Museum, Hugh Grimes went on attachment to Malaya while, at Eton, David struggled to conquer his stammer by filling his mouth with pebbles. Pearl said she had always known Monty would succeed and persuaded Lord Creed, whose affair with the younger woman had broken down, to sell her the Jaguar for £400. Her vision of a Howarth restored was being fed by Monty's success, and Pearl gave the car in gratitude to him: to elegant Monty who went on making money. His fears of the immediate post-war months faded, he blossomed like the wicked, and the skies of his life seemed cloudless.

Sir Nicholas Fenton felt the sweat trickle down his ample belly beneath his vest. He always wore a vest under his shirt, and a waistcoat over it, and his only concession to this warm summer sun was an alpaca jacket left over from pre-war days which was tight under his armpits.

He sat in a deck chair on the terrace of Caton Hall while, high above him, wobbling slightly in the warm air, a Tiger Moth biplane made a circuit of the parkland.

The aeroplane was Lord de Conroy's newest toy. He had learned to fly in South Africa, despising the handicap of his false leg, and now flew a bombing mission over his domain. It was all rather tiresome, Sir Nicholas thought. He had been invited here for a business meeting and his Lordship was buzzing around the welkin in a bright yellow biplane trying to drop flour-bag bombs on to the swimming pool.

The Tiger Moth approached again. Lord de Conroy had the controls, Edward Fenton was in the rear seat with the flour bags. Sir Nicholas kept a wary eye on the machine, suspecting that his son might think it amusing to overshoot and bomb his father instead of the two girls in the pool. Sir Nicholas wondered what effect one two-pound bag of self-raising flour would have on an ample human body in a deck chair.

The engine of the plane roared as Lord de Conroy picked up the nose, Edward released the last missile, and Sir Nicholas watched as it exploded on a neatly clipped yew bush. None of the bags had struck anywhere near the swimming pool, instead there were smears of white up to fifty yards away from its concrete surround. He reflected that Berlin would probably still be standing if his son had chosen the Royal Air Force for his war service.

'Have those geezers finished?' one of the girls shouted from the pool.

'I believe they only had twelve bags,' Sir Nicholas replied. He wondered where Lord de Conroy had found these girls; pretty enough, but with such raucous, common voices. It pained him to think of Edward sleeping with such baggages, but young men would be young men and thank God for penicillin.

Sir Nicholas went back to the papers he was studying and reflected that Lord de Conroy had been right all along. The financial pressure had failed, but the law would now take its inevitable course and the Marquess of Arlington would be ejected from Howarth.

The first paper, recently come to his office, was a letter from the Howarth lawyer. Sir Michael Gooding replied to Sir Nicholas Fenton that there was no truth whatsoever in his allegation, which he had the honour to answer, that the fourth Marquess of Arlington had pre-deceased his son and that the Lord de Conroy, by this fact, should have possession of Howarth. To clear the matter up, and in the hope that Sir Nicholas would advise his client to pursue the matter no further, Sir Michael had the honour to enclose a typed copy of the letter penned by Doctor Andrew Gordon on the day of the fourth Marquess's demise. The lawyer had fired the first shot and been rebuffed, just as he had suspected he would be.

The second paper, stored for almost two years in Lord de Conroy's safe, was the Lady Sophie Howarth's affidavit. 'The Marchioness of Arlington,' the crucial line read, 'telephoned me to say that my father died at 3.43 on the Friday afternoon.' Sir Nicholas thought it most unlike the Lady Sophie to be so precise, but doubtless she had over-egged the pudding at her lover's request. 'The police confirmed to me that my elder brother, the Earl of Mountsorrel, did not die till 4.30 p.m.' Quite so, the lawyer thought.

The third paper was a deposition made by Mrs Olive Mackenzie, a widow from Hull, who had been present at the fourth Marquess's death. 'I am certain that the old man died at around quarter to four in the afternoon because I remember thinking that I would not be late for my usual tea in the butler's pantry.'

The Tiger Moth re-appeared at the park's boundary, losing height, and Sir Nicholas watched as it descended gently towards the turf. It bounced once, again, then was running safe and easy towards the house.

Lord de Conroy had hired a private detective to find the nurse. The matter, Sir Nicholas felt, was beyond dispute. The detective had also discovered a man who was certain the flag over Howarth had been lowered to the half well before four o'clock. The man would not give evidence; no one in the local village would testify against the Howarths, but the evidence would not be needed. Nurse Mackenzie's relief at being in time for her tea was the kind of small peg on which justice depended and great families fell. It was entirely convincing.

The intrepid airman limped from his plane and hooted with derision at the results of Edward's marksmanship. 'Bloody useless, wouldn't you say, Nick?'

'He seems somewhat off target, yes.'

De Conroy dropped his goggles on the table beside Sir Nicholas. 'Working! That's the spirit. Earn your bloody fees, man.'

'I strive to do so.'

Edward said he would go swimming and the Baron slapped his shoulder. 'The blonde one's mine, Eddie!'

'Whatever you say.' Edward grinned at his father and left.

'Wherever,' Sir Nicholas asked, 'did you find those girls?'

'They're tarts, of course,' de Conroy said. 'Drink?'

'That would be a relief.'

A servant was rung for and drinks ordered. Christine wandered on to the terrace and flinched against the strong sunlight. She was thirteen now, thin and mousy, with a plain, shy face and timid eyes. De Conroy, in a fine mood this summer's day, scooped his daughter on to his lap. 'Want a swim?'

Christine shook her head.

'Ride?'

'No.'

'What then?'

She held out a small, pale hand. 'Keys?'

De Conroy laughed, fished in his pocket, and brought out a

bunch of keys on a loop of chain. 'Go on with you!' He watched her go back into the house. 'She likes to sort through her mother's jewellery! Can you believe it? Hour after hour, like a bloody jackdaw.'

'She's a pretty girl,' Sir Nicholas said unctuously.

'Don't be ridiculous! Those are pretty girls,' de Conroy nodded towards the pool. 'Christine's as plain as a pikestaff, but it's wonderful what a bit of cash can do for a plain girl. We'll tart her up when the time's right.' He waited as the steward served the drinks, then nodded at the papers. 'So?'

'Quite splendid,' Sir Nicholas said, 'as far as they go.'

'Don't hold me in suspense! Will they do or won't they?'

'I think they very well might. The nurse's affidavit is the important evidence.' The lawyer frowned judicially. 'But I fear, my Lord, that a court might construe your relationship with the Lady Sophie as being of a nature that might unduly influence her evidence.'

De Conroy scoffed at the thought. 'Arlington won't want the world to know I've whored his sister!'

'Arlington will do anything to hold on to Howarth,' Sir Nicholas said. 'Sophie's corroboration will be important, but the nurse is our key. I'd like another witness, though. Hilary?'

De Conroy swirled his gin and tonic about in the glass. 'She dropped hints to Edward, that's all. If push comes to shove, she'll stay loyal to her uncle.'

'She has the reputation,' Sir Nicholas said slowly, 'of being painfully honest. It might be fascinating to see her under cross-examination.'

'Should we put the thumbscrews on the bitch now?'

Fenton looked pained at the suggestion. 'The Howarth lawyers will be protecting her. No, I fear these are all we have,' he tapped the papers, 'but I think they will serve. I think they will serve very well!' As he made this assertion, he wondered just what kind of defence the family would concoct. Surely, he thought to himself, there was no real defence possible?

De Conroy smiled. 'So what do we do with the papers?'

'I think the best thing all round would be to let the Treasury do our work for us, don't you agree? And so much cheaper if they instruct counsel!' Sir Nicholas laughed. 'I would, then, simply send the statements to the Treasury solicitor.'

'The Treasury will act on it?'

'Of course they will! They'll act on anything! They'd sue if they got anonymous information on used toilet paper!' He added, chuckling, 'I have often thought what an easy time the Gestapo would have had if they occupied England. We betray each other so gleefully.'

There were screams of laughter from the pool. Sir Nicholas looked, looked again, and his eyebrows went slowly up his plump forehead. His son was chasing a dark-haired girl around the pool's margin, trying to flick her rump with a wet towel. She was stark naked, not a stitch on her. 'Dear me,' he said. 'Oh, dear me!'

'Fine lass, eh?'

'Remarkable, indeed.' Sir Nicholas was deeply embarrassed. Grateful as he was for de Conroy's interest in Edward, there were times when the lawyer felt that perhaps his Lordship's influence was not entirely for the good. Edward had graduated well and now worked for de Conroy's accountants. Sir Nicholas had hoped his son would swiftly qualify as a chartered accountant Edward, but instead seemed to be his employer's companion in baser pursuits. He wondered if young Christine was watching the happenings at the pool from some window of the house, then thought it was no business of his how de Conroy reared his child.

'So,' the Baron said, 'what happens now?'

'That's really up to the Treasury, isn't it?' Sir Nicholas forced his gaze away from the squealing beauty still trying to evade his son. 'Naturally they will want the death duties owing to them. They could simply sue for them, but as fraud is implicit in their case, then I imagine they will prefer a criminal trial.'

A slow smile spread over de Conroy's face. 'Criminal?'

'What else? Pearl and the doctor, we presume, conspired to defraud the Treasury! There are two possible charges, conspiracy and fraud, but my own guess, thank you, my dear fellow,' Sir Nicholas took the cigar de Conroy offered, 'is that the Treasury solicitor will prefer charges only against the doctor. It is his handwriting on the letter and Gordon will be easier to prosecute than Pearl.'

The Baron frowned. 'Why?'

'Think of the circumstances! A woman loses her father-in-law, her brother- and sister-in-law, and all in the same week that she has heard her husband is missing, presumed dead. My dear Kynaston, any decent barrister could take those circumstances and have a jury weeping for the woman! Juries are the most uncertain creatures, you know. They have inconvenient emotions.'

'So the doctor would be imprisoned?'

'Possibly.' Sir Nicholas saw, with relief, that the naked girl had leapt into the pool. 'But I should think the judge would know who was truly on trial. No. I imagine the doctor will be given a very steep fine, which the Howarths would be duty-bound to pay.'

'Which they can now afford to pay,' de Conroy said savagely.

'Hasn't our Marquess been clever!' Sir Nicholas spoke with mock admiration. 'His Jewish partner must be the brains, though.'

Kynaston could not bear to think about his rival's sudden and unexpected success. 'So what happens after the trial?'

'The criminal prosecution will have established that the late Earl of Mountsorrel succeeded, however briefly, to the Marquisate. The Treasury will demand, and receive, the death duties of which they were defrauded. They will doubtless demand, and receive, further monies as interest and in legal costs. At that point, my Lord, we will issue a civil writ for the possession of Howarth on the true grounds that the Earl of Mountsorrel agreed to sell the freehold to you, with vacant possession, at his accession to the Marquisate. We will prove that dear Lady Montague had no right, therefore, to negotiate the lease with you.' Sir Nicholas smiled. 'I think I might fairly say that you'll be master of Howarth within the year? And that the Howarth family name will not be worth a bucket of spit.' He raised his glass. 'My sincerest congratulations.'

'Thank you.' De Conroy picked up the two affidavits. 'Shall I have these sent to the Treasury solicitor?'

'Let me, dear fellow.' Sir Nicholas put them into his briefcase. 'I'll have luncheon with him and mutter a few soothing words into his ear.'

Lord de Conroy savoured his coming victory, and found it good. He laughed. 'Fancy a spin?' he said, gesturing towards the biplane.

'Good Lord, no! I do not think flying would agree with me at all!'

'A swim, then?'

The lawyer shuddered at the thought. 'But do have one yourself, my Lord.'

'I'll let you have a look at the blonde, shall I?' De Conroy laughed as he stood up.

The blonde, Fenton thought, was worth looking at. Quite remarkable! He sipped his whisky and soda, listened to the merry cries coming up from the swimming pool, and thought how very silly Lady Montague had been. There could be no defence, none! So sad, so inevitable, and so inexorable. Thus comforted, Sir Nicholas closed his eyes and slept in the sunshine, for Howarth was doomed.

A tow truck had been hired from a local garage. Its hook, harnessed to a winch powered by its engine, took the strain. 'Careful!' Pearl snapped.

Her father, standing beside her in the spring sunlight, thought she was quite mad to be spending so much on Howarth. 'Her head's been turned,' Sir Reginald had told his wife before leaving. 'Daft as a bucket.'

One of the wrought-iron gates stirred on the gravel, grated, then, with its base braced by wooden planks jammed under the tow truck's wheels, swung upwards. 'Gently, Potter!' Pearl snapped again.

'She thinks I'm bloody going to drop the thing,' Mr Potter, controlling the winch, muttered under his breath.

'Did you say something, Potter?'

'I said to mind it don't topple over, your Ladyship.'

The old gates had disappeared in 1940; gone to be melted

down as part of a tank or a warship or an aeroplane. Now new gates would bar the long elm-edged driveway.

They were magnificent, weighing more than two tons each, far more splendid than the gates they replaced. The iron bars were fully fifteen feet tall at the centre of the span, and the spaces between them were decorated with curlicues of delicate metalwork. The tops were lined with spear-points painted bright gold.

In the centre of each gate was the coat of arms of the Howarth family: the quartered shields were lacquered gules and argent and the brightness of their reflections made Sir Reginald squint. 'And how much did they cost?'

'Not very much.' Pearl was watching Potter's winch-handling like a hawk. 'Stop there! Now brace it!'

The farm labourers borrowed for the occasion knew well enough what to do without the imperious commands, but they nodded, braced the gate, and waited while the hook was freed.

'How much?' Sir Reginald, standing by his Daimler, insisted. 'And where did you get the iron from? I can't lay my hands on metal just like that! You're supposed to indent for it. You're supposed to have an M Licence from the Ministry of Supply!'

'I don't deal with ministries,' Pearl said grandly. 'A little man came round and I told him to go away.'

'So where did it come from, girl?'

'Mr Linsky.' Pearl's disapproval was obvious. She thought Solomon Linsky a vulgar little man, but was prepared to tolerate him so long as his endeavours enriched Howarth's coffers. She saw no need whatsoever for Monty to take his partner into society, but accepted that her husband had perverse ideas at times.

'And how the hell does Linsky get iron?'

'I really can't say, father. He just does. The Jews have always been good at things like that, haven't they? I mean if they can find manna in Sinai they can certainly find iron in Britain. Our village blacksmith ran them up. He did rather well, didn't he?'

The winch chain had been draped over a timber joist that lay on the two stone pillars of the gate. Now, very delicately, Potter raised the gate clear of the ground so that the hinge-sockets could be lowered on to the pintles. 'Did you put grease on them, Mr Dyson?'

'I did, my Lady.'

'But it must have cost money!' Sir Reginald's red, heavy face frowned. 'You haven't got money to throw around!'

'As a matter of fact, I have, and I'm restoring Howarth as it should be restored. Is it hanging straight? Put your level on it, Mr Dyson!'

It took two hours to hang the gates. They looked splendid. The lacquer on the shields and the gold of the spear-points hurled the sun back at the onlookers. They emblazoned the family's coat of arms to the passer-by even as they barred him from entering the grounds. 'Very nice,' Pearl said.

'And how the hell do you get in?' Sir Reginald grumbled. 'Am I supposed to get out of the bloody car and open the gates every time?'

'Your chauffeur can.'

'I don't have a chauffeur.'

'Then either you open the gates or else use the Dower House entrance,' Pearl said with barely concealed impatience. 'One day I'll have a gatekeeper here.'

'One day! One day you'll lose the bloody place. De Conroy will take it over and he won't thank you for doing this.' Sir Reginald waved at the gates. 'If you've got money, girl, then you invest it! Put it in gilts, not this frippery.'

For, astonishingly, there was money. It had come in the nick of time, just as de Conroy had secured his Release Notes from the Ministry of Supply and the precious building materials had flowed into Howarth. The surveyors had been meticulous. They had found damp in the internal walls of the east wing. The decorative plasterwork of the octagon's ceiling needed repair. The wiring in the servants' quarters was dangerous and must be replaced immediately. All the gutters needed re-securing, cleaning, and painting.

The stable block's internal walls needed repointing. A new screed had to be laid under the kitchen floor and the walls damp-proofed. The chimneys needed cleaning throughout the house, and there was scarcely a bedroom that did not need redecorating. 'The work,' the surveyors had written, 'especially the fine-work such as the repair of the plaster mouldings, must be done by specialist craftsmen.'

Pearl was angered by the demand. Did they think she would hire butchers to repair Howarth?

The outflow of the ornamental lake was blocked in the sluice tunnel, so the lake would have to be drained, the sluices rebuilt, and the adjoining lawn, spoilt by the flooding, relaid. The steps of the terraces had suffered frost damage and the masonry would have to be repointed. One third of the kitchen garden greenhouses needed new glazing. The list had taken up sixteen closely typed pages. Pearl, reading it, had heard the death knell of all her hopes, then, out of the blue, the money had started to arrive.

So now the repairs were being done, and there was even money left over to dig a new inlet channel for the ornamental lake so that the water was not fouled by de Conroy's vast manure heap which mouldered behind the young willow screen. Some days, happily rare, the wind brought the stench of the rotting manure to Howarth's gardens, but Pearl could afford to ignore the provocation. She had survived. There was still a vast amount of work to be done: carpentry and sewing and upholstery and painting and gilding, but the essential repairs were in hand, the lease was being honoured, and Pearl was secure for the moment.

Sir Reginald grudgingly allowed that his daughter had done a fine job. He still did not understand why she had done it, why she poured money into a house she must lose on behalf of a husband who rarely seemed to be there.

'Monty prefers being in London,' Pearl said equably.

'That's where you should be, then.'

'Nonsense, father.' Pearl poured their after-lunch coffee. 'I have to look after Howarth. Do you know anyone in the central-heating business?'

'Aye. There's Jack Thomas, remember him? Makes boilers up in Walsall.'

'Perhaps you'd persuade him to give us a price for a new system?'

Sir Reginald lowered his coffee cup. 'In twenty-odd years, lass, you lose Howarth, right? It goes! Why in hell's name are you putting in bloody boilers?'

'Because I don't intend to shiver through the next twenty-seven years,' she said. Nor thereafter, for Pearl, who liked taking a long view, was already worrying about what would happen at the lease's ending. De Conroy, she was sure, would never sell the freehold back to the family, so there must be another way. She had not found it yet, but she was thinking constantly. 'De Conroy might die!' she said to herself hopefully, 'and that drab little daughter of his won't want Howarth, I'm sure! Christine wouldn't know what to do with a rabbit hutch!'

She took her father over Howarth after lunch, describing her plans for the house and showing him what small improvements, beyond the essential repairs, she had already achieved. They ducked under painters' scaffolds, edged round piles of timber, and Sir Reginald saw with what an eagle eye his daughter supervised the workmen. She harried them, criticized them, demanded ever higher standards, and left them wondering what good it had done to vote Labour three years before. 'They have to be kept up to the mark,' Pearl said. 'I time their teabreaks.'

'You do what?'

'Naturally. I'm paying them.' She pushed open the door of her bedroom with its massive new four-poster bed. 'Do you like it?'

Sir Reginald made appreciative noises. 'New wallpaper?'

'It isn't wallpaper, father. It's percale and it's over a hundred years old.'

'Looks like that stuff your mother hung in the sitting room. Remember it? With a daisy pattern?'

'Thank you, father.' She closed the door and led him further down the passage.

'What's that noise?' Sir Reginald asked.

'Someone called Frank Sinatra,' Pearl said with distaste. 'Monty bought David a gramophone and I wish he hadn't.' She pushed open the door and ordered the noise to be turned down.

David, fifteen now, jumped with surprise at his mother's voice. He scraped the needle on the record as he tried to turn it off, then smiled at his grandfather.

'Didn't know you were here!' Sir Reginald said.

'Here I am.' David, Earl of Mountsorrel, had fair hair that fell over his forehead and a nervous, quick face that seemed apprehensive of his mother.

Sir Reginald looked approvingly at the open book on the boy's bed. 'Studying?' he asked.

'Yes.'

Pearl crossed to the bed and picked the book up. 'Eton now has the adventures of Captain Hornblower on the curriculum?' she asked acidly.

David blushed, uncertain why he should feel so ashamed. 'Hilary sent it to me.'

Pearl dropped the book, losing David's place. 'I told you to tidy this room. I can't expect Mrs Carline to clean out a pigsty, can I?'

'No, mother.'

Sir Reginald smiled reassuringly at his grandson. 'You've lost your stutter, David!'

'Yes, sir. I have.' David smiled, immensely grateful that his achievement should be noticed. His mother, for whose approval he had fought the crippling stutter, had said nothing about his new fluency. 'Pebbles in the mouth and deep breathing.'

'He's a good lad,' Sir Reginald said to Pearl as they walked down the servants' stairs to avoid the scaffolding that cluttered up the main staircase.

'He improves,' Pearl said grudgingly. 'Though God knows his school work isn't as good as it should be. It's a blessing, I suppose, that Monty's making some money. I can't see David ever being able to hold his own in the world!'

She kissed her father goodbye on the front steps of Howarth that the workmen were not allowed to use. 'Thank you for coming.'

She watched him leave. His Daimler turned into the drive that led past the Dower House just as a Riley, dust pluming from its tyres, sped in the opposite direction. Pearl frowned. She disapproved of people racing on Howarth's long driveways and if it turned out to be one of the workmen or one of the architects who supervised them, she would have some strong words to say.

She rehearsed the words as the car slewed on the wide fore-

164

court, gravel flaying from its wheels, and skidded to a halt with brakes locked. The tyres left deep gouge-marks in the drive, a thing always calculated to make Pearl angry.

Yet to her astonishment it was Mrs Gordon, the doctor's wife, who climbed out of the driving seat. The woman's grey hair was disordered, and her expression frantic. 'My Lady!'

'Mrs Gordon, how very nice to see you.'

'It's Andrew!' Adele Gordon stood at the foot of the steps, staring up at the Marchioness.

'Is he hurt?' Pearl could think of no other reason why this elderly woman should come out so ill-kempt and ill-dressed.

'He's been arrested! For fraud!'

Pearl's blood ran cold. For a few seconds she stood, quite frozen, and her mind refused to acknowledge what she had just heard. She had dared to hope that the small deception over the time of the fourth Marquess's death was now quite forgotten. 'Fraud?'

'The old Marquess's death . . .' Mrs Gordon was almost incoherent.

'You'd better come in. Tea.' Pearl's heart was thumping. If the doctor was arrested, were the police coming for her? 'Taggart! Taggart!' She gave orders that the new gates were to be padlocked, then she sat Mrs Gordon down in the Garden Room and ordered tea.

'But what are we going to do?' The old woman was close to tears.

'We telephone Monty, of course. Your husband needs a London lawyer, not some local incompetent who'll only panic.'

Monty, thank God, was in his office. 'So they've struck, have they?'

'You mean you knew it was likely?' Pearl, telephoning from the privacy of her study, betrayed panic in her voice.

Monty had not told her about Sir Nicholas's exploratory letter, hoping against hope that Sir Michael's reply might have drawn the enemy's fire. Now he calmed Pearl down, telling her to soothe Mrs Gordon's feathers and pretend an absolute assurance.

Monty's calm seemed justified for, within the half-hour, news came that Doctor Gordon, having been charged with fraud, was

165

released on bail. Mrs Gordon, reassured by Pearl's apparent confidence, left the house to join her husband.

Pearl had been calm, superbly calm, but there was terror like a live, clawing beast inside her.

She could not sit, she could not rest, she could only pace the echoing halls of Howarth that slowly emptied of painters and plumbers and electricians as evening descended. She telephoned Monty again, wishing he was at Howarth, and snapped at David and Caroline to take their supper in the kitchens because she wished to be alone.

Pearl paced the high rooms, thick with scaffolding, and knew that all her hopes for this house were threatened by a lie, by a little, little lie told so long ago. The family's name, the family's pride, the family's house, all would go, and all for a little lie, and in the night, alone in the emptiness of her room, Pearl cried like a child for Howarth.

Sir Michael Gooding called at the Monsol offices with his latest news. 'I fear the prosecution will subpoena the Lady Hilary.'

'What unprincipled bastards they are.' Monty poured the lawyer a whisky and looked quizzically at Sol, who nodded acceptance.

'Will you tell Hilary?' Sir Michael asked, 'or shall I?'

'I will. I'm having dinner with her tonight.'

Sol Linsky was suspicious of his partner. 'Are you trying to tell me,' he said as he took his drink, 'that they've been investigating this for four years and you knew nothing?'

'Not a bean, Sol. Not till Fatty Fenton wrote to Sir Michael.' Monty sat in a leather chair and stretched out his long legs. 'I thought we'd headed the bastards off, but sadly not.'

Sir Michael sighed. 'I must say, Monty, that you don't sound worried.'

'Why should I be worried?' Monty sounded truly astonished. 'Innocence is the best defence, isn't it?'

'That rather depends,' the lawyer said, 'on the prosecuting counsel.'

No one replied. A taxi hooted in Dover Street where rain fell

166

to streak the window and glaze the pavements. Sir Michael made a note on the edge of a typed sheet of paper. 'You've undertaken to pay all Gordon's defence costs?'

'Naturally.'

'And we put up the bail,' Sol Linsky said.

The committal proceedings at the Magistrates' Court had been over swiftly. Dr Andrew Gordon, retired, had pleaded not guilty to the charge of fraud. The magistrate, after hearing the prosecuting lawyer, had committed Gordon to trial at the next County Assizes. He released the doctor on a thousand pounds bail, but, before Gordon could step down, the magistrate had solemnly opined that, in his view, the dock was half-empty.

The newspapers had picked up the remark and Howarth was under siege. Photographers waited at the new gates, ambushed every car that left by either exit, and even now waited at Monsol's front door. Doctor Andrew Gordon might be on trial, but every newspaper reader in the country knew that the Marchioness of Arlington was just as culpable. The *Daily Herald* had printed an editorial which, though not mentioning the case for fear of contempt of court, nevertheless pointed out that there was still one law for the aristocracy and another for the rest of the country. The people of Britain, the newspaper said, had not elected a Labour government to see privilege preserved.

'I'm trying to get Trenton Rudge,' Sir Michael Gooding said. Sir Trenton Rudge, QC, was a barrister of fearsome repute.

'Splendid.' Monty hoped the rain was soaking the photographers below.

'But I hear a whisper that the Treasury might have approached him, so I'm talking to Chris Lumley as well.'

'I'm sure he'll do just as well,' Monty said.

Sol tried to judge his partner's insouciance. New affluence had hardly changed Sol Linsky: he still dressed in baggy flannel trousers and preferred a knitted waistcoat to a formal jacket. 'You're really not worried, Monty?'

'The silly sods have got the wrong end of the stick. They've got some daft nurse, Sophie was probably drunk as a judge, and they think they can soak me for a hundred thousand. Bugger 'em.'

'If they win,' Sir Michael said slowly, 'de Conroy will be wanting Howarth back.'

'They won't win,' Monty said scornfully.

Sir Michael wished he could share his confidence. He closed the brief and tied its red laces. 'I'd like to know what the Lady Hilary's evidence will be?'

'It will be the truth,' Monty said blandly.

The lawyer stood. 'I'll know who our counsel will be in two days. You'll have to come to a conference.'

'Of course.'

'And don't say anything to the press, there's a good fellow.'

After the lawyer had gone, Sol Linsky relit a cheroot and looked at his partner. 'I may be a middle-aged Jew, Monty, not worthy to tie your shoe laces, but I always know when you're lying. It's at the moments when you look most innocent.'

Monty grinned. 'Thank you, Sol.'

'So?'

Monty looked at the man who had brought such blessings on his life, a man he had despised at their first meeting, but who was now a friend. He shrugged. 'Pearl lied, and I'm going to perjure myself rotten, and the only person who can disprove me is Hilary.'

Sol frowned. 'I like Hilary.'

'She likes you.' Monty sat behind his desk and cut a cigar.

'And she won't tell a lie,' Sol said stoutly.

Monty lit a cigar. 'She won't?'

Sol, who was not in the least astonished that Monty's innocence was a pretence, sighed. 'She's made honesty the basis of her life.'

'She's family, Sol. Family.'

Sol, who had lost his own family, and therefore prized family above all possessions, was still not convinced. 'She's honest.'

'Yes.' Monty was far more worried than he dared show. 'But you forget something, my friend.'

'Astonish me.'

'We're innocent, and I'm late.'

Sol made a gesture of long-suffering patience. 'Good luck.'

Downstairs the guard of journalists surged forward as Monty came out of the small front door. Did his Lordship have any comments to make? Was the prosecution a surprise to him? Did he know why a country doctor might have wanted to change the time of the Marquess's death? Monty could see Hammond waiting with the car by Brown's Hotel, and he held up a hand to stop the questions as he walked towards the new Rolls-Royce. 'I have a statement.'

The newspapermen crowded round him. Flashbulbs exploded like magnesium shells in his face.

Monty paused at the car door. 'The Marquess of Arlington is deeply worried. He has learned today the wicket is taking spin, and only more rain can save England in the final Test. Good day.'

He grinned as Hammond accelerated away. Sir Michael Gooding feared the press, but Monty would use them. He gave the reporters flippant statements, smiles, and insouciance. Slowly, grudgingly, the mood was swinging towards him. He was painting the impending case as a clash between an innocent, ancient, aristocratic family and the insensitive, faceless, grasping taxmen. The truth, and Monty knew it, was that de Conroy was behind the prosecution and that what happened in court could bring victory to an old enemy.

So he had to win himself.

'You'll wait, Hammond?'

'I will, sir.'

Monty had come to a building with a portico larger than Howarth's. He climbed the great stone steps between the high, grimy pillars, then dived into the warren of backrooms the public never saw in the British Museum. He walked corridors lined with drawers, past rooms where incalculable treasures were stored unseen, and into a small warm room where Hilary was bent over a table. 'Hello, squirt,' he said to her back.

'I can't turn round.' Hilary, using a spatula and tweezers, was lifting the page of a book. 'And try not to breathe.'

'Consider me dead.'

'It's vellum,' she said. 'Bound in the tenth century, and the owner used it to support the leg of a table. Then the kitchen flooded. Ah!' The page peeled away from the rest and she slipped a sheet of tissue paper beneath it. 'It's the story of St Cuthbert.'

'Thrilling sort of fellow, was he?'

'He lived alone on an island and the seals brought him grub.' Hilary was wiping her hands on a towel. 'Hello, you horrid man.'

Monty kissed her and peered at the book. 'I need something good to read.'

'We paid fifty pounds for it, and I don't suppose anyone will ever look at it again, but it's added one whole word to our vocabulary of Old English.'

'Wow!' he teased her.

'To some of us, Monty, that is wow.' Hilary laughed. She disliked London, but she loved this job. At weekends she fled to a small village in Wiltshire where she rented a cottage. 'How are you?'

'To the *Daily Herald* I am the soul of feudal arrogance, but to the rest of the press I am a champion of olde England. You look tired.'

'I am. I'm trying to learn the difference between upward brush-strokes in Japanese calligraphy and downward strokes.' She grimaced.

Monty was impressed. 'And your brute? How's he?'

Hilary's face lit up immediately Hugh was mentioned. 'He's killing communist terrorists in Malaya and having a whale of a time. He really likes it! I've got my ticket, you knew that?'

Monty knew Hilary had been saving for a holiday in Singapore, planning to go out by sea to snatch a few nights with Hugh. Ostensibly she was searching for oriental manuscripts, an excuse necessary for a travel permit to be granted in the continuing post-war austerity and, duly, had been studying Chinese and Japanese. It was typical of Hilary, Monty thought, to take the excuse for travel as seriously as the real object. To do anything else would be dishonest for her. 'When are you going?'

'Two months.'

He leaned on the table, hating to give her the bad news. 'You may not be able to. Not then, anyway.'

Hilary looked at him, fear and shock in her eyes. She had not seen Hugh for a year and Monty knew how desperate she was to travel to the Far East. 'The bloody law case?'

He nodded. 'The defence informed us today that a subpoena will be served on you.'

'Oh, God.' She picked up her spatula and drummed it into the palm of her left hand. 'Monty?' She said it as a plea, as an expression of helplessness.

'I know.'

'I don't think you do know.' Hilary pulled a cloth over the precious book. 'Pearl did telephone me that day.'

'I know.'

'And lied to me later on.'

'I know that, too.'

'I . . .' Hilary shrugged. 'I don't know.'

'Talk about it over dinner,' Monty said soothingly.

She gave a knowing laugh. 'Dinner, champagne, and your golden tongue?'

'Not in that order, but yes.'

Hilary picked up her white coat and pushed at her disordered hair. 'You're telling me that the time of death really was changed? That there was fraud?'

'Of course there was, don't be naïve.' Monty helped her on with her coat. 'Ready?'

'But I am naïve.' The word had obviously preyed on Hilary's mind all the time she was changing, while they had drinks in Brick Street and on the way to their table at the Savoy Grill. 'I hate to sound smug,' Hilary said, 'but I even want to stay that way.'

'You're not naïve with Hugh,' Monty said gently. 'You and Sophie are the only women in my family who live in sin.'

'If only I could live in sin with him! The brute insists on being in the jungle, doesn't he?' Hilary smiled. Her beauty brought envious glances from the other tables. 'But there is a difference, Monty.'

'There is?'

'I'm utterly, boringly faithful to Hugh. And he to me.' She said it with such absolute assurance that Monty believed her. 'And perhaps we will marry one day, but it just doesn't seem necessary. I can't really think that a shared bed needs a priest's platitudes mumbled over it, do you?' She waited for an answer that did not come. 'Obviously you don't. How's Elizabeth? And Henrietta?'

'Much as Carol and Madeleine and Emily are.'

'Madeleine? Is she a new one?'

'I met her at Chantilly. She has a flat near the Opera and says I'm not so very bad for an Englishman.'

Hilary laughed. 'What does she know? You're exactly the sort of man I avoid like the plague.'

'You don't know what you're missing.'

'With Hugh,' Hilary said, 'I don't think I miss anything.' The simple statement, said with humour and love, made Monty suddenly jealous of her happiness, of the contentment that he had never found with just one person. She smiled. 'Can I ask a rude question?'

'Ask on.'

Hilary turned her wine glass, staring at it. 'I don't understand why you put up with Pearl. She lied, she's made all this trouble, and you don't behave as if you,' she shrugged, tangling herself in embarrassment, 'as if you love her.'

'Would you believe,' Monty met Hilary's challenging blue gaze, 'that I put up with her because a priest mumbled platitudes over us?'

She shook her head. 'No. I wouldn't believe that.'

Monty smiled at the First Secretary of the American Embassy who was entertaining at a nearby table. If he lost the case, he thought, then the smiles would fade rapidly and all polite society would shun his company. He shrugged. 'I think I understand Pearl's weakness.'

Hilary grimaced. 'That sounds very patronizing.'

'It is patronizing.'

She shrugged. 'Are you going to tell me what her weakness is?'

'Have you ever seen where her parents live?'

'No.'

'It's a great, ugly brick house without charm or loveliness. It's a rich man's house, and it's very, very middle-class.'

'Hugh's middle-class.'

'Don't take offence. Listen instead.' Monty was leaning for-

172

ward, his voice quiet but intense. 'It's a house that has money but no taste. Pearl hates it. She thinks people would laugh at her if they knew her mother liked curtains with prints of roses on them and used a tea cosy shaped like a thatched cottage. But that's where Pearl came from. Her father made his own money and he still calls lunch dinner. They don't have sofas, but settees. They don't go to the lavatory, but say they need to wash their hands. Pearl's ashamed of her parents!'

Hilary stared at him, saying nothing.

Monty poured more wine. 'But she does have taste. Lord knows where it comes from, but it's good taste. She believes that it's an aristocratic taste, and perhaps it is, but the most important thing in Pearl's life is for no one to ever know that she isn't a born aristocrat. So she tries very hard to behave as she thinks a marchioness ought to behave. She's cold, abrupt, snobbish . . .'

'Rude,' Hilary interrupted.

'Rude,' Monty agreed, 'and at times she's utterly, bloody insufferable, but she's also got more vision, more determination, and more sheer damned guts than the rest of the aristocracy put together.'

'Is that why you married her?'

'I married her for her legs.'

'Monty!'

'I'm almost serious.' He smiled. 'Because she was the most beautiful girl I'd ever met and I thought marriage was a competition between men, and I was damned sure I would win it. I did and, oddly, I don't regret it because, you see, all Pearl's worst qualities come from being married to me, a marquess. She wants to be worthy of that, so she plays at being an aristocrat. She dresses well, she looks wonderful. She's condescending, proud, and utterly terrified.'

'Terrified?' Hilary sounded surprised.

'She's terrified of being found out. Of someone looking at her and seeing that she isn't really an aristocrat at all, but a pretty girl from an ugly middle-class house in the Midlands. So her pretence has to be very, very good. She's like an actress, and she has wonderful props, but the best prop, the biggest of all, is Howarth. As long as she has Howarth then her deception will

173

work. Without Howarth?' Monty shrugged. 'She would collapse.'

'So you keep Howarth for her?'

'I think so. I don't like the place that much. I could live in a brick house and still be a marquess, but not Pearl. And when you know someone's weakness like that, you know them. I don't see Pearl as a cold, arrogant bitch. I see her naked, shivering, and terrified. Like a child. And once, a long time ago, I swore to protect her. So I do.'

Hilary paused, frowning. 'By telling lies in court?'

'If I must, yes.'

There was another pause, even longer. 'And now you're telling me that I must lie.'

'No,' Monty said, 'I'm not.'

She looked up at him, surprised. 'No?'

Monty smiled. 'You must say in court whatever you want to say. I won't tell you what to say, I don't even want to know what you might say! You must do whatever you think is right.'

She stared at him for a long time. 'I wrote to Hugh. He said that the truth is always the best thing to tell, that once we start telling lies we begin to trip ourselves up and worse. We may get into the habit of deception.'

Bugger Hugh, Monty thought. 'Hugh is fortunate if he only knows the theory of the thing.'

Hilary allowed the point. 'True.'

Monty leaned back. 'But you must do what you think is right. Truly.'

Hilary had expected impassioned arguments, but not this bland trust. 'I don't think I can commit perjury, Monty.'

'Then so be it. I'll love you as much afterwards as I do now.'

She grimaced at him. 'Bastard.'

'The angel swears! Did Hugh teach you that word?'

Hilary laughed and leaned back in her chair. She seemed to be released from whatever tension had held her in these last moments. 'That was delicious, thank you.'

'Night spot? Dance? Opium den? Or shall I show you where the white slave-traders ply their filthy trade?'

'I've been to Brick Street,' Hilary laughed at her uncle. 'Can Hammond drop me back home? I've got to sleep.'

'Prude.'

She nodded. 'But a happy prude. Thank you.'

Monty took her home, then went to a nightclub where his friends, jocular and confident, believed his assurances that he would wipe the floor with the God-damned Treasury. Monty was not so certain that he would, for he was not sure of Hilary, but he thought that perhaps, in the great balance-scale of all things, Howarth was not worth Hilary's innocence. So he could only wait and see which way the coin would fall and whether his defence, that he had planned long ago, would stand up to the test and save a family from a rival's enmity and from an honest girl's truth.

Sir Trenton Rudge, QC, had the honour, he said, of appearing for the Crown which was, in this sad case, instructed by the Treasury solicitor.

He deplored the necessity of prosecuting the case at all. It was with the deepest reluctance that he did so. The verdict, and he confided to the jury that the verdict could only be one of proven guilt, would reflect hard upon the Howarth family and Sir Trenton Rudge declared himself not unmindful of the services wrought to his country by the head of that family, the Marquess of Arlington. However, Sir Trenton would remind the jury, the Marquess was not on trial. The Marquess, as some newspapers had seen fit to inform the country, had been abroad at the time when the fraud was committed. It was Doctor Andrew Gordon who was on trial.

Doctor Gordon, dressed in country tweed and his white hair bright in the courtroom, frowned as if some terrible outrage was being inflicted upon him. He was guilty, he knew he was guilty, but he had been persuaded by Monty to protest his innocence, and thus had pleaded not guilty in a confident voice. He had lied once, so long ago, and now he must stay with the lie and trust that the Marquess of Arlington's ingenious defence would suffice.

Doctor Andrew Gordon, Sir Trenton Rudge informed the court, had a long and honourable history in his profession. The defence, and here the wigged head gave a small bow towards the barristers who would oppose him, would doubtless seek to show that the doctor was well loved by his ex-patients and had performed many acts of mercy. The Crown did not seek to deny this. The Crown only sought to show that, on the day of the fourth Marquess of Arlington's death, Doctor Andrew Gordon had falsified the time of the Marquess's death. He had done this, Sir Trenton declaimed, out of loyalty to a family.

'Loyalty is a most excellent thing.' Sir Trenton plucked the edges of his gown and peered across the rims of his half-moon spectacles at the jury benches. 'Loyalty is not to be despised, yet loyalty that leads a man into a criminal act is to be abominated!' His fine voice, which might have earned him a fortune upon the stage were it not that the rewards of the bar had proved so much greater, stilled the fidgeting in the crowded public gallery. 'There might be those who think the wrong prisoner stands in the dock! I am not one of those people! I seek only to prove that a forgery was uttered, a fraud promoted, and that the man who perpetrated the act stands before you, and he, out of misplaced loyalty, did thereby defraud the Crown of monies properly belonging to it! Others there were in that great house, but they, in their grief, did not wield the pen.'

Sir Trenton Rudge paused, his heavy face mournful at the necessity of this prosecution. Then, in harsh, loud tones, he sketched the outline of the case against Doctor Andrew Gordon. The fourth Marquess of Arlington had died at three forty-three p.m. on a September afternoon in 1944. His eldest son, the fifth Marquess, had been tragically killed in a road accident some forty-five minutes later. Doctor Gordon, out of his misplaced loyalty and a desire to save the Howarth family death duties, had written a letter that timed the fourth Marquess's death at five forty-three p.m. It was as simple as that, and the Crown would produce witnesses to demonstrate the truth of the prosecution's case. Sir Trenton finished, paused for a moment as though expecting applause, then, with a fine swirl of his black gown, sat.

It was, Monty thought, a fine beginning, though he suspected Rudge was hiding a nagging concern. This was a criminal trial and the defence had no need to disclose the nature of their defence, nor had they, and doubtless Sir Trenton was wondering

176

what surprises might be sprung on him. Thinking of Hilary in the corridor outside, he wondered what surprises might be waiting for himself.

Mr Christopher Lumley, QC, led for Doctor Gordon. His gown was impressively threadbare and his horse-hair wig magnificently filthy. If such signs of his long experience at the bar were encouraging, then Sir Trenton Rudge's legal accoutrements were equivalently depressing.

Mr Lumley rose to his feet as though unsure exactly what odd circumstances had brought to him to these Assizes. After Sir Trenton's opening peroration, so finely spoken, Mr Lumley's diffident uncertainty seemed pale. The pressmen, crammed into their gallery, had to lean forward to hear his precise, thin voice.

The case, he said, would prove to be mercifully short. Indeed, he believed that it was a nonsense for the case ever to have been brought at all. Mr Lumley paused there, shuffling papers on his desk. Monty, sitting in the solicitors' chairs behind him, saw that the papers were about an entirely different case. Mr Lumley suddenly looked up and, almost apologetically, explained that the defence did not deny the validity of Doctor Gordon's letter, written on the day of the Marquess's death and copies of which had been distributed to the jury, but, as would be seen, the explanation was not only obvious, but trivial. Abruptly, revealing no more, he sat.

There was a stir in the public gallery. Monty looked up and saw a tall figure, black hair gleaming, edge along a bench. The figure turned and Monty stared into the dark eyes of the Baron de Conroy. Then he sat and the thin, handsome face was hidden by a woman's hat. Sol Linsky, sitting further along in the public seats, looked at Monty and shrugged. Monty's face did not move.

Sir Trenton Rudge stood again. 'If your Honour pleases,' he said, 'I would call the Lady Sophie Howarth to the witness stand.'

There was a stir in the courtroom. The opening statements had been predictable, but now the gentry were being called to the bar of Justice and put upon oath.

'Lady Sophie Howarth!' The usher's voice echoed in the corridors.

Monty had not seen Sophie for some months. In a dark blue coat and small veiled hat, she looked oddly small as she crossed the court and climbed into the witness box. She took the bible and, in a clear, cold voice, repeated the oath. When it was done she looked down at Monty and he saw, beneath the veil, how the small lines on her face had deepened. She gave no sign of recognition, no sign that she would give her evidence as Monty had told her to give it.

Sophie turned her eyes from Monty as Sir Trenton, gown wrapped about him like a great bat's wing, asked his opening questions.

She paused, then gave her name and established her relationship with the dead men. Her sharp voice was icy clear in the courtroom; a condescending, aristocratic voice that seemed to ring with derision for the proceedings. 'I first heard about my father's death on the telephone.'

'Who telephoned you, Lady Sophie?' Sir Trenton Rudge, driving the Treasury's nails into Howarth's coffin, was at his most lugubrious.

'The Marchioness.'

'The Marchioness of Arlington?'

Sophie nodded. 'Yes.'

'You're quite certain?'

Sophie paused, as if contemplating some witticism, then controlled herself. 'I am quite certain.'

'And what, Lady Sophie, did the Marchioness tell you?'

Sophie hesitated. Sir Trenton Rudge repeated the question and the judge, seeing Sophie's continued hesitation, leaned forward. 'I find it inconvenient,' he said, 'that the witness is veiled.' Sophie, very slowly, raised the net veil to reveal a face of beauty and scorn. 'Well?' the judge asked, prompting her answer.

There was a silence during which Sir Trenton cleared his throat. 'This is an unhappy duty, my Lord. The Lady Sophie is not here of her own volition.' Sophie, so that no newspaper could accuse her of wilful treachery against her own family, had insisted on being served with a subpoena. Sir Trenton, having established the fact as Sophie had requested that he should, turned again to

178

his witness. 'But you must still answer the question, my Lady. What was it that your sister-in-law said upon the telephone?'

'She said,' Sophie raised her head defiantly, 'that my father died at three forty-three.'

'She used those very words?' There was a stir in the public gallery, a murmur that was drowned by Sir Trenton's voice. 'I asked you, Lady Sophie, whether the Marchioness used those words?'

Sophie nodded. 'She told me that the clock in my father's bedroom had shown three forty-three.'

'In the afternoon?'

Again there was a pause as if Sophie was tempted to some biting remark, probably to the effect that Pearl would not even know that there was a three forty-three a.m., but she bit it back. 'In the afternoon.'

'She was specific? She did not say "at about three forty-three"?'

'She was specific.' Sophie said it firmly, and Monty sensed Sir Trenton's relief. The big barrister asked a few more questions, his examination-in-chief designed to drive into the jury's brains the certainty that Sophie displayed about the time of death. Monty also felt relief because she had kept her word.

When Mr Christopher Lumley stood for the cross-examination he seemed hesitant. He peered down at his papers, as if searching for inspiration, then looked up at the witness. 'Do you remember, Lady Sophie, exactly what you were doing when the telephone call came?'

'I was in the bath.'

There was a small murmur of laughter in the gallery.

'And doubtless,' Mr Lumley said tartly, 'observing the wartime regulation to keep the depth of water in your weekly bath at five inches or less?' Sir Trenton began to rise, but Lumley raised a hand. 'I withdraw the question. Do you normally bathe at three forty-three?'

Sophie's expression was one of utter contempt. 'Normally I bathe later.'

'But that day you were precipitate in your need for cleansing?'

Sophie's voice rode over the gentle laughter. 'Yes.'

'And when, Lady Sophie, you had taken the telephone call,

presumably dripping water on your carpet as you did so, what did you do then?'

'I went back to the bath.'

'How very sensible. You were, of course, alone?'

The judge's head jerked up from the page on which he made notes. 'That is an outrageous question!' He looked at Sophie. 'You have no need to answer it.'

Sophie, who had been sharing the bath with her American lover, bowed her thanks to his Lordship.

'Did you,' Mr Lumley said, 'happen to see a clock on your way from the telephone to the bath?'

'No.'

'So you cannot, Lady Sophie, corroborate what you claim your sister-in-law told you?'

Sophie shook her head. 'No.'

'You saw no clock. You have merely repeated to us what you believe your sister-in-law said to you, but you yourself did not perceive at what time the telephone call was made?'

'No.'

It seemed, to many in the courtroom, a very weak defence. Henrietta Creed, up in the gallery, looked sadly at Monty, wondering why he had not hired Doctor Gordon a more tenacious counsel.

Mr Lumley tugged his gown tighter round him. 'Would you say, Lady Sophie, that your father was an eccentric man?'

'I believe he was.'

The barrister evinced surprise. 'Believe?'

'I had not seen him for many years.'

'Ah.' Lumley stared down at his papers as though the answer had surprised him. He frowned. 'Would it be true to say, Lady Sophie, that, before you attended your father's funeral, you had not stepped foot in Howarth for more than twenty years?'

'That would be true.'

'Thank you.' And that, it seemed, was that. There were no more questions and Lord de Conroy, high above the court, felt a small surge of satisfaction with Sophie's performance. He had found a bookmaker willing to take a bet of five hundred pounds, at odds of two to one, against acquittal, and Kynaston de Conroy could already taste the feast that his winnings would bring.

The next witness was Mrs Olive Mackenzie who, on Sir Trenton Rudge's careful instructions, appeared in the witness stand wearing a high-necked nurse's uniform. She had on a black coat over the severe tunic and looked, and indeed sounded, a most impressive witness. The nurse had a robust Scottish voice, a commanding appearance, and a firm confidence. She told the court she was a widow, born in Scotland but domiciled in Hull, and that she had been hired on the recommendation of Doctor Gordon to tend the dying Marquess of Arlington.

She was quite sure, she said, that the Marquess had died at three forty-three p.m. She distinctly remembered, once the old man's pulse had stopped, thinking that she would take her tea in the staff kitchen before laying the body out.

Sir Trenton smiled encouragingly. 'You are fond of your tea, Nurse Mackenzie?'

'Very fond, sir.'

'And you take a dish of tea each day, do you?'

Mrs Mackenzie, coming from a different social class from Sir Trenton, took cups of tea, but she knew what was meant and nodded vigorously. 'Come wind or blow, sir, I like my tea.'

'And you like it at the same time each day, yes?'

'Indeed, sir, as close to four o'clock as I can decently make it.'

'And you are quite certain, are you, that the fourth Marquess of Arlington had not enjoyed a resurrection during your repast?'

'I'm sorry, sir?'

Sir Trenton smiled. 'The Marquess was not alive after your teatime?'

Mrs Mackenzie scorned the notion. 'As I stand here, sir, I am sure. The old man died before tea, and I remember the doctor putting the time down in his wee book.' The nurse stared a silent remonstration at Gordon.

Mr Lumley, when Sir Trenton had finished his damning examination, again armed himself with a distracted, almost forgetful air. He scratched his wig and seemed unsure what he wanted to say. He sniffed, then peered at the witness. 'Would

181

you say, Nurse Mackenzie, that the fourth Marquess was an old-fashioned man?'

Mrs Mackenzie seemed unsure what to say, the question was so unexpected. Finally, receiving no help from either Sir Trenton or the judge, she nodded. 'Yes, sir. I would, sir.'

'Old-fashioned,' Mr Lumley said ruminatively. 'He did things the old-fashioned way, yes?'

'Indeed he did, sir.'

Then in his most courteous voice, he asked Mrs Mackenzie whether she would therefore describe the fourth Marquess as an eccentric man?

Mrs Mackenzie still seemed bemused. 'Eccentric?'

'If the court will indulge me,' Mr Lumley said, 'let me help you a little. Was he man of small quirks?'

'Oh, definitely, sir. Yes.'

'He would only drink his morning tea out of a shaving mug which he insisted should never be washed. Is that right?'

'A dirty habit I thought, sir.'

'He refused to have a wireless in his rooms, believing that the crystal's oscillation affected his liver?'

Nurse Mackenzie nodded. 'He did, sir.'

'And he insisted that the electric table lamps be removed each day to the lamp-room as though they were oil lamps that needed to have their wicks trimmed. Is that right?'

'Aye, he did, sir,' Mrs Mackenzie said grimly.

'So he was, would you say,' Mr Lumley's voice was very mild indeed, 'an old-fashioned and an eccentric man?'

'Oh yes, sir. Definitely, sir.'

'So it is hardly surprising then, is it, that he should keep the clocks in Howarth at Greenwich Mean Time?'

Mrs Mackenzie, led into it, agreed. 'No, sir.'

'Thank you, Mrs Mackenzie.' Lumley, whose speed over the last question had been pantherish, sat down. The murmur rose again, more excited this time, and the judge frowned for silence. Monty leaned back in his chair and smiled.

Sol Linsky, sitting in the public gallery, stared at him. The clever putz, he thought, the clever, clever putz! Monty looked so angelic, so harmless, yet he had been the only one to spot that

British Double Summer Time, adopted in the war to boost agricultural productivity, meant a two-hour difference between winter and summer clocks. If this lie was believed, and Linsky had just heard the prosecution's chief witness confirm it, then the three forty-three reading of the clock in the Marquess's bedroom, which had been accurately set to Double Summer Time, would be construed in this court as having been set for Greenwich Mean Time and that would translate into a time of death at five forty-three. Clever Monty. Lethal Monty. Sol smiled.

Sir Trenton Rudge rose hastily. 'Mrs Mackenzie. Did the fourth Marquess keep his clocks to Greenwich Mean Time?'

'I really couldn't say, sir.' Mrs Mackenzie was all at sea, her certainty that she would make a splendid witness gone to pieces.

The lawyer smiled on her, knowing that it would only take a few simple questions to bring her to the truth. If this was their defence, he thought, then God help Arlington. 'The Marquess died during the war, Mrs Mackenzie?'

'He did, sir, yes.'

'And did you listen to the wireless for news of the war?'

The nurse's broad, reliable face nodded. 'I did, sir. I had a wee . . .' She stopped suddenly.

'Pray continue,' Sir Trenton invited her.

'I had a son in the army, you understand. I'd listen for his sake.'

'What mother would not?' he said sympathetically. 'And did it never strike you as strange, Nurse Mackenzie, that when the British Broadcasting Corporation read, say, their nine o'clock bulletin, that the clocks at Howarth showed a different time?'

Mrs Mackenzie thought about it, then understanding dawned upon her face. 'They didn't, sir! There was a wee clock in Taggart's pantry, above the wireless it was, and it never showed the wrong time!'

Sir Trenton, feeling like a man who has just hit the enemy's opening bowler for six runs, smiled beatifically. 'You're certain, Mrs Mackenzie?'

'As I stand here, sir, I'm certain.'

Sol Linsky, whose hopes had soared so high just a moment before, felt them drop like a stone. The woman had been led to certainty by the barrister's clever questioning, and Sol believed he had just watched Monty's escape route barred shut.

Monty must have been feeling the same, for he was taciturn during the lunch adjournment which they took in the saloon bar of a pub in the town's market place. Mr Lumley was equally silent over his cheese sandwich.

Monty sipped beer made by a brewery he had once owned. 'Will they call Hilary?'

'Don't see he needs to,' Lumley said. 'He certainly won't want to. It all rather depends on Taggart, doesn't it?'

'Let's hope he isn't drunk,' Monty said without hope.

Taggart, the old butler, held on to the parapet of the witness box after lunch. He was Lumley's first witness and, with true feudal loyalty, he swore blind that the clocks in Howarth were never changed. 'Never!'

Sir Trenton, splendidly fortified by a surprisingly well-roasted piece of beef and a half-bottle of decent claret, stood expectantly when his chance of cross-examination came. 'The clocks in Howarth, Mr Taggart, were never changed?'

'I said so, didn't I?'

'You did indeed,' Sir Trenton said complacently. 'None of the clocks were changed, Mr Taggart?'

Henrietta Creed was shaking her head. Sol was doing the same, but Taggart did not look at the gallery. 'None of them!' he said with stubborn loyalty.

'Not one clock in Howarth,' Sir Trenton said, 'was ever changed?'

'Those were the master's orders,' Taggart said. De Conroy, knowing he was surrounded by Howarth supporters, sneered in triumph.

Sir Trenton, revelling in the moment, raised his voice. 'Yet we have heard evidence, Mr Taggart, indisputable evidence, that the clock in your own pantry was changed.'

'Of course it was!' Taggart said without a second's hesitation, and in a tone that suggested Sir Trenton was foolish to even mention the matter.

The barrister, taken aback, stared at the witness. 'But you have already said that not one clock in Howarth was changed! Were you lying?'

'Howarth is Howarth,' Taggart said, 'and my pantry is my pantry. If the old man had wanted me to do his nonsense in my pantry I'd have told him he was a fool! But beyond that door was Howarth and he could have the clocks going backwards for all I ever cared.'

Sir Trenton opened his mouth, then closed it again. The old man's truculence in defence of his scrap of territory had been altogether too damaging to risk more questions.

Monty felt the case was on a knife edge. Pearl would lie, of course, but the jury would know she had cause to lie, so all now depended on whether they believed the nurse or Taggart. One person, and one alone, might convince them, and it was that person, to Monty's dread, that Sir Trenton Rudge begged the court's indulgence to call. 'I would have called her earlier,' he explained to the judge, 'but I wished to spare the family too great an ordeal.'

The judge gave permission for the prosecution to call another witness.

There was a stir in the courtroom as Hilary took the stand. There was some quality about her, Monty thought, that displayed trustworthiness. Her face was so finely honed, her back so straight, that he was sure the jury would believe her every word. He looked at them: stolid, intelligent, curious, caught up in this odd little drama that was unfolding in the panelled room beneath the great royal coat of arms. Hilary's voice, when she took the oath, was hesitant and nervous. There was not a person in the courtroom, Monty thought, who would disbelieve a word Hilary uttered.

'You are the Lady Hilary Howarth?'

'I am.'

'And you are the daughter of the eldest son of the late fourth Marquess of Howarth?' Sir Trenton, carefully, gave no title to Hilary's father.

'I am, yes.'

'And your paternal grandfather was the fourth Marquess?'

185

It seemed an unnecessary question after the preceding one, but Hilary treated it with solemnity. 'He was, yes.'

'And you can recall the day on which your grandfather and, tragically, your father, died?'

'I can.'

Sir Trenton paused. He shrugged massive shoulders inside his gown, took a great breath, dragged the pause out dramatically, then shot a look over his glasses at the slim, beautiful girl who stood in the witness box. 'Did your grandfather put his clocks forward in summertime?'

Hilary stared at him. She was dressed in a fawn coat and wore a small fawn hat high on her hair. She frowned.

'You heard the question?' Sir Trenton asked forcibly.

'I did, but I don't know the answer.' Her puzzlement was obvious. She had prepared for this ordeal, but she had not thought to have such a question shot at her.

'Do you mean,' the judge, evidently pleased to have such a beauty in his court, leaned forward and adopted his most kindly expression, 'that you don't know, or that you can't remember?'

'I can't remember.' Hilary was frowning, obviously trying to remember. 'We didn't visit often, you see.' She shook her head, her honesty shining, and Monty felt a terrible fear for the next questions and answers.

Sir Trenton Rudge, who had hoped against hope that the girl would remember about the clocks, wondered where this cross-examination would go. The rule, the first shining and un-breakable rule of his profession was to never ever put a witness in the dock whose answers you did not already know, and he was breaking the rule with this girl. She had refused to cooperate with the prosecution and had needed a subpoena, yet, Sir Trenton thought, if there was a truth to be elicited in this courtroom, then surely this girl would reveal it.

'Lady Hilary, let us instead think of that sad day of your parents' deaths. Where were you on that day?'

'In my parents' London home.'

'Not at school?' Sir Trenton smiled indulgently.

'I was on my way to take an exam for Oxford.'

'Which we trust, for Oxford's sake, that you passed?' Sir

Trenton smiled at the appreciative laughter. 'Indeed we know that you did, and that you are now employed in the Manuscript Department of the British Museum, is that right?'

'Yes.'

'So you are accustomed to precision in your work, and we shall hope for precision in your answers. Who informed you that your parents had died?'

'My aunt. Aunt Pearl.'

'And she is the present Marchioness of Arlington?'

Hilary nodded. 'Yes.'

'And doubtless,' Sir Trenton said, 'Auntie Pearl will be called by the defence as a witness.' Again he paused for the rustle of laughter. 'How did she inform you?'

'By telephone.'

So far, the lawyer thought, the girl was saying all that could be expected of her, but it was the next few questions that would decide this case. Sir Trenton seemed to swell beneath his robe and his voice seemed to deepen as he ploughed on. 'And did your aunt also inform you of your grandfather's death?'

'Yes.

'So there were two telephone calls to your house from Howarth?'

Hilary paused, Monty prayed, and the court went very still. Sol Linsky feared for Hilary if she lied, and feared for Monty if she did not.

Hilary did not lie. 'Yes,' she said.

Sir Trenton Rudge pounced like a stooping hawk. 'Two telephone calls. At what time was the first?'

Again Hilary hesitated. Her gloved hands gripped the witness box and Monty, whose eyes she had not met since she had come into the courtroom, saw the tension in those hands. She jerked her head up, almost in defiance. 'The first telephone call came at four o'clock. Or close to four o'clock.'

'How close?'

'It was very close. I had made tea, you see.'

'How that beverage does feature in our case.' Sir Trenton did not say it benignly, but with steel in his voice. He was staring at her. 'And the second call?'

'That was at six o'clock.' She sounded utterly certain.

'So.' Sir Trenton, like a great actor, knew that he had all the poised courtroom in the palm of his hand. There was not a sound as he paused. De Conroy, high above, stared at the girl. Sol dared not breathe. The lawyer looked at his notes, counted to ten, then looked up. 'And was it during the second telephone call, Lady Hilary, the telephone call at six o'clock, that your aunt informed you of the death of your parents?'

She had gone pale. Some people mocked her because she had once vowed to be truthful, because she abhorred dishonesty, and perhaps there was no witness, ever, who had taken the oath as seriously as Hilary.

'I ask you again,' Sir Trenton was merciless, 'was it during the second telephone call that your aunt informed you of your parents' deaths?'

Monty knew the case was lost. Hilary's voice was very soft, but quite audible throughout the courtroom. 'Yes.'

'So what, Lady Hilary,' Sir Trenton leaned forward as though only he and she were in the great room, 'was the purpose of the first call? The call at four o'clock?'

Hilary stared at him. She swallowed. 'My aunt telephoned because she wondered where my parents were. She was expecting them, you see, and they hadn't arrived.' Monty, staring up, saw tears in her eyes.

Sir Trenton knew he had asked the wrong question. 'Did she call to tell you that your grandfather had died?'

'No.' Hilary said it quickly, shaking her head, knowing that she told the truth even if her answer was against the spirit of the truth. Pearl had not telephoned to inform Hilary of anything, but to find Hilary's parents.

Monty was holding his breath. God damn it, he thought, but she is telling the truth, the literal truth! He watched, fearing the next question, but suddenly a tear ran down Hilary's cheek, and that tear seemed to break the tension in the court and the judge was asking if she would like a chair and there were murmurs in the gallery and Hilary was saying no, she did not need a chair, and the usher was handing her a glass of water.

'What you're saying,' the judge, eager to spare this lovely girl

188

an ordeal, smiled at her, 'is that your aunt was enquiring after your parents in the first telephone call, and that the tragic news, the news of the deaths, came later?'

Hilary thought about it and found she could tell the truth. 'Yes, my Lord.'

'There!' The judge beamed at Hilary, then looked at Sir Trenton. 'I think that's very plain, don't you, Sir Trenton?'

'If your Lordship pleases . . .'

'I think it's plain!' the judge said tetchily. He looked at his notes. 'The first call was an enquiry, and the second call brought the news of the deaths. Isn't that so, my dear?'

Hilary could only nod, and the judge, pleased to have helped this beauty who graced his witness box, looked again at the lawyer. 'I find it plain. It mystifies you, Sir Trenton?'

Sir Trenton dug in his heels. 'I wish to discover, my Lord, whether the Marchioness of Arlington told the Lady Hilary Howarth in the first telephone call, the call at four o'clock, whether the Marquess was dead!'

The judge, with a long-suffering expression, looked at Hilary as if to say that she should indulge this pestilential counsel.

Hilary, who prided herself on not being given to tears, was crying now, for now was the moment when she must either lie or dash all of Monty's hopes. 'She telephoned,' she said, 'to ask me where my parents were, and . . .'

'Exactly,' the judge broke in over Hilary's last word, and looked in triumph at Sir Trenton. 'Do you wish to persist?'

Sir Trenton knew that the sympathy of the court had swung utterly against him. He shrugged, he sat, he wondered whether he would have time to play a round of golf when the case was done.

Mr Lumley, thinking that the judge, out of misplaced gallantry, had just done a superb job for the defence, shook his head. 'No questions, m'Lord.'

Monty was shaking like a leaf. God damn it, but she had not lied! The rest was downhill all the way. Doctor Gordon, called in his own defence, said that of course Howarth's clocks were kept at Greenwich Mean Time and Sir Trenton, trying to retrieve a lost match, failed to shift him.

Mr Lumley, with admirable forbearance, begged to inform his Lordship that the defence had a list of witnesses, many of noble birth, who would testify that the fourth Marquess had insisted on keeping his clocks to Greenwich Mean Time. Mr Lumley did not wish to try the court's patience, but if it was necessary it would be done. Lord Mackerson, MC, was available immediately. Perhaps, Mr Lumley suggested, Lord Mackerson would suffice as a witness to this point?

Monty looked up at Sol, whose eyes were gleaming. He could not see de Conroy.

The judge stared pointedly at Sir Trenton who was in earnest consultation with his junior and with the instructing solicitors.

The barrister knew when a fox had gone to earth. He stood. 'The prosecution has no more evidence, my Lord.'

'You wish the defence to produce more witnesses?'

'We see no purpose, my Lord.'

'Then,' the judge said, 'I can have no other duty but to instruct the jury to bring in a verdict of not guilty.' The jurors left the room for the shortest possible time. On their return, the judge looked at them, was rewarded by obedient nods, and, for the first time, he looked at Monty also. 'I order full costs against the Crown.'

Pearl, waiting to be called as a witness, wondered why there was a cheer in the courtroom. Sol Linsky was crying for joy. De Conroy was staring in impotent fury at the royal crest. Doctor Gordon was taking the congratulations of the lawyers. Hilary was trying to calm her heart, and Monty, clever Monty, was smiling.

Howarth had won.

PART TWO

The weathermen pronounced that June 2nd would be the perfect day of 1953. It would be sunny, warm, dry, it would be splendid.

It was cloudy, cold, it rained, but it was undeniably splendid.

Dukes, marquesses and earls, duchesses, marchionesses and countesses, viscounts and barons, lords and their ladies; all the aristocracy of Britain had been ordered by the Earl Marshal to take their places by half past eight in the morning. Brought by taxis or cars, by bus or by tube, they obeyed.

Heads of state, prime ministers, and foreign royalty took their places obediently. Carriages brought the dukes, the princes and princesses of the Blood Royal to Westminster Abbey. A hum of conversation filled the great stone hall where Saxon kings had raised their eyes to God's glory. Trumpeters and heralds, knights and bishops, all waited as Big Ben tolled the passing hours.

The peers had come from their dilapidated homes in the shires, from their castles on the border marches, and from their semi-detached houses in the new suburbs. There were rogues and great men among them, bankrupts and millionaires, fools and wise men, but all were aristocrats, and this day they would flank their monarch in the places of honour. No prime minister, not even Churchill, and no foreign head of state could usurp their privilege this day, for they were the Queen's peerage. Their robes had been hired or taken from long-locked cupboards and the thin smell of mothballs clung to the banked seats where the nobility of Britain waited.

The fifth Marquess of Arlington, his scarlet robe trimmed with black-studded miniver, waited among them. The fur prickled at his neck while the television lights, brilliant and huge, made his ceremonial dress unbearably hot. His neighbour, a fellow marquess, grumbled about the long wait. 'Fellow can't even light up a cigarette, Monty!'

'I noticed the television chaps were using Poets' Corner as a smoking room.'

'Really? Think I might join them.' He pushed his way along the row of seats, leaving Monty his newspaper to read.

The front page was full of triumph because the British expedition had conquered Mount Everest while, inside the paper, the City pages continued the note of unbridled optimism. This was the new Elizabethan age and profits must rise. There was even a promise from Churchill's government that, eight years after victory, wartime rationing would end. Building controls were being relaxed and those who, like Sol and Monty, had bought cheap sites in the wake of war were beginning to reap the profits of their foresight.

'You're sure your damned clocks are right?' A sour voice spoke behind Monty. 'You weren't here two hours early?'

He turned to see the Baron de Conroy's dark face framed in miniver. It was the first time Monty had seen his enemy since the court case, and the Marquess of Arlington, filled with the goodwill of this day, smiled benignly. 'You're not looking well, my dear Kynaston! A touch liverish this morning?'

'That's better than being a bloody bowler hat, isn't it?' De Conroy sneered at the newspaper. 'I've often wondered what tradespeople read in the morning.'

'You want the children's page?' Monty asked innocently.

'Find the property page,' de Conroy snarled. 'Start house-hunting, Monty. Important fellow like you shouldn't be a tenant!' He laughed, pleased with his gibe that had been said loud enough to cause smiles among a dozen peers.

Monty let the words flow off him. The feud had gone into abeyance in the years since the court case, and an uneasy truce now prevailed. He had his temporary possession of Howarth, but de Conroy merely had to wait for the lease to end and victory would be his. He had fled the high taxes of Britain and gone to Monaco where, like a bored monarch in exile, he waited at the gambling tables for Howarth to be vacated.

194

'How do we stop it?' Pearl asked the question obsessively and constantly. She had won her first victory, possession of Howarth for thirty years, but that was not enough. She wanted it restored and returned to the family for ever.

Money was the only answer Monty could give to Pearl: money that would be a weapon in a fight, but how money could cheat the law's inexorable course was a mystery. The lease existed, de Conroy would not sell the freehold, so Monty could only wait upon time and upon the profits that he and Sol made.

Yet today, for once, the future of Howarth was not nagging at the Marquess. Today he was a lord in attendance on his monarch; a day for splendour and for a ritual that began with the Speaker of the House of Commons, in wig and knee-breeches, leading a procession up the Abbey's aisle. The clergy assembled in their gaudy robes.

'A hundred pounds,' de Conroy's voice came clear along the banked seats of the peerage, 'says the Archbishop will forget his words?'

There were no takers, instead he was hushed by a score of men who waited for the uncrowned Queen to come into the Abbey.

She came in a robe of crimson velvet edged with ermine and golden lace. Trumpets sounded, and the great organ seemed to shake the stones of the Abbey as the Queen, preceded by her sword-bearers and followed by her pages and maids-of-honour, walked to where her peers waited to witness her enthronement.

Monty looked towards the peeresses who were bright in their fur and scarlet. He caught Pearl's glance and they smiled. It was a smile of complicity because each recognized the achievement of the other. They had inherited a broken legacy and today, in an ancient Abbey, they could hold up their heads among their peers. And this day, Monty thought, Pearl was in her deserved glory. In Brick Street her parents would be watching on one of the new-fangled television sets and would see their daughter bright with diamonds among the greatest of the land. Pearl looked, Monty thought, as beautiful as he had ever seen her: a woman in her pride, in her glory, in her rightful place. She was also wearing makeup thick as double cream for she had been told

195

that otherwise she would look pallid and wan on the television.

The Archbishop of Canterbury presented the Queen north, south, east and west for the Recognition. 'Sirs, I present unto you Queen Elizabeth, your undoubted Queen. Wherefore all you who are come this day to do your homage and service, are you willing to do the same?'

Monty answered with the other peers, 'God save Queen Elizabeth!'

'See him?' Hilary, sitting on the edge of the sofa in the Brick Street house, pointed at the screen that, for an instant, showed Monty's thin, unnaturally solemn face. 'Look. There!'

Solomon Linsky was in tears. He kept removing his spectacles to dab a handkerchief at his eyes. 'If my wife could have seen it! If she could have seen it!' He was so proud. His business partner, dressed up like something from a Gilbert and Sullivan operetta, was in the Abbey, and Sol was loving every moment. 'She's so pretty,' he said of the Queen, 'so pretty!' Gloria and Sol had insisted on draping Monsol's office façade with flags until, as Pearl had tartly said, it looked like an exploded laundry. But Sol did not care what she thought, for this day he was a proud man.

'There's Pearl, look!' Lady Gall, sitting next to her husband, pointed at the flickering set. 'Doesn't she look good?'

Sol loyally agreed she did, and Sir Reginald wondered just how much money the jewels around his daughter's neck had cost. Caroline, Monty and Pearl's daughter, sat dumpy and silent, just staring.

Hilary was enthralled by the Coronation. 'I wish Hugh could see it!' Hugh Grimes, with a captaincy and an MC from fighting the Communist rebels in Malaya, was now in the highlands of Kenya where the Mau Mau rebelled.

While in London a kingdom's regalia was laid upon an altar; the curtana and spurs, the swords and rod of mercy, the patens and the chalice. Monty was caught up in it, lost in the mystery of the moment as, beneath a canopy of cloth of gold, the Queen was anointed.

The participants moved in slow and stately ritual. Gowns and copes and uniforms and heraldic smocks splashed colour in the Abbey's splendour. The Queen, bereft of her royal robe, was in a simple shift of white linen as the sword of state was presented for her touch, and as the armilla of sincerity and wisdom were put upon her wrists.

A golden mantle, splendid and vast, was draped about her shoulders. The orb of Christ's sovereignty was given into one hand and the sceptre of power into her other. The rod of mercy tempered the sceptre's power and the royal ring with its ruby and sapphire cross was placed upon her finger.

Monty watched. He had seen the dawn cover a desert, and watched the Ganges flood. He had known victory in battle and seen flags fly on a captured crest, but he had never seen a sight to touch this one. He glanced along the rows of his fellow peers and thought that just such faces must have watched, amidst their misting breath on a cold Christmas Day, the crowning of the Conqueror nearly nine hundred years before in this same Abbey. Then the faces would have been framed with steel that now were cradled by fur, but they had been lords and Monty wondered if they too had stared into a long future to fear for their holdings and their houses and their sons.

From the Abbey's High Altar the Dean carried the crown on its velvet cushion to where the Queen waited in her ancient, wooden chair. There was silence as the Archbishop lifted the great crown. Monty's own coronet was in his hand.

For a second the Archbishop paused and a television light slashed a streak of light from a diamond in the crown, then the symbol of majesty descended on to the Queen's head.

There was an instant's silence, then all the peerage put on their own coronets. 'God save the Queen!' They paused, took breath, and shouted it again, louder this time, and as they did so the fanfare pealed from the galleries overhead, bright metal trumpets searing the Abbey's vault with noise while, in Hyde Park and on the Tower Wharf, the great guns began their royal salute. The gunshots echoed through the capital, frightening a million wings into a grey sky, and the bells of every church clamoured out the message that Britain and the Commonwealth had a crowned monarch.

The sound of guns and bells carried to a lavish suite of rooms above Pall Mall. These were the offices of the de Conroy Trust, the place where de Conroy's wide lands and great holdings were administered, and from whence the money was sent to feed the gambling tables of Monte Carlo.

This day, because the de Conroy Trust offices overlooked the circuitous route that the royal procession would take on its return to Buckingham Palace, the rooms were crowded. A champagne buffet was served, while three hired television sets brought the scenes from the Abbey to Lord de Conroy's guests.

Those guests were bankers, lawyers, whores, family, and friends; all entertained this day by the clever young man who administered these offices.

Edward Fenton had changed. He had succeeded to his dead father's position, and the assumption of responsibility had smoothed his old hostility into a courtier's elegance. Edward Fenton had learned the art of self-effacement, moving silent and smooth behind the scenes to provide the money that allowed others to glitter. There had been many who thought the Lord de Conroy foolish to trust so much power into such young hands; it was said, not without cause, that it was Edward's hero-worship of the older man that had earned him advancement, but his foolishness had been justified by Edward's cleverness. No man was better with a balance sheet, no man more skilled at milking fresh income from ancient, tangled finances or avoiding the snares of new taxation.

Today Edward entertained his master's guests and was amused that the Lord de Conroy had invited, along with the men of money, four whores from the brothel he patronized when in London. The girls, as elegantly beautiful as they were expensive, moved easily among the other guests and were mistaken by most for county girls up in town for the Coronation.

The Lady Sophie was not fooled. She watched with a critical eye and was envious of their youthful beauty that, with the poise and manners their trade had taught them, would doubtless catch them rich husbands one day. The four made a cruel context for the plain girl who sat, thin-lipped and alone, on a sofa placed before a television set.

The girl was pitifully thin, had a weak chin, a petulant mouth, and mousy hair. She stared at the television as though too

198

frightened to meet anyone's gaze. Sophie, out of pity, sat beside her. 'Christine! You're looking quite lovely.'

Christine de Conroy gave Sophie a sideways glance, decided that the approach was friendly, so gave a flutter of a smile. 'Lady Sophie.'

'How's school?'

'Frightful.' Christine looked back to the television. She was nearly seventeen and had been abandoned at a boarding school by her exiled father. She spent the holidays with relatives or schoolfriends, rarely going to see him in his Mediterranean lair.

Edward, even though he paid both her school fees and her allowance, was always astonished to be reminded of the girl's existence. There was something mouse-like about Christine. She moved like a pale ghost in her father's shadow, and the contrast between her pallid, wan presence and the Lady Sophie's striking beauty was cruel. Yet even Sophie's beauty was fragile now. Edward knew, none better, the time it took for her to put on a public face and, even with all her artifices, it now showed, at one and the same time, the shadows of age along with the lineaments of youth's beauty.

One of the whores perched on the back of the sofa to watch the royal dukes kiss the Queen's hand. Christine looked up and greeted the girl by name.

'You know her?' Sophie asked in mild astonishment when the girl had moved off.

'I know most of them,' Christine said calmly. 'Father brought them to Caton quite a lot.' From her tone it was obvious she knew the girl's trade and Sophie wondered what such a timid, plain child made of the exotic beauties. It seemed better not to ask and Sophie, whose life had foundered on a sexual indiscretion, felt a sudden pang of pity for this child for whom love had always been monetary indulgence, but never a parent's affection. 'Are you going back to Monaco with your father?'

'Marjory Fleet's taking me to Scotland.' Christine's voice betrayed neither enthusiasm nor distaste at the prospect. She stared at the black and white screen that now showed the senior marquess of Britain on his knees before the Queen. His hands were enfolded by the Queen's hands and he swore, on behalf of all the marquesses of Britain, that he would become her liege man of life and limb and of earthly worship. The picture changed to show the other marquesses kneeling, repeating the words, and Monty's face suddenly filled the screen. 'Is that your brother?' Christine asked with sudden interest.

'Yes,' Sophie said.

Christine studied the face, as if trying to understand the man who was her father's sworn enemy. 'He's handsome.' She sounded surprised.

'Monty always was handsome,' Sophie said bleakly, 'and always will be. That happens to some men.'

The Earl of Fleet's sixteen-year-old son, Basil, sneered at the screen. 'You'll have his house one day, Christine.'

'Yes,' Christine spoke very calmly, 'I will.'

The horses pulled the Queen's coach away from the Abbey and the crowd, packed in their damp thousands, started the cheer that swelled to fill the capital. Behind the coach, resplendent in breastplates and plumes, and with swords drawn, the Household Cavalry guarded their sovereign. 'Look,' Sophie pointed at the television, 'that's David.' The Earl of Mountsorrel endured his National Service in the Cavalry, and his face, solemn beneath the shining helmet, was caught for an instant in the camera's lens.

Christine frowned. 'That's Arlington's son?'

'Yes.'

'And one day,' Lord Basil Fleet sneered, 'a homeless marquess.'

'But he's got his title, hasn't he?' Christine looked sharply at Basil Fleet, expressing her distaste that she, as a mere daughter, could not take on the ancient honours of the twenty-third Baron de Conroy. 'And at the next Coronation,' she said, looking into a future unimaginable to Sophie, 'he'll have his place in the Abbey, won't he?'

Sophie heard the unhappiness in the sharp, thin voice: unhappiness because Christine would never be Debutante of the Year, would never be sought out by the handsome young lords as Sophie had once been. It was the voice of a rich young girl who had been given everything but beauty and affection, and it gave

Sophie a sudden, burgeoning, and ridiculous idea that could reconcile her family with their ancient enemy.

Next day, after a night of dancing and champagne, Sophie curled up on her sofa with a book. She dreamed of a forbidden, secret love, of a feud ended, and a house won. She dreamed of Romeo and Juliet.

Two years after the Coronation, his National Service ended and his first year at Oxford nearly done, David met his Aunt Sophie at a Brick Street dinner. Sophie, made unwelcome at Howarth by Pearl, came often to see Monty. 'Your father always used to complain,' she said to her nephew, 'that Oxford was dreadfully short of girls. Is it still?'

'I suppose it is, yes.'

'And those there are,' Sophie enquired sweetly, 'must be frightfully earnest?' She touched the rim of his wine glass with her red-painted fingernail. 'I really do think it's time we got to know each other, nephew. Would you like to visit me at champagne time tomorrow?'

David, fascinated by this exotic relative, went. Sophie met him at the door with an unopened bottle of champagne. 'Welcome into my parlour, as the spider said. Do you think you can prise that open?'

David was not a bad-looking young man, Sophie thought. He had the fair hair of the Howarths and a pleasant face. It was hard to see anything very distinguished in him, but at least he was well-mannered and elegantly dressed. 'Did you enjoy the Cavalry?' Sophie asked.

'Not much.' David grunted as the cork came out of the bottle. 'I really wanted the Air Force, but . . .' he shrugged.

'The Air Force wouldn't have been nearly grand enough for your mother,' Sophie suggested sympathetically.

'Yes.' He smiled, showing a pale echo of his father's swift charm.

'In my day,' Sophie said, wondering why she used such a phrase to betray her age, 'the Household Cavalry kept their mistresses in Maidenhead. As a joke.'

'Really?' The interest was polite only, the smile perfunctory. Whatever else David Howarth had got out of his National Service, Sophie thought, it was not the dashing, insouciant carelessness of the true cavalryman – who cared for nothing except his horses and his woman, in that order, and took fences like the devil and did not give a damn for the world's convention. Sophie remembered Monty pretending to be the King of Montenegro many years before and could not imagine David playing the same kind of careless joke.

Beneath his carefully polished exterior, he seemed to be a sad, hollow man. Not once, as they spoke, did Sophie elicit a spark of enthusiasm. There was an aimlessness in him, a puzzlement at the world in which he found himself and in which he must make his way. 'After Oxford,' he told Sophie, 'I suppose I'll go into Monsol.'

'So odd, isn't it, to have a Marquess of Arlington who works?' Sophie smiled. 'I imagine the family vault as being full of twirling corpses. I must say you don't sound enamoured of Monty's business?'

'I'm not really.'

There was a kind of pathetic helplessness in him that Sophie thought might appeal to women. In her experience there were two kinds of men. The first sort, Kynaston de Conroy and Monty among them, were the cavalry of men. They seemed not to give a damn, promised a wondrous, if precarious time, and the women, like fools, flocked to the careless call. Such men made better friends than lovers, but they were irresistible. The second kind, David's kind, were more insidious. They used helplessness as a mating call, offering their predicament to a woman's solution, and, like fools, the women responded. Sophie wondered which call Christine de Conroy would answer.

The door bell rang.

Sophie, hiding her nervousness, darted to the window. 'My Lord! I quite forgot. David, darling, pretend you just dropped by. Will you do that for me?'

David, utterly bemused, nodded.

'And be kind,' Sophie said as she went to the door. 'Christine's a sad little soul. She just needs a little love and she'll blossom wondrously. I've seen it happen!' The door bell sounded again and Sophie disappeared into the hallway.

David stood as Sophie brought her visitor into the room. 'This is terribly embarrassing,' she said, 'but I know you'll be civilized. Christine de Conroy, David Mountsorrel.'

David had met Christine years before, when she had been eight or nine, and she still seemed to be the same fey, wistful child of his memory. 'Hello,' he said.

'Too silly.' Christine gave him a quick, thin smile.

'I was just leaving . . .' David began.

'Don't be a bore, David,' Sophie said. 'I won't tell your parents you've been consorting with the enemy. Now be a treasure and work your magic on another bottle of champagne. You'll find one in the kitchen.'

'Poor boy,' Sophie said to Christine when David had gone safely into the back of the house. 'He has the most ghastly mother. Once he's free of her he'll be quite splendid! Now let me take your coat.'

It worked. Sophie leaned back and watched the two respond like flowers to sunlight. The situation was too precious, too full of possibilities, for either to resist. Like enemies meeting in a safe no-man's-land they explored each other and ridiculed the fight that had been thrust upon them.

That David was fascinated by Christine was obvious, and that she found a secret delight in confounding her father's enmity was equally clear. Christine's life was drab. She stayed with the Earl and Countess of Fleet in their damp Sussex house, but in six months was going to a finishing school in Switzerland.

'And after that,' Sophie said brightly, 'no doubt your father will expect you to find a husband in your first season?'

'I suppose so,' she said dubiously.

'Fathers never know what to do with daughters,' Sophie said, 'except push them into some rich brute's arms. You should come to town more often. I'm sure your father would be delighted if you stayed with me. Shall I write to him?' And to Sophie's delight Christine shot a wan look at David as if seeking his advice before she nodded.

'That would be lovely,' she said.

'Then that's what we'll do. Such fun!'

So love, in the next few months, took on the splendour of a thousand suns, and love was all.

Love was sunlit days that went like moments, it was laughter on a river, and tears at parting. Love was more secret than the furthest star and closer than a farewell kiss. Love was all that was forbidden and all that beckoned. Love was all.

Love was small restaurants where no one would recognize them, and it was whispered secrets about families that would not meet, and it was about sharing two lives sundered by enmity. Love was reading *Romeo and Juliet* in an Oxford night.

Love was Jimmy Witherspoon singing the blues on David's gramophone, and Christine wrinkling her small face because she preferred Doris Day singing 'Secret Love', and even David, who liked his music with a sharper edge, adopted the song as their theme tune.

Love was a forbidden, piquant secret, and love was a dare. Above all things it was the risk that gave spice to love.

One day, so they promised each other, there would be no need for secrecy. One day their love would be shown to an envious world. 'I can't think,' David said in Oxford one day, 'why my parents would disapprove.'

'I don't suppose they would.' Christine could sometimes sound acid on the subject. 'After all I'd bring them Howarth, wouldn't I?'

'I wouldn't care if you brought nothing,' he said. His Aunt Sophie's words, that this girl needed only a little affection to blossom into beauty, had sunk like a ripe seed into his soul.

Their punt floated among water lilies and between banks heavy with wild roses. Christine, curled on the punt's cushions, stared at David from beneath the brim of her straw hat. 'My father would kill me if he knew.'

'No,' he protested.

'He told me I was never to have anything to do with a Howarth, except for Sophie. He thinks your family cheated in court.'

David balanced the huge, dripping pole, then thrust it down, pushed, and let it trail as a rudder to correct the punt's course.

'I don't know what happened in court,' he said truthfully, 'but if Howarth was mine I'd give it to you.'

Christine laughed. She liked the way that David fussed around her, the way he cared for her comfort. She was learning that all she had to do was ask, and the gift would be given. He treated her as she had never been treated by anyone, as if she was fragile and precious. Her father had always been generous, but his gifts were bribes to make her content while he lived his own separate life. David was the first man Christine had known who could be manipulated, and she revelled in the power, just as she adored the secrecy of this forbidden love. She lit a cigarette. 'But if your parents knew, they'd tell someone, and they'd tell someone else, and then the telephone would ring in my father's suite, and I'd be in trouble.' She stared innocently up at David.

'Yes.'

'So no one must ever know.'

'Of course not.'

Yet while Christine was the one who insisted that their love was so forbidden that it must be a dark secret, she also loved to risk the secret. She delighted in dares. In Oxford she would walk arm in arm with him down the High as if careless that someone would recognize them, and when he came to London she insisted that he take her for tea in Brown's Hotel or the Ritz. To Christine the risk was part of the secrecy and of the thrill, for love was dull without thrill and commonplace without risk. They were in love.

'You'd almost think,' Pearl said to Monty that summer, 'that he's in love.'

'David?'

'Who does he see in London, tell me that?' Pearl was sitting on Howarth's terrace lawn with watercolours on a folding table beside her. She was painting Howarth, wondering why her hand could never quite translate the vision in her head. 'He spends his life in town! I thought he was supposed to be studying.'

'When I was up at Oxford,' Monty said lazily, 'there was only ever one reason for running into town.'

'I can imagine,' Pearl said. She mixed some burnt umber with white, wondering if that was the shade of the shadowed stonework about the windows. 'I can't imagine what any girl would see in David.'

Monty, stretched in his deck chair, opened his eyes and frowned in reproof. 'Oh, come!'

'He's so torpid!' She sat perched forward on a stool, her back as straight as ever and her bare arms turned the faintest golden hue by the sun.

Monty watched Pearl, thinking that he had never tired of looking at her beauty, and wondering at the same time how any woman could be so unrelenting. She had expected the highest standards of her children, simply because they were her children, and now she would not see past their faults to praise their virtues.

Not, Monty thought, that Caroline had obvious virtues. The girl was catatonic, but her brother was cut from a better cloth. 'David's the quiet sort,' he said.

'He's torpid,' Pearl insisted. 'Name one thing he's interested in, apart from that wretched gramophone?'

'Curiously,' Monty said, 'Monsol.'

She looked away from the easel. 'Monsol?' Her astonishment was obvious.

'He said he'd like to work for us during his vacations. I thought he might shadow one of the negotiators.'

Pearl made a scornful noise and turned back to her painting. 'Which would mean living in London, of course. He's just using it as an excuse to get to London.'

'There's nothing wrong with that.'

The umber mixture was not right and Pearl frowned at the result. 'He's weak, Monty.'

'Quiet.'

'He's weak and he's easily led. He'll just get into trouble in London.'

Monty stretched, stood, and wandered to where he had discarded a golf club and a scattering of balls. He picked up the wooden driver and sent a ball arcing over the lower terraces to bounce in the rough parkland. 'When you're young,' he said mildly, 'London's just the place to get into trouble. Good God! David spent long enough in barracks there! Do you want him tied to your apron strings?'

'Of course not.' Pearl did not want her son at Howarth, but it galled her to think of him enjoying London's pleasures. She did not believe David had earned his pleasures. He had drifted through school, been undistinguished in his National Service, and had barely scraped into one of Oxford's lesser colleges. He was a young man without evident ambition and of few perceptible talents, and there was a Calvinist, hard streak from Pearl's past that rebelled against others presuming an easy assumption of privilege and wealth.

Pearl also suffered the shame of having children who showed no signs of excellence. Other young men, David's contemporaries, already shone in the world; they had wit and manners, interests and enthusiasms, while her son, behind his gentle, shy shell of courtesy, seemed to have nothing. 'Are you going to let him work in Monsol?'

'Of course I am.' Monty drove another ball.

'He'll stay with you in Brick Street?' Pearl asked the question with an edge of bitchiness, knowing full well that her husband liked to keep the London house for his mistresses.

'Sol's found a small house off the King's Road. It'll do the boy perfectly.'

Pearl laid her brush down. 'You're giving him a house?'

'Only a small one.'

'He hasn't deserved such a thing!'

Monty pulled another golf ball towards him. 'My dear Pearl. By being your son he has deserved Howarth. One day, if I can go on squeezing money out of Monsol, I will buy this house back. And another day I will die. On that day, whether you like it or not, David will be Marquess. So he might as well start with two bedrooms now.'

The mention of buying Howarth back mollified Pearl. That was her ambition. It seemed to her to be the likeliest outcome of the rivalry between the two families, for she could not imagine defeat. De Conroy's self-imposed exile in Monaco had encouraged her hope, for surely a man who wished to live abroad would not want to keep a great, empty house in England? He no longer used Caton Hall, so why should he want Howarth?

That was Pearl's reasoning, and it was spoilt by just a single fly in the promising ointment: de Conroy's daughter. Would Christine want Howarth? 'How old would that girl be now?' she asked suddenly.

Monty knew exactly whom she meant. 'Seventeen? Eighteen?'

'She'll be coming out soon.' Her voice was suddenly bright. She saw Christine de Conroy presented at court, then entering the marriage market of her first London season.

Pearl's tone of voice conveyed her thoughts as economically as the effort Monty needed to hit a sweet drive that arched towards the ornamental lake. 'Don't even think about it!'

The ball splashed into the lake and Pearl, invigorated by her idea, stood. 'It's the perfect solution, Monty! You know it is!'

'Kynaston de Conroy would rather drown Christine than let her marry a Howarth. Besides, would you want her as a daughter-in-law?'

'She was a sweet child.' She would take the snake-haired Medusa as a daughter-in-law if it meant keeping Howarth.

'I saw her at Ascot,' Monty said. 'She was being towed around by that dragon Marjory Fleet. The girl's got nothing, Pearl, nothing! She's a drab, sly-looking little thing.'

'Her looks aren't important,' Pearl said stubbornly.

'You want me to tell David that he's got to marry some pallid infant without tits just to make you happy? There's nothing between her nose and her knees. I looked. Flat as a board and about as interesting.'

'Being thin was very fashionable before the war, and I'm sure it will be again.'

'She isn't fashionably thin, she's emaciated. She probably wears a lifebelt in the bath so she doesn't get washed down the plughole.'

Pearl was undeterred. 'Sophie must know her?'

'I'm sure Sophie does.'

'Then . . .'

'My darling.' Monty dropped his golf club and walked over to his wife. He put his hands on her shoulders and kissed her nose. 'If Sophie introduced Christine to David she would lose her income, her house, everything. Kynaston will marry the girl off to a poxed sailor before he lets her marry David. Now please, for me, do not pin your hopes on such a mad idea. I hate to see you disappointed.'

'But you could ask her?' Pearl persisted.

'If you insist.'

A week later, in London, Christine giggled. 'Did you know your father asked Sophie to introduce us?'

'He did?' David was surprised.

'Sophie said she couldn't, because my father would be angry.' Christine wandered about David's new house, envying him such a wonderful gift. 'She said that if your parents knew then father would be bound to find out.'

'I suppose so,' David said.

Christine turned from the back window that looked on to a small derelict garden. 'You sound disappointed!'

'I sometimes wish we could be honest.'

She laughed. 'Secrecy is so much more fun.' They were denied the accoutrements that gave elegance to other aristocratic lovers. They could not meet at friends' country houses, or whirl dizzily from nightclub to race-course or from town house to ballroom. Christine and David were doomed to shroud their love in darkness, and in the private world in which they shared the resentments of their past, they also explored each other. They became secret lovers, for that was the only place their love could go. It could not become friendship, but only passion, and that too was part of the delicious risk.

They were silent the first time. It happened on the day before Christine was due to leave for Switzerland and they drew the curtains of the downstairs living room and, in shyness and daring, undressed.

David had visited the whores patronized by his officers' mess, but he had never taken a girl in love before and there seemed something sacred in the slow, silent care with which he handled her body. She had a white, thin body with tiny breasts that were smooth to his fingers, thin, bony thighs, and hips as narrow as a child's. He thought her frightened, but the dare of it drove them on, and afterwards when they lay in the curtain-shadowed gloom of the small room, they were both silent.

David felt guilty. They had dared to taste the ultimate of

209

forbidden fruits and he stared into her shadowed, bruised-looking eyes and wondered what change had been wrought by their clumsy lovemaking. He looked shyly at her slight body, at the dark shadows on her white skin, and felt a welling of the most tender affection. He would protect her against all unhappiness, against all evil, and in the shadow of his protection she would blossom.

Christine rolled over to look at him. 'Did you like it?'

'Yes.' He poured all his tenderness into the word and kissed her small breasts. 'You're beautiful.'

She laughed, then sat with her knees drawn up to her chin and her arms clasped about her thin shanks. 'I don't see why nice girls shouldn't do that. It was good.' She smiled, then dragged her handbag across the floor and took out a packet of cigarettes. Somehow her voice and actions broke the sacramental mood that had come over David in their lovemaking. She clicked her lighter. 'They always said it was quite fun.'

'Who did?'

'The women daddy brought to Caton, of course. I told you about them.' Christine liked to remember the girls from London with whom she used to have breakfast while her father still slept. 'They were awfully nice.' She giggled, as if she now shared their secret and was glad. 'Do you really think I'm beautiful?'

'Yes, I do.'

Christine half-smiled, searching his face as though trying to determine the truth of his words. 'You're so sweet.' Suddenly she reached for his jacket with a thin white arm and, as she talked about going to Switzerland, took out his wallet and counted the notes. David, watching her, knew she would take half the money without asking, but he did not mind, for he was in love and he took a delight in her foibles. She folded the pound notes. 'Will you miss me?'

He gave her the answer that he always gave. 'More than I can say.'

'But you can come to Switzerland?'

'Yes.'

'And we can do this again?' Christine spoke with sudden eagerness.

David spoke the refrain of their love. 'And for ever.'

For they were lovers, cleaving the enmity of their families, and daring all in the shadows of a feud. Romeo and Juliet, and for ever.

Love was the pain of separation. Love was jealousy and obsessively wondering what men pursued Christine in Switzerland. But love was also Christine forging letters from her father that released her for long weekends and it was David catching the strange, romantic trains in the boatsheds at Calais.

The journey was always a delicious apprehension as each beat of the steel wheels took David closer to the girl he loved, until, at last, with gouts of steam whiter than the snow on the Alps, the long train shuddered into Zürich's station and the small precious face, swathed in a collar of fur, came running towards him.

Love was pastries in warm shops while sledges clattered on icy cobbles outside. It was tumbling from skis and drinking mulled wine in beamed chalets while the snow, gentle as love itself, sifted on the slopes outside. Love was small hotels and great billowy eiderdowns and games of love in strange beds.

In January Christine cabled David, insisting that he come the next day, but explaining nothing. So he took the boat and train and when he arrived in Zürich she rushed him towards a smaller, local train. 'What's the excitement?' David said.

'You'll see.' Her eyes were bright, her mood excited. She mocked her school to David as the small train jerked out of the station. She told him about the fashion and cosmetics classes, the deportment class, and the endless lectures about who took precedence in society. 'An Irish baron is lower than an Italian count but higher than a Bulgarian bishop!' Christine squealed with delighted derision. 'Did you know that if a lady comes into a room a man should never give up his own chair to her, but find another?'

'No.'

'So she won't feel his bum warmth through her clothes!' She rocked with laughter at the thought and David, seeing her happiness, thought his Aunt Sophie had been right. All Christine had

211

needed was affection. Love, he thought, solved all, and love was a conspiracy against the adults who had forgotten its power.

The train puffed through valleys deep with glittering snow. The day faded beyond the train windows and the few lights in the deep valleys were like bright stars in the shadowed land. It seemed to David, lulled by the wheels of the train, that they voyaged into a dark heaven of delight. 'Where are we going?' he asked as Christine leaned her head on his shoulder.

'The Badrutt's Palace, of course.'

'The Palace!' David's expostulation made Christine sit up.

'Why ever not?' She laughed.

'We'll be recognized. Half London stays there!'

'Don't be silly.' She put her head back on his shoulder. 'Did you know that an English royal duke takes precedence over a German prince?'

But David was suddenly imagining his worst daydream come true: the one in which an angry Lord de Conroy snatched his daughter away from his arms. He shuddered, knowing that again Christine was daring the risk because the risk was the joy of secret love. It was foolish to go to St Moritz, to the fashionable hotel where the society of Europe feasted and played, but to refuse, even to disagree, was to risk Christine's contempt and so David, despite his forebodings, followed her up the hotel steps. There was no one he knew in the lobby and it was with relief that he closed the door of their bedroom.

Christine was filled with delight as she whirled about the lavish room that looked towards the Corviglia. 'We're dining in someone else's suite,' she said. 'It's all arranged.'

'We're doing what?'

'Will you stop worrying, my darling?' She kissed his nose. 'You'll see.'

And waiting in the suite were two other girls from Christine's finishing school. One had brought an Italian count, the second a French viscount, but Christine was declared the winner for she had produced an English earl. 'Don't you understand?' she said to David. 'It's a game!'

'But . . .'

'Six girls were to take part. Whichever of us produced the

highest ranking escort this weekend won! Simple! Obviously the others failed miserably. Isn't it too wonderful? I knew I'd win.'

'But suppose someone talks!'

'You're so nervous! Isn't it fun?' And it was fun, because for the very first time they had dinner with other couples and David felt as if they were open lovers at last. He applauded as Christine was presented with the magnum of champagne that was the prize for this game, but privately he could not wait for the day when they dared to tell Christine's father and when such games of high risk were abandoned for the joys of marriage.

David was certain they would marry, for they had shared their bodies and that was a pledge against the future. Her daring made him nervous, but in bed nothing seemed at risk.

They were avid lovers and, because they were young and had the appetites of the young, they made love constantly. They made love in the morning and in the evening, and in the night's heart, in the moments before dinner and after lunch and between the time when the waiter brought in the breakfast trolley and the time they removed the silver covers from the chafing dishes. Their stolen days began and their secret nights ended with the twining of legs and the hard thrust of bodies that needed the touch of the other's flesh. They explored the unspoken and forbidden mysteries of love and there was not an inch of her body David did not know by the winter's ending and nothing that roused Christine that he could not perform, and yet it still seemed to David that they made love like children, in innocence and delight, yet terrified that the grown-ups might find them.

To David she was beautiful. He never tired of watching her pale, slight body move about a hotel room. Christine was more restless than he, more energetic, and she would pace naked, always talking, and he would watch the muscles move beneath her white skin and would think her so very beautiful. Later, when he recalled that first winter, he hardly remembered either of them dressed. They were in love.

Love was jealousy. Love was another girl glimpsed by David in a street, a girl with long legs beneath a summer skirt. It was a tall Italian man, climbing from an Alfa-Romeo with a lazy ease, whose eyes caressed Christine with the smiling promise of a stranger's hand stroking pale skin. Love was confusion and bitterness, arguments that left each exhausted and nerve-tight. It was reconciliation in which their bodies were so much more expressive than their words.

Love was a year gone, Christine back from Switzerland, and David feeling a swift cut of jealousy because the Lord de Conroy, stirring himself to his paternal duty, decreed that his daughter, her education finished, should have a coming-out ball in London. David could not bear to think of his loved one dancing in another man's arms.

'Then come,' Christine said carelessly. She was in David's London house.

'I couldn't!' If Kynaston de Conroy discovered them, that would be the end to their love.

'You couldn't!' she mocked him. More and more Christine matched David's resolve against the declarations of his love, and more and more he felt himself driven by love into actions that he feared. She manipulated him, and he did not see that her enjoyment came from that manipulation. Risk and discomfort added their own spice to the piquancy of a forbidden love. He looked for an excuse to avoid going to the ball, but the thought of his attendance gave Christine a sudden and energetic vitality. 'If I persuade father to give a masked ball,' she asked, 'will you come?'

So David went to the Hurlingham Club in mask and cape and danced with his secret lover beneath the Chinese lanterns, and his heart beat nervously because the Lord de Conroy, nodding approval upon his daughter, asked her masked partner if they had ever met and David pretended to be a Frenchman.

'French, eh?' De Conroy seemed pleased. 'I think the Froggie Ambassador's here somewhere. You must meet!'

So David had fled into the night and the next day, lying in bed with Christine, they laughed about it. 'You were very good.' Christine stroked his face with her thin, tantalizing fingers. 'And my reward for not betraying you is to go to Howarth.'

'Howarth!'

'I want to see it again!' she said petulantly. 'Tomorrow.' She stared at his face, then smiled. 'You're not frightened, are you?'

214

David was terrified, but he dared not show it to Christine. To show fear was to risk losing this love that he had convinced himself was his one great achievement in life. 'Tomorrow,' he said with a calm he did not feel.

By luck neither the Marquess nor the Marchioness of Arlington were at Howarth the next day. Monty, as ever on a weekday, was working in London and Pearl had gone to visit friends. David deliberately took Christine in the afternoon, for Howarth's servants were under strict orders to finish their work by midday and then leave the family quarters empty. With his mother away, a fact he had elicited by telephone that same morning, he knew he should find an empty house.

He parked his MG in the stable block and took Christine into the house by the West Wing entrance. The windows were open to a bright spring day and tall curtains stirred in the scented breeze to fill the rooms which had once been the American hospital.

The walls were hung with paintings now, the pillars gilded, and the floors polished to a brilliant shine. David pushed doors open, taking Christine deeper into Howarth's splendours. 'I remember it,' she spoke of the times when, as a little girl, her father had brought her to Howarth during his courtship of Pearl, 'as crummy.'

David smiled at the word. 'It was, but your father insisted on repairs. There's still a lot to do.'

'There is?' Christine sounded astonished.

David touched one of the white, gold-streaked pillars. 'It's paint, not gold leaf. Mother wants real gold, but . . .' He shrugged.

'But not if my father gets the house in seventeen years?'

He smiled. 'Exactly. And no doubt, when you do, you'll remove the dung-heap.' He pointed out of the window. 'Luckily we've got an east wind today.'

Christine laughed, then admired the Music Room where the restored plaster cornice seemed as fresh as the day when Italian craftsmen had made the cherubs, lutes and trumpets that ringed the ornate ceiling. She turned beneath the coloured glass panes of the Garden Room, admiring the acanthus leaves of iron that supported the roof, and paced the floor of the Long Gallery, loving the light that streamed through open windows to fall on inlaid tables and Persian rugs. 'It's all so light,' she said. She seemed entranced by Howarth and turned with wonder to each new delight. 'It's white and light and lovely.'

David, pleased that she was so solemnly happy, smiled. 'Isn't Caton like that?'

Christine shook her head. 'Caton's dark. Full of guns and mouldering animal heads. It's a man's house.' David smiled at the conceit, but she nodded. 'It is. The lavatory seats were always left up. Always.'

She raced him up the curve of the Grand Staircase, past the statues on their niches, up to the corridor that led to the bedrooms. She threw open the doors, seeing the undecorated rooms that Pearl would not spend money on while the lease threatened. Here, where visitors were less likely to come, there was still much evidence of Howarth's old dilapidation. 'Where do you sleep?' Christine asked.

He took her to his bedroom and she ran a thin hand along the cardboard sleeves of his records. 'You've got as many here as in London!'

'Eight hundred and thirty-two.' David was meticulous with his records, cataloguing each one and preserving them from dust and bad needles.

Christine opened a cupboard to see scores of Dinky toys on the shelves. 'Don't you throw anything away?'

'Not really, no.'

She bounced on his bed. 'This is where you dream of me?'

'Of course.'

'Where does your mother sleep?'

The demand made David nervous. Till now, if his mother should have come home unexpectedly, he could simply have said Christine was a friend who had wanted to see the house and even have trusted to the likelihood that she would not recognize de Conroy's daughter whom she had not met for so long. But Pearl regarded her private suite as sacrosanct and woe betide anyone found there without permission.

'Well?' Christine demanded.

He shrugged. 'It's always locked.'

'Let's try.' She held out her hand. 'Well?'

David could not appear timid before Christine so he took her to the end of the East Wing and pretended astonishment that the door was already open. He felt all the old fear of his mother surge up as he led her into the beautiful room that faced east and south and was dominated by the huge four-poster bed hung with Chinese silk.

Christine adored the room. She rubbed a hand on the newly cleaned cotton percale, then found Pearl's notebook on the dresser. She read aloud from it. ' "Tell Rowlands stable clock ten minutes slow." Who's Rowlands?'

'The new butler.' Taggart had retired, gone to a brand-new bungalow that Monty had bought for him as the wages of perjury.

' "Caroline, doctor?" What does that mean?'

David shrugged. 'Mother thinks Caroline needs a nerve tonic, something to perk her up.'

'She should do what I did, shouldn't she? Find a lover.' Christine laughed at the thought, then sat in Pearl's chair and stared into Pearl's mirror. She opened jars, trying the creams on the back of her hand, then painted a fingernail with Pearl's lacquer. She stared at it critically. 'I like that.'

She tried Pearl's lipstick and mascara, leaving all the bottles and tubes uncapped. She used Pearl's powder brush, then opened the drawers to discover Pearl's lesser jewellery. 'That's nice.' She pulled out a chain of gold from which hung a golden net studded with seed pearls. She tried it on and it hung in a great blazon of gold on her blouse. 'That,' she said, 'should only be worn by a naked woman.'

'It must be rather wasted on mother,' David said tartly.

Christine walked into Pearl's dressing room, opening the cupboards and touching the cambric bags that protected the Parisian dresses. Then, restless still as if these rooms had not yet yielded up their secret to her search, she went into the private bathroom. She tried the taps and opened the cabinets, smelt the soap and put foam-crystals down the lavatory, flushed it, and laughed to see the bubbling chaos that resulted.

David, sensing that this high trespass was being done to dis-

217

comfit him, tried to find the right caps for the cosmetic tubes and bottles. He spilt powder and put a smear of lipstick on the linen cloth that covered the dresser as he tried to repair Christine's damage.

'I like the bed,' she said to him.

'For God's sake don't make an apple-pie bed.'

'Here,' she said.

He turned. Christine was standing inside the four-poster, only her face visible between the silk curtains that she clutched at her throat. David smiled. 'We should go.'

'Really?' She said the word slowly, teasingly, then opened the curtains to reveal her body naked but for the pagan gold that hung between her small breasts. Her wiry body was white against the shadowed bed behind.

She let go of the curtains and fell backwards, keeping her body rigid so that she bounced on the thick mattress as the gold bounced on her pale skin. 'Come on,' she said, 'I dare you.'

David looked nervously through the half-open bedroom door, but the house seemed deadly quiet beyond it.

'If you don't make love to me now,' Christine said, 'I'll run screaming through the house. Naked.'

David knew she was capable of carrying out the threat, but he could not imagine making love on his mother's bed. 'My room?' he suggested.

'Here,' Christine said harshly. 'Now. Or are you frightened?'

'No,' David lied. He climbed on to the bed, his shoes on his mother's lace bedspread, and slowly, fearfully, undressed.

Christine's clothes had been dropped on to the bolster at the bed's head and he threw his own on top, then turned and pulled the curtains closed so that they were enclosed in a dusky, multicoloured tent of Chinese silk.

Christine watched him, then slowly opened her straight legs like scissor blades parting. 'You don't love me. I can see you don't.' She laughed. 'Come here.'

He knelt beside her, but she pulled him down and kissed him hard on the mouth. He wanted this over and done with, finished, and he used small ceremony and abandoned his usual gentle tenderness. She gasped, then hooked her legs round his and

218

clawed at his back with long nails. 'You're good! You're good!' She cried out as she twisted him, her small body surprisingly lithe and strong, then she was above him and her fingers scratched down to his belly. 'You're so good.'

This was sacrilege, but suddenly he did not want to end it because never before had he known lovemaking like this. It was as if they had found a new ecstasy and David wanted to laugh because he had dared to enter his mother's Holy of Holies with the daughter of his father's enemy and it was a revenge for all the days of misery she had given him.

'Oh God,' Christine moaned, 'but you're so good.' She twisted him over again on the rucked, crumpled ruin of the bedlinen.

'I love you,' David said, 'I love you,' but then a crisp, sharp voice called out just a few yards away in the corridor outside the bedroom. 'Phillips! Phillips! I want you!'

David went rigid with a sudden fear that sent a chill coursing through his veins. 'My mother.' He mouthed the words to Christine, not even daring to whisper.

Footsteps sounded, the small creak of the bedroom door being pushed wider open, then an audible intake of breath.

Christine, beneath David, stared up at him. She seemed as terrified as he, as cold and frightened and motionless as her lover who lay, shrivelling, on top of her thin body.

More footsteps sounded. 'My Lady?' Margaret Phillips, Pearl's maid, came into the bedroom.

Pearl was staring at her dressing table. 'Did you do this?'

Margaret Phillips saw the disordered cosmetics and smears of colour on the linen and her eyes registered shock at the horrific trespass. 'No, my Lady!'

'Then who did?'

Margaret shrugged helplessly. 'Don't know, my Lady.'

'Then think!' Pearl's voice was a whiplash. 'Did you take away my breakfast tray?'

'No, my Lady.'

'Then find out who did, and if they were also responsible for that filth then they can have their cards and go!'

Assuming that the inquisition was over, the maid bobbed a curtsey. 'Yes, my Lady.'

'Well don't vanish, Phillips! I need you to pack some clothes. An evening dress, two day dresses, and something for the mornings. All black. Pack them, with everything else I need, and have Rowlands put them in the car.'

Margaret Phillips bobbed. 'Yes, my Lady.' She opened the dressing-room door. 'It's not bad news, I hope?'

'My father died this morning,' Pearl said without a flicker of emotion. She did not believe in showing emotions to servants.

'I am sorry, my Lady.'

'And in the Yellow Room you'll find a book called *The New Men* by a man called Snow. I'll take that. And you'd better find a black coat as well.'

David lay like a statue, his weight pressing on Christine who moved her face, very slowly, to lick his ear. He gave the tiniest shake of his head to discourage her, but the ripeness of the moment overcame her terror and she shifted her hips to rouse him again.

David could not be roused. He heard Phillips clattering hangers in the dressing room, then the sound of his mother dialling on the telephone 'Hammond? This is the Marchioness.' A pause. 'Monty? Thank God you're in.' There was the tiniest hiatus, then the curt delivery of the news, 'I'm afraid my father's died.' Another pause. 'I know it's wretched timing, but the Lawrences will understand.'

David heard the sound of a suitcase being unlatched and clothes being folded in tissue paper, then his mother's sharp voice sounded again. 'I was with Julie Witherspoon. Rowlands was bright enough to find me there.' More tissue paper, then a louder thump that David thought must be shoes being packed in the suitcase. 'I think the funeral's on Monday,' Pearl was saying. 'It would be too inconvenient if it's later. Will you stay overnight in Coventry?' There was the sound of a drawer being opened, then Christine pushed her hand down, trying to stir David while the gold that lay between her breasts dug into his chest. 'I have to spend the weekend there, Monty. Mother's being quite hopeless. David will have to come to the funeral, of course. Do you know where he is?'

'I do,' Christine whispered. Her hand, as light as a bird's wing, played with him, rousing him even though he did not want to be roused.

'No one ever knows where David is these days,' Pearl said.

'Not true,' whispered Christine who moved her hips and opened her eyes wider as she pushed her body on to David's.

'Wait a minute,' Pearl said. She turned from the telephone. 'I don't need a black nightdress, Phillips! I'm not going to the grave in lingerie! Use the one you laid out yesterday! I'm sorry, Monty, you were saying?'

The curtain on the right side of the bed, farthest from Pearl, was suddenly jerked back.

Margaret gasped. She looked at David, naked as the day he was born, thrusting slowly into a thin, brown-haired girl who first smiled at her, then put a finger to her lips.

The maid blushed, shut her eyes, then groped between the coverlet and the pillows. Christine helpfully raised her head.

The nightdress was withdrawn, the curtain fell, and David felt Christine shake with silent laughter. He was shrivelling again and his heart was banging in his rib-cage like a steam hammer.

'Keep going!' Christine hissed.

'I'll phone you in the morning,' Pearl said. 'And can I leave David to you?' A pause. 'Of course I will. Goodbye.' There was the sound of the telephone going down.

'Why don't you wait downstairs, my Lady?' Margaret asked sympathetically.

'Don't be ridiculous, Phillips! You expect me to turn up at my mother's house in yellow? That may be the way they do things in your family, but not in this one. Bring me the silk Hartnell, the day dress we took to Paris.'

Pearl walked into her dressing room and David, given a tiny respite, let out his breath.

Christine was writhing slowly beneath him. She took his right hand and put it on to her left breast. 'Come on. I dare you!'

David's head was spinning in the rainbow darkness of the Chinese silk. He could see the colours reflected on Christine's body, and suddenly, despite himself, he was roused. He watched her pale-lashed eyes close in the way he knew so well and moved his hand from her breast and clamped it over her mouth so she

221

would not cry out as she usually did. Then he felt her teeth bite into his palm and slowly, so very slowly, they subsided together and her body was slick with sudden sweat and she was licking the blood on his hand. 'You are good,' she said.

'Sh!' He flinched because she had spoken in a normal voice.

Christine smiled mischievously, loving the dare of it, the flaunting of the moment.

They lay together, tangled and spent, and David listened to the murmur of his mother's voice, made indistinct by the dressing-room door, and let his hand flicker gently on Christine's breast.

He had no idea how long they waited, letting the wetness dry from their skins, till suddenly, making them jump, Margaret's voice sounded just beyond the curtains. 'You silly fools!'

'Has she gone?' David asked.

'Yes.'

David felt the tension flow out of him with more force and relief than any lovemaking had ever given him.

'And you can clear this mess up!' Margaret said.

'When we've finished,' Christine said, 'we might.'

A scornful noise came from the other side of the Chinese silk, then the sound of footsteps receding down the passage.

'Well done,' Christine said.

David laughed weakly. He could not, he thought, go through that again, not for anything. He twisted off her body and kissed her belly. 'We have to tell them,' he said.

Christine smiled. 'Why?'

David, his head on her taut belly, looked over the shallow contours of her breasts at her small face. 'We have to tell them,' he said, 'so that we can get married.'

She turned her face into the imp-mask of mischief that David loved, but was beginning to fear for the trouble it boded. 'We could,' she said, 'go to a registry office and shock them.'

'Like John Fitzsimmons?'

'Why not?' She wriggled from under him and sat with her knees apart and ankles crossed. Her voice had a sudden enthusiasm. 'You've got to go to this boring funeral, obviously.'

'Obviously.'

'But if you were in London on Tuesday you could get a special licence, couldn't you? And we could be married a week later and then tell them!'

David smiled. 'But John Fitzsimmons, remember, was disinherited.'

Christine thought about it. 'Fuck.' It was a new word to her and one she loved to use. 'OK, so we tell them.' She fingered the gold at her neck. 'But I want a ring from Asprey's.'

'Of course.'

She jerked the curtains aside and stared into Pearl's room. 'And I want this room.'

David, appalled, said nothing.

Christine laughed and slid from the bed. She pranced her thin nakedness about the bedroom. 'Howarth is ours anyway, not yours. So I'll want rooms here!' She turned. 'You agree?'

'Of course.'

'We'll need bedrooms, dining rooms, servants' quarters, guest suites, kitchens, everything! And this wing is so nice! I think I'd like this room. I feel at home in it.' She spread her arms and turned around on Pearl's carpet and David, watching her pale body spin about, thought that perhaps Sophie, the secret begetter and encourager of this romance, might help break the news.

Christine, lithe as a dancer, leapt back on to the bed and kissed his forehead. Till now she had played with David as a child plays, but this visit to Howarth, following so close upon the coming out that marked her as a girl ready for marriage, had sparked off a new idea. She had forgotten Howarth's beauty, had forgotten the lust that the house stirred among those who would possess it, yet now Christine could do what her father had failed to do in the courtroom. She could put the three martlets of de Conroy back on Howarth's walls.

They had travelled the path from innocence to experience, and now they would put rings upon each other's fingers to end a feud between their families. They would marry for love, and for the three birds of de Conroy's crest that would come to roost, once more, in their proper home: in Howarth.

Sol Linsky was close to sixty now, with grey hair and a spreading waistline over which a gold watch chain stretched, but his face still retained the sprightliness of youth and still reflected his mercurial moods. Now he was embarrassed and his eyes were sad. 'I don't like it, Monty. I don't like it one little bit. I'm losing sleep over it.' The two men were taking a pre-lunch stroll in St James's Park.

'I'm sorry.' Monty spoke gently. 'I'm not sure I like it either, but I don't know how to refuse.'

'You could say "no"!' Sol said without any real hope that he could.

'And the money would be very useful. Very.'

'Money!' Sol said as though it was an irrelevance.

'It's a windfall!'

'I grant you that,' Sol said. 'But it's the wind I don't like.'

Pearl was the wind. She had inherited a fortune from her father and had suddenly expressed the wish to invest the money in Monsol. 'It's likely to be a million pounds after tax.'

'A million!' Sol said scornfully, as though a million pounds was a mere bagatelle.

'It could make us the biggest property company in London,' Monty said.

'And it will bring her on to the board.'

'Yes.' That was the rub, for Pearl insisted that, in return for her investment, she be made a full director of Monsol with voting rights and an office. Damn her father's heart, Monty thought.

'But I like our arrangement!' Sol turned to Monty. 'Just you and me. No contract on paper, but a handshake and trust! That's good!'

'That won't change.'

'Ha! You see? The old putz still comes out in you.' Sol shook his head. 'I mean with respect, if you weren't married to her, Monty, would you want her on the board?'

'No.' He smiled.

'What does she know about property?'

'She's always taken an interest in the business,' Monty said mildly.

'A wife should be interested in her husband's work,' Sol said, 'but she shouldn't try and run it! It'll be like having Genghis Khan on the board!' He pierced a scrap of litter with the ferrule of his umbrella and shook it into a wastepaper-bin. 'So she'll live in London?'

'I hope not,' Monty said fervently.

'That would cramp your style!' Sol laughed. 'But she'll visit, won't she? And she'll want to change things. We'll have to vote! And I'll be outnumbered!'

'Don't be ridiculous,' Monty said. 'When do I ever disagree with you?'

'Now?' Sol asked.

Monty stopped and looked at his friend. 'Listen, if you say no, that's it. I've already told Pearl that the decision's yours, not mine. But if we get that million we'll make waves! We'll own bloody London!' He laughed. 'And you and I can always outvote her. Always.'

Sol acknowledged what Monty said, yet he feared that a friendly partnership would become a battlefield. He knew Pearl's force and the tactlessness with which she could insist on having her own way. 'She doesn't even like me!' he said truthfully.

'But you will think about it?'

'Oh, I'll think about it,' Sol said airily. 'She's got a million reasons for making me think about it.'

'And it'll take time,' Monty said soothingly. 'The will won't be out of probate for months and she won't sell the factories till she gets her price.'

'I said I'll think about it,' Sol promised, 'and then I'll toss a coin.'

Monty smiled. He shared all Sol's reservations, yet the influx of capital could turn Monsol from a successful small entrepreneurial company into a massive force in the property market. He would like that. The old piratical, post-war days might have passed, but Monty still enjoyed outmanoeuvring London's money men, and Pearl's legacy was money to make yet more money. And, he reflected, if he was ever to take Howarth back then he would need it. One day he would tempt Kynaston de Conroy with an offer that no man could turn down. On that day Howarth would become safe and the banner of Arlington would be secure on its staff.

The hope was a distant one, and Monty knew it. What he did not know was that, even as he spoke with Sol in the park, his sister was travelling south through France on a mission that would change everything.

For Christine and David had gone to Sophie and told her they wished to marry, and that they needed her help in breaking the news.

The Lord de Conroy had a new toy this summer: the Lacewing, a millionaire's plaything that towered above the smaller craft in Monaco's harbour. It was a yacht with rakish lines, a winged bridge, and two rows of portholes studding its long, dazzling white hull. Sophie walked down the quayside to where de Conroy waited at the head of his gangplank. 'You like it?' He greeted her and gestured at the sparkle of brass and gleaming paint in his new craft.

'It's very dinky, darling.'

'It sleeps twenty.' De Conroy gave her a perfunctory kiss and stumped off down the deck. 'Drawing room in there, dining room, bloody great kitchens. I got twenty-four knots out of her yesterday. Want to see my bathroom?'

'That's exactly why I came, Kynaston.'

He led her through the vast cabin filled with Empire furniture and into a bedroom that was papered with pale gold and had a semi-circular bed against a bulkhead. 'In here.' He pushed open a door and a girl in the bath screamed. De Conroy ignored her, grinning at Sophie instead. 'A sunken bath! How about that, eh?'

Sophie smiled at the brunette clutching her arms to her breasts in a bath that was, indeed, sunken. 'It's frightfully sweet,' she said. 'Is that the maid?'

226

'That's Estelle.' He leered at the girl who gave a nervous smile back. 'My secretary.'

'I thought she was the plumber.'

'Always wanted a sunken bath,' de Conroy said. 'That's why I bought the yacht.'

'Did Estelle come with it? Part of the crew, perhaps?'

'She's a good girl.' He led Sophie back through the lavish cabin that was larger than Sophie's bedroom in London. 'When you get to my age,' de Conroy said self-pityingly, 'you need the odd creature comfort, you know. I roughed it for long enough! So how's England? Raining? Cold? Miserable?'

'As ever, my love.' Sophie followed him to the awning-shaded poop deck where a steward brought glasses, ice and whisky. Lord de Conroy tossed the ice overboard. 'Bloody boat belonged to a Yank so the damned crew serve ice with everything.' He poured two generous measures of whisky, then looked at her. 'So what brings you to my lair? Just passing through? Or did you come especially to see me?'

'I came to bring you this.' Sophie reached into her handbag and brought out the letter that Christine had written two nights before. She pushed it over the table and waited nervously as he read the childish, spiky handwriting.

Kynaston de Conroy's hair was grey at the temples now, adding distinction to a face that had otherwise aged badly. The whisky had given him pouches under the eyes and broken blood vessels in his dark skin, but Sophie thought he was still a handsome man. There was an unmistakable force about his looks, a hint of savagery beneath the sun-darkened skin. She could only hope that his evident joy at the acquisition of the Lacewing would soften any anger that Christine's words might provoke.

Yet de Conroy's immediate reaction was not anger. He read the letter twice then let it drop on to the table. 'How long has it been going on?'

'At least a year, I think. I'm not really sure.' Sophie was determined to play the innocent. If de Conroy set his face against the match then anyone involved in it would incur his displeasure, so she would pretend to be nothing but a messenger.

De Conroy stared at her. 'Is the girl in trouble?'

'Good Lord, no!'

'You're sure?'

'I'm quite sure. It's a ridiculous thought, Kynaston. Christine isn't like that!' Sophie gave a brief, brittle laugh. 'I'm sure David isn't either.'

De Conroy shook his head. Behind him the white city climbed up its expensive hill and the sun lanced shards of light from a myriad of windows. The hum of traffic reached the Lacewing across the harbour's rippling water where an American yacht, sails still furled, headed towards the hazy horizon. He sighed. 'It's my fault, I suppose.'

'Yours?' Sophie sounded astonished.

'I gave Christine freedom, didn't I?' Lord de Conroy lit a cigarette. 'Didn't want her cluttering me up. Been different if she'd been a boy, of course.'

'Well, naturally,' Sophie said.

A man came out of the galley and jettisoned garbage over the side. Gulls screamed down to fight on the water's surface and de Conroy stared at them. 'Does she love him, d'you think?'

She poured herself more whisky. Her nervousness had made her drink the first glass much too quickly. 'She's besotted.' It was the only answer she could give. Sophie was certain that David loved Christine, but she had not been sure that the love was returned. Christine had sat in her house and talked of Howarth, of possessions, but if that was what the girl wanted then Sophie would translate it into a love for David. 'They're frightfully sweet together.'

A frown appeared on Lord de Conroy's mottled skin. 'He was always a weak sort of lad, I seem to remember. Stuttered, didn't he?'

'That's gone,' Sophie said. 'And he's really very nice. Nothing like his parents. And I assure you that he adores the very ground that Christine treads.'

De Conroy nodded. 'Probably perfect for her, then. Perfect. Someone to go on spoiling her. That's all women want, isn't it? A pat on the backside and a diamond every now and then. Must be bloody simple being a woman.' He stared at Sophie, thinking

228

that she, like him, looked old. 'Why didn't she tell me earlier? Is she frightened of me?'

'The tiniest bit!' Sophie said it brightly as if to soften the answer. 'Well, you can't blame her, can you? If you'd known she was sweet on David Howarth you might have been very angry, Kynaston.'

The Lacewing shuddered slightly as the wake of a smaller craft gently butted the yacht's hull. De Conroy frowned suddenly. 'Were you behind it?'

'Me? No!' Sophie drew the word out. It was the question she had feared and, to cover her nervousness, she fitted a cigarette into her holder and bent forward for a light. 'I suspect it was really rather inevitable, Kynaston. Romeo and Juliet? Young love. They're very touching and innocent together.'

De Conroy liked Sophie. There was spunk in her, and wit, and in her day she had been a great beauty with the skills to make her beauty ravishing, but he was no fool. He had brooded on the court case and he knew now that this woman was as clever with lies as she was with her body. 'It would suit you, wouldn't it? Howarth marrying de Conroy. Don't tell me you're not the fairy godmother, Sophie. It would amuse you.'

'Kynaston!' she protested. 'How could you possibly think such a thing?'

De Conroy still had a savage temper that could flare with sudden force. It flared now. The ebony stick crashed down on the table, shaking the bottle and glasses. 'Were you behind it?'

Sophie jumped at the horrid crash of the stick, but stuck to her pretence of innocence. 'Why on earth should I be?'

'Because it reeks of you, that's why! Because it puts you back in the bosom of that family, doesn't it? So were you?'

Sophie gave the tiniest of shrugs. 'Well, maybe just a little bit, yes.' She watched the anger in his face and thought that she had failed.

'And his family?' de Conroy asked. 'Are they behind it?'

'No,' she said quickly.

He raised the stick again. 'Are they behind it, Sophie?'

'Kynaston.' Her voice was almost pleading now. 'They know nothing! Nothing! David's terrified of his parents. He can't stand his mother and he thinks he'll never be like his father. Can't you understand? David and Christine did this, no one else! They're in love. Or perhaps you don't remember what that is?'

De Conroy lowered the stick. 'I remember.' His bad temper disappeared as fast as it had come. 'All that damned effort, Sophie. All that energy! All those hopes and fears and bloody nerves. Love!' He shook his head. 'So the Arlingtons don't know?'

'They don't have a clue.'

He grunted ironic laughter. 'It isn't a bad thought.'

Sophie hid her relieved surprise. 'Does that mean you approve?'

De Conroy paused a long time before answering. 'I've been thinking about Howarth. I don't suppose I'll live there again, Sophie. Oh, I'd visit. I'd fly the damned flag and prowl around the corridors, but the cold and those damned taxmen would drive me out again. And Christine? Would she want to live there? I never thought she would. I mean it's a damned great place for anyone! Mind you, I never thought anyone would want to marry her.'

'Kynaston!'

'She's not a beauty!' de Conroy said indignantly. 'I suppose someone would have come along for her money, but would they want Howarth? Perhaps they'd sell it. I wouldn't want to see it as a hotel or a school or a bloody lunatic asylum! If she marries this boy then at least they'll stay at Howarth, won't they? And my crest stays on the house for ever!' He scowled, as if ashamed of betraying such softness towards his enemies. 'Mind you, she'll be a handful. Christine looks so prim, but there's more to that girl than people see. She's got de Conroy blood, and that was never thin.'

'I know she'll be delighted you approve,' Sophie said. 'She really didn't want to upset you and I think she's genuinely in love. Truly!'

De Conroy sneered at the thought. 'She's always had what she wanted. Spoilt rotten! Why shouldn't she marry whom she wants? But tell her there'll be no marriage without settling our differences! If that damned family think they'll get Howarth outright because David beds Christine, they're wrong! Understand? And if that bitch Pearl is involved then I want the contract signed in b!ood! Her blood!'

'Of course, Kynaston.'

De Conroy fell silent, brooding over his whisky. He growled suddenly, 'Edward can deal with Pearl. He's bright! Clever! Needs to be clever if he's dealing with those bastards!' Then he frowned, shaking his head. 'She really wants to marry him?'

'Yes.'

He fell silent again. Water lapped against the hull in a comforting, monotonous rhythm. Gulls flew overhead, their cries lonely in the cloudless sky. 'I was never a good father, Sophie,' he said suddenly.

'Of course you were, Kynaston!'

'But I love her!' He stared at Sophie as though challenging her to defy his statement. 'And I won't see her unhappy! Tell her to come down here. Next week! And tell her to bring the boy, right? I want to see them together. I want to judge them!'

'That's very wise, Kynaston.' Sophie discovered she had finished the second glass of whisky, so poured herself another.

There was a burst of music from the cabins, then the door opened and Estelle, wearing a black two-piece bathing suit and high heels, came on to the deck. '*Bonjour!*' she said brightly as though she had not been interrupted in her bath, then draped a towel in the sunlight and lay down, stretching out her long, tanned legs for de Conroy's inspection.

'Ready for dictation, is she?' Sophie asked.

'It's going to be a long engagement,' de Conroy ignored her gibe. 'A very long engagement.'

'If you insist.' She was puzzled.

'Long enough,' he turned his gaze from Estelle to Sophie, 'to test whether this boy really wants to marry her. Because if he doesn't, Sophie, and if he breaks it off, I'll have them for breach of promise. And I'll sue them for everything! I'll crucify them.'

Sophie flinched at the quick gale of temper. 'They're in love, Kynaston! You don't have to worry.'

'Love! They're children!' He suddenly gave her a sinister,

wolfish smile. 'Clever Sophie. Too clever sometimes. But you do amuse me.'

'Thank you, Kynaston,' she said primly. 'You'd like me to do a soft-shoe shuffle? Or does Estelle do those little things for you?'

He laughed, but there was no humour on his face. 'And if it goes wrong, Sophie, and Christine is hurt, I'll hurt you. You understand me? I'll make you pay for her pain.'

The words made Sophie shiver. She had thought that she did a sensible thing, that she brought together warring families, but suddenly she sensed that the negotiations would be hard and bloody and that her future depended on two children who claimed to be in love, but who would now be at the mercy of lawyers and accountants and men like Edward Fenton who would be de Conroy's harsh champion in the struggle of the marriage settlement.

But Kynaston had said yes, love had triumphed, and so the second battle of Howarth could begin.

David drove to Howarth on a Friday just when the leaves were beginning to turn. He parked his MG at the foot of the pedimented steps and went nervously into the great house where he found his mother rearranging the pictures in the Long Gallery. She seemed somewhat annoyed by his coming. 'I hope you haven't parked on the forecourt?'

'Yes, I have.'

'Dyson's spraying it for weeds today. You really ought to use the garage anyway.' She ordered a Lely to be taken down and stacked against the wall, then glanced again at her son. 'Aren't you supposed to be at Oxford?'

'Yes. But I was hoping to see father.' David had telephoned Monsol and been told that Monty had already left for the weekend.

'He is around, somewhere.' Pearl turned away from him to order that the Lely be put back up. 'I wanted to speak with you, anyway.' She led David on to the terrace. 'Monty tells me you never visit the Monsol offices.'

'Not a lot, no.'

'But you were provided with a London house for precisely that reason. Do you imagine that wealth grows on trees?'

'No,' he said.

Pearl walked briskly. 'We can afford to live in this house because your father works! And if you don't, then you won't be able to live anywhere. Have you come to ask for money?'

'No.'

Pearl stopped outside the Small Dining Room where a parlour-maid had laid luncheon. 'I'll order another place. And you can move your car.'

'Yes, mother.'

'And do comb your hair before you eat.'

David obeyed all the instructions. He wondered why his mother always filled him with such terror. He had realized once, talking with Christine, that Pearl had never, so long as he could remember, hugged him. The deprivation had left him with a great well of sympathy that he wanted to pour out on Christine.

'David!' Monty greeted his son in the Small Dining Room. 'How very nice. Come for the weekend?'

'Not really.'

'Pity.' Monty would rather have welcomed a diversion this weekend, for he was in the ticklish position of having to explain to Pearl that Sol Linsky still had not made up his mind about her investment.

But the news David told them over the asparagus soup would drive Pearl's investment clean out of Monty's mind for weeks. 'I'm hoping to get married,' he said shyly.

'Oh, my God!' Pearl stared at her son, wondering what disaster was presaged.

'Congratulations,' Monty said.

David blushed. 'Well, I . . .' He stopped, not sure how to break the news.

'Come on, then!' Pearl glared at him. No doubt some slut wanted a title and had snagged this fool in her claws. 'Who is it?'

David laid down his spoon. 'I'm in love with Christine de Conroy,' he said defiantly.

There was utter silence for ten slow ticks of the clock on mantelpiece. 'Good God!' Monty said.

233

'Kynaston's girl?' Pearl asked in disbelief.

'I didn't tell you,' David said hastily, 'because it really had to be a secret. If her father had found out there'd have been a dickens of a row.'

'You love her?' Monty asked.

'Yes.' David smiled shyly.

'Good God.' Pearl was staring at her son as if he was the prodigal returned. She smiled. 'Christine! How very clever of you!'

Monty still looked at David. 'Does Kynaston know?'

'I've just got back from there, actually.' He blushed. 'Asked his permission and all that.'

'And he said yes?' Monty asked in astonishment.

David nodded. 'Everything has to be arranged, of course. I don't understand all the details. I just wanted to tell you before his people make formal contact.'

'Good Lord!' Pearl blinked at her son. 'I think we should celebrate!' She rang the bell, ordered champagne, and then to Monty's astonishment stood, walked round the table, and kissed her son's forehead. 'You really are very clever, David. Very clever.'

'I am?'

'But of course.' She was elated. Howarth was safe! Her joy was a swelling bubble of happiness that defied comprehension. She stared at her son, trying to believe his good news; suddenly realizing that all the hopes and fears and dreams and struggles of the years since the war had been brought to triumph by David. Now, instead of merely repairing the house, she could lavish refinement and beauty on to it. Howarth was safe and Howarth was Pearl's. 'I always knew you'd come out right in the end,' she said happily. 'So you bearded Kynaston?'

David had rather thought he was the one who had been bearded, but he managed a smile. 'Yes.'

'Was he frightfully rude?' Pearl asked. 'He can be.'

'He was really quite pleasant. I mean he wanted to know if I was serious.'

'Naturally,' Monty said.

'But he's delighted. As long as everything else is all right.'

'Of course it will be!' Pearl said. 'And she's such a delightful girl, don't you agree, Monty?'

'Oh, yes,' Monty said, then turned to take the champagne from Rowlands.

'She has such fashionable looks. So slender. You're really very fortunate, David.'

'Thank you.'

'And so very clever.' Pearl was in heaven. At a stroke her son, her despised David, had cut through all the long agony of waiting and brought her Howarth on a plate. 'I think you should telephone your sister. Tell her the good news!'

Pearl had sent her daughter to live with her widowed mother. It removed the annoying Caroline from Howarth, just as her request for David to telephone his sister removed him from the Small Dining Room. 'The first thing,' she said quickly, 'is that there'll be no marriage unless the lease is annulled. Don't you agree, Monty?'

'You can tell the damned Howarths,' de Conroy said to Edward Fenton three days later, 'to take a flying poke at the moon.'

'The Lord de Conroy,' Edward said to Monty a week later, 'has reservations about abandoning the lease, my Lord.'

'Tell him his titless daughter can marry a bloody tramp, then. Good day to you.' Monty put the telephone down.

But this was precisely the task that Edward could do well. His patience would have worn down a saint, and his subtlety confused a sinner. He was under orders from Kynaston de Conroy to drive a harsh bargain, and these early skirmishes were nothing but a reconnaissance to see where the enemy might yield.

In the end he proposed to form a new charitable trust that would take over the freehold of Howarth. The trust would designate who could live in the house. Lord de Conroy would donate Howarth, together with its park, gardens, and farms, to the trust while Monty would donate half Howarth's value to de Conroy. A month was spent arguing about Howarth's valuation, but in the end a sum was agreed.

'It's no bargain,' Monty said gloomily to his partner. 'The

235

bastard's screwed at least fifty per cent more than the damn thing's worth out of me.'

'I'm just happy for David,' Sol said, 'so happy! I'm sure she's a nice girl!'

'She looks like a streak of damp string,' Monty said. 'God knows what he sees in her.'

The trust would be called the Conroy-Howarth Trust and Lord de Conroy would be its chairman. 'Bugger that,' Monty said.

'If you allow Lord de Conroy that small pleasure,' Edward said, 'then I'm certain that he'll give way on the date of the trust's formation.'

'Fix it,' Monty said.

De Conroy wanted the trust formed immediately, while Monty insisted that it should not be made until the marriage was consecrated. That way he would avoid being trapped as de Conroy himself had been trapped at the war's end.

'You don't have faith in love?' Sol was shocked.

'I have total faith in love,' Monty said, 'but it doesn't mix well with cash.'

De Conroy agreed to delay the trust's formation, but insisted that the cash was paid to him on signature of the agreement. To Edward's relief Monty agreed without a fuss.

Kynaston was chairman of the trust. He insisted that he should appoint two further trustees of his own, while Monty and Pearl could only have two seats. 'It's ridiculous,' Pearl said to Edward in Paris where she had gone for the auction of a splendid Renoir. 'He can always outvote us!'

'I'm afraid he'll insist on it, my Lady.'

'Tell him no! If he has three seats, then we shall have three seats. It's my final word, and I'm sure Monty will agree.'

But de Conroy would not give in. He named the Earl of Fleet and Edward Fenton as his other trustees, and demanded to know whom Monty would nominate. Monty put forward his own name, Pearl's, and that of Solomon Linsky.

'Tell him his bloody son can look for another bride,' de Conroy said. 'I don't care.'

'I'm afraid he's adamant,' Edward said to Monty.

'It won't do!' Pearl was back from Paris, the Renoir safely

236

purchased. 'The trust will decide who lives in Howarth. They could put anyone in here, anyone! I will not play musical chairs with this house!'

'The cow can stay there till she drops dead,' de Conroy said. 'What's the bloody fuss? I won't sling her out, but I'm damned if she can have as many votes as me!'

Edward, who was travelling between Paris, Monaco, and London like a steel ball on one of the new pinball machines, took the proposal to Monsol's offices. 'His Lordship, my Lord,' he said, 'is willing to give an undertaking that you and the Marchioness have tenure of Howarth, subject to the divorce clauses, and that it would take four votes to remove you for any other cause.'

Monty, bored with the whole thing, nodded. 'Agreed.'

Edward smiled. 'Lord de Conroy wants half Howarth to be given to his daughter now, though.'

'Jesus Christ,' Monty said.

'Over my dead body!' Pearl said that night in Howarth. Her sticking point was reached. Christine wanted the East Wing with Pearl's light-drenched suite of rooms, and her anger at the demand was fearsome. 'Who does she think she is, Monty? She's a child, and a very graceless one I'm beginning to think. Of course she can't have half Howarth! What's wrong with Caton Hall?'

Edward, apprised by Monty that the Marchioness had expressed some mild reservations, opined that it was not unreasonable, surely, for Earl and Countess of Mountsorrel to have rooms in Howarth.

'You telephone,' Monty said, 'and tell her.'

Edward did. 'They can have rooms,' Pearl said dismissively, as if she might find a boxroom and an attic where David and Christine could be squirrelled away. 'But if you think I shall let my son and that girl take over my house, you are wrong! They can have the Dower House.'

'Tell Pearl,' the Lord de Conroy said in Monaco, 'that she can go to hell in a wheelchair.'

'He feels we should explore the point further,' Edward said to Pearl. 'Would it help if I motored up to you?'

237

'If you insist,' she said, 'but I'm not surrendering the East Wing!'

Edward walked the long halls of Howarth at Pearl's side. He was Lord de Conroy's man, but these negotiations had given him a glimpse of the new wealth that Monsol was making, and he had seen possibilities in that wealth. One day, he knew, David and Christine would control both Lord de Conroy's legacy and the legacy of the Arlingtons. Neither child, Edward considered, would know what to do with that money, but he would know. He lusted after that wealth and, for once, was ready to offer a compromise that might save the marriage. 'Perhaps,' he said, 'if we were to put a flagpole over the West Wing?'

'A flagpole?'

'From which Lord de Conroy can fly his banner when he visits,' Edward said. 'It's closer to the main road, so more likely to be visible. And if you were to uncover the old de Conroy crests beneath the plaster? Say in every room west of the Octagon?'

He had proposed about twenty rooms, none of them the great rooms of state, and Pearl, influenced by Edward's subtle flattery, finally agreed. Howarth less twenty rooms was better than no Howarth at all.

'The flagstaff,' de Conroy said, 'must be higher than theirs.'

'Of course,' Edward said. He decided not to pass that demand on; it could wait till the couple was married and would give the happy family something to fight over.

Christine objected, but was told that one day death would bring all of Howarth to her, east, west and middle, and she took consolation thereby. 'But if I can't have the West Wing now I want Ash House.'

'Agreed,' Monty said to Edward. 'Damn place is empty any-way.'

'And they want the Dower House,' Edward said.

'They think this is Monopoly?' Monty knew that Kynaston de Conroy would give the couple a town house and, naturally, there was always Caton Hall at their disposal. 'Let them have it, Edward. God knows what they'll do with all those houses.'

'Fill them with your grandchildren, my Lord?'

'So long as they don't have bawling infants in Howarth,' Pearl said with a shudder.

If divorce preceded the birth of children then the fate of Howarth would be decided by the trustees, which meant, Pearl knew, that Christine would be given all of Howarth. 'Suppose she decides to marry, then divorce straightaway? It's exactly the kind of filthy trick that family would devise! We'll be evicted! It won't do!'

Even Edward was getting tired by now, but it was agreed after five weeks of acrimonious wrangling that the trustees would be duty-bound to give due weight to the findings of a divorce court as to which partner was the guilty party. 'It isn't watertight,' Monty said, 'but it'd be a hell of a legal battle, and you can tell de Conroy that I'll chase his damned tail into the House of Lords on that case!'

'The Marquess finds that an acceptable compromise,' Edward told de Conroy.

It was detail after detail, but it worked. Edward and the lawyers, with the patience of Job and the fees of Croesus, hammered out the agreement until the day came when he could at last raise a glass of champagne to Pearl and pronounce the thing finished.

'Howarth's mine?' Pearl asked.

Edward rather blanched at the simplification, but he decided not to argue with it. 'Except for the apartments in the West Wing, Howarth is yours.'

'Then my son can marry,' she said grandly. 'And you can tell Lord de Conroy that he should visit us. We have a wedding to discuss.'

'The bitch will make me pay for a lot of God-damned non-sense!' de Conroy said. 'But well done, Edward. You stitched the buggers up, right?' He looked at Monty's cheque that paid him back all that he had spent at the war's end on Howarth's freehold, and gave him a sweet profit besides. 'You're a clever man! And you're making sure that flagpole's erected?'

'Indeed, my Lord.'

Love had survived the accountants and endured the lawyers' quibbles, and so, in *The Times*, to the astonishment of a society that had thought a de Conroy would never meet a Howarth in amity, an engagement was announced. The Earl of Mountsorrel, only son of the Marquess and Marchioness of Arlington, would marry the Honourable Christine de Conroy, only daughter of the twenty-third Baron de Conroy. The games were over, love was made public, and Romeo could marry his Juliet. Howarth was safe.

Sol Linsky, in full evening dress, waited for Monty in the grubby pre-fabricated huts that were the passenger terminal of London's Heathrow Airport. The flight from New York was late and he kept standing on tiptoe to see whether Monty was among the travellers emerging from the customs hall. 'Don't worry,' Hammond told him, 'I'll make the time up on the road.'

'Bloody BOAC!' Monty said when he finally appeared. 'The bloody Comet broke down so we landed in Newfoundland while they found a new rubber band. Have you got my penguin suit, Hammond?'

'In the car, sir.'

Monty kept his good news until he and Sol were ensconced in the comfort of the Rolls-Royce. 'They signed. Twenty-three shillings a square foot! Can you believe it?'

Sol clapped his hands with delight. American companies, moving tentatively into Britain's reviving economy, were proving wonderful tenants. 'I didn't think you'd get more than a pound! What did you do? Flash your coronet at them?'

'Only once or twice.' Monty grinned. 'I said they could use Howarth for a summer party next year. It worked a treat.'

'So long as Pearl doesn't mind,' Sol said dubiously.

'I'll pack her off to Baden-Baden,' Monty said, 'for her annual injection of scorpion venom.'

Sol laughed. He had still not made his decision about Pearl's directorship of Monsol, but he knew it could not be delayed much longer. Her negotiations with Sir Edward had ended, but they had renewed her taste for such wrangling and she wanted a swift decision out of Solomon Linsky. 'She telephoned me four times while you were gone. Four!'

'One million, one hundred thousand, two hundred and sixty-three pounds, fourteen shillings and sixpence,' Monty said. 'Right?'

'And I've found a property in Manchester begging to be bought! Begging!'

Monty shrugged. 'It's your decision, Sol.'

But Sol was still thinking that Pearl would destroy a friendly partnership. He wished the money had never been offered, just as he wished he had not been so quick in accepting the invitation to this lavish party that celebrated the engagement. 'She'll ask me tonight!' he said fearfully.

'Toss your coin,' Monty said. 'You know how Pearl loves gambling.'

Sol laughed. The only consolation he could find in the whole matter was that Pearl was suddenly being wonderfully polite and considerate to him. 'Perhaps I can string her along for ever?'

Monty, as the car reached the motorway and accelerated on to it, stripped off his suit and shirt. 'Are we wearing decorations, Hammond?'

'Gawd yes, my Lord! All the glitter! It's in the attaché case!'

Motorists were entertained by the sight of a Rolls-Royce containing a man stripped to his underwear and struggling into evening dress.

Sol, watching Monty adjust a sash that bore a diamond-crusted decoration, smiled. 'I'm so happy for David!'

'If he's happy, I'm happy,' Monty said neutrally. The few times he had met Christine she had not impressed him. He thought he detected a predatory gleam in the girl's eye, but David seemed blinded by love so he would say nothing. Besides, she brought Howarth in her train and removed a vast load from his mind.

'And you don't mind meeting de Conroy?' Sol asked.

'He's not a bad fellow,' Monty said. 'Bit hot-headed. Shoots well. And he's got some damn fine ground in Scotland. Maybe we'll go up for the grouse, Sol?'

'Me and a shotgun? You're tired of life?'

Monty laughed. He was not tired of life, far from it. He even believed this marriage would give him a new lease of life, letting him relinquish some of Monsol's day-to-day business because, with Howarth secure, there would be no need to make more and yet more money. He anticipated country days, fishing in chalk streams and riding to hounds twice a week in the season. Howarth would have its Home Farm restored and he thought of the pleasure that land would give to him. He had enough money now; he could do what he wanted and let the world drift by in happy contentment. He put his head back on the leather headrest, anticipated the lazy days to come, and slept.

He woke as the Rolls crunched on to the gravel of Howarth's drive between the opened, boldly crested gates that led to Pearl's proudest achievement.

Howarth shone this evening. Every window was uncurtained and every light, on her orders, was switched on. The house sparkled like a constellation, while the turning circle of gravel, where once the long teams of horses had swivelled the carriages about, was thick with cars.

Two families had come together. They had come from Scotland and the Welsh hills, from the stone-walled Cotswold country and the high moors of Yorkshire. They had come from London and Bristol, from the valleys of Devon and the great hunting counties of the Midlands. They had come to celebrate an engagement that David and Christine had feared to announce, but which, in the simple elegance of its implications, had at last been welcomed by the two families.

Pearl greeted Monty in the Entrance Hall that gleamed with polished marble. 'How was New York?'

'Damnably hot, but very welcoming.' He kissed her cheek. 'You look utterly beautiful, my dear.'

She did look beautiful. The de Conroys had come to Howarth and Pearl had dressed to kill. She plucked at her dress. 'It's just something I picked up in Paris.'

'Not a bad frock,' he said. The dress was of silver pleats that fell from her neck to her ankles in a shimmer of expensive cutting. 'But it hides your legs. I married you for your legs.'

'Thank you, Monty,' Pearl said patiently. 'Solomon! How very nice. Perhaps you'd take me into the ballroom and find me some champagne?'

Sol, revelling in her sudden charm, offered his arm. Pearl was a head taller than he was, but he stalked with proud dignity beside her graceful stride.

The party might be to celebrate an engagement, but the moment that every guest waited for, the moment that had been postponed through all the negotiations until this happy night, was the meeting between the Marquess of Arlington and the Baron de Conroy.

De Conroy, slightly stooped, stood with his daughter. His dark, broken-veined face twitched slightly as Monty's elegant figure appeared in the ballroom's open doors.

Very slowly a hush fell on the room. At least half those present remembered the last meeting of these two men in this room, a meeting when violence, quick as a summer storm, had shattered a party.

Christine, beside her father, stared at Monty. Light, reflected from the vast chandeliers, slashed from the decorations on his breast. He was tall and slim, with that easy elegance that David, she thought, would never have.

Pearl, standing with Sol to one side of the room, looked between the two men, seeing how alike and yet how different they were. These were two proud men, one dark and one golden, who now must bury an ancient enmity. The silence became absolute, edging towards embarrassment, then Pearl realized Monty had deliberately allowed the tension to rise.

Monty bowed. 'Ten guineas, sir, says you'll slip bonnet over boots on this polished floor before the night's out.'

Every eye went to de Conroy, who smiled his twisted sardonic smile. 'De Conroys don't gamble with Howarths.'

'You've learned something from life, then.' The tone was light, the smile disarming, then he was walking forward, hand outstretched, and there was a release of breath in the room, a feeling that the men had carried the difficult moment well, and Monty was suddenly shaking his enemy's hand. 'You're most welcome, de Conroy.'

De Conroy nodded. 'You know my daughter, of course.'

'I was enchanted to discover,' Monty took Christine's hand and kissed it, 'that David has inherited my excellent taste in women.'

243

Relieved laughter rippled about the room. Christine was dressed in white and wore a fillet of silver in her hair. But nothing, Monty thought, could hide that she was a plain child, with a chalk-white face and a flat chest and stick-like arms that stuck incongruously from her puffed sleeves. 'I apologize,' he said, 'that I was late.'

'Not at all,' she said politely.

Monty turned, caught Pearl's eye, and beckoned her forward.

For de Conroy this formal greeting was a worse moment, but Pearl behaved as though she had anticipated the reunion with delight, and perhaps she had, for, with the cold kiss that was briefly, formally exchanged between them, she changed Howarth's fate. 'You look delicious,' the Lord de Conroy said gallantly, and gallantry, it seemed, was to be the night's theme.

The band major of the military band rapped his stick on the music stand and the first waltz filled the glory of the ballroom. David, shy under the gaze of the assembled families, took Christine in his arms and, his eyes on her eyes, danced with her beneath the scintillating crystal of the vast chandeliers. The Lord de Conroy, eschewing dancing because of his leg, bowed Pearl on to Monty's arm and slowly, like hostile armies mixing upon the declaration of an armistice, the two families met, bowed, and danced on to the wide floor.

The terrace was draped with lights. There were rowing boats on the lake, each one with a lantern mounted at the prow so that, after dinner, it seemed as if magic lights floated on the still water. The guests, over four hundred of them, had the whole house as their playground; they had all the magnificence of Howarth that was the purpose of this marriage.

'Christine's got very nice bones,' Hilary said to Monty.

'Don't be ridiculous!' Monty said. 'She's got no tits, a face like a dyspeptic rabbit, and I doubt she could say boo to a goldfish. Where's your gorilla?'

Hilary smiled happily. 'Hugh's coming. He's doing a refresher course in Scotland on how to kill people in new and interesting ways. He's riding his motorbike down. Good grief! Is that Edward Fenton?'

'Sir Edward since his father's death. He did most of the

negotiations. He's got a mind like a steel trap.' Monty spoke with grudging admiration. 'I can't say I like him much, but he's damned good. Pearl rather took a shine to him, but she always does like men who look as if they bathe in Brylcream.'

Hilary grimaced. 'Oh God, he's seen me. I suppose I'll have to make my peace with him.'

'There are plenty of bedrooms,' Monty said helpfully.

Hilary made a face at him just as Edward approached. He bowed, and there was a hint of a smile as he asked her to dance. The smile spoke of regret for the past, and a recognition of the irony in his question. Hilary, her distaste for this man long forgotten, echoed the evening's spirit of reconciliation by smiling her acceptance and offering Edward her gloved hand. 'My uncle tells me you've been the marriage broker?'

'I have, yes.' Edward, as she would have expected, danced superbly well.

'Was it easy?' Hilary asked.

'Not particularly.' He glanced at David and Christine who, to approving glances from reconciled families, waltzed together. 'Not that they cared. But the parents all had to have their say.'

'I'm glad for their sake it all turned out well.'

'If you ever need a marriage broker,' Edward said easily, 'then you must look me up.'

'I think Hugh's the type to drag me off to the hills and hit me over the head,' Hilary said. 'I can't see him making too much fuss.' Edward, she noticed, held her a primly respectable distance from his body, unwilling to take the smallest liberty. He bowed to her as the music ended, then gestured towards the terrace where liveried footmen moved among tables. 'Champagne?' It was a night for peace to be made, hatchets to be buried, and Hilary had taken care to let him know that Hugh Grimes still existed. So, with their new peace wary between them, they walked on to the terrace from where, later in the evening, the guests would gather to watch the fireworks.

'You're not tempted by marriage?' Edward asked when he had fetched the champagne to the table. 'Not even the caveman variety?'

'Lord, no!' Hilary said. 'Hugh would be scared stiff! He'd

rather walk through a minefield than up an aisle. And I've never really wanted to force him.'

'No?' He had forgotten just how beautiful this woman was. It was beauty worn so carelessly that it hurt. 'Why not?'

'I have love,' Hilary said simply, 'why do I need more?' She laughed, as if she did not expect Edward to understand. 'And you? You're not married.'

'I still wait for you.' He said it lightly, as nothing more than a gallant reply, and Hilary took it as such.

The Earl of Fleet came up to the table and wanted to know if Edward had seen his son, Basil.

'I haven't, John. Do you know the Lady Hilary Howarth?'

'Dear lady,' Fleet bowed gallantly. 'I had spotted you. I was hoping for a dance.'

But Hilary was staring into the lantern-strung gardens, watching a single headlamp speed along a gravel path. 'Oh God!' she said happily. 'Pearl will kill the fool!'

Edward twisted in his chair. 'Who?'

'It's my thug, making an inelegant entrance.' She gave both men a lovely smile. 'I'm sorry, you'll have to forgive me. If I don't head the brute off he'll probably ride that monster into the ballroom.'

The Earl of Fleet watched her run down the terrace steps, then gave Edward an inquisitorial look. 'Yours?'

'If only, John, if only.'

Fleet laughed. 'Basil saw her and went weak at the knees. He's a randy little sod, Edward. I told him she was too old for him, but I think he's ready to attack anything. Who's the lucky man?'

'Called Grimes. A nobody.'

The nobody braked the big Triumph, took it out of gear, and grinned. 'Some idiot told me to come round the back. What am I supposed to do? Park it in the roses?'

'He meant the stable block, you fool.' Hilary lifted Hugh's goggles and kissed him. 'Your face is covered in squashed insects!'

Hugh licked his lips and pretended enjoyment. 'Hello.'

'You look awful!' She laughed because he had ridden the long journey in his evening dress and his jacket was spattered with dead moths, tar specks, and dust. 'The stable block's back there.'

'Why don't I just leave it here? So much more convenient if we decide to elope.'

'I'm a romantic,' Hilary said, 'and I only elope on horseback.' She pulled up her skirts, put her leg over the pillion and her arms around his waist. 'Turn it round and I'll show you where to go.'

'Don't get your frock caught in the wheel!'

'Just drive,' she said.

Sol Linsky, watching Hilary and Hugh from a window of the Banquet Hall, smiled seraphically. 'Now there's a happy couple, my Lady! I do like Hilary!'

'One could only wish that one or the other would suggest marriage!' Why on earth Grimes was riding a motorbike in her lantern-lit garden, and what possessed Hilary to show a length of thigh beneath her bunched-up dress Pearl could not imagine. She looked back at Sol, thinking how ridiculous it was that this little man should have the power to decide the fate of her inheritance. 'Monty told me you'd discussed my proposal in the car?'

Sol, after the polite glass of champagne at the beginning of the evening, had tried hard to avoid Pearl. 'Yes, we did.'

'And?' Pearl had decided that she had been polite long enough and that the time had come for a frontal attack.

His spectacles flashed circles of light as he looked up at her. 'A delicate thing, isn't it?'

'I really can't see that it's delicate, Solomon. Either you welcome fresh capital or you don't.'

'There's David,' Sol looked past his hostess, 'and I haven't had a chance to congratulate him.'

'I'm sure David's happy to wait.' Pearl had him cornered, trapped in the deep window's bay, and she would not let him slide out of this confrontation.

Sol knew there could only be one answer: that Pearl was too dangerous as an enemy, but he dreaded losing the friendly arrangement with Monty. Monsol would change. New people would be hired, new rivalries begun, but he knew it had to be so. Yet knowing that he would surrender did not mean he would make her triumph easy. He fished in his trouser pocket and consoled himself that Pearl, even on the board of directors, could surely not come between Monty and himself.

'What on earth are you doing?' Pearl asked.

'I'll toss you for the answer,' Sol said. He balanced the bright double-headed penny on his bent thumb and forefinger.

'Mr Linsky,' she began, but Sol's thumb flicked and the coin, spinning light, sped into the air.

'Heads and you're in.' He caught the coin and slapped it on to the back of his left hand, keeping it covered with his right. 'Well?'

'This is ridiculous!'

Sol smiled. 'You wanted a decision now, my Lady.'

'I will not accept the toss of a coin on a matter of such importance.'

He raised his right hand to reveal the penny. 'You're sure?'

Pearl saw King George V's head and a pulse of pure pleasure went through her. 'Thank you, Solomon. I assume I'm joining the board, then?'

'As soon as the money's paid.' There was no way that he would let her come in and wrench his world apart until the million pounds was in Monsol's keeping. He watched Pearl walk away. 'Putz,' he said to himself. 'Silly bloody putz that you are!' But Monty, Sol thought, would be relieved that the matter was decided.

Monty was in the Library, where the Knight of Swords still hung on the wall. The Lord de Conroy had his back to the playing card and leaned intently over a leather-bound book. 'Good God! You did the Triple Crown?'

'Twice,' Monty said modestly. The Triple Crown was to shoot a stag, catch a salmon, and bring down a brace of grouse all in the same day.

'Starting with a twenty-five-pound salmon!' de Conroy said jealously. 'What fly?'

'Blue Doctor.'

De Conroy turned the pages of Monty's game book, looking at the pre-war record of pheasants and snipe and woodcock and deer and grouse. 'I fish a bit still,' he said, 'when I'm in England.'

'You've got a beat on the Test I hear?'

'I have, yes, indeed I have.'

248

'I wouldn't mind a thrash some day.'

'Quite so.' The Lord de Conroy had given up his daughter, the lease, and possession of Howarth to this man, and now he was being asked to sacrifice an even greater gift: the use of his river for a day. But nothing, he decided, should mar this night's pleasantry. 'I'll tell my bailiff you're welcome anytime!'

'That's really most kind.'

'Not at all. I'm not the fisherman I was. The leg, you know? And the water could do with a bit more interest.' The long-case clock in the library whirred, then struck eleven, and the thin chimes made de Conroy stare at the timepiece. 'Always wanted to ask you about your bloody clocks.'

'It's a Tompion,' Monty said smoothly.

'But did it go forward in the war, eh?' de Conroy bared his yellow teeth to show that though he asked with a smile, there was also the hint of a snarl in his voice. 'Did it?'

'I thought no gentleman ever changed his clocks,' Monty said lightly.

'Arlington!' Kynaston's mood veered downwards as his hand came up to point at him. 'The truth, damn you!'

Monty smiled his most charming smile. 'The old man was quite mad and he would not change the clocks in this house.'

The Lord de Conroy seemed to test the words for their veracity, then he shrugged. 'True or not, man, don't cheat on Christine, you hear me? Or I'll have the dogs on you!'

'She will be treated,' Monty said, 'like a queen.'

And Pearl was indeed planning a most royal marriage. 'A spring wedding. They can wait that long. The band of the Scots Guards will play. Naturally David and Christine will travel in carriages to the Dorchester.'

'Let's hope they clean it up first,' Lady Mirabelle Hare said.

'The biggest problem, as I see it,' Pearl said, 'is where to get the girl's dress made.'

'The church might find you a miracle worker,' the Countess of Fleet said acidly. 'Christine was not exactly endowed with beauty, was she? I used to despair when she stayed with me. I found a few pretty things in the children's department at Harrods, but I don't suppose they have wedding gowns. But she's very sweet.'

249

'David must think so,' Lady Mirabelle said, 'he looks so lost without her.'

The ladies turned to look at David. He had left Oxford with a dutiful third and was now employed full-time at Monsol. He did indeed look forlorn as he stood at the ballroom's edge. 'Who?' the Countess asked, 'is that dreadful man with him?'

'Hilary's,' Pearl said bleakly. 'He's called Grimes. He's a soldier.'

'Oh what fun! He looks more like a crow scarer. And talking of such things, where on earth is Sophie? Have you barred her from Howarth again?'

Sophie was not barred from Howarth. She wandered the great house, thinking that it was her cleverness that had brought peace to these lavish rooms and graceful halls. She could see the work that Pearl had poured into Howarth, and knew that it had only just begun. Secure now in this house, she would put splendour unlimited into its fabric. Howarth had been repaired and now it would be made magnificent.

Sophie climbed the stairs and found the room that had been her bedroom as a child. Nothing had changed here. Pearl had burnished the private rooms and the rooms of state, but there had been neither the money nor the will to decorate the many guest bedrooms that were still as dingy as ever they had been.

Standing in the room's depressive silence, Sophie wished the wedding was sooner. She wished the wedding was next week, but Pearl would have nothing but the best, and the best had to be booked long in advance and so David and Christine must wait. Sophie, who had seen the marriage from the very first as a chance of uniting her divided and warring loyalties, feared what might happen when their love, that had been hatched in secrecy's darkness, was now exposed to the harsh light of the common-place. She suddenly felt immensely tired, and pressing her face against the window stared into the night. 'But they're in love,' she told herself, 'in love.' She said it like a talisman to convince herself that it was true.

*

250

Christine was in David's room, staring at the gramophone records: shelf after shelf of records, box after box. 'He's very boring about records,' she said. 'He knows a lot about them, but he's got such strange taste!'

'Oh God, oh God!' Lord Basil Fleet, the earl's twenty-year-old son whose face was still scarred by pustules, replied.

'He wastes so much money on them!' she said. 'Are you coming already?'

'Jesus!' Basil, his trousers round his ankles, heaved one last time, opened his eyes wide, then exploded. 'Oh God!'

Christine absent-mindedly patted the back of his jacket. 'That's better, isn't it?'

'Oh God.' He collapsed on her, his head in the crook of her neck and his right hand on her breast beneath the crumpled dress. 'Oh God.' His breath came in huge gasps. 'Was that all right?'

'Well, it was your first time,' Christine pulled his hand out from her dress, 'but it was a bit fast.' She grimaced as she pushed his slack body off hers. It was the secrecy she loved, the dare of it, the sweet risk of exposure. 'It'll be better the next time.' She dressed herself slowly, then peered into David's mirror to re-arrange her hair. The idea had come just an hour before. What better way to celebrate an engagement than by taking a risk in her fiancé's own bedroom? The thought had been delicious, and she still relished it. Risk was all. It gave life to life itself.

She picked the silver fillet up from the floor. 'Once I'm married,' she said, 'I'm not having my house full of David's bloody jungle music.'

'No.' Lord Basil Fleet, trousers wrinkled about his ankles and dress shirt rucked up on his belly, watched as she took a record off the shelves and out of its sleeve.

'Chuck Berry!' Christine said scornfully. 'Noise!' She put a tooth of the silver comb on to the black disc and, slowly and deliberately, gouged across its grooves. She laughed, then slid the record back into its place and the fillet into her hair. She smoothed her skirts, then bent to give him a swift kiss. 'Wait ten minutes.'

'For ever,' he sighed.

Christine walked downstairs, demure and wan, and met Sophie on the half landing. 'I was exploring,' she said. 'Such a big house!'

Sophie frowned, as if not expecting to meet the girl. Then, strangely, she raised her dry, bony hands and placed their palms on Christine's cheeks. For once the older woman was not brittle or witty with her. 'Don't let me down, Christine.'

Christine smelt the whisky on Sophie's breath. 'Too silly,' she said, then giggled.

The guests had gone to the terrace to see the first fireworks explode above the lake. Applause rippled the night as Christine slipped a small white hand into David's. 'Happy?'

'Yes,' he said. 'It's all gone very well, hasn't it?'

'Yes,' Christine said, 'indeed it has.' She turned her shy face to the sky where fireworks splintered the night with dying stars.

For love had come true, a feud was ending, and they would be married.

'If I was you,' Sol said, 'I'd pull out that schlock. Put in a double drainer. Stainless steel? I know a man in Peckham who does lovely sink units. And an electric stove. One with an eye-level grill. You'd like an eye-level grill?'

Hilary smiled. 'And the floor, Sol?'

Linsky tapped an experimental toe on the wide, uneven flagstones. 'Screed the lot,' he said finally. 'Put in a baseboard and linoleum. Kitchens look good with linoleum. You want me to talk to Harry? He could do you a lovely job. And he could fill in that big fireplace and give you a tiled number with a mounted electric fire.'

Hilary picked up her tray then stooped to kiss his balding pate. 'Peasant.'

Sol followed her into the living room. 'And you don't want beams, Hilary! Think of all the dust they catch! Put in a false ceiling.'

'Shall I concrete the garden, Sol?'

'Good idea!'

Hilary laughed. A dozen people had come to the house-warming, Sol among them, and it pleased him to tease her with his ideas for improvements. 'Wouldn't you concrete the garden, David?'

'Yes, Sol.' David looked at his watch. Christine had said she would be here by lunchtime, but it was already two thirty and there was no sign of her.

'I'd take out these.' Sol made a dismissive gesture at the small-leaded windows. 'Put in steel frames, Hilary!'

'God knows why we bought it, Sol.'

The house was in Gloucestershire. It had been built in the fourteenth century and modernized in the seventeenth. It had stone walls and a stone roof, rambling rooms and twisting corridors, spiders in the bath, moths in the bedrooms, and mice in the wainscots. It had six acres of garden, a small orchard, and a paddock where two horses were out to grass. A stream wandered past the garden towards a tributary of the Thames, dogs roamed the downstairs rooms, and Hilary was in heaven.

David was in misery. He had twice walked to the pub where the nearest public telephone had brought him no respite from his agonized worries. Christine was not at her London flat, not at Caton, and he was beginning to think that her car must have crashed on the way here. 'She probably forgot she was invited,' Hugh said.

'I reminded her yesterday.'

'I wouldn't worry,' Hugh said with rough sympathy. 'Time to earn your lunch!' he said to the room at large.

David tried not to worry, but Christine's absence nagged at him. He could not enjoy the conversation, he found the other guests positively irritating, and he kept stooping at the front windows to peer up the lane that twisted its way between winter-bare trees.

'He's hopeless, Sol,' Hilary said.

'He's in love.' The two of them had followed Hugh into the back garden where scythes, machetes and rakes were being distributed to the guests. The house-warming party doubled as a garden-clearing effort, and Hugh was relishing the making of a vast bonfire. 'The wonderful thing about the countryside,' Sol said, 'is that if you're not killing something, you're burning it.'

'If you're talking about the leg of lamb,' Hilary said, 'I'm sorry.'

Sol laughed. He stared at the house that was so very beautiful and so perfect for Hugh and Hilary. 'If you pulled it down,' he said, 'I could give you a very good price for a brick bungalow.'

'I adore you, Sol Linsky. Take that.' Hilary gave him a pair of garden shears. 'We're doing the hedge.'

Sol was allowed his jokes. The building societies did not look kindly on unmarried army officers living in sin and, discovering Hugh and Hilary's troubles, he had insisted on lending them the money himself. Now he made a few futile stabs at the frosted hedge with the clippers. 'It's all going to be a disaster,' he said.

'I don't know, Sol. Hugh can do the rewiring himself and we don't want mains water.'

'Not this shack,' Sol said, 'Pearl.'

'Oh,' Hilary smiled. 'Has she got her money yet?'

'She will in a couple of months.' Sol dropped the shears and lit himself a cheroot. Alone in the garden he was dressed in city clothes, scarf tucked into a black overcoat and polished shoes smeared with grass and mud, but, despite his inappropriate appearance, he was an entirely happy man. There was no one he liked more than Hilary. 'She'll be insufferable,' he said of Pearl. 'She'll get Howarth next spring and Monsol this winter. The woman's an ogre.'

'Monty can control her.' Hilary slashed down with a sickle.

'No one else can,' Sol said gloomily. 'If he went under a bus, God help us all.'

'I rather think that Christine might prove to be her match. Do you think it's true that boys marry girls who remind them of their mothers?'

'How would I know?'

'Because you're a very wise man. Now get out of the way.'

Sol stepped out of the sickle's way. 'Christine just needs a little love.'

'I think,' Hilary said, 'that she's a sly little thing. David spends a fortune on her!'

'He does, true.'

Hilary was raking the brittle cuttings into a heap. 'And he's so miserable!'

'He'll be all right when he's married,' Sol said. 'He just needs to settle down with her.'

Marriage was Sol's answer to the ills of the world, a ringing declaration of faith rooted in his own memories of a happy wedded life, yet marriage was one of the matters that was contributing to David's misery.

He listened to the telephone ringing in Christine's flat then, putting the handset down, he wandered back towards the house-warming party and tried to convince himself that all was well with his engagement. He told himself that it was not Christine that worried him, but the marriage itself. His mother had gone to town on her wedding plans and it terrified David. St George's, Hanover Square, was not good enough for Pearl, nor was St Margaret's, Westminster. It had to be the Abbey or nothing, so every string had been pulled until the dean, pestered beyond endurance, had answered yes.

Westminster Abbey, the Dorchester, horse-drawn carriages, a Guards band, and the Royal Philharmonic for the dancing through the night. The dresses were being made in Paris, right down to the tiny frocks that the children would wear as they carried Christine's train. Page boys, dressed in silk stockings and velvet cutaway jackets, would process with the bridesmaids. Royal choristers would hymn the nuptials, no one less than a bishop would be allowed to bless the bride, and Pearl was even hopeful of a royal presence. 'Perhaps not top-drawer royalty,' she had said realistically, 'but someone respectable. After all we went to their wedding, so the least they can do is reciprocate.' It would be the most fashionable wedding of the year, a celebration of aristocracy, and it terrified David.

Yet the wedding plans were just a single strand of a tortuous knot of worries. He let himself into Hugh and Hilary's new house and stood in their hallway, listening to laughter from the garden, and was miserable.

Hanging from hooks in the hall were shooting bags, rods, waterproofs, dog leads, bridles, and a great canvas fishing bag replete with beeswax, spoons, reels, lines, and ancient river licences. It spoke of country matters, taken softly and with passions ruled by reason's pleasures, and David was deeply, hopelessly envious.

Somewhere, he thought, he had lost such honest pleasures.

Christine and he had taken their delight in darkness. Their love had been a secret, its ecstasies forbidden, and now that the curtains had been drawn back it seemed to him that the strong light of society's approval had made their love pallid. It had certainly made it circumspect.

Circumspect. That was Christine's word of the moment. She said again and again that they had to be circumspect. There had been a time when she would risk anything, when she would make love in his mother's bed or run naked through Howarth's corridors, but now circumspection was all. 'I mean if one of those filthy gossip columnists find out about us, you can just imagine what they'll say!'

'But,' he would say to her, 'what if they'd found out before?'

'Exactly, David,' Christine would say as though it should have been obvious to a child of five. 'We weren't engaged before, now we are. We don't want to spoil the wedding with a lot of filthy rumour, do we?'

So they were circumspect, which meant Christine would only meet David when others were present as chaperones. Rarely now did she come to his house alone, and when she did it was with a dramatic guile as though all the gossip columnists of Europe were at her heels. Waiting for her, wrapped on the pillow, would be David's latest gift: some bauble like a diamond pendant or a bracelet of ivory panels linked with gold or earrings of blood-red rubies. He would tempt Christine with gifts, murmuring of their existence at dinner tables in the hope that, when the evening ended, she would come in secrecy to his house. There had been a time when a day apart from each other was an eternity of torment, but now they were circumspect.

Circumspection meant evenings alone for David while Christine did he knew not what. He had seen her once, driving with the Earl of Fleet's son in an Austin-Healey, and she had laughed at him when he taxed her with it. 'Are you jealous? Davey-poo's jealous?'

'Don't call me that.'

'Davey-poo, Davey-poo. You can't be jealous of Basil! He's a moron!'

But David was jealous. He was jealous of those who spent

time with Christine while he, through circumspection, was barred from her company. The jealousy obsessed him, destroying his pleasure.

'You're back!' Hugh had come into the house, his face reddened by the wintry cold. 'Any news?'

'No, none.'

'I wouldn't worry.' Hugh was rooting about in a cupboard. 'I need some petrol to light the fire.' He backed out with a jerry can. 'Damn silly place to leave it, but I'm not squared away yet.' He saw the worry on David's face and smiled. 'She's probably had a puncture! Do you want to be in charge of the afternoon's arson?'

'I might go and look for her,' David said lamely.

'I wouldn't do that.' Hugh spoke brusquely. 'You mustn't treat people as if they're helpless. Either she's coming or she isn't, and if she isn't then she'll have a damned good reason. You might as well just enjoy yourself.'

It was rough, sensible comfort, but useless to David. He envied Hugh his certainty. It was impossible to imagine him jealous, or for Hilary to give him cause for jealousy. There was a trust and a liking between them that David might apprehend but he could never imagine feeling for Christine. Instead, he was ruled by jealousy and immured in unhappiness.

'Coming, then?' Hugh asked.

'In a moment.' David waited till Hugh was gone into the back garden, then left by the front door. He slid into his car, released the handbrake, and let it roll down the driveway. He did not want people to know he was leaving, he did not want to explain, he just wanted to go. He started the motor fifty yards from the house and accelerated towards London.

Hugh and Hilary's happiness was a goad to David's misery. He wondered if marriage would give Christine and himself the same quiet contentment. Perhaps marriage, defeating circumspection, would bring happiness, but there was a dark, inchoate suspicion that he had made a vast mistake; that in Christine he had found someone who would never give him the peace and security that he craved.

He dared not face that truth. He clung to the memories of

happiness and yearned for her body in his bed. There the touch of skin against skin drove out all other thoughts. Happiness was the achievement of coition; nothing more.

It started to rain. The wipers flicked back and forth and the road stretched glistening before him. He saw the mocking image of Christine in Basil Fleet's Austin-Healey, her laughing face bent towards the driver, and flinched as if from a blow at the memory. Of course it was nonsense. Time and again she told him it was nonsense and that there was no need to worry, none.

The winter dark was settling over the countryside as he drove between the avenue of limes in Burford and turned on to the London road. He was taking a risk. Perhaps Christine was driving the other way, perhaps she was even now arriving at the house where Hilary would be preparing the big dinner, Hugh uncorking the wines and the bonfire casting its glow on the cleared garden. Yet David could not wait in that company. He needed to be moving, he needed to search, and so he drove fast in the wet darkness to London.

There was no answer from Christine's flat so, hope dampened and worry stretched to a new tension, he went to his own home where the walls were like an echo-chamber for his lonely unhappiness. He poured himself a whisky, then sat and stared at the wall. Some music, he thought, might help.

He crossed to the gramophone, and stopped.

The arm had been abandoned on the inner groove of a record. He frowned, lifted the needle clear, and saw that the record was Bing Crosby's 'Changing Partners'. Christine had been here.

He twisted, looking through the archway into the dining room, and saw two glasses on the table. One was smeared with lipstick, the other had a trace of wine in its base. The kitchen was a mess, with broken eggshells abandoned on the work-surface and unwashed plates and pans left in the sink. Two plates.

The house was silent. David pulled his shoes off and mounted the stairs, remembering his father's advice on how to creep about country houses at dead of night without being heard, the trick of which, Monty always said, was to keep one's feet at the edge of the stair-treads.

David told himself a hundred times each day that there was

nothing for him to be jealous about. Yet he was jealous. Christine was so often busy these days, so often away for weekends, so often brusque when they met. Circumspection made him jealous. Basil Fleet made him jealous. Seeing Christine laugh at another man's jest made him jealous.

He reached the landing, scarcely daring to breathe, and saw that the bedroom door was an inch ajar. A red glow from the burning gas-fire showed inside.

He pushed the door open with his foot, and felt a pang of pure, wonderful relief.

She was here, she was naked, she was sleeping, and she was alone.

Christine lay on a disordered bed, sheets and blankets rucked into a heap, and her skin was given a glistening sheen by the hissing fire. She lay spread out, like a discarded doll, her thin legs straight, her tiny breasts elongated, and one arm trailing on the bedroom floor. The room was as hot as a glasshouse.

David stared at her.

Love had changed. Passion had become circumspection, but of this David had never tired. He could not drive this image of her whip-thin body from his mind, any more than he could live with the thought of other men writhing with her on white sheets. He watched her shadowed ribs rise and fall as she breathed. Then, on tiptoe, he crept forward and bent to kiss the taut white skin of her hollow belly.

She twitched, drew up her legs, and opened her eyes. 'David!'

He hugged her, all the relief pouring out of him. 'Where were you?'

'Here of course! Waiting for you! What's the time?'

'Half past seven.'

'Jesus!' She twisted away from him and picked up her watch from the bedside table. 'I thought you were driving me to Gloucestershire!'

'We were meeting there!' David protested.

'Davey-poo!' She kissed him. 'You've got a memory like a sieve. Never mind. I thought you'd like to find me here. Like this.' She stretched herself catlike on the bed. 'Surprise!'

'It's a lovely surprise,' David said.

'Then do something about it.'

He obeyed. Secrecy had once given spice to lovemaking, but the passion had not changed, and David, needing her, went to her and was reassured that she was still his, that she still wanted him, that this pleasure would be his to time's ending.

They lit cigarettes when they were finished, then lay on the bare bottom sheet and listened to the tap of rain on the window.

'You had lunch here?' David asked in a bland tone, but the question was driven by jealousy.

'With Julie Massey. She is a bore! She wanted to see the dress designs. You don't mind?'

'Of course not.' There was a wedding file downstairs, and in it were some sketches of bridesmaids' dresses that Pearl had considered, then rejected. It was odd, David thought, that Christine should have been so careful to put the file away when she had been so careless with everything else, but he thrust the jealous thought away as unworthy.

Christine rolled on to her side, propped herself on a thin elbow, and started shrivelling the hairs on David's chest with the tip of her cigarette. 'What was the house-warming like?'

'Very energetic. I didn't stay long.'

She dabbed with the cigarette. 'All jolly hockey sticks, was it?' She sneered. 'Hilary being her enthusiastic self?'

'Exactly,' David said disloyally. 'Ouch!'

'I didn't really want to go,' Christine said. 'Seeing other people enthuse about damp houses isn't my idea of fun, and I can't stand Hugh Grimes.'

'He's all right.'

'No, he isn't. He's such a hypocrite! He goes to church, pretends to be honest, and he won't marry her! I don't call that decent behaviour.' She drew on the cigarette then brushed ash off his chest. 'And I suppose they're living off your father's money.'

'I don't think so. Hilary's got her rare book business now, and Hugh's got his salary.'

Christine smiled. 'What do you know, darling? You're so honest and you think everyone else is.' She shrivelled one last hair then twisted round and dropped the cigarette into a glass of water. It was a habit David hated. She always went to bed with a glass of water, never drank it, and always filled it with cigarettes that turned the water brown. She kissed him. 'I'd much rather be here than with all those bores.'

He ran his fingers over her breasts, touching the bone between them, loving the feeling of her body. 'You'll stay tonight?'

'If only I could. I promised Julie I'd make up a dinner party for her. Such a bore, but I thought you'd abandoned me for the day.' She looked at her watch again. 'I'm late.' She scrambled off the bed, suddenly filled with energy.

David propped the pillows behind him and sat up. 'But you are coming to Howarth this weekend?'

Christine froze, one leg half into a stocking. 'This weekend?'

'Father's hunting thrash.'

'Shit! I thought it was next!'

'Christine!'

'Darling.' She came round the bed and kissed him. 'Daddy wants me to go to Monaco! He's leaving for South Africa next week so I won't see him all winter! I absolutely have to go. But we're going skiing in the New Year, aren't we? A whole week and no prying journalists!'

David was not sure why, if Christine believed that the gossip columnists might dog her every step in London, she should think that a week of unmarried love in St Moritz would go unnoticed, but he nodded anyway. 'A whole week.'

'It'll be like old times.' Christine pulled a jumper over her head. 'Just like old times!'

She finished dressing, then tugged a vast black coat from beneath the blankets and sheets that had been pushed on to the floor by their lovemaking. David wondered why she had brought it upstairs, but again said nothing because he knew that jealousy was an unworthy, destructive thing. She swathed herself in the coat, turning up the collar so that her face was almost entirely hidden by its high points. A black hat, pulled low on her head, finished the outfit. 'My disguise.'

'Disguise?'

'So no one recognizes me. Circumspection is all!' She giggled, pulled the collar aside to give him a kiss, and was gone.

David pulled on a bathrobe and carried the discoloured water downstairs. The house was empty again, lonely, and he told himself, as he had told himself unnumbered times in the last few months, that love was a flower born to fade into affection and that marriage was a compromise and that when they were married, and circumspection was no more, they would be happy. Just that, no more, but nevertheless: happy.

The double-leaf doors of Howarth's Octagon had been sent to London to be stripped and re-gilded, and temporarily replaced by thick velvet curtains that kept the smell of paint and varnish from seeping into Howarth's living quarters.

Monty pushed the curtains aside, then froze in the deep doorway.

'Froze', he thought, was entirely the wrong word. Howarth's new central-heating radiators had been turned on to their greatest heat, while three electric fires, all bars glowing, were arranged in a semi-circle around the mantelpiece in which, crackling and bright, a fire blazed. It was late December, a frost rimed Howarth's park, but this close-curtained room was like a Turkish bath.

Monty inched forward and raised his eyes. A scaffold had been built above the fireplace, making a platform eight feet high upon which he could see a pair of legs.

They were very long legs, very smooth, very shapely, and very bare.

He took another half-pace forward and could now see a girl, dressed in a two-piece bathing suit, standing on the platform with her back towards the door where Monty stood. It was a very nice back, he thought, entirely fulfilling the promise of the long legs. She was a tall girl, and her extraordinarily long, jet-black hair was twisted into a single plait that fell to her polka-dot clad bottom. She was doing something, he could not see what, to the high moulding above the fire.

Monty, dressed in jodhpurs, boots, shirt, stock, waistcoat and pink tailcoat, felt the first prickle of sweat on his forehead. The room was like an oven. 'Good evening to you!'

'Jesus!' The girl jumped in fright, her hands twitched, and an object fell to shatter in the fireplace. 'Now look what you've done! Can't you knock?'

'Not on velvet,' Monty said. The girl had an American accent which might explain, he thought, the heat in the room. Much as he adored visiting America he could never understand why its natives liked to live in temperatures of extreme and debilitating heat.

'There's a lintel, isn't there?' the girl protested. She was scrambling down the scaffold, giving Monty a splendid view of her long legs that were well worth watching. She crouched in the fireplace, her body lit by the leaping flames, and examined the broken pieces. 'That's an hour's work down the tube. Thanks.' She twisted her head to examine him, seeing a mud-spattered man elegant in spurs and boots and hunting pink. She grinned. 'Am I chewing out the boss?'

'You're doing it rather well,' Monty said.

She backed away from the flames, brushing her hands clean. 'You're the Marquess?'

'I am. Hello.'

'Hi,' she smiled. 'I'm Grace.'

'How do you do.' They shook hands. She had a face, Monty thought, like a Madonna's face: oval and smooth and heartachingly lovely. 'Will you forgive me,' he said, 'if I observe that you seem to be keeping the room rather chilly?'

She laughed. 'That's what her Ladyship said.' Monty doubted whether Pearl had used those exact words, but he said nothing. The girl, with a lovely lithe stride, was crossing to a work table at the far side of the room. 'It isn't for me,' Grace said, 'but the plaster. You want it to dry out, you got to heat it.' She waved at the stucco fireplace that she was restoring. The Octagon had been part of the US officers' club in the war and the moulded cherubs had been too tempting a target for after-dinner games. She was making new cherubs and Monty had startled her just as she was fixing one of the wingèd babes into place.

She took a cigarette from her busy work table, lit it, then looked again at his superbly tailored, mud-drenched clothes. 'You always dress like that to go horseback riding?'

263

Monty waved the riding crop absent-mindedly. 'Canoeing, actually.'

Grace considered his answer, decided it would be polite to laugh, so laughed. She wrapped a cotton robe round herself, thus reducing the pleasure quotient in the heated room. 'I work semi-naked because it's easier to wash skin than clothes, right?'

'I would be the very last to complain.'

'Some people have,' she said tartly. 'I was told I was lowering the tone.'

'My wife's tone is easily lowered.'

This time Grace laughed quickly, then nodded towards the almost finished repair work. 'So what do you think?'

Monty appraised the fireplace that towered towards the ceiling. 'I think you've done marvels.'

'Genius, that's me.' She frowned. 'I guess I have to call you my Lord, right?'

'It's sort of polite to hurl one in at some point in the conversation,' Monty said, 'but I don't insist.' He turned back to the fireplace and tried to distinguish between the new cherubs and the old. He really could not. 'How do you get the colour to match?' The original stucco was not quite a true white.

'Tobacco juice,' Grace said.

'Truly?'

'Cross my heart and hope to cough. I just spit in the mould. My own discovery,' she said proudly. 'I told you I was a genius.'

Monty laughed. 'And what on earth is an American girl doing in Howarth?'

'I was at Bryn Mawr, you know? The place where they try and turn us into good little Europeans. I got kind of fed up with it, came over here, enrolled in a school of art, and I am now your sculpture adviser's senior assistant. Aren't you impressed?'

'Enormously. And working on a Saturday!'

'I've got classes on Monday. Student, right? This has to be finished, so here I am, slaving away.'

'Then I mustn't interrupt you,' Monty said. Pearl, now that Howarth's future was assured, was pouring money into Howarth. Gilders and upholsterers and half-naked American girls lavished

264

their skills on the house, putting decoration over repair, restoring it to a pristine magnificence.

He crossed the room, on his way to the Entrance Hall where his hunting guests were gathering for tea, then turned again to the American girl. 'Are you staying in the house?'

'I've got a hutch in the attic. Where the maids used to live.'

'I think I've been up there once,' Monty said. 'You're taking meals in the servants' hall?'

'The kitchen,' Grace said, 'claim they eat better than the toffs.'

'That's usually true in country houses.' He paused. 'But if you'd like to join the gentry tonight?'

'Really?' She seemed delighted.

'My son's fiancée has let us down, so we're a place short.' He smiled, releasing all his charm. 'I'd be most pleased if you would join us.'

'So would I,' Grace said, 'but I don't have a thing to wear.'

'Why is it,' Monty said, 'that all women, of all races and all ages, all say the same thing?'

She laughed. 'You want me to come in trousers?'

'There's someone called Hilary staying in the Orchid Room. Tell her I said you were to borrow a frock, OK?'

Grace smiled. 'OK.'

'You did what?' Pearl demanded of Monty an hour later.

'I invited a most beautiful American girl to dinner.' He lay in his bath, hunting clothes strewn on the floor, sipping a whisky.

'But she's a tradesgirl!' she protested. 'We're paying her!'

'Think of her as an artist, a genius.'

Pearl pushed his filthy clothes into a pile. 'There are times when you astonish me, Monty. We go to immense pains to make a civilized evening, and you invite some American girl to whom we haven't got any kind of introduction! She may not have manners! Most American children don't.'

'She's not a child,' Monty said. 'And anyway most English children don't have manners these days. Manners are out of fashion.'

'I doubt very much she'll know how to behave. So if the evening turns into a vulgar brawl, you can thank your own insensitivity.'

Monty smiled and gestured at the bath. 'Want to join me?'

Pearl's face flickered distaste. 'Thank you, Monty. I shall just hope that Hilary has nothing that fits this girl.' She swept out of the room.

Hilary had a blue dress that Grace had somehow made fashionably startling with the addition of a scarf and a wide black belt. 'I never look good in it,' Hilary said to Monty as they gathered for cocktails in the Yellow Drawing Room.

'Nonsense,' Monty said. 'You look delicious in anything.'

'She is very beautiful,' she said appreciatively, 'where did you find her?'

'Naked up a ladder.'

'Oddly,' Hilary smiled, 'I believe you.'

This was the kind of evening Monty loved. A sprinkling of family and a host of old friends, most of whom had hunted with him through the day. He felt refreshed by the long cold day in the saddle, he expected good conversation, and the evening could only be enriched by the addition of a good-looking stranger. 'You like her, Hugh?'

Hugh Grimes turned to look at the American girl. 'I'm sadly loyal to Hilary. But it seems she has an admirer already.' Lord Creed had closed on Grace like a hound on a stray vixen.

'How's the new house?'

'Bloody marvellous, Monty! I can make the barracks in an hour on the motorbike, perfect!' Hugh, a major now, had a home posting. Promotion and experience, Monty thought, had not changed him. He still had the same battered face and the same honesty in his eyes. He had ridden a big roan to the hunt, a horse that tended to demolish fences like a tank rather than soar gracefully over them. It was a pity that his son did not have the same toughness as Hugh. David, as likely as not, would wait to file his horse through a field gate rather than follow his father over some high hedge, but in fairness he had restored Howarth to the family. What a strange thing, Monty thought, love was.

David, bereft of Christine for the weekend, was making desultory conversation with Lady Creed, and Monty, trying to cheer his son up, took him aside. 'There's someone I want you to meet.' He led David to Grace, who had been temporarily abandoned because Pearl had demanded Lord Creed's opinion of a Stubbs painting she had purchased at Sotheby's. 'It occurs to me,' Monty said to her, 'that I don't know your surname.'

'Dunwoody.'

'Grace Dunwoody, this is my son, David.'

'Hi.' Grace gave him a brilliant smile. 'Do I have to call you my Lord?'

'Absolutely,' David said.

'You're the one who's getting married, right?'

'Yes.'

'And she stood you up?'

'She's in Monaco,' he said.

'Guess I'm the replacement, then.'

Pearl saw David with the girl and, brusquely abandoning Tom Creed, beckoned Monty towards her. 'Are you entirely mad?'

'Whatever do you mean?'

'Introducing them!'

'Don't be ridiculous,' Monty said. 'David obviously doesn't fancy that type! He likes skinny girls with flat chests! She hasn't got a flat chest, I checked.'

'You make it all into a joke, Monty. And it isn't!' She was terrified that the engagement would be called off, and that all her restoration of Howarth would be wasted. 'God knows why we're supposed to entertain her in the first place. I don't suppose she knows which knife and fork to use.'

Grace did know. Pearl deliberately sat the girl far away from David or Monty, placing her between the Honourable John Lancaster and Lord Creed: both men, she thought, who would pursue the American unmercifully. When the ladies withdrew to the Drawing Room for coffee, Pearl tried to freeze Grace out of the company, but Hilary insisted on sitting with her.

Back in the Dining Room Lord Creed cracked a walnut. 'The American girl's yours, Monty?'

'Lord, no, Tom!' Monty would never start an affair in his wife's presence. 'I just found her wandering the halls.'

'I wish crumpet like that strayed into Marchdene,' Creed said gloomily.

And afterwards, when the port had gone round thrice and the

cigars had burned evenly down, the company gathered once more and the day's hunting was relived. Some of the men drifted to the Billiard Room, others stayed with the ladies until, at a quarter to midnight, Monty stood. 'Bed. Church party musters at ten forty-five, right?'

'Right,' Hugh said.

'Heathens can linger over breakfast with me.' Monty thought it had been the perfect day. 'Goodnight all.'

Some of the guests stayed up, playing bowls in the Long Gallery with tennis balls or practising cannons in the Billiard Room. One by one, or two by two, they melted upstairs.

Lord Creed tried to teach Grace the rules of billiards, and when she seemed bored by the game John Lancaster wondered if she would like to see the Lelys in the upper gallery. Grace said she would rather see the famous Renoir that the Marchioness had bought recently, but Lancaster did not know where it was hanging, so David was summoned.

'It's in the Terrace Room,' David said.

'You'll show me?' Grace asked him. She looked at John Lancaster. 'I'll be back,' she promised.

She walked with David through the shining halls. 'I guess I'm tonight's star prize, right?'

'I'm sorry?'

'Those guys back there. They think I'm the donkey and they're gonna pin their tails on me.'

David smiled. 'I'm afraid that's all part of the country weekend. Especially for Tom Creed.'

'He really thinks he's something else, doesn't he?' Grace grimaced, and then they were standing before the lovely Renoir that glowed like a spring day. She stared and stared, half frowning, wondering how a man could find such beauty in his head. The clock struck half past one. 'Hickory dickory dock,' she said.

'I'm sorry?' David was distracted, tormented by thoughts of Christine in Monaco.

'Nothing.' Grace walked to the window and pushed her nose against a pane. The night was crystal clear, bright with stars, and white with a new frost. 'I'm going for a walk.'

David smiled. 'It'll be cold.'

'So I'll shiver,' she said. 'You want to come?' She threw the invitation out very casually.

David fetched coats and boots and scarves and hats from the cloakroom by the gun room, then unlocked the passage door and they stepped into a freezing, still night in which the stars arched above them like a smear of scattered diamonds.

They walked across the upper lawn, their boots making dents in the frosted grass that would show as bruises until springtime. They went down the terrace steps and headed towards the lake that was a sheet of silver in the moonlight.

'It's beautiful,' Grace said. She had turned to look at Howarth, but her praise encompassed all the wide countryside that was sifted with frost and sharp-edged beneath the moon.

'Yes,' David said.

They walked along the lake's margin, beside the white spear-points of frozen reeds. Their boots crunched the newly iced puddles. 'It's like a big private joke,' Grace said suddenly. 'I mean everyone knows everyone else and you feel such a fool, you know?'

David frowned. 'I don't know.'

'I mean they were sweet, or most of them.' Grace had wanted his company as a shield against the pestering in the Billiard Room. 'Hilary's nice.'

'Yes.'

'But it's a private world, isn't it? And no one's going to explain the rules.'

David had not sensed any insecurity in the girl during the evening, but as she spoke he saw how a stranger might find Howarth a closed and privileged world. He wondered how old she was, guessing twenty-one or two, but he did not like to ask. He felt obscurely pleased that she had abandoned Creed and Lancaster for his own company.

They had reached a small, white-stone summerhouse that faced an arm of the lake, and sat on a bench. Grace, answering David's desultory questions, told how her sculpture lecturer had been made Pearl's adviser for the restoration of Howarth's carvings, and how, as a result, she had found this part-time job working

269

on the stucco's restoration. 'I guess your parents are God-Almighty rich, right?'

'They weren't always,' David said. 'At least not really rich. But my father's been rather clever in the City.'

'Like my father,' Grace said. 'He's a big guy on Wall Street.' She stared at the lake as she talked, and David stared at her. It was dawning on him that this girl had a beauty that was rare and extraordinary.

She spoke of her work, and her voice was gentle and intelligent, but there was a raw streak of ambition that she did not care to hide. She wanted, she said, to be a sculptress, but not just any sculptress: the best. 'Not this old stuff,' she waved deprecatingly at a statue of Ceres pouring stone water towards the freezing lake. 'Metal, I think. I like working in metal.' She turned to him, her eyes reflecting the cold light of the moon, and smiled. 'I guess you don't have to work?'

'I do.' David had his hands thrust into his coat pockets. 'Not very seriously, though.'

'What does that mean?'

He shrugged. He told her about Monsol and said that, since leaving Oxford, he had worked there full-time, but that his impending marriage had taken the pressure off him. 'They don't really expect me to make money now.'

'Because you're marrying it?'

He nodded.

'Lucky old you,' Grace said. 'But you're not gonna do nothing, are you?' She sounded incredulous.

'I know what I'd like to do,' he said wistfully.

'What?'

So David told her the things that Christine always scoffed at, his dream of musicians and records and concerts. It was a dream that had grown slowly, a dream of managing singers or groups and steering them to success. Christine despised the ambition, calling it David's jungle-music pipe dream, but Grace, with a leap of vivacity, clapped her hands. 'You like rock 'n' roll?'

'Yes.'

'And me!' She listed her favourite records and David knew them all, and when he said he had a new American pressing of an unknown singer called Elvis Presley she looked at him in awe as though, at last, in the magnificence that was Howarth, she had found something truly remarkable. 'Then why don't you do it?'

David laughed. 'What? Start my own business?'

'Sure! Hell! If you're an earl those guys'll eat out of your hand!'

'I hadn't thought of that.'

'What would you need?' Grace was suddenly all enthusiasm. 'An office, right? And a small studio, nothing big. Just somewhere to make a demo' tape. Couldn't you hire them?'

He smiled. 'I've got room in my house.'

'There you go, David! Go get 'em!' She twisted on the stone bench, eyes alight and face eager. 'Why not?'

He shivered in his coat. 'I'm not sure my family will approve.'

'Hell, you're the heir, aren't you? What are they gonna do? Throw you out?'

'And Christine doesn't like it.'

'She's the fiancée, right?'

'Right.'

Grace seemed to subside. 'That's too bad. You're supposed to be all posh, I guess.'

David smiled at the word. 'Yes.'

Grace stared into the cold night where the only moving thing was the gelid ripple of tiny waves at the lake's centre. It occurred to her that she was watching a lake freeze, whitening from its margins to its silver-dark centre, and she held her breath as if she dared not disturb this cold, still night beneath the ice-bright stars. Then she broke the silence with a laugh. 'I know what you mean. My family want me to be respectable. That's real important in Westfield.' She laughed. 'Get married, have kids, don't let the neighbours think you're odd. Shee-it. That's why I'm here.'

'So you can be odd?'

She shrugged, half smiling. 'So I can do what I want to do. Only I don't have a house like you. I don't have a studio. I share this garbage dump with a mad Dadaist and a cubist who thinks he's God's gift to women.' She shuddered. 'Still, it's better than the junior league and the welcome-wagon and all that shit.'

'You mean,' David said, 'that you're not here with your parents' blessing?'

'Sure! They're sweeties! But hell, they'd rather see me married to some clean-cut guy with a low golf handicap and a high mortgage.' She nodded towards the lake. 'If you watch that real carefully you can see it freeze over. It's weird!'

David leaned back to watch, not the lake, but Grace's profile. Moonlight silvered her parted lips and put cold fire in her wide eyes. The night was freezing, but he did not notice, for a great hawser was pulling apart his life to sunder him away from Christine.

He shivered suddenly and the thought struck David that he was sitting and talking with a girl as comfortably and casually as Hugh talked with Hilary. Even more startling was the realization that this American girl liked him, that she treated him with amusement and interest. He stared at her. For years he had poured all that he had and all that he wanted to be into Christine, yet now, as suddenly as the fall of a shooting star, he was looking at this girl's profile and feeling the agonies of yearning and it was as if a great light burgeoned in his head. Then, dream shattering like fragile ice, he knew he had denied himself choice, that he was trapped, and that the hawser could not be cut because upon his marriage depended Howarth and all its future.

'It's getting cold,' Grace said suddenly.

'Yes.' They walked slowly back towards Howarth and David feared that when they reached the house he would lose this girl for ever. He was lonely and she had responded to him with enthusiasm and he could not bear to think that this starlit meeting would be their only time together. 'Are you staying here long?' he asked.

'Hell, no. I have to be on a London train tomorrow.'

'I'm driving to town tomorrow. Would that help?'

She gave him her quick, vivacious smile. 'That'd be great. Thanks.'

'About six?'

'That'd be just perfect.'

He opened the door and ushered her into Howarth's warmth.

At the foot of the servants' stairs she paused and turned. 'Thanks again.'

He took her hand and, thinking himself daring, kissed it. 'Tomorrow.'

'Tomorrow.' She climbed the stairs into darkness, and David went to the Yellow Drawing Room, sat before a dying fire, and smoked a last cigarette. He was in love, and he was trapped, and his daydreams had a new focus and a new hope because he had met Grace.

Christine arrived in Monte Carlo to find Sir Edward Fenton staying in the Hotel de Paris where her father had his suite. Sir Edward had come to finalize the financial arrangements consequent on Lord de Conroy's South African visit.

'Have the Howarths started decorating the rooms?' de Conroy asked Edward at dinner.

'Indeed, my Lord.' Edward had visited Howarth and established that the rooms in the West Wing were being made ready for Christine and David. 'Your coat of arms is in every room.'

Kynaston laughed. 'And you're getting what you want, Christine?'

'Yes,' she said. She had demanded Chinese silk wallpaper in her bedroom and, though Pearl had protested, the expensive request had been granted. 'I thought you might like a sunken bath in your suite, daddy?'

'I fancy that.' De Conroy seemed delighted. 'Look after it for me, Edward. Gold taps. Something vulgar to offend Pearl.'

'Indeed, my Lord.' Edward made another jotting in his notebook that was filled with instructions for the care of Caton Hall, for this suite, and for the Lacewing that was moored in the harbour below. There were servants and pensions to pay, whores and old mistresses to be looked after, as well as the important task of making sure that the terms of the marriage contract were being obeyed.

Kynaston poured himself more wine. 'They're spending money like water on the damned place. Where does he get it all?'

273

'Some is Pearl's money, but their property firm is damned successful.'

'Must be the little Jew,' de Conroy said. 'Bloody clever of Arlington to find a tame kike.' He looked at his watch. 'My guests are coming. You want to stay, Edward?'

'No thank you, my Lord.' On winter nights the Lord de Conroy played poker with a retired American broker, a Frenchman who had made his fortune out of brothels that served the German army in the war, and a man who claimed to be an exiled Rumanian prince, but whom de Conroy suspected of being a professional gambler who simply wanted to add a little glitter to his otherwise drab life. Such company was not to Edward's taste.

'Perhaps,' his host said, 'you'll be kind enough to give Christine a nightcap?'

'I'd be delighted,' Edward lied. He had other plans for tonight, but he dared not refuse Christine's drab company. He took her down to the lavish bar beside the *Salle Empire* and was gentleman enough not to look ashamed of his companion.

Christine ordered a champagne cocktail and Edward a brandy. 'How does Arlington make his money?' she asked suddenly.

'Property,' he replied shortly, fussing with a cigar.

'I know that.' There was a hint of sharpness in Christine's voice. 'But how?'

Edward sighed. He had the telephone number and address of one of Monaco's finest houses, a place where women from throughout the Mediterranean catered discreetly for the most jaded of tastes, but first he must amuse this pallid girl. He willed her to drink the champagne cocktail swiftly, then take herself off to bed. 'It's really quite simple. Monsol owns a building. They sell a lease on it to someone who wants a guaranteed return for their money. Suppose the lease-holder wants a rental income of five hundred pounds a month?' He deliberately used a low figure to make it easier for Christine to grasp. 'The price of the lease is set by that rental return, but the clever bit is that Monsol leases the buildings back for the five hundred. So they sell the building and guarantee the return on the investment by paying it themselves. Then they sublet for seven hundred and fifty a month. Add a few noughts and that's the trick.'

274

Christine's face showed no reaction for a few seconds, then she nodded as if understanding had dawned. 'So they sell it and rent it at the same time?'

'Yes.'

'Clever,' she said.

'And very, very profitable.' Edward had caught some glimpses of Monsol's books during his negotiations with Arlington, and what he had seen had impressed him immensely. Sol Linsky had bought shrewdly in the years after the war, and Monsol had a portfolio of property that ranged from scarce sites in London's financial heart to wide tracts of provincial high streets that were now being developed into new self-service stores. Edward also had a hunch that the future would make Monsol's present profits look puny, and he was wondering how he could involve himself in those profits.

'Do you think,' Christine asked, 'that David will take it over after his father?'

'I don't think he's interested,' he replied casually.

'No.' Christine lit a cigarette, rather surprising Edward who was old-fashioned enough to dislike women smoking in public places. She frowned. 'But someone will have to run Monsol.'

'David can always put professional managers in.'

Christine thought about it. 'I might take an interest.'

'Why not?' he said patronizingly.

'David's useless!' she said scathingly. 'Someone in the family will have to protect the finances, won't they?'

Edward was startled by the sudden venom of her reply, and unsure how to react. Till now he had thought Christine's spite a girlish trait directed only at getting her rooms in Howarth decorated precisely as she wished, but now he heard an utter scorn of her fiancé that rather shocked him. 'Is he useless?' he asked cautiously.

'Entirely.' She said the word slowly and cuttingly.

Edward, who had been bored till this moment, frowned. 'If it isn't a rude qestion, why . . .'

'Because,' Christine cut in, 'he makes me a marchioness, doesn't he?'

'Indeed he does.'

'And you,' Christine stared at him, 'will make me a rich marchioness.'

Edward had never suspected the steel that was inside this small, pale girl. 'I will?'

She still held his gaze, challenging him, daring him to contradict her. 'You're clever with money, they say. Father can't live for ever and I'll need the best advice, won't I?'

'Indeed you will.'

'And father's not making money. It seems to me that if we take his property and Monsol's management skills then we have a perfect marriage, don't you agree?'

Edward was rapidly changing his opinion of Christine de Conroy. Far from being the wan, lost child of his previous appraisal, he was seeing a shrewdness that was startling. 'Yes.'

She smiled with thin lips. 'So in, say, twenty years I could be the richest woman in Europe? Apart from the Queen, maybe.'

'Yes.' Edward felt oddly trapped, as if her stoat-eyes were hypnotizing him. Yet what she said was true. To take de Conroy's vast holdings and add them to Monsol's arcane skills was a recipe for a fortune beyond imagination, and Christine, despised Christine, had seen it. This quiet, docile girl had grasped the real point of the marriage and Edward was quite sure that she had not shared this new wisdom with David. Except that Christine was not as docile as he had thought. There were very sharp teeth in that rabbit mouth, and a brain like a razor beneath the mousy hair. She had discovered the dream that he thought was his alone, for Edward, early in the marriage negotiations, had seen his chance to manipulate David when David inherited his wealth. Now, it seemed, Christine wished to do the same.

'I left a coat in the Lacewing,' she said abruptly. 'Will you walk down and fetch it with me?'

'Of course.'

She wanted to know more about the property business and, as they walked through the cool night beside the dark water, she quizzed him about plot-ratios and rents and leases and options and Edward was impressed by the swiftness of her understanding. He was also impressed by her ambition.

It was a searing, terrifying ambition, born out of the derision with which the world had treated her. Society had thought her plain, so society had pitied and despised Christine, counting her for nothing, but Edward saw now how this girl was quietly planning to use the money of her inheritance, and of David's inheritance, to take her revenge on the world.

They walked past the shrouded, dark shapes of the moored craft. A police car slowed down, but, seeing Edward's white silk scarf over his evening dress, accelerated on. Water lapped beneath the quay and creaked the ropes that held the expensive toys fast. 'I think it's a fair exchange,' Christine said abruptly.

'What is?'

'David wants Howarth, and I want Monsol.' She laughed. 'All he needs is amusement, nothing else. And he daren't divorce me! They lose Howarth if he divorces me, don't they?'

'Indeed they do.' Edward's astonishment reached new levels. This girl was more calculating than her father, greedier than Pearl, and more heartless than himself.

She took a key from her bag and unlocked the gate that barred the Lacewing's gangplank. The yacht was darkened and empty, its crew paid off for the winter, but the power was still connected to the dockside and Christine switched on the lights in the main saloon. 'I told the dockyard we'd be here.'

'That was thoughtful,' Edward said drily.

'I'll have a brandy.' Christine gestured at a cupboard, then went into the companionway that led to the cabins where, Edward presumed, the coat had been left.

He poured two brandies, then sat. He waited. The wind sighed in the radio aerials and the water made small noises on the hull. Monte Carlo in winter, he thought, was the end of the earth.

He considered Christine. It was a sneaking, bitter ambition that she had revealed and he saw how, given power, she would become a despot like Pearl, but with no Monty to restrain her. David would be no match for Christine, none. The Howarths had taken a vixen to their bosom and she would gnaw and claw at them until she had consumed them.

He finished the brandy, frowned, and looked at his watch. Nearly ten minutes had gone. He twisted to look into the companionway, but could neither see nor hear anything. 'Christine?'

'Have you got my brandy?' she called out.

Edward carried it down the passage. 'Where are you?'

'In here!' she called from the main stateroom.

Edward pushed open the door, stepped over the sill, and stopped. Christine lay on the bare mattress of the semi-circular bed with a blanket, evidently taken from a cupboard, covering her body.

'I wasn't feeling well,' she said. 'I'm sorry.'

'The brandy might help.'

'Yes.' She lay still and straight, her head on two pillows, making no effort to reach for the glass.

Edward sat on the bed. 'Here.' Her arms were still beneath the blanket. She seemed to be shivering and he wondered if she had a fever. 'Do you want it?'

She nodded, but made no other move.

'Here.' Edward put a hand beneath her head and put the glass to her lips, but it was still no good. 'You'll have to sit up,' he said. She was shaking and he wondered if he should call for an ambulance. 'Can you sit up?'

'I can't.'

'I'll help you.' He put the brandy beside the bed, turned back to her, and put his hand beneath the blanket to the small of her back, then froze.

She smiled. 'Well?'

Edward swallowed. His left hand, instead of encountering the wool suit she had worn at dinner, was on bare flesh.

'Well?'

'But . . .'

Her left arm snaked out from beneath the blanket and pulled his face down to hers. Edward, lost in confusion at the crazy events, let her pull his lips to hers. She kissed him fiercely, bruising his mouth with her small teeth, and her other arm linked behind his head and pulled him with surprising force down on to the bed.

Edward put his arms around her and, despite himself, caressed her thin body. The blanket slid down as she wrenched over him and he saw that she was utterly naked, white as a fish's belly, and he slid his hands to her small, hard breasts. She pulled at his

278

shirt front, snapping the studs, and he made one last effort to stop what he knew was wrong. 'Christine!'

'What?' She smiled. It was odd, Edward thought, but stripped bare there was something sexual about Christine, something provocative. Perhaps it was the very thinness of the body, or else the brazenness with which she flaunted it. There was nothing shy here, only a confidence that what she bestowed, he would enjoy. 'Well?' she asked.

'I shouldn't.'

'Of course you shouldn't,' she said. 'But I want to see if you can. You seem such a dry, dull thing, Edward. So quiet and smooth.'

The criticism stung him. He might be a courtier, knowing how to mix obsequiousness with useful skills, but in bed he prided himself on his abilities. 'Wait.' He pushed her away, swung himself off the bed, and undressed.

She watched him, her tongue just showing between her lips, then her white skinny arms reached for him and he went down on her. She writhed up to meet him and Edward, who thought he had paid for every experience a woman could give to a man, suddenly found there were pleasures he had not known existed. She was skill incarnate.

They finished on the floor, half-wrapped in the blanket, and she smiled at him, proud of herself. She saw the exhaustion and the admiration on his face, and kissed him. 'You were very good, Sir Edward.'

He laughed softly. 'And you. Did David teach you?'

'David!' she said scornfully.

'Then who?'

'Wouldn't you like to know?' Then, unable to resist the boast, she smiled. 'I bed who I like and when I like and I especially like doing it in Howarth or in David's house.' She watched his face to see if he was shocked, then reached up, found her bag, and took out her cigarettes. She lit one, blew smoke past Edward's face, then kissed his mouth. 'I think we can work together, don't you?'

'Yes,' Edward said. He would not have dared say anything else.

279

'I want Monsol, you see. I want Monsol, the trust, and my father's holdings. If they can be united, Edward, and administered from one office, they'll make a fortune. I want a small staff and a very discreet one.' She smiled at him. 'Like this. I want you and me to work together.'

Edward, still entangled with her, saw the vast extent of her dreams. 'And David? Howarth?'

'David can be kept happy. And once his father's gone, what does Howarth matter? I don't think there's a future in Britain, do you?' she asked seriously.

'Not much of one.' Edward tried to convince himself that this conversation was really happening and bent to kiss one small breast as if to shatter the dream. The dream did not shatter. Christine, her legs twined hard round his hips, was calmly discussing the empire she would build when Monty was dead and her husband had inherited the wealth of Monsol. 'Will that little kike Linsky be a problem?'

'He can be bought out,' Edward said.

'You think about how we do it,' Christine said. 'And I want daddy's accounts sent to me from now on. You can do that?'

It was a hard request for an accountant to refuse when he was engaged in coition with a client's daughter. 'Of course.'

Christine puffed at her cigarette, then turned her face to his. 'If I had my chin built up and my eyes reshaped, what would you think?'

Edward, ever gallant, smiled. 'How could you be improved, my dear?'

'I will be,' Christine said. 'When we're finished, Edward, we'll have the damned world at our feet.' She smiled. 'And then we'll kick it.' She dropped the cigarette into the brandy glass, then tightened the grip of her thighs. 'Are you glad you took me for a nightcap?'

'Oh yes,' Sir Edward said, for this night had decided his future and tomorrow, when he returned to England, he knew just what he must do.

For Edward, shrewd behind his careful, calculated exterior, saw that this girl was not a maker or a builder, but a destroyer of lives. She would use every man and when she had sucked them

280

dry she would spit the husks out to make way for her next conquest.

He knew what time to scotch a snake, not when it was fully grown and fanged and hissing, but when it was in the egg. That time was now, and Christine had shown him how. He was glad he had come to this cabin and that he had lain with this girl-child because now he would betray her; because, if he did not, she would destroy him.

The Lord de Conroy laid down a straight flush, his daughter clawed at Edward's back, and, in the balances of greed and lust, Howarth trembled.

Monty did a good deal of quiet soothing that winter in preparation for Pearl's joining of the Monsol board. No one in the company's new St James's offices relished the thought, for, though her money might bring expansion and opportunity, it would also bring the Marchioness.

She arrived in a brand-new, pearl-grey Rolls-Royce with a chauffeur in matching uniform. He opened the car door while a commissionaire, medal ribbons bright in the winter's gloom, held open the office doors, and thus Pearl, with a brand-new briefcase of Spanish leather in her right hand, made a dignified entrance to her new responsibilities.

Gloria Cockerel had been deployed to meet her Ladyship on the top floor. 'That coat ain't 'arf lovely!'

Somehow the greeting rocked Pearl who, in truth, was as nervous as any of the people who awaited her coming. 'Thank you.'

'My mum had one like that. She got it in Southend.' Monty had picked Gloria as the official welcomer, reckoning that no one short of a crowned monarch would manage to subdue her. 'Well, me dad got it really. Off the back of a lorry, if you know what I mean.' Gloria gave a huge smile. Her husband had done well out of Monsol contracts, but she would not give up working for Sol. 'The board meeting's in 'ere,' she said.

'Thank you.' Pearl wondered why she had not insisted on more politeness.

'It's all right, I'm coming in. I take the minutes, see?' Gloria pushed into the room behind her. 'You want the coffee now, Monty?'

'Please, my darling.'

Sol grinned. So far, he reckoned, so good.

Pearl waited for Gloria to take her coat, but the offer was not forthcoming so she hung it herself on a bentwood stand. Southend, indeed! The coat, a powder-blue cape with leg of mutton sleeves, had come from Rome!

The coffee was served. Sol was jacketless with metal expanding rings holding up his shirtsleeves. The smoke from his cheroot drifted towards Pearl who was caught between it and moving closer to Gloria. Snobbery won over suffering and Pearl stayed where she was.

'If we're ready?' Monty said. 'Chairman?'

'Chairman?' Pearl bristled at the word.

Monty smiled. 'Sol.'

'But . . .'

'We voted before you arrived,' he said. 'Sol and I cast two votes so I don't think we can be outvoted.'

Pearl closed her mouth. It was ridiculous that a man like Sol Linsky should be Chairman of Monsol instead of the Marquess of Arlington, but she recognized that Monty was protecting Sol's pride and she was sensible enough to say nothing more.

The early business was dealt with swiftly enough and without clashes. Pearl had always taken an interest in the firm's affairs, and found that she could follow the discussion even when Sol became technical and began talking about reversions and head-leases and shell companies. To her surprise Gloria chipped in often, usually about technical building matters, and was heard with respect.

Sol had expected and dreaded a show of strength from the Marchioness, but after the first *frisson* when Monty announced

282

the chairmanship, she was wonderfully subdued. Even when Sol sought the board's formal approval for the way he had invested Pearl's million pounds, she gave her nod without the smallest query. Pearl had oddly allowed the money to be invested without any involvement in the decision herself and Sol took it as a sign of her commercial naïvety.

Thus the board meeting was surprisingly pleasant-tempered and Sol reached the end of his jotted agenda with a feeling that he had misjudged Pearl. Put her in Howarth and surround her with the trappings of majesty and she became a tyrant, but in this man's world of a boardroom, with its cigars, cheroots and whisky waiting for the meeting's end, she was as tame as a de-clawed pussy-cat. He smiled. 'That's all, then, isn't it?'

Monty nodded and Gloria closed her notebook.

'There is one other matter,' Pearl said.

There was silence.

Gloria looked to Sol and Monty, received no help, and so re-opened her book. 'Do I call it Any Other Business?'

'Yes,' Sol said, 'you do.' He looked at Pearl. 'My Lady?'

'Tax,' Pearl said firmly, surprising both men. 'Last year a company we own,' she looked at the papers before her, 'the Exeter Magneto Company, paid over fifteen thousand pounds in tax. Why?'

Sol shrugged. He patiently explained that shell companies, defunct businesses bought off the shelf in the Stock Exchange, could not offset old losses if the nature of their business was changed. Exeter Magneto, whatever its old name, was now a property company, one of the slew of such companies that existed so that Monsol could circumvent the controls on financial borrowing. 'So we've cleared its debts,' he said, 'and now we can use the company to . . .'

'I know that,' Pearl said brusquely. 'But if we'd declared a small profit in year one we could have offset the losses in year two. We'd have paid none of the tax.'

Monty frowned, hearing an expertise he had not suspected. Gloria scribbled. Sol, fighting down his resentment at Pearl's imperious tone, thought about her statement and found that the Marchioness spoke good sense. 'Yes,' he said slowly, 'it could well mean that. We'd have to check with Bradley and Mallermine, of course.'

'Bradley and Mallermine,' Pearl spoke the accountants' names scathingly, 'are letting us down. We should not take such ideas to them, they should bring them to us before the loss is incurred. I propose a new accountant for the firm. Someone who can bring some expertise to this board.'

There was silence. Both Monty and Sol had been wrong-footed. They had played their small game with Pearl, making Sol chairman and using Gloria to puncture the Marchioness's dignity, but it seemed Pearl had not come as empty-handed as they had thought. What was more she was not just discussing a change of accountants, but had mentioned the word 'board'. She wanted a new director.

'Who?' Sol's hostility was obvious.

Pearl sprang her surprise. 'Sir Edward Fenton.'

'No!' Sol said. 'No. No and no and no. No.'

'I take that,' Pearl said cuttingly, 'as a single vote against my proposal. Monty?'

Monty stared at his wife. She was a clever woman, and she had a good business mind, but he had never before heard her express any knowledge of company tax. 'You've spoken to Fenton already, haven't you? You've shown him our statements.' He could not hide his astonishment that his wife should have shown confidential papers to an enemy of the family. Perhaps David's marriage made him into a wary ally, but the marriage was still four months off and, till then, and until the trust was formed, Monty would avoid entanglements with the likes of Sir Edward Fenton.

Pearl matched his stare. 'A person investing a million pounds in a business has every right to seek whatever advice she chooses.'

Monty's voice was stark. 'And what price did you offer for Sir Edward's advice?'

Pearl, for the first time since she had proposed Fenton's name, looked uncomfortable. 'He's an ambitious young man.'

'And I'm a suspicious one,' Monty snapped. 'If you've offered any undertakings on behalf of this board, any, then we have a right to know.' Sol opened his mouth, but he motioned him to silence. 'Have you made any undertakings?'

'Of course not,' Pearl lied.

Monty knew it was a lie, but equally he knew that the lie could not be exposed here and now. Pearl was playing some game and she was keeping her cards hidden. He would not have it, and shook his head. 'I vote against.'

Gloria winked at Sol, who smiled with relief. Monty, as Sol had known he would, had stood by him. 'I think,' he said mildly, 'that the motion is defeated.'

Pearl smiled an acid smile. 'I doubt whether Monsol would endure if I withdrew my funds now?' Her voice, like a whip, rose above the mounting protests. 'And it can be withdrawn, which would force you to borrow heavily and over-extend.' She paused, and both men now understood why she had let her money be invested before this board meeting. The market now knew of the injection of capital, and it would turn on Monsol if the capital was suddenly withdrawn. Pearl, pleased with her carefully prepared threat, smiled. 'I really cannot see the wisdom of frittering away my few savings in a firm that will not use the best possible advice on taxation. Still, if that is this board's decision?'

'You can't . . .' Sol started.

'Pearl!' Monty said at the same time.

'I intend to withdraw my money.' Pearl stood. 'And I shall announce it to the financial press this afternoon. Good day.'

'Wait!' Monty snarled.

'I do not care to be spoken to . . .'

'I said wait! Gloria? Take her Ladyship to her office. It's time you saw it, Pearl. You can decide what wallpaper you want.'

Pearl shot Monty a savage look, but she sensed that the men would change their minds about Edward if she left them alone and so, with a shrug, she let Gloria open the door and lead her down the corridor beyond.

The two men sat in silence for a few seconds.

'Sod it,' Monty said.

Sol, agitated, shook his head. 'I knew it! I knew it!'

'Sol!'

'She goes behind our backs! It's all arranged, isn't it? Who

285

cares what Sol Linsky thinks? He's just an emotional old Jew and one day he'll die and Pearl can take the bloody firm!' Sol stood and began pacing the office. 'And Fenton! A sneaking little anti-Semite! He hates me! Oh, he's clever! He should be Jewish, he's so clever. But he's a snake, Monty!'

Monty nodded. 'What happens if she withdraws her cash?'

'Nothing!' Sol said, but his nervous anger belied the word.

'The banks will hammer us!'

'Firms have taken a hammering before! We'd survive.'

Monty rubbed his face. 'Not if the banks called in their loans, Sol. We'd be dead.'

'You see? You're on her side. Blood!' Sol said the word dramatically, 'it's thicker than water, yes? Thicker than friendship! There'll be me, Sol Linsky, and all you goys! All my work, all my hopes, all for some toffee-nosed boy who thinks the SS were boy scouts in sharp uniforms!'

'Sol . . .'

'Last week,' Sol said, unable to check his grief, 'it was you and me. Just you and me! Now it's her, and now it'll be him! All against me! All! I knew it would happen! I knew!' He turned on Monty. 'You think she's right, don't you? You think we ought to have Fenton!'

Monty stared at the table. 'I think she's promised it to him, and I don't know why. But I think she'll carry out her threat if we don't support her.' Sol's grief, he thought, was not aimed at Sir Edward Fenton, whom he hardly knew, but was a lamentation because Pearl had come on to the board. It was Pearl Sol disliked, but loyalty would not let him attack her to Monty so he had dug his heels in against Fenton instead.

Sol sniffed and sat down. 'Now we're all respectable, we have to have a knight on the board! We mustn't let people think a little Shylock runs Monsol, not while Lady Pearl is there. How soon before you all vote me off, eh? Tell me that?'

'Sol . . .'

'No! You think I don't know! You think I'm a putz!'

Monty leaned over and took Gloria's notebook. He found an empty page, tore it out of the book, and scribbled on it. He read the words aloud as he wrote. 'I hereby relinquish my vote on the

286

matter of appointing Sir Edward Fenton on to the board of Monsol Ltd and its associated companies, and assign said vote to Solomon Linsky, friend and putz. Signed, Arlington.' He pushed the paper towards Sol. 'There. Now you can outvote her.'

Sol stared at the proxy vote, trying to see the catch. 'Why?'

'Because we're friends,' Monty said with simple truth.

Sol, as Monty had known he would, sniffed back tears. 'You want Fenton, don't you?'

'I don't think we can endure the withdrawal of Pearl's money,' Monty said quietly, 'and I think she's made a bargain with him and I'm damn sure she won't tell us what it is, at least not before the vote. I also think that what can be voted for today can be unvoted another day. So I'd vote yes, but I don't have a vote any longer.'

Sol nodded understanding, but still frowned. 'It'll be two and two, Monty. We can't vote him off! And when you're away, Monty, it's two of them against me, isn't it? And you tell me you won't be here so much! You've got Howarth now, so you'll go off and kill God's creatures! And leave me to her and Fenton!'

'Trust me,' Monty said. 'You won't be outvoted.'

'You think I'm that much of a putz?' Sol smiled. 'OK, so I am. Shall we bring the ladies back?'

Pearl was suspicious as she came into the room, and even more suspicious when she saw the smile on Sol's face. She looked at Monty. 'So?'

Monty said nothing. Instead he stood, walked to the window, and lifted a slat of the blind to stare down into a wintry St James's.

Sol cleared his throat. 'We have a proposal on the table to appoint Sir Edward Fenton to this board. I suggest that we now vote on that proposal, and accordingly cast my vote against. Lady Arlington?'

Pearl frowned, sensing that something was wrong, but unable to trace it in Sol's formal words. 'I vote for, most strongly.' She looked at Monty's back. 'Monty?'

He turned from the window and smiled. 'Sol has my vote. He can do what he likes with it.'

'But . . .'

'Sol has my vote!'

Pearl, appalled, gathered her handbag. 'In that case . . .'

'I haven't finished yet!' Sol snapped the words. 'I have used my vote, but not Monty's. I need to think.'

'This is ridiculous!' Pearl said.

'I have to think,' Sol said, 'what is best for this company.' He leaned back in his chair and clicked his lighter to his recalcitrant cheroot. He puffed smoke towards Pearl. 'We've always been a friendly company, my Lady. We use each other with respect. I think the best thing is if we try to go on using each other with respect. Board members who threaten to use their wealth to destroy the company are behaving childishly, stupidly, without respect! Don't you agree?' Pearl, hearing these words spoken in front of Gloria, said nothing, but merely looked daggers. If this was the price she must pay to win, then she would pay it because Edward on Monsol's board was an Edward who had the power to keep the bargain he had made with her just two weeks before. Sol smiled. 'I don't know how Monty will vote on this thing, but I have to cast his vote, so,' he pushed a hand into his trouser pocket and brought out some coins, 'I'll toss for it.'

'Monty!' Pearl said, 'stop this nonsense!'

'But I'm enjoying it,' Monty said.

'This is no way to run a company. You're making a mockery out of it!' She stared at the bright penny Sol had selected.

Sol shrugged. 'Heads and Sir Edward joins the board. Agreed?'

Pearl said nothing. 'Agreed,' Monty said.

'You don't have a vote, Monty, so be quiet.' Sol flicked the coin and let it fall on his blotter. It bounced once, twisted brightly, then settled.

'Heads,' Pearl said triumphantly.

'Then I use my second vote,' Sol said, 'in favour. The motion is carried two to one.'

Pearl had won her victory.

Monty sat at the table again. 'One other thing. When I'm away, as I intend to be away from time to time, my vote at board meetings will be used by the Chairman.'

'Agreed,' Sol said.

'And in the event of a tied vote,' Monty said, 'the Chairman has the casting vote.'

'Shall I put that down as carried?' Gloria asked.

'Please,' said Sol. He collected his papers, then smiled at Pearl. 'A very satisfactory first board meeting, don't you think?'

Pearl, despite her victory, did not think so. When she was left alone with Monty she exploded with pent-up anger. 'You humiliated me! Deliberately! In front of that girl! I will not be spoken to like that, Monty, I will not . . .'

Monty brought his right hand down on to the table like a gunshot. The noise, with its hint of violence, shocked Pearl into silence. His voice, when he spoke, was angrier than hers had been. 'I have lied for you, cheated for you, and worked for you. Whatever you wanted, Pearl, you have had. I will go on doing that. I will go on paying for Howarth and I won't raise a single objection to anything you do with the house. I will even welcome that titless little wonder into my family as the price for Howarth. All that I will do, Pearl, but if you ever again decide to make me choose between you and Solomon Linsky, then I will divorce you, I will expose your lies, and I will kick you out of Howarth and back to the brick house you came from. Do you understand?' Monty paused, but she said nothing. He stood. 'So what price are we paying for Edward?'

Pearl, crushed by his implacable voice, looked up at him. 'Price?'

'Don't fool with me!' Monty snapped. 'We don't give Edward Fenton a director's fees because he's got a pretty face and can add up. What arrangement have you made with him?'

'I haven't made any,' Pearl said. 'I think he will be most useful to this firm, that's all.'

Monty was silent for a second or two, then spoke in a chill voice that was far more terrifying than his earlier rage. 'Until David's marriage, Pearl, Howarth is leased to the Arlington Trust of which I am the principal trustee. If you do not answer me to my satisfaction in the next thirty seconds then I will relinquish the lease and lose you Howarth tomorrow.' He spoke the threat with a calmness that made the incredible credible. 'I will not have people making arrangements behind my back, and I do not propose to reward you and your friends for deception. Make up your mind. Howarth or the truth.'

Pearl chose the truth, for she dared not lose Monty. She was a director of the firm now, and a wealthy woman in her own right, but without Monty she had no position in society, none. So she told him all that Edward had told her, all.

Christine was a whore. Not in the strict sense, perhaps, but in every other sense. Christine only wanted Monsol, and Monsol's money, and one day she would even abandon Howarth as a drain on her resources.

Monty listened, at first disbelieving, then slowly convinced. He had watched David these last months, through the painfully long engagement, and everything that Pearl so hesitantly said made sense. 'Why did Edward tell you?'

'Because he thinks Christine will take everything.'

'Leaving nothing for him?'

She nodded. That also made sense to Monty. Edward Fenton was ambitious. He wanted power and money and influence, but not through Christine, for he had perceived that she would not share her influence with anyone. Edward, seeing the future that Christine had planned, wanted to change sides.

'So what you're saying,' Monty said carefully, 'is that when the trust is set up, we'll have Edward's vote?'

'Yes.' Pearl stared beseechingly at Monty. 'Don't you understand? We'll have three votes and de Conroy will only have two!'

'Which will only matter,' Monty said scathingly, 'if there's a divorce. Are you planning on a divorce, Pearl?'

Pearl said nothing. Tyres hissed on the sleet-wet street outside, a taxi engine throbbed then whined away, and still she said nothing.

Monty sat opposite her. 'You'd let your son marry a whore?'

'For Howarth,' Pearl said softly, almost in a whisper.

'A whore?'

'Why should we lose Howarth because she's a slut?' She blazed the question at Monty. 'If they don't marry I lose Howarth. If they do marry I keep it, and if David has to divorce her for me to keep Howarth, then he'll have to do that!'

'No!' Monty slammed his hand on the table again.

'No?' Pearl had recovered her spirit now. 'This isn't a marriage about love, Monty! It's about property! It's an aristocratic marriage!'

'You'd know about that, wouldn't you? Where did they teach you about aristocratic marriage, Pearl? At Sunday school? Keep your knees together and hang on to the deeds of the house? Is that what you think aristocratic marriage is?'

'Yes!' She spat the word out. 'What would you call our marriage, Monty, if not an arrangement?'

Monty rubbed his face. In some ways Pearl was right. The point of an aristocratic marriage was to amass a fortune to surround the family's pride so that, no matter how hard the taxman cut, the blade could not reach the heart. Younger sons could marry for love or, as Monty had done, for lust, but not the heir. And David, by marrying Christine, was marrying well. She might be a slut. She might, if Edward was right, open her legs to any man who wandered past, but she made Howarth safe. 'She has to be curbed,' he said tiredly.

'Curbed?' Pearl asked.

'Curbed.' Monty repeated the word because the pride of a family was more than its house, more than its coat of arms, more than all its possessions. A marquess could marry a whore and make her a lady, but a lady who became a whore never changed. 'She must be taught how to behave,' he said at last.

'You'll talk to her?' Pearl was shocked.

'I'll talk to both of them.'

'Monty!' Pearl's voice was a wail, for she saw Howarth lost.

'The girl's a fool,' he said, 'but I've seen what foolishness unforgiven does to a woman.' He was thinking of Sophie. 'Christine deserves her chance.'

'But . . .'

'God damn it! I should break the engagement off, shouldn't I?' His anger was back. 'But I've got your greed, Pearl. I'm caught in it, soiled in it, because I want Howarth, too! But the least we can do is pay the price we agreed for the house, and that price is Christine. And David has some say, doesn't he?' Monty waited for an answer he knew would not come. 'Good day!'

Pearl sat for a long time when he had gone. Snow began to

fall softly in the street outside, then turned again to sleety rain and she wondered how she could survive if the engagement was broken and her hopes for Howarth were no more. But there was nothing to be done, nothing but to wait and let Monty pursue his damned chivalry and give Christine her chance that could break Pearl and the house for which she had married, for which she had borne children, and which she might now lose. Howarth.

It was the kind of day Monty loved; a cold day on which the winter light gave the countryside a metallic gleam of white and grey. The clouds were hazy and the sun was nothing but a pale silver disc low in the southern sky. Walking a stubble field with a gun under his arm and dogs at his heels, he pointed to a reed-thatched cottage half hidden by a stand of alders. 'There used to be an old fellow in that cottage who made game kites. Ever seen one?'

'No.' Sir Edward Fenton, dressed in carefully contrived tweeds, was nervous. He had been invited to Howarth for this day's rough shooting, but he suspected that the fate of far more than a few pheasants and partridges was involved.

A game kite, Monty explained, was like a child's kite, but smaller and made from black cloth cut and stretched into the shape of a hovering hawk. One man would fly the kite from behind a hedge and the enemy shape, quivering in the sky at the end of its string, would freeze partridges in the stubble. Partridges were nervous, fast birds, difficult to poach, but once immobilized by the sight of their natural enemy they were easy prey for the second man who would simply walk the field and knock the birds over.

'Fascinating,' Edward said.

'Yours.' A questing dog had startled a cock pheasant which, tail feathers drooping, climbed fast into the wintry sky. Edward took it high and late, neatly dropping the bird with a head shot that killed it instantly. 'Well done,' Monty said.

The retriever fetched the bird and dropped it at his master's feet. Edward put it into his game bag. 'You saw the revenue proposals I made?'

'Indeed I did.' Monty broke his gun, knowing that Edward's shot would mean no new targets for a few moments. 'Why don't we cut towards the Meal Dyke?'

'Of course.'

'The proposals seemed excellent,' Monty said, 'quite excellent. If Sol gives his approval, we'll implement them.'

'Good.' Edward's nervousness increased with every moment that Monty did not discuss Christine. Edward was now a Monsol director, but he sensed that without Monty's support he would be nothing.

Far behind the two men, silvery pale in the wintry haze, Howarth was beautiful. Monty stopped at a gap in a frosted blackthorn hedge and stared at it. 'That's the game kite, isn't it?'

'I'm sorry?'

'Howarth. Everyone knows I want Howarth, so they hold it above me like a threat in the hope that I'll freeze. And who's sneaking round my back, Edward?'

'My Lord?'

Monty's gaze, as cold as the winter's day, turned on him. 'Pearl tells me that Christine wants to win the pot. She wants to take her father's money, my money, and Monsol. She's doing quite well, isn't she? She's obviously Kynaston's heiress, she's marrying my heir, and now she's got a lover on Monsol's board. Clever, very clever.'

Edward was embarrassed. 'It's not like that.'

'So you say,' Monty said equably. 'Mine.' He closed his gun, raised it, and dropped a brace of high pheasants with the same efficiency that Edward had shown earlier. 'But how do I know it's not like that, eh?'

Edward said nothing, but merely followed Monty around the edge of a ploughed field towards the glimmer of water beyond.

'Oh I know you tell us your vote is ours at the right moment,' Monty said, 'but how do I know? After all, Pearl bribed you with a directorship, so why shouldn't Kynaston bribe you back again? I think you're sitting rather pretty, don't you? All your options are open, Edward. You can pick your own side now and give it victory.'

'It isn't like that,' Edward repeated feebly.

293

'If you say so, but how have you explained your new appointment to Kynaston?'

Edward shrugged. 'I wrote and told him that it gives me an insight into your finances.'

'Exactly. De Conroy thinks you're spying on me, while you tell me that in truth you're on my side now. But I want proof of that.'

'Proof?' Edward wondered what proof he could offer other than the revelations he had brought about Christine. He rehearsed them again, telling Monty all that she had boasted of, and describing, with assumed self-disgust, his own evening on the Lacewing. He told of Christine's ambition, of his own conviction that, given power, she would share it with no one.

Monty listened to it all without any show of surprise. 'But what happens,' he asked mildly, 'if the marriage doesn't take place?'

'Doesn't?' Edward's voice betrayed his shock. 'But if . . .'

'If they don't marry,' Monty said, 'I lose Howarth.'

'Yes.' Edward stared at the Marquess.

'Do you really think,' he gestured at the beautiful building that was so serene in the half mist, 'that Howarth is worth a whore in the family? Don't you think, Edward, that the decent thing is to call off this shambles of a marriage?'

Edward did not. David's happiness was not of the smallest concern to him, and David, by marrying Christine, could unite the great fortunes that he wanted one day to control.

Monty understood what was happening. He could sense that the younger generation, like leashed hounds, manoeuvred for the moment when the leashes would be slipped. David alone seemed uninterested in inheriting great wealth, while Edward had glimpsed that his chance of control lay in being Monty's protégé, not de Conroy's, for Christine would take her father's power. 'You'd call off the marriage?' Edward asked with shock.

'Not my job. That's up to David. But if it is called off I'm going to be in trouble, aren't I? De Conroy's going to sue for breach of promise. He's going to tell a court that his titless daughter was promised a life in Howarth, money, and that, with the engagement broken, she will have suffered emotional grief and financial loss. I don't give a tinker's curse for her grief, but I care like hell about giving up Howarth and paying the little whore cash. So what I need is a weapon to defend myself against that. I need proof that Christine opened her legs during the engagement. I need an affidavit from you, Edward, duly sworn, duly signed, and duly in my safe.'

Edward's reluctance to provide the document was not because he planned to double-cross Monty, but because he did not relish dictating his memories of the Monaco night to a lawyer's secretary.

Monty misunderstood his hesitation, and his voice took on a silky edge of pure menace. 'If I don't have the document within a week, Edward, then you will no longer be on my board, there will be malicious rumours in the City concerning your standards of honesty, and Kynaston de Conroy will hear of our conversations. I think we might stroll back, don't you?'

The document, duly signed and sealed, was with Monty inside the week.

He felt the temptation not to use it, to let sleeping dogs lie, but he also thought he could not see his son destroyed by a sly bitch. So, on a cold day, he drove to Howarth where he knew Christine was furnishing her private apartments. He used his key to let himself into the lavish drawing room that was now dominated by the de Conroy crest of black martlets on a yellow field. Pictures were stacked against the walls, waiting to be hung, and new furniture was still shrouded in its protective paper wrapping.

He heard laughter upstairs, the rush of feet, then silence. David, Monty knew, was in London.

He had made no sound entering the private rooms. Christine's fur coat was dropped on a chair, her handbag beside it, while a man's coat was discarded on the floor.

He moved, silent as a hunter, to the foot of the stairs. He could hear voices, quieter now, murmuring from the upper rooms, and he sensed that all he needed to do was climb the stairs and he would find her in bed.

Christine was a whore. She liked to risk things, Edward said. She liked to use the beds of Howarth, or David's bed; she liked the taste of daring in her life. Monty had known such girls before. He remembered one, now a duchess, who had slept with him during her own honeymoon. He had been young then, stupid as the duchess herself, but sense and discretion had come in time. Perhaps, he told himself, discretion would come to Christine, too.

He knew he should climb the stairs. The honour of Howarth was in his grasp, but so was its future, and he hesitated.

The marriage solved so much. It saved Monty from the need to work like a dog for the remote chance that de Conroy would one day sell him Howarth. He had already warned Sol that henceforth he would be in London less for, with no need to amass a vast fortune any more, Monty dreamed of days in wintry mists as the hounds gave tongue and the horse's ears pricked forward to the huntsman's horn, of coming home to buttered toast and anchovy relish, and to whisky by a big log fire: country matters in a country house.

Yet those pleasures would be bought by the body of a girl who despised David, despised Howarth, a whore.

So Monty hesitated at the foot of the stairs. If he climbed them now and found Christine then he could only do one thing: cancel the wedding.

Laughter sounded again, then there was another rush of feet on the carpet, and the sound had the light quality of bare feet running, and Monty turned abruptly away.

He let himself out of the apartment as silently as he had entered it and despised himself all the long road to London.

'Brick Street, my Lord?' Hammond asked.

'Limerston Street.'

It was almost dark when the Rolls stopped in the quiet Chelsea street and Monty climbed the steps and knocked on the green-painted door. He was not sure why he had come here, or what he could say, but he knew he could not let David walk like an innocent to the slaughter.

'Father!' David seemed astonished and more than a little embarrassed by his unexpected presence. 'Come in, please.' He led Monty into the living room. 'You know Grace, of course.'

'Hi!' Grace Dunwoody, dressed in a fetching white sweater and with jeans tight on her long legs, uncurled from the hearth-rug.

Monty could not place the girl for a moment, then he recognized the legs. 'You're the sculptress!'

'That's it! Still chiselling away, my Lord.' She leaned over and, with a gesture that spoke of her familiarity with this room, lifted the gramophone arm from a record. 'I guess you don't want jungle music, right?'

Monty smiled at her. 'I wonder if you'd be very kind and let me talk with David?'

'Sure!' Grace scooped up a coat and handbag. 'I was going anyway. I'll see you, David.' She grinned at him, raised an eyebrow to Monty, and was gone.

'She was just returning a record,' David said in some embarrassment.

'I'd rather forgotten about her,' Monty said. He stared into David's tiny back garden and saw that someone had designed a stone bench around a raised flower bed. Somehow the care and neatness of the design did not match David's character. 'You see a lot of Grace, do you?'

'Oh, no,' he said a little too swiftly.

Monty turned from the window. 'She's extraordinarily beautiful.'

'Is she?' David said altogether too innocently. 'Yes, I suppose she is.'

Monty fingered a small, black-lacquered, metal sculpture that stood on top of a bookshelf. 'Hers?'

'Yes.'

'She makes rather a contrast to Christine.'

'I suppose she does, yes.' David, dressed in faded corduroys and a shabby cricket sweater, blushed.

'Bedding her, are you?' Monty asked suddenly.

David started at the question, then blushed even more deeply. 'No.'

'I wouldn't blame you. The first time I saw her I thought she'd be worth trying. But not in front of your mother.' He smiled. 'Is that whisky?'

'I'm sorry.' David hurried across the room and poured two whiskies.

Monty sat on the sofa that was covered with a rather good piece of quiltwork. 'American?' he asked fingering it.

'I think so.'

Monty caught his son's eye, held it, then laughed. 'You lucky bugger!'

David, too embarrassed to say anything, just shrugged.

Monty thought how full of surprises the world was. Two weeks ago he had thought David and Christine a shy, ordinary couple, yet now he had discovered that both were having affairs. The knowledge made this visit somewhat easier. He sipped his whisky. 'Do I take it that things aren't too clever between you and Christine?'

Thrown by this sudden visit and unused to such intimacy with his father, David frowned. He felt as if he had been caught out, like a small boy scrumping. 'They're all right.'

'All right,' Monty repeated. 'What does that mean?'

David looked into his father's eyes. He had detected a harder note in the last question, and he supposed that his father feared that Howarth might be lost if the engagement was broken. 'I mean all right,' he said stubbornly. 'She's away a lot, though.'

'And Grace?'

'She's a friend,' David said defiantly.

Monty stared at his son. He disliked David's nervousness that so annoyed Pearl, yet he also saw a stubborn streak in him, deep down, and one day, when it surfaced, it might yet prove to be made of unbreakable steel. 'Have you fallen out of love?' he asked gently.

'Love?' David paused as if making a decision where to lead the conversation. He could keep it light and untruthful, or plunge into the discomfort of honesty. He chose prevarication. 'We've rather manhandled that word, haven't we? I'm not sure I know what it means.'

'So you have fallen out of love,' Monty said flatly.

'I don't know,' David said. He stood and walked to the window and, staring at the garden Grace had made, plumped for honesty. 'I think I felt pity for Christine and confused that with love. But

298

she's not really as helpless as everyone thinks. Then everything got rather venal, didn't it?' He shrugged. 'I mean it started as love, but it became a marriage to suit a board of trustees.'

Monty thought he heard echoes of long, agonizing talks into deep, exciting nights and he imagined the American girl curled on the rug, talking and talking, and he rather admired his son for having won such a rare prize. Perhaps, Monty thought, David was one of those sons who always show a better face to strangers than to their parents. 'You sound as if you don't want to marry Christine any more.'

'If I had the choice today?' He turned from the window, then stopped.

'Well?'

'I wouldn't,' David said defiantly.

Monty smiled to show that he was not angered by the answer. 'Has she done something to annoy you?'

'No. I wish she had.'

'And Grace?'

There was a flash of anger on David's face, as though Grace was a subject too precious to be discussed. 'She doesn't want to marry me,' he said bitterly.

'So you did ask her?'

David paused, then, in the mood for sour truths, nodded. 'Yes.' He crossed to the table and found his cigarettes. 'But she's too busy with her work. I'm just a friend.'

'So,' Monty said gently, 'what conclusions do you reach in the long soul-searching nights?' He saw his son's startled look, and smiled. 'We all had them, David. Maybe your mother didn't, but I did. Mine was a rather pretty Scottish girl. We talked till the words went round in circles, talked and talked. All the world's ills, all our own ills, then she buggered off and married a travelling salesman. So?'

David was in no mood to smile. He stared at the carpet, then shrugged. 'I have asked a girl to marry me and she has said yes. By marrying her I bring Howarth back to the family, and for that small gift I assume that my mother will give me peace. I will also become rich and, because I am not like you, and doubt whether I can ever be like you, I am grateful for that. I shall doubtless

299

become an eccentric peer and I shall doubtless come to a compromise with my wife. Will that do?' David had nerved himself to make the speech and, because it hurt his real desires to speak it, there were tears in his eyes as he finished.

'But you'd rather marry Grace?'

'Yes!' He shouted the word, then, ashamed of showing emotion in front of his father, shrugged. 'I'm sorry.'

'Don't be.'

David sat again. 'But Grace doesn't want to marry.'

Monty smiled. 'But she could presumably stay as your mistress after marriage?'

David shrugged as though the question was distasteful.

Monty stood. 'It isn't actually any business of yours, but I don't think I've shared a bedroom with your mother more than a dozen times in the last two years.' He saw that David wanted to protest, so he held up his hand. 'No, let me speak. It doesn't matter, David. The marriage works. We have one thing in common, Howarth. It's insane, if you like, but we're enslaved to it. We work to keep it intact and we bred an heir to fill it when we're gone. That's our duty, you see, because we're aristocrats. We have to entertain the populace and die for our country. We're also part of the scenery, and people want us to live in damned great museums. And you're right. That's why we marry: to keep the damned houses.'

'You don't have to convince me,' David said grimly.

'Perhaps I have to convince myself, then. I've had a dozen mistresses I'd rather spend my life with than your mother. I've got one now. I tell her my fears, I weep on her shoulder, I laugh with her.' David looked up at the word 'weep'. Monty smiled. 'Far better than marriage! But not one of them, David, not even the best of them, would have been one tenth as good as your mother at looking after Howarth.'

'Yes,' David said, though he sounded unconvinced.

'The trick of the thing,' Monty said, 'and I suppose you know it already, is to secure your damned position with a marriage, then go off and find your pleasure. Then the rule is discretion. The wife appears in public, sloshes champagne at the palace, and breeds the next poor sod who has to repeat the damned process.'

300

'And the poor sod,' David said bitterly, 'is brought up by nursery nurses, governesses, Eton, and Oxford?'

'Exactly. And you'll be astonished how well they turn out.'

The compliment, coming from so unexpected a source, made David smile. 'I wouldn't know.'

'I have great faith in you. Aren't you going skiing with Christine next week?'

'With the Fleets, yes.' David sounded unhappy at the prospect. He had been trying to find an excuse not to go, preferring to be with Grace, but he had thought of nothing convincing.

'Talk to Christine,' Monty said. 'Lay it all out for her. I wouldn't mention Grace to her yet, but make it plain what you expect out of marriage.'

'What I expect?' David frowned.

'What you just told me! You're marrying for Howarth, for the land, and for the money, and just so long as both of you behave discreetly then the marriage will last. Make your arrangement now, do it cold-bloodedly.'

'But . . .'

'Isn't that what you want? Christine brings you wealth, Grace happiness? It's what I've got, roughly, so why not you? So talk to Christine. If she won't give you the marriage you want, then you'd better come and talk to me.'

David stared with genuine puzzlement at his father, sensing that there was more than a casual reason for this visit, but unable to perceive it. 'I'll talk to her.'

'Good!' Monty finished the whisky and stood. 'That's filthy Scotch.'

'I'm sorry.' David walked with his father into the tiny hallway.

Monty stopped at the front door and did a thing he had not done for fifteen years. He hugged his son. 'I know. It's a bugger being a bloody peer, but a damn sight better than not being one.'

'Yes.'

Monty sat in the back of the Rolls. 'Brick Street,' he said.

He felt tired. He had fudged the issue and he knew it. He had kept Christine's secret because she would bring him Howarth, and the lust for Howarth was too deeply embedded to be given up so easily.

301

He should have told David the truth, but instead he had pointed his son towards compromise. So be it, Monty thought. Once Christine was married, and once Edward's vote made the trust a safe instrument to keep Howarth in the family, Monty would force discretion on Christine; he would scare her out of her wits as sometimes Pearl had to be scared.

That was Monty's compromise, but he was not proud of it. He had not dared face Christine's truth, so he would keep it locked away in his safe as a key for the future.

Yet Monty also feared, for he saw in these events an echo from the past; there were affidavits and talk of marriage, court cases looming, and treachery. Sophie had appeared to change sides once, and now Sir Edward turned his coat. Monty saw the feud stretch on past his death to sour a family's future, and he did not know what he could do to end it except give up Howarth, and that, out of stubbornness and pride, he would not do.

So David must marry his whore, Monty would whip her into line, and Howarth would be safe.

Spring came to wreathe the hedgerows with flowers, mist the trees with emerald and clothe the chestnuts in Howarth's park with white and pink. The manure heap, that had mouldered so long on the far side of the dyke, was at last being carried away.

The Lord de Conroy laughed to see the smeared earth that was left when his dung-heap had gone. 'It was young Edward told me to put it there! He was wrong, eh? Wind doesn't come from there anyway!'

'It was nauseous at times,' Monty said, not wanting to disappoint his old rival.

De Conroy barked a laugh. 'It's all nonsense, all stuff and nonsense!'

'The feud?'

'No! Lord, no! That was serious!' Kynaston leaned more heavily on his ebony stick these days. His face, deep tanned by the South African sun, was more savage, more lined, only pleasant with those men, like Monty, whom he perceived to be of his own kind. 'No, I'm talking about marriage, Monty. What a bloody fuss, eh?'

'What a fuss, indeed.' The two men paced the park to which Monty was thinking of bringing back deer.

'Weddings!' de Conroy said. 'Bloody flibbertigibbet nonsense to please the ladies. My first marriage was in a parish church. Priest wore cricket flannels under his clobber, spliced us, then went and scored a half-century on a turning wicket! No nonsense there, Monty. And my second was in a registrar's office. It was quite adequate! Can't see the need for all this flummery.'

'The ladies like it, as you said.' The ladies, at this moment, were at a council of war in Howarth's Garden Room, planning the finer details of the most lavish wedding London had seen since Princess Elizabeth's nuptials. Monty thought it was a hollow sham, for the girl who would be arrayed in white silk and lace was nothing but a slut, but one that he would welcome into Howarth because she brought him security of tenure. Monty despised himself, and found some small consolation that David expected nothing from the marriage.

'God knows why women don't attend weddings on their own!' de Conroy said as though he had discovered a wonderful idea that would galvanize the world. 'Why have men there at all? I mean you wouldn't go if Pearl didn't give you marching orders, would you?'

'I'd rather be fishing.'

'Any sensible fellow would! I suppose the groom ought to turn up,' Kynaston added grudgingly, 'to have his tackle blessed.'

Monty smiled dutifully. The trick of it would be to whip Christine into line. Wait till she was married then scare the living hell out of her thin bones. 'I'm sorry Christine couldn't come today,' he said blandly, 'but do you like the way she's decorated the rooms?'

'Very nice! Very nice!' De Conroy had searched the lavish apartments in the West Wing that would be used by David and Christine. The arms of de Conroy, lacquered in yellow and black, appeared in every room. 'Mind you,' he said, 'I won't be staying here much, Monty. Not much. I'll live in Monaco, as ever. The hotel's good to me and I've got a damned fine secretary down there.' He paused, evidently brooding on the long-legged Estelle. 'The fact is, Monty, I think the sun keeps the juices flowing. Know what I'm blathering about, do you? And I like the Lacewing. You and Pearl should take it for a jaunt! Get your juices flowing, eh?'

'That's very kind of you.'

The Lacewing, at this very moment, was sailing from the Mediterranean to the Caribbean, laden with every delicacy Fortnum and Mason could cram into her refrigerators and storage cupboards. David and Christine, two weeks from now, would fly to Nassau and spend their honeymoon on the yacht among the islands. 'It's costing a damned fortune,' de Conroy said, 'a God-damned bloody fortune. Thank God I only whelped one daughter.'

'It's costing us all a bloody fortune,' Monty said. Flowers would be flown in from the Scillies, the Orders of Service had been embossed, and the menus gilded with the linked arms of Howarth and de Conroy. The dresses had gone for their final fitting in Paris, the photographers had been booked, and police hired so that casual spectators would be kept away from the Abbey's entrance as the happy couple walked to the waiting carriages. Pearl had insisted on match greys to draw the polished coaches.

The money did not end there. An orchestra, a Guards band, and a cabaret singer had to be paid for. A bishop, a dean, and a slew of lesser clergy needed their fees. The ring had been made, like royalty's, from Welsh gold. Champagne was coming from France and caviar from the Black Sea, and all, Monty thought grimly, to legalize a bounce in bed that had doubtless taken place months ago.

'David's bearing up under the onslaught, is he?' de Conroy asked.

'I'm packing him off to Scotland to get drunk,' Monty said, 'because a sober groom will only make a subservient husband.'

'Very good! I like that! Ha!' Kynaston stared at the house where the women were gathered with their swatches of cloth and their dreams of flowers and their plans for glory. 'It's good for the women, though,' he said grudgingly. 'Makes 'em feel useful, eh? Gives them something to do.'

Pearl had poured all her organizational genius into the marriage, even down to decreeing just how many minutes late Christine could be at the Abbey. It was traditional for the bride to be late, but Pearl's timetable would be wrecked if the girl dallied more than three minutes. 'I've talked to the bishop,' she said, 'and told him I don't want a lot of sentimental nonsense.'

'Quite right,' Sophie said.

Pearl had other reasons for eschewing a romantic sermon, for she, like her husband, knew how sham the wedding was. Christine wanted her title and her fortune and would discover, when the knot was tied, that her plans had been forestalled. By marrying David she became a Howarth and Monty was the head of that tribe and would crush the girl into a formal, loveless marriage that kept Howarth safe.

David, sitting in his mother's study, was writing short, formal thank you notes for the wedding gifts. Each brief note was written on a piece of paper embossed with the quartered arms of de Conroy and Howarth, and the envelopes would be posted while he and Christine were on their honeymoon. He checked another name off the list. From the Earl of Fleet had come a silver table-centre, ornate and lavish, suitable to grace a lordly dinner. The Creeds had sent an oil painting that Pearl remembered failing to reach its reserve price at Christies. Solomon Linsky had given the couple a softly romantic Corot landscape of which Pearl was jealous. From the tenants of Howarth's farms there was a canteen of silver cutlery, while Major Hugh Grimes and the Lady Hilary Howarth had sent a greenheart fishing rod and written to say they had a pointer bitch on heat and would give the couple the best of the litter. 'You'd think they could do better, wouldn't you?' Pearl showed the list to Sophie.

'I don't think they're very rich, Pearl.'

'And it's what I asked for,' David put in.

'It was very kind of you,' his mother said tartly, 'but the least I'd have expected was a piece of silver as well. Still, no doubt if Hugh ever has the decency to make an honest woman out of Hilary, they won't expect very much from us.'

Sophie had given them a Queen Anne escritoire which she suspected had been knocked up in the Brighton lanes in the last

305

five years and given a mock antique finish by being shot full of wormholes and distressed with a chain. The piece nicely cut the fine line between betraying poverty and pretending generosity, which was the normal dilemma of those giving wedding presents.

The Lord de Conroy, with a spark of malicious pleasure, was giving them the gold dinner service that had once been presented by the Czar of Russia to the first Marquess of Arlington, and which he had bought after the war when Monty had been forced to sell it. Pearl, not to be outdone, had given a Chippendale dining table, with twenty chairs. 'You might like to show it to Sophie?' she said to David now.

'Of course.' The furniture was the only present in Howarth, the rest were on display in Brick Street, guarded by Hammond who had given David an antique pistol with a chased silver handle that Monty had found in Bond Street. 'If the wife gets out of hand,' Hammond had said, 'you can clock her one.'

David walked through Howarth with his aunt, and Sophie saw just how much money Pearl had poured into the house since the engagement party. It must now rank with the best houses in the land, she thought, and perhaps no stately home had ever been given so much care. 'Are you happy?' she asked David.

'I ought to be.'

'That doesn't sound very jolly, does it?'

David smiled, said nothing, and threw open the door in the Octagon that led into the private apartments. He was not happy, of course he was not happy, but he told himself, over and over, that he did not marry for happiness, but for Howarth.

He had talked with Christine in Switzerland and found her eager to accept his father's formula. She had called it adult and sensible, but David secretly found it mean-spirited and sad. He knew now that he was not in love with Christine, and when, in Switzerland, he had seen her laughing head bent close to Basil Fleet's, he felt no jealousy at all, none.

Instead he had been jealous of Grace, wondering what she did in London while he was in St Moritz. He had imagined her with art students, in coffee bars, in bed. He wanted Grace, not Christine, because he needed the possession of the one he loved as a means to his own security. He was too ashamed to admit that to his father, for Monty would not understand the weakness, but it tortured him all the same. He told himself that it was fate that had brought Grace into his life, and fate which had made her face match the blueprint of beauty that was imprinted on his soul, and he believed that fate should not be crossed, for it would bring revenge. He was in love again.

But he was trapped in marriage for a house and an heir.

'You're very lucky,' Sophie said.

'I am?'

She looked at the high, gracious rooms and mocked the de Conroy crest with a shrug of her shoulders, then threw open double doors to see the next room's new splendours. 'Will you live here much?'

'I don't know. I suppose we'll use the rooms fairly often.'

'I can't imagine Pearl wanting you to raise children here,' Sophie said. 'She was never fond of children, but then nor was I. I suppose Christine will have to drop one heir, though.'

'I suppose so.' David was thinking of Grace, only of Grace.

Sophie was insensible of her nephew's anguish, for she could see at last the end in sight. De Conroy and Howarth, the two sides of her warring life, would be united and Sophie would know some peace. She looked in a gilt looking glass, grimaced at the lines of age on her face, and wondered whether these rooms, if David and Christine did not choose to use them, could prove the safe haven of her old age.

She turned and stared through the window at Monty and Kynaston in the gardens, two men who had once fought, but who now made peace. It was odd, she thought, how well they got on.

De Conroy stared at the house. 'Which one's highest?'

'I'm sorry?' Monty said.

'Flagstaff, man! Which flagstaff's highest?'

Monty looked from the central staff on which his banner now flew to the empty, waiting pole that had been placed above the West Wing. 'Yours is six inches higher than mine.'

'Splendid!' Kynaston seemed to take enormous pleasure in the fact. 'I should have made it ten feet higher, yes?'

'Why not?' Monty smiled. In fact his own flagpole was a foot higher than de Conroy's, but there was no point in stating the fact.

'We'd better be off,' de Conroy said. He and Sophie were meeting Christine for dinner at Caton that night, and the next time he came to Howarth it would be as part-owner and his banner would fly above his daughter's rooms.

For the feud that had been started by a game of cards had but a fortnight to run; then would come marriage and, in the long, fading echo of the wedding bells, peace.

Each morning, when Hugh was away, Hilary's day began with the feeding of two horses, five dogs, three cats, and thirty-eight chickens. The two sheep that kept the lawn mown looked after themselves. She said good morning to the bees in their hive in the orchard for, like other country folk, she firmly believed that courtesy towards bees fended off trouble. The postman usually arrived just as she was taking warm eggs from the straw in the chicken-house and she sometimes suspected, without any grudge, that he deliberately waited until that moment so he could be rewarded with a couple of large brown eggs for his tea. 'Not much this morning, my Lady,' he said a week before the wedding. 'One from the Major in Germany. Two from America, they'll be wanting books, won't they? And a rate demand.'

'Tea, Jimmy?'

'I haven't got time really,' he said, as he said every morning.

'But you'll have some anyway.' And in the kitchen, as she always was at eight o'clock, Mrs Joyson from the village shop was reading *The Times* she delivered for Hilary. 'Do you know this Harold Macmillan?' she asked. The village somehow assumed that Hilary knew everybody, even new prime ministers.

'Never met him.' Hilary put the egg basket on the table and saw that Mrs Joyson had already wet the tea. Hugh called these gatherings Hilary's Parliament and was secretly glad that people dropped in on the huge kitchen whenever the fancy took them. She claimed that the house was just a convenient stopping place, halfway between the village centre and the outlying farms, but whatever the reason, people did seem to gather there and share the local news.

'Major will be back on Thursday, will he?' Jimmy asked.

'He's not looking forward to it,' Hilary said. 'Nor am I.'

'It'll be lovely,' Mrs Joyson said. 'The Abbey? And all that fuss? I think you're ever so lucky.'

By half past eight the Royal Mail, with two added eggs, was on its way again and Mrs Joyson's bicycle carried two *Daily Mails*, one *Telegraph* and one *Daily Herald* out to the furthest farms. Hugh had written about an exercise his battalion had just finished in the German plains, 'two nights in a turnip field, rain, not much fun', while one American professor from Indiana wanted to know whether Miss Howarth could find him a first edition of *Pilgrim's Progress* and a second, from San Diego, wanted a *Natural History of Selborne* that Hilary knew she had in stock.

The rare book business occupied an hour and a half that morning, then Hilary, feeling domestic and vaguely broody, made bread dough that she put into the airing cupboard to rise. After that she took Mistle for an hour's ride, taking the mare up to the ridge behind the house where a wide tract of grassland stretched beneath a Cotswold sky. The may was in bloom and the hedgerows were beginning to take on a clouded, white appearance as the bright green curls of cow parsley came into blossom.

In the half-hour before lunch she cranked the outside pump and carried pails of water to the vegetable patches. The vet called, not to deal with any particular problem, but to see if the kettle was on and to tell her that the vicar's dog would have to be put down. 'He might like one of your pups, my Lady.'

'Three pounds for a dog, five for a bitch.'

'I'll tell him.'

It was, Hilary decided, a quiet day. She ate cheese and an apple for lunch then, reluctantly, got out her sewing basket. She did not mind sewing, but she resented making the dress she

309

would wear to David's wedding. Weddings, to her, should be joyous occasions, but there was something sour in the air of this marriage. David seemed so quiet about it, derelict almost.

By half past two the dress was as finished as Hilary intended it to be and she took the risen dough out of the airing cupboard and shaped it into loaves that then went into the Aga's oven. At three o'clock, when the day was as warm as it would be, she took a book into the back garden and fell asleep.

Which was how her visitor found her: one English lady, asleep in a deck chair, with dogs and cats littered about her like some pastiche of the life of St Francis. 'Hello!' the visitor said nervously. 'Hello?'

Hilary opened her eyes. At first she could not quite place the tall, dark-haired girl wearing trousers and a patchwork shirt. She had a sacking bag over her shoulder and looked oddly out of place in the spring softness of the countryside. 'Hello.' Hilary pushed the cats off her lap and stood up.

'I'm Grace.'

'Of course you are!' Hilary hid her astonishment. 'We met at Howarth, didn't we? Good Lord! The bread!'

Grace, nervous as the two sheep that had taken refuge from the newcomer beneath a hornbeam at the top of the garden, followed the panicked Hilary into a vast, beamed and flagged kitchen where her Ladyship, much relieved, took out two huge hot loaves that she set to cool on a rack. 'Just in time! You like new bread?'

'I love it.'

'Hugh says it's bad for you, but what does he know? There's butter in the scullery. Green door over there.'

Grace went into the big, cool scullery and wondered why the British believed possession of refrigerators, like central heating, to be evidence of low moral fibre. The butter was in a dish beneath a beaded muslin cover and she took it back to the kitchen where Hilary had hacked two chunks off one of the loaves.

New hot bread, soaked in butter, was one of those rare treats, but Grace was in no mood to relish it. She was nervous. She had come here on impulse, travelling by train and bus, and now she

310

was not sure that she should have come at all. 'It's nice.' She gestured at the kitchen.

'It's wonderful,' Hilary said. 'It's the happiest house I've ever lived in. How did you find me?'

'David's address book.'

'Oh! You're friends, are you?'

'Yes.' Grace gave a quick, nervous smile. She would not sit down, but roamed the kitchen almost as if she was looking for an escape. Hilary, watching her, thought what a restless and exotic creature the American girl was; beautiful and strange. Not a girl, she thought, for the countryside, but for city salons and artists' studios. Hilary thought she remembered Grace saying something about sculpture on the evening she borrowed her blue dress at Howarth.

'I guess I should have telephoned,' Grace said.

'You couldn't. The Post Office promised a telephone two months ago, but it's still a promise. You have to leave messages at the Crown and Anchor.'

'I wanted to talk to you, you see.' Grace said it defensively, as though Hilary might bridle at the suggestion.

'David?' Hilary made the guess to help the girl's nervousness and saw, from Grace's startled glance, that she had scored a bull's-eye.

'Yeah. David.'

Hilary did not try to guess further. Whatever the problem was would doubtless emerge. Instead she lifted the Aga's lid and put a kettle on the hotplate. 'Tea or coffee?'

Grace did not respond. She had at last sat down in a broken-springed armchair where the pointer bitch spent her nights. She stared at Hilary with big, oddly violet eyes, then shrugged. 'I'm pregnant.'

'Oh, Jesus,' Hilary said without thinking. 'Scotch?'

'Better than tea, I think.'

Hilary went to the dining room and fetched a bottle from the drinks cupboard. She paused in there, trying to adjust to the news she had just heard, and when she reached the kitchen again saw Grace pushing a handkerchief into her sleeve. 'Scotch,' Hilary said, 'and tell.'

311

Grace lit a cigarette. Slowly, haltingly, the story came out, all of it, right back to the night when she had watched a lake freeze.

She had been fascinated by David. He was the first aristocrat she had ever met, and that was a challenge, and he was also so lonely and unhappy, which was another challenge. It was his broken-winged appeal, rather than his coronet, that had made Grace go beyond sympathy's duty. 'Just stupid, really.'

'No,' Hilary said. 'I met Hugh in Oxford on a Saturday and we were lovers by the following Friday.' Not that it had happened because Hugh had been broken-winged, the very opposite in fact, but Hilary thought it best not to mention the contrast between the two men.

'But you didn't get pregnant,' Grace said bitterly.

'No.'

'And if you had?'

Hilary sighed. The one-eyed foxhound bounded through the door, wagged its stern, then chased out into the sunlight again. 'If I became pregnant,' she said, 'we'd marry.'

'Just like that?'

'Yes.' Hilary smiled. 'Hugh and I are both orphans, you see, and perhaps that makes a difference. We haven't got parents to push us into a white wedding, and the only other reason I know for marrying is so your children don't get teased at school. I think I also like the freedom of not being married.' She thought about it, cradling the beaker of whisky in her two hands. 'I'm actually the most married woman I know, but I can pretend I'm not. Does that make any sense at all?'

Grace nodded. 'So you don't really want to be pregnant?'

'I'm not sure. Sometimes I do,' she said wistfully. 'I was feeling rather broody this morning, as a matter of fact, so it's probably a good thing that the brute's in Germany.' She smiled. 'Hugh would want a boy, of course, but I'd like a girl. I'd call her Lucy.' Lucy had been Hugh's mother's name. Hilary shrugged, knowing that Grace did not want to listen to such ramblings. 'Do I assume you don't want to be pregnant?'

Grace shuddered. 'I do not!' She spoke of her dreams and ambitions, of her wish to be a sculptress famed throughout the West. It was a dream that did not include, as she put it, diapers

312

and comforters. She wanted to be a free and celebrated spirit, stalking the art world in a blaze of colourful fame. Now she was pregnant. 'The kids in college, right? They told me about this crooked doctor in Catford. Seventy-five quid and no dirty knitting needles.' Again she stared at Hilary with defiance.

Hilary stared back, giving nothing away. 'And?'

'So I went, right? Twenty-five quid down, he gave me a physical, and you're lying there with your feet in the damned air and this dirty bastard having a feel. I'm meant to go back tomorrow night.'

Hilary smiled. 'And you don't want to go back.'

'No.' Grace shuddered. Much as the birth of a child would wreck her careful, glowing ambitions, there were also strange tendrils of motherhood invading her feelings. She could not bear to think of her child being swabbed, like garbage, down a drain. 'I mean I don't really object to abortion, right? But . . .' She shrugged.

'I think I know what you mean,' Hilary said mildly. She herself believed abortion to be the most selfish act imaginable, but Grace did not need her views, merely a sounding board to discover her own. 'Why did you come to me?'

'Because,' Grace was embarrassed. 'I don't know. You were nice that night.'

'I'm the nice Howarth.' Hilary laughed. 'I assume, from what you're saying, that David doesn't know?'

'No.'

Which explained why Grace was here. She needed a Howarth's view, an interpreter of the family. 'You want a walk?' she asked. 'You can bring your drink.'

They walked round the garden, Grace with her glass and Hilary carrying the sword of honour that Hugh had won at Sandhurst. She used the engraved blade to slice dead heads from daffodils and cut back the encroaching nettles. 'Why didn't you tell David?'

And that produced a complex answer that took two whole circuits of the garden and left most of the important things unsaid. Hilary, cleaning the blade of plant sap, frowned. 'You mean you're not sure you'd want to marry him, even if you could?'

'I guess so.'

David, Grace said, was a dreamer. He dreamed of launching his own music business, but did nothing about it. He dreamed of love, but claimed to be trapped in a loveless engagement. He dreamed of things he said could not be, but all of which were possible with just a little work.

'I'm not sure you're right,' Hilary said. 'I agree he's a lost soul, but lost souls do find themselves.' She had brought the bottle of Scotch out to the garden table and they sat opposite each other, sword and glasses between them, in the fine evening sunlight that stretched the hornbeam's shadow across the finely cropped grass. 'And I'm not sure how any boy could survive Pearl.'

'The wicked witch of the north, right?'

Hilary smiled. 'She terrifies most people. But I think David inherited her insecurities, oddly. The thing is, did he inherit any of his father's certainty?'

'You tell me,' Grace said.

'I don't think I know him as well as you,' Hilary said and they both laughed. 'I suppose,' she went on, 'we should be thinking about Lord Fred or whoever.'

'Lord Fred?'

'In your tummy.' Hilary smiled. 'What would happen if you went home?'

Grace shuddered. Kind as her parents might be, she did not think that her safe, conventional town would welcome a pregnant girl. The shame would enwrap her family, and the child would be an oddity from the start.

'So,' Hilary said, 'I suppose we're back to the choices. There's Catford, or home, or staying in England and having the child, or there's marriage.' She shrugged. 'If it helps, you're welcome here. I won't notice another mouth to feed in this damned menagerie. And Hugh won't mind. He'll growl a bit, but I've got him right under my thumb.'

Grace did not respond immediately. She poured herself more whisky. 'Don't people think you're strange round here?'

'Because we're not married?' Hilary thought about it. 'Not really. I'm a Lady, which helps enormously because the English think that the aristocracy has its own rules. I like dogs and horses, so I'm not too obviously weird, and Hugh bellows out the hymns

314

in church so he's obviously not entirely strange. I think most people assume we just forgot to get married and they're much too polite to mention it.'

Grace smiled. 'But they'd think I was strange?'

'Oh, yes! You're very exotic. The pub would talk about you for ever.'

Grace tried to imagine living in an English country village as an exotic stranger and, much as she liked this pretty, blonde woman who was so extraordinarily sensible and welcoming, she knew it would never work. It would be running away and delaying the inevitable day when she would have to face her own fate.

Hilary let the silence stretch on. House martins, beaks full of nesting materials, were fluttering at the eaves, while the marmalade cat was stalking a bluebottle that buzzed away as soon as it pounced. Hilary could hear a tractor on the Glebe fields and guessed that an early hay crop was being cut.

Grace sniffed. Hilary had the impression that the American girl could cry at any moment, but instead she lifted her face towards her and gave an odd, crooked smile. 'I really thought I had it sorted out, you know? Down at Catford, raise my legs, and kiss the little bastard goodbye. But I can't do it.'

'Perhaps you'll forgive me if I say I'm glad?'

'So what do I do? Tell David?'

Hilary reflected that it had taken nearly three hours to reach the real question. 'If he knew,' she said carefully, 'would he want to marry you?'

'He talks about nothing else.' Grace said it with a trace of bitterness. 'I think he's got something like this in mind.' She nodded at the cottage, so cosy and tight in the evening sunshine. 'Domestic bliss, right? New bread in the oven, cats on the doorstep, and honeysuckle on the wall.'

Hilary ignored the note of scorn. She understood well enough the nature of the trap Grace was in: a choice between ignominy and a marriage she did not really want. 'I suppose,' she asked the question very carefully, 'that you're utterly sure the baby is David's?'

'Oh yeah! I even know which night it was! He came back from

skiing and he was so damned miserable! Like a whipped puppy, so stupid here has to give him his cuddle.'

Hilary smiled. 'You could stay his mistress, couldn't you?'

'That's what his father suggested before I was pregnant.'

Hilary laughed. 'He would.' She reflected that Monty would probably be glad to pay Grace off, without rancour, and ensure that she had a sufficiency to live on and with which to raise the baby. That, in Monty's view, was the aristocratic way, and thus another woman would be given the imprimatur of a peer's whore, branded for life by her bastard.

'The thing is,' Grace said suddenly, 'that there are times when I really do want to marry David, you know?' Hilary did not, but said nothing. 'I mean he's so grateful! He's always so affectionate, and I kind of wonder what he could do if he was really happy. Shee-it. I don't know.' She shrugged. 'I guess I can't marry him anyway.'

'It would cause a certain amount of fuss,' Hilary said with remarkable restraint. 'They'll lose Howarth, but you know all about that.'

'Do I not?' Grace shuddered and lit herself a cigarette.

'My aunt won't be happy,' Hilary said, 'but that's not important. What's important is the baby, you, and David. What makes the greatest happiness for the three of you?'

'A bottle of gin and a hot bath?'

'If you like,' Hilary said, 'but preferably not in my bathroom. It might scare the spiders.'

They talked on through the dusk, as Hilary shut up the chickens in their fox-proof house and as she cooked the dinner. The next morning, when Hilary's Parliament gathered, Grace slept in upstairs and, when she appeared at lunchtime, she started talking again. 'The real point,' Hilary said the next evening, 'is that if you truly want to be the Countess of Mountsorrel, then you'd better do something quickly, hadn't you?'

'Countess,' Grace said with surprise. 'I guess I would be a countess!'

'You'll get much better service at Harrods,' Hilary said drily.

'And one day,' Grace said, 'I'd be Marchioness?'

'Oh, yes.'

The scales were tipped by that realization, and Hilary watched the decision forming in Grace's uncertain mind. None of the choices was satisfactory, none, but they never were with unwanted pregnancies. Yet perhaps, Hilary thought, when the fuss had all died down, marriage might be the best answer. It might not prove the happiest marriage, for Grace's intelligent ambitions would sit uneasily beside David's cosier dreams, but David would have the woman he wanted and Grace would have the title she saw as a consolation for an inconvenient marriage.

Grace laughed. 'I guess that being an American countess would be one hell of a selling point for my work.'

'Undoubtedly,' Hilary said.

'But it's a bit late, really. I mean the poor bastard can hardly back out of the marriage, can he?'

'You've only got to ask.' Hilary wondered what trouble she caused by the mild suggestion.

'I was wondering,' Grace said hesitantly, 'whether you wouldn't tell him.'

'Me!'

'He kind of reacts strange to me, you know? He puts me on a pedestal.' Grace shrugged. 'I mean I don't want to pressure him, I really don't. If he wants to do it, then he should do it calmly, shouldn't he? And I sort of wondered whether you wouldn't be a bit more objective than me.'

'Me,' Hilary said again.

'Would you? He's up in Scotland somewhere. His father sent him up there to get drunk.'

'Shee-it,' Hilary said, thus causing generations of ex head-girls of her old school to turn in their graves. 'If you want me to, I suppose I'd better.'

'I'm really sorry.'

'It's what the family's for,' Hilary said bleakly. 'Starting fights, that sort of thing.' She wondered where Monty might have sent David for a week's carouse. 'Suppose I can't find him?'

'I guess I have to think of something else,' Grace said.

'Four days,' Hilary said hopelessly.

Four days to cause chaos, to find a groom, and to make a decision that might lose Howarth for ever and give the family an

317

heir conceived on the wrong side of the blankets; which was not, Hilary reflected, a bargain likely to appeal to Pearl, but it was not Pearl's decision. It was David's, and thus Hilary, with Grace left behind to look after the livestock, set out to find him.

The organ started softly as the organist exercised his fingers with running trills and snatches from a Bach fugue that would later thunder among the high arches.

A white silken rope was being stretched across the south transept, east of Poet's Corner, and curious tourists were told that a wedding was to be celebrated in one of the retrochoir chapels and that no one, without a pass or an invitation, would be allowed through until midday.

Pearl would have liked to use the Abbey's High Altar, or at least Henry VII's chapel, but she had to be content with St Edward's Chapel where the Coronation Throne stood. The white altar frontal was brushed and the carpet swept.

Vans drew up at the west front and great urns of white flowers were carried up the nave and past the verger who guarded the white rope. The early morning sunlight lit the dancing dust motes in the nave and glowed through ancient stained glass.

This was the place where Henry III and Eleanor of Castile were buried; where the Tudors lay with their enemy, Mary, Queen of Scots. The banners of the Order of the Bath hung in the splendour of Henry VII's chapel, and chairs were carried beneath Henry V's chantry that crossed like a bridge over the south ambulatory. Westminster Abbey.

Choirboys were practised, clergy rehearsed, and the sun was unmisted by cloud. A perfect day for a wedding in the greatest church of England in the very heart of London.

'Well?' Hilary, back from her first errand of the day, asked Hugh, who had just returned from his.

Hugh frowned. 'I don't know.' It had taken Hilary two days to find David who had taken refuge in a hunting lodge belonging to a friend of the family. She had brought him south and Hugh had taken over as his mentor in London. 'He keeps asking me what to do!' he complained. 'I can't make that kind of decision!

318

Still, I took Grace round there this morning and perhaps she'll tip his hand.' He looked at his watch. 'I just wish he'd make a decision one way or the other! Good God, he can't wait till she's prancing up the aisle, can he?'

'Better then than later.' Hilary drank some of Hugh's coffee. They were in the kitchen of a friend's house where they sometimes stayed when they were in town. 'I've got to go to the British Museum for Monty.'

'You've got to do what?'

'Never mind.' Hilary paused. 'I must say he took it remarkably calmly!' Hugh and Hilary had privately agreed that Monty must be forewarned of the struggle going on inside David, and she had taken on the dread task. 'I'll tell you everything later. I've got to run.' She gave him a kiss, snatched up her handbag, and was gone.

The guard of honour would be formed by dismounted troopers of the Household Cavalry, hired for the morning, who now polished breastplates, helmets, boots, and the swords they would hold as a glittering tunnel over the bride and groom as they left the Abbey.

The royal trumpeters were ready and waiting for the truck that would carry them to the Abbey where their pennanted silver instruments would celebrate a wedding. Eight pairs of grey draught horses were being combed and brushed, their manes plaited, and the open landaus were given a last gloss before their proud ride from the Abbey to the Dorchester Hotel.

In the Savoy Hotel Lord de Conroy ate his breakfast in bed. His false leg was propped against the wardrobe where his morning suit was hung. 'Bloody waste of time,' he grumbled.

'You like it,' Estelle said. She sat beside him in bed, quite naked, with toast crumbs on her rosy skin. She disliked London and could not wait to board the train that would take them south again when this day's festivities were done.

'I added it all up,' de Conroy said, 'and reckon this damned weddding is costing me fifteen thousand pounds. Fifteen thousand! That would pay for a decent whore every night for more than four years!'

'In that case,' Estelle said, 'you owe me thirty thousand pounds because French whores are twice as good as English ones. I will take a cheque.'

'You'll take nothing,' he grumbled. 'I suppose my daughter is up?'

'I heard Christine's breakfast being taken in. And in a minute I will help her dress.'

'You want to know what that damned frock cost me?'

'You are a disagreeable old man,' Estelle said, 'so it's a good thing you're rich.'

In the vast kitchens of the Dorchester the *sous-chefs* began their work. Six hundred hors d'oeuvres of quails' eggs and caviar had to be fashioned on six hundred plates. White linen was unfolded from laundry baskets to drape the serried tables. A score of Rolls-Royces, garaged all over London, received a final polish. Silver Ladies were draped with white ribbons and chauffeurs adjusted white carnations in their buttonholes.

'Did I hear Hilary's voice?' Pearl, staying in Brick Street for this occasion, had come downstairs in a silk dressing gown. She lifted the lid of a chafing dish and forked out a devilled kidney.

'She dropped by for an early cup of coffee,' Monty said.

'I do hope she's got something decent to wear. And not that yellow rag she thinks is so fashionable.'

'She was wearing wellies and trousers this morning.'

'Very funny, Monty.' Pearl brought her breakfast to the table.

'She was really here to warn me that there might not be a marriage.'

'She's always had a strange sense of humour.' Pearl turned to the share prices in *The Times* and saw with pleasure that the market had risen. 'Have you telephoned David yet?'

'I imagine he's got a hangover. I hope he's got a hangover. I had a hangover when I married you.'

'You were drunk,' Pearl said. 'You slurred your words and tried to put the ring on my middle finger. I'm glad we bought those Imperial Chemical shares.'

'Making us rich, are they?'

'Moderately.'

'Enough to buy a house to replace Howarth?'

Pearl frowned. 'You're in a very strange mood this morning, Monty.'

'It's not every day one's son gets married.'

'Thank God.'

'And you also hear that he's knocked up some girl who wants him to call off the wedding and legitimize her bastard.'

Pearl froze, a fork with half a kidney impaled on its prongs quivering six inches above her plate. 'I'm not sure I understand you.'

Monty sipped his coffee, wondering whether it had been altogether wise to pass this news on. 'David's put a bun in a strange oven, wants to marry her, and can't make up his mind. Hugh and Hilary are baby-sitting him.'

'Monty!' The fork dropped.

'I've asked Edward Fenton to call.'

'I don't understand!' Pearl's fine, stern face had gone pale. 'Why Edward?'

'Because if David does call off the wedding, my darling, Edward's my best chance of saving Howarth. I assume you do want Howarth saved?'

'What girl?' Among the thousand confusing thoughts jumbling in her head Pearl seized on that one.

'An American,' Monty said calmly. 'Rather a pretty thing. You might remember her? She dined at Howarth last winter. David's been having a thing with her ever since. Damned careless to get her pregnant, though.'

'You introduced them!' The accusation was searing.

'I did, rather.'

'And she's pregnant? It could be anyone's! She's just a gold-digging slut!'

'I thought Christine was the gold-digging slut.'

Pearl paused, with frantic thoughts of Howarth lost going through her head. She knew Monty's restraint was assumed, and she tried to match it with an icy calm herself. 'Are you serious about this girl?' she demanded.

'David might be.'

Pearl stared at her husband. 'Are you telling me that there's a real chance this wedding won't take place?'

321

Monty thought about it, then nodded. 'Yes.'

'And you're doing nothing! Nothing!'

'I've sent for Fenton. Hilary's kindly running a small errand for me. I wouldn't say I was doing nothing.'

'You should be talking to David! Go there now!'

Monty shook his head. 'I talked to the boy before, didn't I? If I'd been honest then, Pearl, I'd have told him to abandon Christine. I don't really see why he should marry some scrubby little whore without tits just because we don't want to move house, do you? But I didn't say that. I should have done, but I didn't. And if I went this morning, Pearl, I'd probably say it. I'd probably tell him to marry Grace. He'd be damned lucky to get her.'

Pearl listened to this long speech with disbelief at first, then anger. She held her breath when he had finished, as if about to explode with anger, but instead she twisted away from the table and snatched open the door. 'Hammond! I want the car in five minutes! Five!'

Monty pulled Pearl's plate over the table and ate the remaining kidneys. It seemed a pity to waste them, and he had a feeling he would need all his strength today.

David, with a hangover made dreadful by misery, sat in his small living room. He was already half dressed and his waistcoat hung over his dress shirt and the braces of his grey trousers. Grace, left alone with him, sat and watched the indecision that had plagued David ever since Hilary had fetched him back to London. In one hour he was to be at the Abbey where Hugh would be his best man and they would stand at the altar and wait for the Rolls-Royce that would bring Christine from the Savoy. There were guests on trains, guests in cars, guests breakfasting in hotels, all waiting for that moment when Christine de Conroy would decide Howarth's fate.

David stared at Grace. She was pregnant and the baby was his, and he tried to balance that tiny, precious thing in her belly against the magnificence that was Howarth. 'Do your parents know?'

Grace shook her head. 'I guess I'll tell them after today, right?'

'Right.' Which only made it worse, for it threw the decision on to David's shoulders and he did not know what he should do.

On the one hand was all he thought he wanted: the bliss of domesticity, a family of his own, and the absolute utter possession of this beautiful girl. On the other was duty. There was Howarth and a future insured against his mother's cold rages; there was money to indulge his whims, and there was no fuss, no fuss at all. He tried to imagine cancelling the wedding now, risking his mother's rage and his father's anger, and he tried to anticipate the fury of Lord de Conroy and the spiteful rage that would spring from Christine's disappointment. He tried to imagine the newspapers, the shockwave it would send through society, and the effort to see all those things made him shudder.

'Listen, honey,' Grace touched his knee. 'It's not a big deal, OK?'

David frowned, not understanding that Grace's compassion was trying to ease his decision. His stomach churned and his hands shook.

'Listen,' she said. 'I guess your old man will see me right, won't he? I mean, shee-it, I can't pay for the baby and all that.'

'I can do that,' David said.

'And we talked about this, didn't we? You and Christine get married and you have a civilized agreement. Just like Monty! I can live here, and you can still come and see me. I mean it won't be any different, except there'll be a rug-rat crawling round the floor.' It was not what Grace wanted, she was not entirely sure of what she did want, but she could see that David was too terrified to make a decision, so she must make it for him.

She had opened the easy door for David and, like a coward, he was ready to take her convenient answer. 'I suppose so,' he said miserably.

Grace, obscurely disappointed, thought that Fred in her belly had just lost a title. She stood and walked to the front window. Her long talks with Hilary had convinced her that perhaps marriage was the answer, that she could parlay David's place in society to her own benefit. Grace had few illusions. She knew David was as kind a man as she was ever likely to meet, and as a lover he was tender and concerned, but she also knew there was a void of loneliness in him that she doubted she could fill.

323

Perhaps, she thought, the baby would help fill it, and perhaps, if David received tender, compassionate love he would find a new confidence. Except that he would not surrender Christine because he was frightened. 'Is Hugh fetching you in a Rolls?'

'I don't know.'

'Well, there's one outside. Oh, my God!'

'What?'

'It's your mother!'

'Oh, Christ!' He stood, looking for escape, but there was none. Then the front door was shaken by the brass knocker, Grace fled into the garden, and David, the day's groom, went to meet Pearl.

The Lady Sophie, splendid in a Parisian dress of soft grey cloth that fell wide-skirted to her black-stockinged ankles, poured herself a martini. She had been up since six o'clock putting on a careful face and now, the outer appearance secured, she wished to fortify the inner self. It would be a long day. She hated the Abbey. It was such a vulgar place to get married in, but typical of Pearl. Pearl had such middle-class taste. Why did the silly woman not see that if it had to be a London wedding then St George's, Hanover Square, was really the only place? In the country it would be the parish church with all the tenantry loyally cheering, but not the Abbey! The Abbey was for tourists.

Sophie looked in the mirror, thought she looked old and, to console herself, finished the martini and then poured four more fingers of gin into the glass. She sometimes toyed with the idea of writing scandalous memoirs called 'Martini for Breakfast'. Or perhaps 'Alcohol is a Girl's Best Friend', in recognition of alcohol's two great qualities of diluting the conscience and dulling the memory.

The telephone rang.

Sophie ignored it, intent on putting just a single drop of vermouth into the glass. The telephone went on ringing. 'Damn.'

She walked into the hallway and lifted the receiver. 'Methodist Home for the Aged, Matron speaking. Monty! Good Lord, brother. Don't worry, I was up with the lark. I'm even sober.'

'Stay sober,' Monty said. He spoke for five minutes and at the end of the conversation Sophie felt so sober that she swallowed the second martini straight down. Somehow the news was too good to keep silent so she poured another one, this time splashing the vermouth in any old how, then went back into the hall to telephone Lady Mirabelle. Monty had telephoned to warn Sophie in case Lord de Conroy turned on her for immediate revenge, and had told her to tell no one else, but Sophie could not leave such a titbit of gossip unspread.

Sol Linsky was washing up his breakfast things. 'You'll love it!' he said to the young man who, rather clumsily, dried up the plates and cups.

Oscar Melnick was nervous as hell. He was one of Sol's orphans, plucked from the ruins of the Reich, and since the day when he had watched his parents and family dragged off towards the ovens in the Polish camps, his life had taken a privileged course. Rescued at the war's end, he had been sent to the States where he had received a brilliant education. Now, partly to research his MA thesis on the convoluted machinations of London's Commodity Market and partly to meet his benefactor, Oscar had come to London. He was short, plump, with a froglike face and myopic eyes and a mind as fast as a striking snake. 'The Marchioness sounds pretty frightening.'

'She'll be in a wonderful mood today, wonderful! She gets everything she wants, doesn't she?' Sol was in a fine mood. David was getting married, the sun was shining, and he would take his protégé, whom he loved like a son, into England's finest abbey. 'I'll make sure you have a chance to chat with the Marquess. Don't be scared of him! I want you to impress him, OK?' He wanted to bring Oscar to England when the young man's studies at Harvard were finished.

'I'll try.'

'And don't worry about the Marchioness,' Sol said. 'She'll purr like a pussy-cat! I wouldn't be surprised if she invites us all to Howarth!'

Pearl was not purring. The sight of her son's dishevelled clothes, bleary face, and unkempt hair engendered a slow, sinister burn of temper that she struggled to control. 'Your father tells me you've got cold feet.'

325

'Cold feet?' David frowned.

'About the wedding.' Pearl had dressed swiftly, but she still looked superb in a coat and gloves that matched her lilac dress and dark hat. 'It's quite natural, David. Everyone feels nervous about getting married.' She had told herself, on the way to Chelsea, that she should begin by being pleasant to her son. 'So this is where you live? It's very charming.'

David brushed a lock of hair off his forehead, but said nothing.

Pearl smiled. 'It's nonsense, is it not?'

'I'm sorry?'

She resisted the urge to shake him. 'It's nonsense, surely, that you've got cold feet?'

David wondered why his mother had the ability to turn him into a quivering mass of nerves. He shrugged, thinking that honesty was due on this day that would settle his life's direction. 'I'm not very happy about it. I should have said something earlier . . .'

'I'm not sure I believe what I'm hearing!'

David shrugged again, then picked up a packet of cigarettes.

'And don't smoke when you're talking to me!' Pearl's temper frayed and ran free. 'If you think, David, that you can simply walk out of this wedding just because you've made some American slut pregnant, you can think again!'

David blinked. 'She's not a slut.'

'Don't interrupt me!' Her fury blazed now. 'Is that what you're thinking? That you'll abandon Christine? Well, is it?'

He gestured helplessly towards his top hat as if to show that the accoutrements of the ceremony, far from being abandoned, lay ready to hand.

Pearl took the gesture to reflect her son's indecision. 'I am here to tell you that you will do no such thing, do you understand me? I want you to understand me.' She took a menacing step closer to David, who stepped back towards the half-open garden door. 'You will not abandon Christine, you will not disgrace me and your family in front of society. You will not lose us Howarth! Is that understood?'

'Yes,' David said obediently. It was the decision he had tentatively reached with Grace in this room just minutes before.

326

Another woman might have left it there, victory complete, but Pearl could not leave an opponent with breath in their body. 'Do you know how much you risked?'

'Risked?'

'By your foolery? Suppose de Conroy had heard of your affair?' She said the last word with utter disgust. 'Suppose your dirty habits had reached his ears, what then?'

David said nothing.

Pearl, conveniently forgetting that she had heard of Christine's affairs and decided to do nothing because to act on that knowledge would have risked her possession of Howarth, raised her voice. 'Suppose they'd broken the engagement because of your actions! They'd have sued us! They'd have had us in court and we'd have lost Howarth, lost everything! And all because you cannot keep your hands off some American drudge who's blaming you for her pregnancy!'

'She's not!'

'Not what, pray?' Pearl suddenly spoke with icy coolness, sure that she had her son running and cowed.

'It is my child,' David said.

'No one,' Pearl said in tones that suggested she was stating an obvious rule, 'who has a child out of matrimony can be sure of the father's identity. Don't be such a pathetic fool!' She stared at him, despising his weakness, hating his appearance, wondering yet again why fate had given her such undistinguished children. 'And there's another thing,' she said.

David showed he had heard by a vague gesture with his hand, nothing more.

'I have gone to extraordinary lengths to ensure that if this marriage goes badly, we do not, as a family, lose Howarth.' She referred to her agreement with Edward which, in Pearl's mind, had become her own achievement, almost as if Edward had never approached her with his bargain and nor had Monty nailed it down with the affidavit. 'Nevertheless I cannot protect you against yourself. I trusted you! I thought, God help me, that you'd seen sense for once. Now I find you have a grubby, secret life! If you parade that dirtiness after marriage then it is quite possible that the trustees will be forced to see things differently.

327

You could lose Howarth!' The last words were almost screamed at David, who flinched under them. Pearl shook with anger. 'You will never, ever, see this American girl again. You understand me?'

David raised his eyes to stare at his mother. He looked oddly puzzled at that moment, as if he was only just beginning to understand the situation which had brought the Marchioness so hastily to his door.

'Do you understand me?' Pearl asked. 'You will give me your word, as a gentleman, that you will never again see that slut. Or any other slut. You will not risk Howarth.'

There was silence, except for a creak as the garden door caught a gust of wind.

A car drew up outside and there was the sound of a handbrake ratchet, then the slam of its door. David stared at his mother. She threatened the one consolation he would take from today's marriage: that Grace would stay his mistress and friend, that he might even build some life with her while keeping the façade of his marriage intact.

'I want your word, David.' Pearl, knowing she had him cornered and finished now, made her voice reasonable, as though she asked very little of him and as if, once his word was given, a mood of sweet reason would pervade this day of wedding and celebration.

'Piss off,' David said, astonishing even himself. A moment before he had been ready to give in to duty's pressure, to abandon Grace's child, to follow the tedious path of marriage, but Pearl had gone too far.

She slapped him. 'You will never –'

'Shut up! And get out of here! Out! Out! Out!' David's own temper had boiled over. He snatched up the hired top hat and hammered it into shapelessness with his fist. 'I'm not marrying her, I'm not going to the fucking Abbey, and I don't give a fuck for Howarth!'

'David!'

'It's over, mother, over! No marriage, none!' He stripped off his waistcoat and threw it into the hearth. 'Now get out!'

She tried to strike him again, but David caught the blow on

his forearm and his anger, suddenly so savage, took away her advantage. Years of resentment seethed in him and Pearl, faced with a strength she had not suspected, stepped backwards. 'David!' Her voice betrayed a *frisson* of fear, a hint that she knew she had gone too far and that all she wanted was now in danger.

Hugh Grimes, finding the front door open, came to the living-room door. 'Am I interrupting?'

'No,' David said, suddenly decisive. 'My mother is just leaving.' He had gone to the corner of the room, found a telephone directory, riffled its pages, then dialled Covent Garden 8080.

'What are you doing?' Pearl asked.

'What I should have done a year ago.' David lit a cigarette and listened to the ringing tone.

'David!' Pearl lunged for him, but he turned his body to shield the telephone.

'I want Christine de Conroy's room. She stayed with you last night.'

'David!' Pearl turned on Hugh. 'Stop him!'

'Leave him alone.' Grace had stepped into the garden door. 'Leave him alone!'

The sight of the tall, calm American girl seemed to freeze Pearl. She feared to lose her dignity. She would lose everything else, but she could not scrap like a fishwife in front of Grace, who stepped into the room, lit a cigarette, and watched David.

'Christine?' His voice was oddly calm.

Pearl gave a tiny whimper, but no other sound.

'I didn't sleep at all.' He paused, and Pearl dared to hope that, at this final moment, he would lose his sudden confidence.

'David?' She whispered his name pleadingly.

'I'm sorry,' he said into the telephone, 'but I won't be at the Abbey. I suggest you don't go either.' His voice had sounded strained at last, almost breaking, but he had forced the words out. The hand holding the cigarette shook.

He paused again. Pearl wanted to snatch the telephone away from her son, but Hugh stood beside her and the American girl came closer, and she could only stand utterly still while her dream was shattered.

'I've said I'm sorry.' David was suddenly harsh. 'I owe you an explanation, but not now. I'm not marrying you, and that's the end of it. The end!' He put the telephone down, his face suddenly drained of everything.

'David!' Pearl wailed.

'Go away,' David said. 'Just go away.' He walked to Grace, for whom he had found his courage, put his arms about her and held her very tight as though this tall, calm girl could protect him against all the chaos he had just made. 'I'm going to marry you,' he said, 'in America.'

'OK,' Grace said. 'That sounds good.'

The front door slammed as Pearl left, then Hugh, coughing to make sure that Grace and David knew he was in the room, went to the telephone. He dialled Brick Street. 'Monty?'

Monty listened, then asked to talk to his son. When the conversation was over the Marquess went back into the living room. He guessed he had ten minutes before the telephone began to go mad and before Pearl came screaming in for David's punishment. 'Edward!'

'My Lord?' Sir Edward Fenton, summoned to the house, was nervous.

'This is the moment when you earn your directorship. You understand me?'

'No, sir.'

'The wedding is cancelled.' Monty said it curtly, then sat at the table, took a sheet of notepaper, and wrote swiftly. 'You will therefore take 'this note to de Conroy at the Savoy. If he's not at the Savoy, find him. You will give it to him.' He finished the note, folded it, and put it inside a crested envelope. 'You will find, Edward, that the Lord de Conroy is already planning a suit for breach of promise against my son. He will undoubtedly want immediate possession of Howarth and a great deal of cash. Tell him I'm offering him both things immediately, on condition that he meets me at four o'clock this afternoon in the library at Howarth. If he does not come, then tell him I will fight him in the courts and I will win.'

Edward, who had provided the evidence for Monty's victory, nodded.

'Naturally, you can deny your affidavit. That would mean you have become my enemy.' Monty pushed the sealed envelope across the table. 'That is the invitation. If de Conroy is at Howarth this afternoon, then I will know that you are not my enemy and I will look forward to a long, happy, and profitable partnership with you. Think carefully which family offers you the brightest future.'

Edward took the envelope. 'Suppose he won't accept your invitation?'

'I'm offering him everything he wants! No scandal, victory, and double the amount of cash a court would award him. Make up a figure, you know the sort of thing. I'm sure he'll accept. Now go!'

Monty sat motionless at the table after Edward had gone. He took a risk and it frightened him, but it was a risk that just might bring him Howarth.

The door to the dining room opened, feet sounded on the carpet, and hands massaged the stiff muscles of his shoulders. 'Poor uncle.'

'No,' Monty said. 'I've cheated for Howarth, I've lied for it, and I expected David to solve my problems for me.' He turned, took one of Hilary's hands and kissed it. 'You got it?'

'The Museum authorities aren't at all happy,' she said, 'but as a trusted ex-employee they allowed me to borrow it.'

'Good!' Monty stood, smiling. 'I think I'd better go to the Abbey and head off the crowds, don't you? And perhaps you'd be very kind and telephone Sol for me? Ask him to come to Howarth as soon as he can. Oh, and when Pearl gets here tell her to meet me at Howarth at half past three sharp. And be there yourself, my love. I need someone honest.'

'How's David?' Hilary asked.

'He's happy. God knows how long he'll be happy. She's much too good for him, but at least he's doing the decent thing.' Monty pulled on his jacket, then plucked out the buttonhole and tossed it away. 'Time to go. Time for the fun to start.'

'Good luck.'

'I'm going to be an honest man,' Monty said. 'It should be rather interesting. And by tonight, my love, I will be the owner of Howarth or I'll be nothing.' He gave her a dramatic bow, a grin, and was gone.

Hilary did not think she had ever seen Monty so happy. He bubbled with a mischievous delight, greeting each new arrival as if, instead of being summoned to Howarth, they did the Marquess great and joyous honour by being there. 'My dear Sol! How are you?'

'I'm upset! Upset!' Sol, like Monty himself, was still in his wedding finery. 'It's terrible, terrible!' He wrung the Marquess's hand as if by so doing, he could share the grief of the day's tragic events.

'Nonsense,' Monty said cheerfully, 'it's nothing but a broken engagement. And look on the bright side!'

'Bright side?' Sol said gloomily. 'There is one?'

'David's new girl has proper tits. Really a vast improvement!' Monty looked at the second figure who climbed from Sol's Daimler. 'You must be Oscar Melnick?'

'Yes, my Lord.' Oscar, brought along by Sol, was too nervous to say anything more.

'Splendid. I'm sorry you find us a little distracted today, but it's not every week that one's son abandons a girl at the altar. Why don't you go and find a drink? Can I suggest the Garden Room, Sol.'

'You wanted me to do something?' Sol asked.

'I do indeed, old friend. I want you to slosh some gin down your gullet, then sit down and work out just how much of Monsol I own. Tell me how rich I am, Sol. Cheer me up!'

The next to arrive was Hugh, driving David and Grace. He was in full dress uniform, David in dress trousers and a tweed jacket, while Grace wore a long skirt of dyed wool and had on a man's shirt instead of a blouse.

David had been terrified of this meeting, but his father was kindness itself. He hugged him, then kissed Grace. 'I think that's allowed if you're in the family way. And I must say I envy my son.'

Grace blushed. 'I guess I'm sorry.'

'Nonsense, my dear Grace! If I must have a daughter-in-law, then let her be beautiful to console my old age. You have nothing to apologize for, nothing to regret. You will probably wish to avoid my wife, so I suggest you join Sol in the Garden Room. Have a drink there. This is meant to be a happy day.'

Hilary joined Hugh and, in answer to his raised eyebrow, merely shrugged to show that she could not tell him the reason for her uncle's frenetic happiness. Monty shook Hugh's hand. 'I want you to do something for me.'

'Of course, sir.'

'In the West Wing somewhere, in the rooms we got ready for Christine, you'll find de Conroy's banner. Nasty thing in yellow and black. Would you be very kind and search for it, then bend it on the central flagpole?' Monty gave Hugh the keys to the private apartments.

'What are you doing?' Hilary asked Monty suspiciously when her lover had gone on his errand.

'I'm throwing Kynaston off balance,' he replied. 'He'll come steaming in for revenge and see his flag fluttering. He'll be suspicious, won't he?'

'Pearl won't like it.'

'That makes me wish I had two of his banners to fly,' Monty said cheerfully. 'Have you had lunch?'

'Not a thing.'

'Come and raid the kitchens with me. I've upset half of London so I might as well make my cook's day a misery.'

Monty had gone to Westminster Abbey where some two hundred guests had arrived early. He had made his short, bleak announcement, then left the ushers to pass on the shocking news to the later arrivals. Organist, choristers, clergy, hotel, liverymen, guard of honour, orchestra and trumpeters, all had to be called from the dean's house, and then the first journalists started their enquiries.

The telephones were now off the hook, the gates were locked and guarded by gatekeepers, and Howarth was under siege. The wedding of the year had been abruptly cancelled, without explanation, and only Sophie's rumour, hissing across London's telephone lines, offered any explanation.

Sophie arrived to find Monty and Hilary eating cold lamb in the huge kitchen. 'Want some?' Monty said.

'What's happening, for God's sake?'

'I'm doing what an aristocrat should do,' he said happily. 'I'm entertaining the vulgar crowd. This should be worth special early evening editions of the *Standard* and *News*, shouldn't it?'

'David walked out on her?'

'Yes. Swore at his mother too!' Monty seemed delighted. 'I didn't know he had it in him.'

'Jesus.' Sophie sat. 'Kynaston will kill me.'

'Nonsense,' Monty said. 'Now do you want some lamb or don't you?'

Hugh had found de Conroy's banner in a cupboard beneath the stairs, and he climbed to the platform at the top of Howarth and raised the folded bundle to the head of the staff. As it reached the very top he saw Pearl's grey Rolls-Royce being admitted through the main gate and he jerked the hallyard to slip the binding knot and the vast spread of yellow and black streamed in the wind.

Monty, warned by Rowlands that the Marchioness's car was approaching the portico, took his sandwich and waited at the head of the steps. 'My dear!'

Pearl, grim-faced, came towards him. 'Have you seen our gates? They're swarming with journalists!'

'Rabid fellows, aren't they?'

'And that flag? Is this some kind of joke?'

'De Conroy owns the house, doesn't he?' Monty took her arm. 'I thought he'd like to see his banner where it belongs. He's coming, by the way, or at least I hope he is.'

Pearl snatched her arm from his grip. 'What are you doing, Monty? For God's sake, what are you doing?'

Monty smiled seraphically. 'I suspect we've rather knocked him off balance, don't you? Always best to negotiate with people when they're off balance. Anyway, I've invited the old bugger for four o'clock and we can only wait and see if he arrives. Want a spot of lunch?'

Pearl ignored the offer of his half-eaten sandwich. 'Where's David?'

'He's here,' Monty said cheerfully. 'With his new fiancée. I must say she's a pretty thing! I quite envy him!'

'He was vilely rude to me!'

'So Hugh said.'

'I want him out of this house, out of these grounds, and I want him punished!'

'Don't be ridiculous, my dear.' Monty took Pearl's arm again and led her to the top of the steps. 'I've got quite enough on my plate today, dealing with de Conroy. I will not start another feud just because you fell out with David over a trivial thing like a cancelled marriage! Anyway, I've already welcomed them both to Howarth.' He spoke with just a hint of intransigence in his otherwise light voice. Monty was in command now, and he would not have Pearl spoiling what he had planned. 'Why don't you change your clothes, my dear? That always cheers you up.'

Pearl said nothing. She stormed into Howarth and Monty, left alone on Howarth's entrance pediment, looked around the spread of the front gardens and thought how much he loved this place.

For Pearl it was pride, but for Monty it was attachment. Howarth was filled by his family, its walls hung with their portraits just as its corridors were sometimes chill with the passing of their ghosts. Howarth was Howarth, and he was Howarth. But Howarth had once been Conroy, and Conroy ghosts must stalk its halls too, and Monty thought how once a Lord de Conroy had stood on this same spot and watched the great wagons take away his possessions. The thought made him realize how saddened he would be if he had to leave it.

But if he was not prepared to lose it, then he did not deserve to keep it. All now depended on Edward. If Edward was still on de Conroy's side, then he would deny the affidavit and there would be no angry Kynaston coming up the drive at four o'clock. If, on the other hand, Edward saw his future with Monsol and with its burgeoning profits, then Monty expected a visitor and a fight. He turned back into the house and made a long telephone call to the lawyers in London.

At five minutes to four Monty asked Rowlands to assemble all the guests in the library. 'Perhaps you could serve champagne?'

'Indeed, my Lord.'

Only Pearl was not present. Sol, with his nervous protégé, sat at the library table. He had jotted down some notes, but Monty waved away the financial statement for the moment. 'I may not need it, Sol.'

David and Grace, both nervous, stood by the fireplace where the Knight of Swords hung in its frame. Sophie sat at the far side of the hearth, shrunken into a leather chair. Hugh and Hilary stood with Monty. The champagne tasted oddly flat.

At five minutes past four Pearl swept into the room. She had chosen a dress of black silk, robes of mourning, and as she entered she saw her son and stopped.

They stared at each other. Pearl took a breath, as if about to open the battle again, then thought better of it and, with splendid disdain, stalked past him to the far end of the room. 'Champagne?' Monty asked. She did not deign to reply.

Grace nervously lit a cigarette. The Tompion long-case clock ticked ominously, its minute hand visibly jerking towards the quarter.

When the quarter struck, Pearl gave a brittle laugh. 'Is this charade over?'

'Gentlemen are never on time in England,' Monty said. 'I think I might have some more champagne.'

Tyres crunched on the gravel and Monty checked himself from going to the unshuttered windows to see who the new arrival was. Sophie, her face suddenly seeming ravaged, came to the table and poured herself yet another drink.

A single leaf of the double doors was opened by Rowlands. 'Sir Edward Fenton, my Lord.'

Monty hid his disappointment. He wanted de Conroy here, for if de Conroy did not come then the lease would tick on to its ordained end and Howarth would be lost. 'Well?'

'He said he'll come.' Sir Edward seemed shaken by the day's events.

'And what did you tell him?' Monty had taken Edward into a corner of the library where their voices could not be overheard.

'Simply that you were ready to treat, my Lord.'

'You didn't mention the affidavit?'

Edward shook his head. He had not needed to betray his part

in Monty's plans for, astonishingly, the scribbled letter to de Conroy had said that the Marquess of Arlington was prepared to give up Howarth instantly if the Lord de Conroy came this afternoon. Edward understood none of it.

Monty went back to the table. He caught Hilary's eye and grinned. No one except Sophie seemed to be drinking the champagne so, to show that he was not worried, he tossed back a flute and poured another.

The first gunshot sounded. Then the second.

There was an undignified, curious rush to the windows. Kynaston de Conroy had arrived.

His Rolls was parked outside the main gates of Howarth and, with his chauffeur acting as loader, he was using two matched shotguns to pepper the great coats of arms that Pearl had put on to the gates.

The first shot had gouged the lacquer and gilt of the right-hand crest down to the bright metal, the second flicked holes of brilliant sunshine in the shield. De Conroy changed guns, and went on firing and changing until he had used twenty cartridges of heavy shot and the gates were like twisted, torn colanders. The photographers, starved of any other news, clicked delightedly. When he was done, de Conroy shouted for the lodge-keeper to open the damned gates.

'That was rather stylish,' Monty said.

Pearl said nothing. She had been humiliated before all London, and now the newspapers would carry pictures of this fresh insult, and she could have clawed out her son's eyes and thrown him from Howarth for ever, but her husband, at his most bland and confident, was holding the room in thrall.

'What are you going to do?' Sol, suddenly nervous, asked Monty.

Monty listened to the crunch of tyres on the gravel, then smiled. 'I'm going to end the feud, Sol. I just thought we needed a witness or two.' He lifted a briefcase from the floor and put it on the table.

Grace, one of the two strangers in the room, was appalled by the intensity of unstated emotion in the room. There was anger and fear, anticipation and amusement; the last from the tall,

337

elegant man who alone seemed to be enjoying the afternoon. She watched Monty with an artist's eye and saw him as one of nature's princes among common men; one of those heroes who had brought civilization to Italy, or thrust the railroads across America. The elegance, she thought, was a lovely façade that hid a cruel yet generous soul. He was a man who made his own rules and Grace suddenly found herself wishing, with a passionate hope, that it was Monty's soul that inhabited the child in her womb, and not the more timorous, gentle personality of his son.

'Monty!' Pearl, hearing the slam of a heavy door deep in the house, turned on her husband to make one last effort to control this day's events for her own good, but he raised a hand.

'I think I hear our guest. Shall we try and look solemn? It must be a hard thing to have your daughter rejected.'

Silence fell: a silence broken only by the clock's tick and the sound of an approaching ebony stick rapping on Howarth's marble floors.

David was shaking with nerves, terrified of this new ordeal, but Grace put an arm around him.

Pearl made her face into a mask of unconcern. Sophie drank her champagne and was glad that she had taken three extra glasses.

Hilary took Hugh's hand.

Both double doors opened inwards. Rowlands, as formal as a bishop at his own altar, stood between them. 'The Baron de Conroy and Miss Estelle Charpentier.'

'You've come!' Monty sounded both delighted and surprised. 'My dear Kynaston! How very kind! And Miss Charpentier? You're most welcome.'

De Conroy waited until Rowlands had closed the doors, then, ignoring Monty's effusive welcome, he searched every face in the room. He looked past Pearl with disdain, stared at Sophie with undisguised threat, ignored Hilary, Hugh, Sol and Oscar, and found David. 'You miserable little bastard.' His daughter, locked in her Savoy suite, was weeping, while Lord de Conroy's bloodshot eyes looked at Grace, then went back to David. 'Is that your whore, boy?'

'I see you've brought your own,' Monty said. 'Didn't we meet in Nice, mademoiselle?'

Estelle, too terrified to reply, clung to de Conroy's arm. He shook her off and stalked further into the room. 'I've come to see you grovel, Arlington. I'll take your damned house, and your damned money, and I'll put a whore in her Ladyship's bed tonight. No doubt the mattress needs the exercise.' He stared defiance at Pearl, challenging her to answer, but she would not meet his gaze. Her timidity pleased de Conroy, who looked back to Monty. 'Flying my flag, Arlington? Have you surrendered?'

'It's your house, my dear Kynaston. I thought it would please you. Now! I suspect you know most people, but that's Mr Oscar Melnick, who's strayed here from America, and Miss Grace Dunwoody, likewise from the States. You'd like some champagne?'

'Damn your champagne.'

'Some whisky, then?'

'What I want,' de Conroy limped forward until he stood opposite Monty on the far side of the table, 'is immediate possession of this house and two hundred and fifty thousand pounds.'

'Fine. But would you like a drink first?'

Monty's apparent agreement checked de Conroy. 'You heard me?'

'Immediate possession and five hundred monkeys.' He smiled at the Lord de Conroy. 'About that whisky. I seem to remember you liked the Islay malt. You'll have a drop?'

De Conroy, assailed by Monty's affability and lulled by his agreement, laid his stick on the table. 'I'll take your malt, then your house.'

'Splendid!' Monty crossed to the tantalus. 'Do you take water with it, Kynaston? I don't recall.'

'Of course I don't take water! I'm not a pansy!' De Conroy watched as the drink was poured, perhaps expecting poison to be put into it.

Monty poured two glasses of the fine whisky, took them to the table, and pushed one across the shining surface. He sat. 'How much did you want?'

'You heard.'

Monty took out his cheque book. 'I'm good for it, am I, Sol?'

'Indeed.' Sol watched him with a pained expression.

Monty uncapped his pen, then frowned sympathetically at de Conroy. 'I fear we must have cost you a packet today, Kynaston. All those flowers wasted. How much did the wedding cost you?'

'Twenty thousand,' he said quickly.

'Am I good for that, Sol?'

Sol could only nod.

Monty wrote out the cheque, speaking aloud as his pen scratched on the paper. 'Pay the Baron de Conroy two hundred and seventy thousand pounds. Signed, Arlington.' He blotted the cheque. 'And what was the other thing you wanted, Kynaston?'

De Conroy, expecting a trick, looked round the room. Pearl was as white as the paper on which the cheque was printed, David was biting his lower lip, while Sophie was swallowing champagne. 'I want,' he said forcefully, 'this family out of Howarth. Now.'

Monty leaned back in his chair. 'I suppose, Kynaston, that the best thing to do is just tear up the lease, don't you agree?'

De Conroy hesitated, saw no catch, and nodded.

'Right!' Monty searched in the briefcase and found the thick, creamy document that Pearl had signed in this room at the war's end. This was the lease that she had lied and fought for, the lease that had given her time to plot the return of the house to her family, and Monty now calmly proposed to destroy it.

'Monty!' Pearl could no longer contain herself, but he ignored her. He showed the lease to de Conroy, then, with extraordinary strength, ripped the thick sheaf of documents into ragged halves.

'I suppose I'm your guest now, Kynaston,' he said. 'Nice place you've got here.'

'Get out!' de Conroy said.

'In a minute.' Monty smiled. So far everything had gone just as he had expected it to, but now he entered the realm of surmise and surprise. 'I will go, de Conroy, but if I do then I shall have my son sue your daughter for breach of promise. We shall be asking for possession of Howarth and a payment to us of two hundred and seventy thousand pounds. And you might recall that I have a habit of winning my court cases?'

De Conroy stared at Monty, then began to laugh. 'You do try it on, Monty, I'll give you that! A rare one, you are! You may be a fly bastard, but I'm not a fool. So get the hell out of here.'

Monty smiled. 'Edward?'

'My Lord.' Sir Edward started nervously from the library steps where he had taken refuge.

Monty did not look at him. Instead he stared at de Conroy as he spoke. 'Do I have evidence that would support my claim that Christine broke the engagement and gave my son cause to behave as he did today?'

There was a long, long pause. Edward's loyalty was on the line and the future of a great house was balanced on a knife's edge.

No one spoke, no one moved, no one took their eyes from the two men who faced each other across a wide, ancient table.

'Yes, my Lord,' Edward said from the corner of the library. He had made his choice for Howarth, and he repeated the words more loudly. 'Yes, my Lord.'

'And do I have evidence,' Monty raised his voice, 'that will brand Christine de Conroy as a scheming, libidinous little bitch who planned to abandon Howarth when her father was dead?'

'Yes,' Edward said.

Monty smiled at de Conroy, as if to suggest that things were not quite as simple as the torn lease and the cheque on the table might suggest.

De Conroy still held his gaze. 'I'll crucify you, Arlington. I'll have your damned guts for this!'

Monty took an envelope from the briefcase. He laid it on the table. David, puzzled, stared at it.

Monty smiled. 'I'll destroy it, if you like.'

De Conroy also stared at the envelope. For all he knew it could be empty, but he would not reward Edward's treachery by asking for an explanation, nor demean himself by opening the envelope to read its contents. He looked at the cheque beside it, then up at Monty. 'What are you playing at?'

'I'm warning you,' Monty said, 'that I can yet cause you trouble. The feud will drag on, Kynaston, it will go from generation to generation, and even if you take Howarth now then I will take it back from your daughter. It will go on for ever, Kynaston, unless we end it now.'

De Conroy took a cigar from his pocket. 'Well?'

'It was always a rotten idea for a marriage,' Monty said. 'They were both unfaithful to their engagement, Kynaston, and I don't give a bugger for it. But we were wrong to expect our children to solve the problem, weren't we?'

'You sound pious all of a sudden!' De Conroy laughed through a cloud of cigar smoke. 'And you wouldn't win your court case, and you know it. So bugger off.'

'And spread nasty scandals about the last of the de Conroys?' Monty said. 'I don't think so. How much am I worth, Sol?'

Sol Linsky looked at his notes, lit a cheroot, and shrugged. 'At a guess, I'd say three and a half million.'

'It's astonishing what thrift and sober living will do for a man,' Monty said. He uncapped his pen again, and once more wrote out a cheque. 'Pay the Lord de Conroy three million pounds. Signed, Arlington.' He blotted the cheque, tore it from the pad, and put it with the first cheque. 'That's for Howarth, Kynaston. An outright sale with immediate possession and I will burn that envelope now, and no courtroom will hear tales of your daughter's exploits.'

De Conroy looked at the cheques that lay in the centre of the table. The price was far above Howarth's worth and it pleased him to pick up the second cheque and, with scorn on his face, tear three million pounds into shreds. 'The house is not for sale, Arlington, and you can spread your damned filth.' He shot a look of withering scorn towards David. 'So what if she did cheat on him? I don't blame her!'

Monty smiled and wrote again. 'Pay the Lord de Conroy three million, five hundred thousand pounds. Signed, Arlington.' Again he blotted the cheque, and tore it from the pad. 'Well?'

Pearl held her breath. At that moment all she wanted was Howarth and the price did not matter, but de Conroy shook his head. 'No sale.'

Monty nodded. 'I thought not. Hilary?'

Hilary jumped, as if startled, then opened her handbag. She

342

brought out a small packet wrapped in ancient yellowed paper and sealed with a dark red wax seal and placed it before Monty.

Monty ignored it. 'It seems to me, Kynaston, that we've treated you badly. This morning must have been hard, very hard. We behaved clumsily at best, foully at worst, so I thought I must make amends. Suppose I offer you two hundred and seventy thousand pounds, immediate possession of Howarth, and the destruction of that envelope. How does that suit you?'

'It suits me fine. So get out!'

'There is a small condition.' Monty pushed the packet across the table. It measured some four and a half inches by two and a half and was a half-inch thick. 'Open it,' he suggested.

De Conroy broke the seal, unwrapped the old, brittle paper, and spilt the contents on to the table.

'No!' Pearl startled everyone in the room, making de Conroy smile.

On the table were playing cards.

'No! Monty, stop this!'

Monty turned a bland face to his wife. 'Why ever should I?'

'No!' Pearl, dignity gone to the winds, was beseeching him, for she knew what her husband suggested, and she saw Howarth lost for ever. 'I forbid it, Monty!'

De Conroy sifted through the cards. He seemed pleased that Pearl was distressed.

'My lawyers,' Monty said conversationally, 'tell me that a gambling debt is not enforceable in law, but I think we're both gentlemen, de Conroy. I shall honour the outcome, of course, but perhaps you do not have the stomach for it?'

De Conroy, an inveterate gambler, smiled. 'Howarth. Its farms, gardens, park, and Dower House. And three and a half million pounds. That's what I'll play for. Nothing less.' He looked up at Monty, gauging the risk his rival ran, and to prove his point tore up the first cheque, just leaving the one huge amount on the table. 'I'll play you, Arlington, for a chance to break you. Nothing less. Do you have the stomach for that?'

Monty heard the mocking question and knew he had misjudged his man. He had guessed de Conroy would not accept any price for the house, but would be unable to resist a gamble, but he had thought that Howarth was stake enough. But now de Conroy wanted more. He would go for Monty's jugular.

'Well?'

Monty still hesitated. He was prepared to lose Howarth, for its possession had forced him into connivance in perjury and close to forcing his son into marriage with a worthless slut, but now the price could be all that he owned.

'You don't have the balls,' de Conroy sneered. 'Your blood's thin, Arlington. You're a coward.'

Monty smiled into the triumphant face. 'It's how the feud started, Kynaston, and it seems the best way to end it. I agree. Howarth, and all its land, against my fortune.'

Pearl gave a small cry, like a dog screaming, but no one else moved.

De Conroy smiled, then looked from the cards in his hand to the mounted playing card on the wall. Monty laughed. 'I have to thank Hilary. She persuaded the British Museum to lend us their only complete pack of late eighteenth-century Spanish cards. It was the same kind of pack that was used in the original game. No queens, you see, just king, knight, and knave. And the suits are cups, coins, batons and swords. There's no ten. Ace to nine, knave, knight, king. Understand?'

'Stop it!' Pearl was shaking. 'Monty! I beg you!' All her hopes, everything, her whole life was on the table in the steel-etched, hand-painted playing cards that had been made by an artist in Madrid over a century and a half before.

Monty ignored her. He reached over and took some of the cards from de Conroy, curious about the things Hilary had borrowed from the storerooms of the British Museum. They did not have the smooth modern finish and so would not slide easily over each other. The court cards were printed just one way, no double-ended kings. The kings and knaves stood, while the knights, just like the Knight of Swords that was hung on the mantel, were mounted on prancing chargers. 'Well?' he asked de Conroy.

Kynaston hesitated, then nodded. He liked this challenge. All he could lose was a house he did not live in, while if he won he would take all Arlington's fortune and the world would know that a great revenge had been taken for the humiliation of this morning's cancelled wedding. 'Agreed,' he said. 'And do we play the game our ancestors played?'

'You know which game it was?' Monty asked.

De Conroy gathered all the cards with practised fingers and put them in a stack face-down on the table. 'It was a Russian game, because only the Russians would be mad enough to invent it. They called it *La Mort*, death. It was popular with soldiers. They could play it on an upturned drum in battle.'

'And the rules?'

'There are no rules,' de Conroy said. 'You name a card and I name a card. One by one we reveal the cards from the top of the pack and the man whose card appears first wins. Simple. It was the classic gambler's game, Monty. Whole estates, as we well know, were lost by it. It took great courage. Are you sure you have that courage?'

Pearl shook her head. 'Stop it!'

Monty ignored her. He took the stiff cards and laid them face upwards on the table, in order of their suits, and looked at Lord de Conroy who, satisfied that all the cards were present, nodded his head. He then turned the cards over, and pushed them in an untidy pile towards Hilary. 'Shuffle them.'

'If you touch those cards, Monty,' Pearl said, 'I will leave! I will not be treated like this! If you lose Howarth I'll leave you!'

'Every cloud has a silver lining,' de Conroy laughed. He watched with hawk eyes as Hilary clumsily piled the cards in heaps and shuffled the jumbled heaps, then cut the pack again and again.

Hilary, finally satisfied, put the cards before Monty who pushed them towards Estelle. '*Mademoiselle?* You'll cut them for us?'

She leaned forward, cut the pack, then reassembled it. Monty straightened the stack of cards in the table's centre, then looked at the man who was his enemy. 'Are we agreed that we end the feud now? That we abide by the cards, and that there will be no action, none, taken in a court of law?'

De Conroy looked up from the pack. 'Agreed.'

'Then name a card, my Lord.' Monty spoke with an odd formality.

345

Kynaston sipped his whisky. 'I am a drinking man,' he said slowly, 'so I choose the Knave of Cups.'

Monty paused. 'Knight of Swords.'

'How predictable you are.'

'Monty!' Pearl broke in again. For the first time in years he saw a dishevelled woman. There was agony on her face. If the Knave of Cups was turned up before the Knight of Swords, then Howarth was lost. It would be lost irretrievably, with all its land, and all Monty's money. Pearl could buy a house with her own money, but all the world would know it as a lesser house inflicted on her by defeat. 'I've spent money on this house,' she suddenly cried. 'You can't gamble with my money!'

Monty looked at her as though she was a stranger. 'How much have you spent? Ten thousand?' He did not wait for an answer, instead he turned to Sol. 'Dear friend, as my money is tied up in this game, would you lend me ten thousand?'

'No!' she screamed, but Sol, his face drawn with worry, had taken out his cheque book and pen. Hilary went to Pearl's side and held her shoulders.

'I think we can begin,' de Conroy said with amusement. 'I chose first, so you turn first.'

Monty, quite casually, turned the first card. The four of swords. It was only fitting, he thought, that this was how it should be settled. The feud had begun thus, and thus would it end. De Conroy's pride would not let him sell the house, so it must be played for.

De Conroy turned. Seven of cups.

Monty turned. Three of batons. So far it did not seem real that any of the plain-backed cards, turned, could lose a house and three and a half million pounds.

There was an utter silence. Pearl, her eyes closed, refused to watch.

'The devil's tickets,' de Conroy said. 'That's what they call the cards, isn't it?' He turned the ace of coins.

'Is it?' Monty turned over the king of coins. There was a shudder in the room for it was the first court card and everyone thought it might be de Conroy's knave.

Kynaston chuckled. 'Not an unexciting game, is it?'

'It has its moments.' Monty was slowly realizing that this was real, horribly real, that Howarth and his fortune depended on these cards, and the elegant insouciance that had been his trademark through life was beginning to fray. He could feel the tension in his arms and his breathing was coming ragged.

De Conroy turned the two of swords.

Monty showed the six of batons.

De Conroy drank his whisky, looked for a refill, and waited while Hugh crossed 'the room with the decanter.

'It's your turn,' Monty said.

'Impatience, impatience!' De Conroy drew on his cigar, then, with a tantalizing slowness, turned a card. Five of swords.

Monty seemed to watch his own hand go forward. With every card now he expected to lose, expected to see the mocking drinker's card: the Knave of Cups. He turned the ace of cups.

'I always wanted to do this,' de Conroy said. 'I admired those old buggers, you know. Brave chaps! Put all their fortunes on the table, everything! One day they were rich as Croesus, the next they had nothing! Good behaviour, that. Damned exciting, too!' He turned the nine of swords. 'Enjoying it, Monty? I don't suppose two aristos have sat down to a game like this in a century and a half!'

'I suppose not.' Monty turned a devil's ticket. It was a court card and he saw the standing figure and the cup, he heard the gasp in the room and saw the smile spread on de Conroy's face. 'King,' Monty said.

There were sighs of relief. Pearl had opened her eyes, and now she turned from the table, fidgeting with her necklace. She was pale as chalk.

'Two of coins,' de Conroy said as he turned it.

Hilary tried to count how many cards had been turned, but she could not see the discards clearly.

'Six of cups,' Monty said.

'If I take Howarth,' de Conroy said, 'will I find it warm?'

'The central heating's very efficient.' Monty was surprised to hear how calm his voice sounded, for he was shaking inside.

'I can't bear the cold, you see.' De Conroy reached for the pack, took a card, paused, then flipped it over. 'Eight of coins.' He sounded disappointed.

Monty leaned back in his chair, suddenly unable to turn another card. 'Edward? You might bring me a cigar.'

'Frightened?' de Conroy asked.

'Don't be absurd, Kynaston.' Monty lit the cigar carefully, drew on it, then placed it in the ashtray. He wished he had never started this. He had wanted to show a carelessness in the face of the day's disaster, to end this thing so it did not drag on to mire the lives of his children and his children's children, but suddenly the breath of defeat was cold in the room and he was terrified to think that he had really put all his work, all his hopes, everything on to the devil's tickets. He had not meant to stake so much. He would risk Howarth to stop the feud souring the next generation, but he had not expected to be sitting here with millions at stake. He turned the next card.

There was an instant's silence, a gasp, then a cheer. The first knight had turned up, a knight holding aloft a baton instead of a sword. The cheer died. 'They're better designed than the old Italian packs,' de Conroy said in a frighteningly calm voice, 'but they can still be confusing. The French gave us the pack we know. Hearts instead of cups, diamonds for coins, clubs for batons and spades for swords. From *espadas*, swords, of course. Nothing to do with shovels.' He chuckled and turned over the three of swords.

Monty was terrified. It took all his courage to push his hand forward, to lift the corner of the next card, and turn it.

Ace of batons.

Each card that was not the Knave of Cups gave him relief, then instantly the relief was replaced with agonized worry again. No wonder they had called the game death. His heart was beating too fast, a muscle in his leg twitched, and he could feel the sweat prickling at his flesh.

De Conroy's hand came forward, turned, and the moment of relief came again. Six of coins.

'I often wondered,' Kynaston said, sounding unaffected by the game, 'whether the clocks in Howarth were changed in wartime.

Do tell me, my Lord.' The bloodshot eyes stared at Monty. 'This is a time for honesty, is it not?'

Monty forced his hand forward. He could swear it was shaking. He took the next card between finger and thumb and was ashamed that there was sweat on his hand.

'Well?' de Conroy said.

Monty turned the card. Eight of cups. 'They were changed,' he said. The relief flooded through him, then the suspense came surging back.

'Then I congratulate you on a well-told lie. And perhaps fate will seal your retribution.' De Conroy turned the next card with a flourish.

Hilary groaned. The onlookers peered, but the knave stood impudently beneath his coin. 'Knave of coins,' Monty said.

'You are nervous,' de Conroy said. Pearl suddenly sat in a chair and stared at the wall. 'Are you well, my Lady?' Neither Pearl, nor anyone else, answered, and de Conroy smiled. 'Your card, my Lord.'

Hilary, like de Conroy, saw the nervousness in Monty. She could see his left hand twitching and the sheen of sweat on his forehead. She did not think she had ever seen a figure so tense.

Monty's right hand did not seem to belong to him. He watched it go forward, turn the card, and the relief was there again. The ace of swords.

'All the aces gone,' de Conroy said. 'Or have you not been remembering the discards?'

Monty said nothing.

'Nor have you. Bad practice in a card game, but you never were a gambler, were you? You used to play the horses though, didn't you?'

'That was all.'

'Shall we double the stakes, then? Shall we say Howarth and all its pictures?'

'Monty!' Pearl twisted round in the chair. 'Monty!' It was a wail, a sob.

'Most of the pictures,' Monty said, 'belong to Pearl.'

'Then your pictures. The family portraits. You've got a fair Gainsborough, haven't you, that would look good in Christine's

349

lavatory? So all the fittings that are yours, Monty, all the paintings, carpets, everything. The horses in your stables, the cars in your garages, everything down to your damned cuff links. You can keep the clothes you're wearing, of course, but damn little else. Shall we agree that?'

'Monty!' Pearl stood, shaking.

Monty knew he was being goaded. He stared at the pack and saw how shrunken it was. The odds might still be even, but the moment when one or other of the two cards must be turned was getting inexorably closer and Monty was certain that he faced defeat. It was a hard, foul feeling.

De Conroy watched his rival and saw the signs of nervousness. 'Well?'

'Turn the card.'

'Are we doubling?'

Monty looked up at de Conroy, resisting the temptation to swear at this man who grinned crookedly as he dared him to risk yet more. 'I'll add those things,' Monty said, 'all of them, if you throw in the gold dinner service and Lady Sophie's house.'

Pearl sank into the chair, sobbing, and Hilary crouched by her but could offer no comfort.

De Conroy laughed. 'I agree. Everything you possess, my Lord, against this house, Sophie's hovel, and a dinner service.' He turned the next card.

Monty stared at it. Oddly there was no noise, perhaps because de Conroy's dare to raise the stakes had silenced everyone in the room. Kynaston shrugged and his voice was very bitter. 'It seems you have a lucky card.'

The Knight of Swords. *El caballo d'espados*. Monty's card. Howarth's card.

Victory had slipped into the room very quietly, very softly. A Knight of Swords.

Sol sighed with relief and the noise seemed to wake the room and there was a cheer. Pearl turned to the table and her hands clapped sharp with relief and victory.

'Quiet!' Monty shouted. He looked at his enemy. 'I'm sorry, Kynaston.'

'It was fair.' De Conroy stared at the gaudy little knight who held the sword aloft. 'I almost chose that card to stop you picking it. But I thought the cups would be luckier today.'

Monty brought out his cheque book again. 'I can . . .'

'Damn it,' his anger flared, 'we're gentlemen! We had an agreement!'

'Yes.'

De Conroy blinked, then shook his head. 'I always wanted to know what those fools felt like when they gambled for everything. House, park, everything. What was it like, Monty? Tell me.'

'Damnable.' Monty was still shaking. Oddly he wished he was alone with Kynaston de Conroy now. 'It was awful.'

De Conroy stood and took his ebony stick. 'Damn your eyes, Arlington, damn you to hell, and well done. I'll send the deeds to you. You'll burn that?' He gestured at the envelopes.

'It was a bluff.' Monty opened the envelope, and tore it apart. It was empty. 'I'm sorry. I just wanted it all finished, Kynaston, so I apologize most deeply for any unfair and untrue slur upon your daughter that I may have used to provoke this game.'

De Conroy stared at him, then, silently, bowed his head. 'The trouble with you, Monty, is that when you look like a saint I know you're telling lies, and when you look evil, I know you tell the truth. Good day to you.' He plucked Estelle's elbow. 'Come!'

Monty looked up, almost asking his enemy to stay, to talk, to finish the whisky. He thought how he would miss the enmity that had driven him from poverty to riches, but now it did not matter.

He stood up when de Conroy was gone. It had still not sunk in that Howarth was won, that the old game had been replayed and won. Sophie was in tears, seeking his embrace, and Monty hugged her, then shook his son's hand and kissed the girl who would be his daughter-in-law. He embraced Sol and watched as Edward uncorked a fresh bottle of champagne.

Monty took a glass. He raised it, seeking silence, and held it towards Pearl. 'To my wife,' he said, 'who knew this was the only way it could end.'

Pearl, startled by the words, turned and stared at Monty.

He smiled. 'You played your part well, my darling. If Kynaston had thought you approved, I doubt he'd have played.'

Pearl took her cue. She accepted a glass, raised it, and drank

351

to her husband. 'Perhaps now,' she said in a voice that betrayed none of the day's agony, 'the flag can be changed?'

Monty turned. 'Hugh?'

They watched from the terrace. One flag came down and another rose to break splendid into the wind: the banner of Arlington.

Howarth had never looked so beautiful. 'I wish,' Monty said to Hilary, 'that it could be yours.'

'I'd give it away,' she said lightly.

Monty ignored her words. 'You're strong enough to hold it.' He spoke too softly for anyone else to hear. He had won it, but the next generation must win it again, and Monty, watching his son, wondered what battles David would have to fight if the banner was to stay on the high staff.

But that was a gloom unfitting to this day. He had won. Arlington had triumphed and Howarth was his.